PRAISE FOR THE STEALING

"*The Stealing* is a finely c[illegible]prises with emotional and psychological depth for its readers. It is brilliant and shrewd with a mesmerizing, captivating narrative that arises from the author's close attention to the intimate details of the lives of regular people and the private struggles for personal power and self-love in relationships between women and men. Once begun, it is almost impossible to put aside and so absorbing you can lose yourself entirely."

—Zenetta S. Drew, *executive director, Dallas Black Dance Theatre*

"*The Stealing* stole my entire day! Almost on cue, I finished reading just as a heavy storm blew through, leaving a beautiful rainbow behind. Masterful storytelling. I enjoyed the characters, the masculine dynamics, and the humorous brotherly love."

—G. M. Newsted, *engineer and aviator*

"Gripping and enthralling from start to finish."

—Niti Prothi, *VP*

"I found *The Stealing* to be captivating and could easily visualize where it's taking place. It is beautifully written and masterfully crafted."

—Alisa O'Banion, *CEO, Texas Microfiber, Inc.*

"Entertaining, unpredictable, and fun. *The Stealing* captured my attention quickly, and I kept turning pages for hours at a time. Five stars."

—Simon Fidler, *author,* Camsterdam: How I got Caught in the Crosshairs of the War on Terror

"This is an amazing book. The characters are so richly developed that I found myself thinking about them even when I wasn't reading the book."

—Margaret Sevadjian, *CEO, Charles Alan, Incorporated*

"*The Stealing* delivers all the gothic promises wrapped up in a modern package. Sarah isn't beautiful; she is sublime. Her stunning good looks inspire fear. The setting was powerful, especially concerning the lighthouse and its history. The narrative is beautifully written with lots of fabulous imagery."

—Robert Baker, *writer and book blogger, TheRomanceBloke.com*

"A beautiful story and impossible to put down."

—Patricia Drake Bryant, *author,* What Happened to My Perfect Life?

THE STEALING

THE STEALING

S.A. SUTILA

Advantage.

Published by Advantage, Charleston, South Carolina.
Member of Advantage Media Group.

ADVANTAGE is a registered trademark, and the Advantage colophon is a trademark of Advantage Media Group, Inc.

Printed in the United States of America.

10 9 8 7 6 5 4 3 2 1

ISBN: 978-1-64225-268-2
LCCN: 2021919068

Cover illustration by M. L. Kolbe
Cover design by David Taylor
Layout design by Mary Hamilton
Author photo by Thaddeus Harden

This is a work of fiction. All characters appearing in this work are fictitious. Any resemblance to real persons, living or dead, is coincidental. Any likeness of places and historical figures, events, including locations, have been used fictitiously.

Warning: This publication contains the following: bullying, child abuse and abandonment, attempted suicide, suicidal thoughts, homicide, death, female oppression, underage drinking, and profanity.

For Loretta ... my sister of the road.

CONTENTS

AUTHOR'S NOTE . . . . *XIII*

FOREWORD . . . . *XV*

1971 . . . . *1*

ACT I

CHAPTER ONE *9*
DEAD END (1984)

CHAPTER TWO *19*
TORTURE

CHAPTER THREE *29*
DRIFT NET

CHAPTER FOUR *37*
LIFEBOAT

CHAPTER FIVE *45*
SWEPT AWAY

CHAPTER SIX 49
HUNTED

CHAPTER SEVEN 55
REBIRTH

CHAPTER EIGHT 63
COSMOS

CHAPTER NINE 71
TRANSFUSION

CHAPTER TEN 83
VIRUS

ACT II

CHAPTER ELEVEN 93
WANDERLUST

CHAPTER TWELVE 111
SWARM

CHAPTER THIRTEEN 127
WARNING

CHAPTER FOURTEEN 149
ICE

CHAPTER FIFTEEN *161*
MIMOSA

CHAPTER SIXTEEN *175*
REDLINE

CHAPTER SEVENTEEN *191*
SKY

CHAPTER EIGHTEEN *207*
SIREN

CHAPTER NINETEEN *219*
FLANKED

CHAPTER TWENTY *229*
BROTHER

CHAPTER TWENTY-ONE *241*
ENVY

CHAPTER TWENTY-TWO *257*
THE PIT

ACT III

CHAPTER TWENTY-THREE *277*
SECRET

CHAPTER TWENTY-FOUR 295
BLOOD

CHAPTER TWENTY-FIVE 315
LIGHTHOUSE

CHAPTER TWENTY-SIX 327
DEATH

CHAPTER TWENTY-SEVEN 345
AFTERLIFE

EPILOGUE 359
THE TRANSIENT

ACKNOWLEDGMENTS 361

ABOUT THE AUTHOR 365

ABOUT PAULETTE REDDICK TURNER 367

ABOUT MITCH KOLBE 369

Q&A WITH COVER ILLUSTRATOR
MITCH KOLBE 371

AUTHOR'S NOTE

The journey begins on a dead-end road.

The Delaware coast is a haunting beauty. Ghosts appear to rise from the salt marsh and linger long past sunrise. The isolation and fear caused by the global pandemic stirred the darkest human emotions. A new kind of gothic novel, created by the dense, seeping fog of my childhood, is reclaimed for the modern era.

Beware the undercurrent of horrific realism. This novel is a work of fiction. The characters appear to come to life but are not real. A character's suicidal ideation is a symbolic attempt to escape a fictional life.

In the face of despair, discover the elusive, invisible, but real connectedness. In the wake of misery, find love within and relentlessly search for the joy in life.

FOREWORD

Growing up as a teenager, I loved Agatha Christie's books and read as late as my mother would allow (and sometimes later!). There was always intrigue and mystery—the triumph of good over evil. As I matured, other authors grabbed my attention, and I still love a good mystery.

Enter first-time author Sharon Sutila, with a refreshed gothic romance genre. The book is riveting with intertwining themes that keep you totally engrossed as you turn the pages. It's the story of all that makes us human. It encompasses our experiences, our failings, the driving desire to take second and third and fourth chances, our ultimate triumphs, and participation in the recreation of new life. The book tells the story of the messy complexity of living and moving through the physical, spiritual, emotional, and psychological realms of this world and learning and failing and persisting and growing through each experience. It brings to memory Newton's third law of motion: for every action, there is an equal and opposite reaction. We see the ripple effect as each character impacts the other just by living.

The reader is moved personally on a visceral level by the dynamics of the characters.

My story connected with *The Stealing* as I read the heroine's search for fulfillment and acceptance. It mirrors my search for truth as I strive to better myself. It's been a journey of finding my voice and my place while overcoming society's drive to victimize me because of the melanin in my skin. It's a reminder of my journey of being born in segregation and being told the lie of separate but equal, only to confirm what I unconsciously knew. In America, segregation was the epitome of separate and unequal. It's my story of persisting nonetheless, time and time again, and adapting to discover more of who I am. It is the story of never relenting despite hardship, systemic and institutional injustice, or people who would try to take away your power.

Are you looking for a good read that heightens your awareness of the physical and spiritual world and opens you to the possibilities of perceiving beyond your human capabilities? My prayer is often, "Open my eyes that I may see, my ears that I may hear, my mind that I may perceive, my heart that I may receive." In her first novel, Sharon Sutila captures all your senses, so you taste the ocean spray and smell the stench of the oyster catch and see the colorful panorama of the coastline. If you close your eyes, you can almost hear the call of the horn on the ocean ferry. Sutila uses her memory of growing up close to the seashore in Delaware and couples that with extensive research to entertain us and enlighten us.

My prayer is that you will read *The Stealing* for the entertainment it is and search for those opportunities to be enlightened, those opportunities to dig deep, to lose, and to find yourself. This book is the beginning for first-time author Sutila. It leaves me wondering about the ending of the story. For in this life, "We are hard-pressed on every side, but not crushed; perplexed, but not in despair; persecuted, but not abandoned; struck down, but not destroyed" (2 Corinthians 4:8–9). I have the blessed assurance that, in the end, my personal story will reflect the triumph of good over evil.

After reading *The Stealing*, my prediction is that you, too, will reflect on the ending of your story and find oneness to become who you are meant to be.

—**Paulette Reddick Turner,** *founder and president,*
Integrated Leadership Concepts, Inc.

1971

The five-year-old girl took one look at the hairbrush and ran. Kick—bang! The flimsy metal door sprang open, stamping a new groove in the sheathing of the single-wide trailer. The girl's momentum launched her over four cinder-block steps. She pedaled an invisible bicycle through the air, wobbled when she hit the ground, but remembered to balance this time. Victory achieved in the Battle of the Hairbrush—the escapee kept running. The fresh scabs from her last attempt to flee were long forgotten, and she sprinted onto the paved street without looking in either direction.

The thought of freedom from her mother's merciless brushstrokes injected power into her pale, thin legs. Wearing her triumphant crown of matted auburn hair, she found the center of the road with her feet and aimed for the rise to the sandy beach. A few neighbors, quenching their thirst under shade trees, witnessed the girl explode from her home. They held their breath, waiting for her mother to give chase, but she did not.

Today the girl had an accomplice for her getaway—a new pair of white-cotton tennis shoes. Her old pair with the flapping-open toe, effective only in scooping gravel, had thwarted all previous attempts to run. Her stride now was long and quick. This time, she promised herself, she would make it all the way to the waves on Killington Beach.

After passing a few houses, the girl looked back once; the door to the trailer, now closed, blocked a return to the refrigerator. She stopped for a moment. Her belly groaned, urging her to march back home and endure the inevitable punishment in exchange for food. But no. She celebrated her freedom instead and continued up the hill, skipping at a bright pace. The "Bingo" song came to mind, and the urge to sing was too strong to shake. She sang "*B-I-N-G-O*" three times, paused to fill her lungs, and yelled, "Bingo was his name-*O*."

A green-eyed German shepherd lying in the shade of an oak tree surveilled the freckled little girl with the faded denim shorts and the polka dot tank top. The girl, caught up in the sound of her own voice, didn't notice the dog until it was too late. The eighty-pound beast lunged with its fangs bared. The girl screamed, but the dog ran out of rusty metal chain and flipped itself in reverse. The girl pointed a motherly finger at it and yelled, "Bad dog!" The Battle of the Dog won, she continued her journey as the dog retreated to its confinement in the cool dirt under the tree.

When the girl reached the top of the knoll, she was met by powerful wind gusts and struggled to stay on her feet. She clung to a roadside sign and imagined being blown into the sky above the clouds. No beach today. Losing the Battle of the Wind—temporarily—she vowed to return someday soon.

The path back to her trailer dungeon was not an option; the evil hairbrush and wooden spoon awaited, ready to pounce. The bluish-green bruises on her thigh still hurt—days earlier, she had refused to drink milk and had earned the colorful badge. The milk she hated taunted her thirst. She touched her lips, angry at herself for having such human weakness. *If only I could live without food and water, I would never go back there*, she thought.

No. She was not going home. That was final. Between the sand dunes of the beach and the edge of the woods to the west, she spotted three young children, two girls and a boy, playing a game of hide-and-seek.

The children, including the girl who watched them, were blissfully unaware of the dangers bordering their field of play. The Delaware Bay, on one side, routinely claimed the lives of swimmers with its strong current. The creatures of the forest, to the other side, were as thirsty and hungry as the bay.

Venomous snakes, fanged predators, and birds of prey readied themselves in anticipation. The oblivious children should have been warned off by the swords of twisted, crooked branches, crafted by coastal storms, but they did not heed them. Hidden under the shade of the wind-battered trees was a carpet of marshland mud strong enough to grip—and hold fast—the children's small feet.

The creatures of the forest loved the games children play. The raucous children bowed together under the soldier's arm of a tree and then ran to hide, ready to be lost—and found.

The little girl, who would not return home, tiptoed to the edge of the woods in search of the children. Moving a branch to peek into the forest, she winced at the stench of skunk. She listened, but there was no sign of the children. Instead of following the trail, she decided to sneak into the woods through the brush.

Unaware of where her feet were planted, the girl stood on a sacred rock at the mouth of an ancient passage through the woods, now overgrown. Beneath her new tennis shoes, an opalized keystone covered in grime depicted a carved petroglyph of the cosmos: two concentric circles enclosed by a diamond shape, split horizontally into two triangles. The girl balanced on the rock; it marked an unseen boundary. She steadied her hand on a moss-covered wooden pillar, revealing an engraved triangular-headed snake.

The little girl ignored the small yet significant carved-snake warning: a primordial being protects the earth. When last this being visited the land long ago, he witnessed no earthly threat by the land dwellers and grew bored. He set the rock-tripwire in the forest and departed. The girl's trespass now summoned his return. Only a child, but still—an inspection was overdue. She stood alone on the line between life and afterlife, and she was named Orphan. The orphan, a curious spirit, was deemed suitable. Her life was chosen as a means to observe and take measure of the latest earthly inhabitants.

Earth's guardian hid in shadows and followed her as she wandered through the woods.

ACT I

CHAPTER ONE

DEAD END (1984)

The boat captain's daughter drove her truck at a reckless speed, half asleep and on autopilot, directly into the rising sun. Jarred to alertness by the crunch of gravel, she narrowly avoided a rock ledge. The balding tires of the rusted Chevy pickup found pavement again and continued bouncing over the pits of Port Mahon Road, passing the Dead End sign that had marked her life since moving here from nearby Killington Beach as a kindergartner.

The abandoned lighthouse grew large as she neared the dock. The iconic symbol of Port Mahon wasn't tall and round like most lighthouses but, rather, square and boxlike with an octagonal lantern tower.

A cloud of sand dust followed Sarah as she arrowed toward the Shucking House. Navigating the slippery coastal curve required two hands on the wheel and acute focus. She fought the possessed steering wheel as it jerked left and right. The truck shimmied, rattled, and skated on the uneven ground until she stomped on the brakes, locking them tight, having arrived at her destination. The onslaught of sand rear-ended the truck as she jumped out and ran to the dock, where the commercial fishing boat awaited.

The young and hearty men stood on the boat throwing daggers at her with their eyes. The Captain was kneeling below the floorboards, checking the engine when she stepped onto the boat. He did not comment when his daughter arrived late, and the crew's silent contempt festered.

The blazing sun was a big, fat tattletale. Someone was always late to the dock, and this day it happened to be Sarah; she had slumbered too long, dreaming of college dormitory life—longing for the Saturday she could sleep past five o'clock in the morning. Graduation was only weeks away, but it felt like an eternity.

The boat was already loaded, fueled, and ready to go. Sarah had missed breakfast, so she foraged for crackers in the cabin. Avoiding ten minutes of work this way, she knew the whole mutinous crew would be plotting their revenge. Her thoughts reciprocated disgust. *The men on the boat are morons—why else would they be working on a smelly fishing boat?*

The crew misconstrued the Captain's lack of reprimand as a privilege afforded his only daughter; the truth was, he had nothing to say to her because he was disappointed that she had not been born a son.

Captain Rex Vise, on several drunken occasions, had expressed regret that his daughter was unable to follow in his footsteps. She was smart enough, no doubt, but her father would not entertain the idea she could ever be a boat captain. He was adamant on the topic: at sea, in rough weather and emergencies, the men would never respect a woman. Lives would be lost.

The *Outlaw*, a forty-foot deep-*V* hull commercial fishing vessel, was the Captain's one true love. When she roared to life, her inboard engine, an Oldsmobile 442, vibrated the whole craft, bow to stern. Off the back of the boat, a pully system with a motorized winch stood ready to pull crab pots. Under the boom, with the help of gravity, hundreds of pots would soon open over a large culling box to reveal the day's catch.

"Nice day, isn't it?" Sarah asked the unfamiliar and equally unfriendly new crew member. Her encouraging smile did not tempt him to answer back. *Probably missing half his teeth,* she thought. The Captain routinely lured dim-witted thugs to the boat for what he described as "great pay for an honest day's work." Memories of past young men who had bitten for the Captain's lure provided a steady source of amusement for her.

Sarah chuckled when the mooring line dropped. The daily grind began. She knew two unwelcome surprises were in store for the men. Surprise one: The weather.

A cool, pleasant breeze now blew out to sea. The boat skimmed easily across Delaware Bay's calm surface. They could have canoed the waters that morning. But she had learned the hard way to look up the weather and tidal forecasts in advance. The Captain rarely informed anyone about bad weather; forewarning the crew often led to last-minute desertions on the worst days. Today the weather at dawn was only a mirage. Change was coming—and soon. But rain or shine, three hundred crab pots would be tended that day.

Sarah choked on the dry crackers as she looked out over the deck rail. Soon her clothes and skin would be covered in flecks of blood, slime, and rotten fish guts. The very thought of the smell of her fingers at the end of the day made her want to vomit, but she had been born with a sailor's steel stomach. Mentally she threw up often, but physically there was no need.

The bow lifted and jumped from the mounting waves as the boat turned southeast toward the first crab pot on the first line of the day. Sarah claimed her spot at the stern's port side, next to the culling box and first mate, Dave. The worst part of the day: Putting on the cold, slimy rubber gloves someone else had sweat in the day before. Sarah had forgotten her own gloves in the truck, but she knew complaining was futile; unless someone died, they would not be returning to the dock early. *Then again,* she thought, *even if someone did die, the Captain would likely finish the lines, figuring the dead were in no hurry to be buried.*

Sarah's job was to sort through all the noncrab creatures that became trapped in crab-pot prison and fell into the culling box. The pots collected anything and everything attracted to the bait of fish heads. Fortunately for most of the captured critters, they were rejected and thrown back to the deep by the crew. When time allowed, she launched the rejects high into the air; they flew among the birds before plopping into the bay. She told herself the discarded critters were probably delighted to take their one and only opportunity to soar the sky.

Ultimately, however, it was the seagull gatekeepers who determined the fate of each thrown creature. When Sarah pitched unappetizing sea life at their heads, the gulls keened their disappointment. They were good at making quick decisions and usually let the nastiest treats fall away—but not always. She laughed at their rare, painful mistakes.

"Stop that," the Captain yelled. He saw her teasing the gulls but was too busy driving the boat to do anything about it.

The more pots the crew collected, the cloudier the sky grew.

The object of the Captain's quest that morning was the blue-claw crab. The males of the species were prized for their taste, and he saw dollar signs affixed to their flat, double-pointed heads. What remained of the captured bounty was discarded for being ugly or prehistorically creepy. When in doubt, the criterion for either tossing a creature into a basket for keeps or hurling it out over the waves as a flying fish was whether the critter looked tasty enough to boil and drench in lemon butter or dip into red cocktail sauce.

There was nothing pleasant about being the judge and executioner of captured prey. Sarah routinely got soaked in salt water by the abrupt braking of the pot above her head. Unsuspecting jellyfish often hitched a ride on the crab pot. Their cloudy snot dripped from the wire-mesh holes and coagulated below among the slimy, flipping cow turds called toadfish. With their Pac-Man heads, rows of sharp teeth, and beady eyes, toadfish landed squarely in the prehistorically creepy category. Sarah believed the creature had lived on Mars before the planet had dried up into a dusty, red ball. Nature, inexplicably, decided to include two poisonous barbs at the fish's dorsal fins—just in case the thing wasn't unappetizing enough already. Nothing hunted the toadfish; it was safe from extinction for another million years.

A few unlucky flounder flopped into the box, followed by a slow-crawling spider crab covered in barnacles. But the five male blue crabs were able warriors with their large, powerful claws. They held on tight to the inside of the wire-mesh cage. Dave shook the pot, and the Captain yelled at him; when a crab is threatened, it sometimes drops its claw to get away and thereby devalues itself.

Sarah picked up a shovel and scooped the unwanted guests from the culling box. The seagulls fought over the flounder. The largest of the crabs took a defensive position in the corner; it had experience. She could see how it had lived so long in the hostile bay. She sacrificed the health of her finger to move the creature to the wooden basket. She endured the maddening pain, but she dared not shake its claw loose. The loss of the devil's precious regenerative arm was not her concern; she feared the death grip of the abandoned claw. Only a pair of pliers could detach a pincher from a finger, and the slow removal process brought involuntary tears of pain as well as gales of laughter from the crew.

As the Captain accelerated to the next pot, the boat lunged forward and slipped sideways. The overcast sky darkened to a dense slate gray, and the wind picked up. The white tips of the waves now rocked the boat, and the downpour began. Only half the lines tended, but the fun must go on. The Captain wrinkled his nose in the wind and let the rain pelt him as he pushed the *Outlaw* forward with a full throttle in search of the next cork. As the men raised more black-metal pots, heavy with crab, the old salt appeared gleeful—the wet men did not.

Sarah struggled to keep up with an overflowing culling box while the crew closed multiple bushels and provided an endless supply of new baskets to fill. Rain poured from the end of her nose. When she could no longer keep up, the Captain called a break for the men. As her work continued, despite the dreary conditions, she was thankful for the rain; it spared her having to hear the men pissing off the side of the boat.

When the culling box was nearly empty, break time was over. The Captain snagged the next floating cork with a hook attached to a long pole and handed the captured rope to Dave. The first mate wrapped it around the winch a couple of times, pulled the rope, and dropped the slack at his boots.

When the crab pot dangled above Sarah, it drenched her with a new coat of cold, repulsive slime. Dave banged the old, rotten fish bait out of the empty pot—the filth spit in her face. He dutifully waited for the Captain's signal to roll the pot off the stern. Sarah involuntarily tasted the putrid specks of decay clinging to her lips.

The rainstorm continued, and the boat rocked and bucked, but the crew made the chaos appear relatively controlled. The greenhorn, however, spent an inordinate amount of time holding on to whatever solid object he could find or pulling himself off the floor. The Captain yelled at him about bending his knees, but strangely enough, he was not learning anything by being endlessly berated.

At one point while Sarah was looking down, the iron edge of a crab pot collided with the side of her head. The first word of the day she heard from Dave, besides the occasional curse word, was an abrupt "Sorry," but he continued to work without pause. She was sure it had not been an accident; he'd taken the perfect opportunity to collect payback for her earlier slacking—when the Captain was preoccupied with steering. The stinging salt water seeped into the fresh gash and washed a drizzle of faint pink blood into the box, blending with the entrails and sewage already sloshing around in there.

The crew snickered. The deeper the box of crabs grew—and the more she was bit and stung—the angrier she became. Her first enraged thoughts were to shove Dave off the boat, but that was too good for him. She imagined looping a rope around his throat and wrapping it around the electric winch, making sure it was good and tight.

But why do the dirty work when gravity is happy to help? The crew rarely paid attention to their feet, and the ropes often snared unsuspecting swabs. She spotted one lying near Dave's feet when he glanced over to look at her wound. *Admiring your handiwork?* she thought. She returned his insincere grin, plotting her own revenge.

When the first mate looked to the Captain for the signal to throw the pot overboard, she covertly spun the rope ahead of his raised boot. The rope formed a loop, waiting for him to step forward. Dave threw the crab pot overboard, and the attached rope zipped off the boat. He took a small step forward, and the rope snagged his foot, causing him to stumble backward into a steel motor housing. The long rope, still flying off the boat, buzzed past his ear, searing his neck. He yelled, and the Captain idled the boat, but it was still moving forward.

The momentum continued to carry the rope overboard until the large orange cork smacked Dave in the head, and he fell to the deck. The cork catapulted into the air, belly-flopped into the water, and caused a big splash. Dave pulled himself off the deck, hugging the winch's drum. Instead of moving to help him, the Captain yelled, "You never listen. If you don't watch your feet, I'll be pulling your goddamn dead body out of the water."

The only remorse Sarah felt was disappointment. She'd hoped to see Dave flying off the boat, connected to the rope of a crab pot, but she'd have to settle for the rope burn on the side of his neck and the red mark on his head instead.

When the rain slowed, there were over fifty bushels stacked on the deck, leaving a sparse area for the crew to maneuver in. Except for the Captain, who was navigating from the cabin, the whole crew huddled in the back, soaking wet. Studying the new guy's greenish tint up close, Sarah knew she would never see him again.

The Mahon River lighthouse no longer housed a beacon—its light had been removed in 1955—but was still a useful landmark for guiding them home. The boat raced, fully loaded, to the Shucking House. It was only now that the second "surprise" of the day revealed itself; the dock was missing over eight feet of water. Sarah never got used to the eeriness of a dock standing so tall. In solidarity, the whole crew cursed Mother Earth. With the tide out, they had to move the cargo over their heads onto the soaring planks of the dock. Low tide also exposed the thick, muddy marsh soup, and the insects showed up for the feast, along with the alluring aroma of rotten eggs.

The crew thought of Sarah as the lucky Captain's daughter, but they were unable to fathom her onerous world; they sampled her life only eight hours at a time. The lost minutes they lamented over in the morning were the petty concerns of paid labor, not family. The crew tended a few hundred crab pots, lifted fifty bushels over their heads, emptied the boat, and then extended eager hands to the Captain for their wages. Sarah was jealous of every one of them but especially the greenhorn, who ran from the building without even stopping to collect his cash.

The Captain's daughter touched her painful wound; she didn't have the luxury of quitting. And because Saturday night was not a prime recruitment slot for men to work the boats, the Captain always needed her to work the Saturday night fishing trips. That meant within four hours from now, the overworked boat would start another shift. A thousand pounds of striped sea bass, also called rockfish, caught in the anchor nets offshore, would have to be boxed and iced before she would go to sleep that night.

Near midnight, Sarah dragged herself to her truck, her second work shift finally over. She was thankful for the new law making it illegal to crab on Sundays, but she still had work to do in the morning: wire brush the eel pots, paint the corks, and clean the walk-in cooler. And the Captain reminded her when leaving the boat—as if she could forget—that she had to finish making the new drift net before Monday night's fishing trip.

The only thing lifting the spirit of the Captain's daughter was knowing graduation was around the corner, and soon she would be off to college. She had applied to two universities, one in Delaware and one out of state, and both had accepted her. Although her father was reluctant to let her go, she was desperate to leave.

Late on Saturday night, on her way home, she imagined what it would be like to have a desk job in an air-conditioned building. Her father would never let her be captain, but she dreamed of one day having a title, like his, she could be proud to earn. Her fate, however, was in her father's hands, and he benefited much more by making her stay. She harbored hope, but deep inside she knew—he would never let her escape the isolation of the dead-end road.

CHAPTER TWO

TORTURE

The Captain snored on his tattered recliner, wiggling his yellow, cracked toenails and pointing them toward the television. At the kitchen table, Sarah, afraid to wake him, carefully turned the page of her calculus book. Her father was a light sleeper. Before she could finish reading the first paragraph of the page, he woke himself with an abrupt, piglike snort. He surveyed the room and smacked his lips. Spotting her sitting at the table doing nothing important, he said, "I need you to take the rent over to Viktor."

"I'm studying," Sarah replied and planted her finger—hard—in the book to keep her place.

"All they teach you is crap anyway. We have calculators now," he said.

"You know I hate going over there," Sarah said and resumed reading but kept her finger rigid on the page. Her loathing of the landlord's family was a weakness her father would not tolerate.

"Boys will be boys. Stop being so damn sensitive," he said, getting up to fiddle with the antennae on the television set.

Sarah pounded her forefinger's fury into the page again and glared at her father. Every time she tried to read a book with her father in the room, he interrupted her midsentence. He lumbered away from the TV. The recliner caught his fall, and he focused on a field of TV static that vaguely suggested a football game. "Get me a beer," he said.

Sarah slammed the book shut with a loud *crack*, and he jumped an inch off his seat—but did not ask why she was angry. Nor did he seem to care.

While Rex immersed himself in the staticky suggestion of a football game—a long pass, judging by the camera movement—Sarah tossed her own pass: a cold beer that landed hard in his lap. In his scrambling to prevent the can from tumbling onto the floor, he missed the outcome of the play, and whistles blew on the field. His face turned purple in rage.

"Do it now!" he yelled, practically frothing at the mouth. "Take that damn money down to the Eriksens before I—"

Sarah was as enraged as he was but knew when her father had reached the point beyond which further provocation might be dangerous. He was, after all, more than twice her size. Without further objection, she scooped up the damp envelope, full of fish-blood money, and left.

A thunderous slam of the door behind her accentuated her displeasure. The rental house rocked, and its foundation vibrated ever so slightly. She wished the house would crumble behind her with her father in it, but the old house was sturdy. Hand-delivering money to the landlord was an insufferable indignity piled onto old wounds of shame.

The local fishermen—even the old-timers like Sarah's dad—were mostly renters, coming and going with the tides. The farmers were the landowners. The power dynamics between the farmers and the fishermen created long-standing resentments that simmered below the surface.

In Sarah's case, the resentments were more recent and specific. *I have more important things to do than to be humiliated by the Eriksen brothers today*, she ruminated as she walked to the truck.

The rainstorm had passed, and the sun triggered a natural sauna. Sarah looked across the field, on the same side of Port Mahon Road, at the white, two-story farmhouse with the haint-blue shutters. The landlord and farmer, Viktor Eriksen, lived with his wife, Clare, and their three sons: Lance, Brody, and Grant. Sarah reached for the truck handle and paused. If she drove to the Eriksens, the errand would be over too soon for her father to cool off. Instead, she decided to walk the short distance and enjoy the sun.

Sarah's reluctance to visit the Eriksen home was not only because of the humiliation of being the lowly, paying indentured servant living on their property. There was also the fact that all three Eriksen boys were vile bullies. The echoes of their laughter at her expense over the years rang in her head so loudly that she was forced to cover her ears to stop the painful flow of memories.

Sarah walked without haste on the narrow paved road with corn planted on both sides, hearing only the sprightly violin of grasshoppers, the buzz of bees, and the percussion of her footsteps. Over the short, young stalks, she saw the Eriksen boys up ahead, clustered around a truck with an open hood.

Sweat made her clothes cling to her skin. The Eriksen brothers were merciless, but they were also undeniably impressive physical specimens. The knowledge that she would never see any of them again after graduation reduced her apprehension.

When she neared the house, she thought about just walking past it, but instead, she aimed for the middle of the Eriksen pack, leaving her humiliation on the side of the road.

The hobbled silver Chevy four-wheel-drive echoed Grant's own feeling of vulnerability as it sat facing the road with its hood up and engine exposed. Grant saw Sarah before his brothers did; he wiped the oil from his hands with a rag and stepped away from the truck. She was also a high school senior but rarely in the same class with him. He was surprised to see her here on foot; usually, she tore past the house in her pickup without a glance or wave.

Sarah hated Grant, he knew, and he had earned it—he and his brothers—through years of tormenting, teasing, and downright bullying. Beset by guilt, Grant had long been yearning to apologize and make amends, but Sarah had skillfully and intentionally avoided being alone with him for the last half of high school. With his brothers listening, he dared not try to make amends in front of them; the price to pay would be too high.

The dead-end road had made the Eriksen house impossible for Sarah to avoid over the years. Grant remembered how, as children, the Eriksen boys would ambush her with prepared insults when she passed by. The sadistic desire to ridicule and demean her was on a par with the boyish need to kill ants with a magnifying glass. The boringness of the road, with its few distractions, made matters worse. The boys would call her Fish Face, Stinky Fish, and Crab Cakes. Worse than that, they would mock her for having been abandoned by her mother and for having to rent their house. For years, the boys had been addicted to a horrible predatory game, and she had served as their easy victim.

In high school, however, something had changed: Sarah had become Grant's tormentor. Not with her words but with her beauty and persona. He was forced to watch, at close range, her transformation from an uncombed, wild-haired, redheaded kid into a drop-dead-gorgeous high school senior. All the guys in town, Grant and his brothers included, routinely kicked themselves for failing to foresee how beautiful she was going to turn out. It was as if she had willed herself to be the prettiest girl in the state for the sole purpose of extinguishing all the happiness they'd accrued from the devilish amusement they practiced as children.

"Damn," said Grant, acknowledging the effect she had on him. Her thick, wavy auburn hair; greenish-hazel eyes; small collection of sun-kissed freckles; and wide, infectious smile melted his sanity. Grant felt driven to prove he was no longer the same inhuman child who had teased her. Graduation was around the corner, and soon they would head to college—in different directions. He needed to make his apology before it was too late, and he was running out of time and chances.

Before she could change her mind, he sprinted down the driveway to meet her.

His father, Viktor, and her father, Rex, frequently talked over beers on the Eriksen front porch. When not complaining about onerous fishing regulations that made it impossible for him to earn a living, Rex bragged about his exceptionally talented, gorgeous daughter. And the boys tuned in. Just the other day, Rex said to Viktor, "She is a heartbreaker."

Grant wholeheartedly agreed.

Sarah's talent, in her dad's eyes, lay in her net-making ability. Fine art—to a local commercial fisherman—was a Sarah Vise fishing net. If her nets were not so valuable for catching fish, they would be hanging on walls all over town to be admired. When Sarah turned eighteen and announced she was planning to leave for college, the fishermen panicked, as did all the boys in town.

The more Rex talked about Sarah, the more she became a mythical character; she knew how to tie all the knots and read nautical maps and was strong enough to lift a hundred pounds over her head.

In Grant's mind, she embodied divine lineage. Her porcelain skin; heart-shaped face; long, whimsical hair; and round green eyes reminded him of a goddess. One day, he thought, all the brothers would sit in chairs as old men, like their father and Rex, and talk about the one that got away: not a mythically large fish, but the Captain's astonishingly beautiful daughter.

But the story of Sarah was still being written, Grant reminded himself. He extended his hand toward her, absurdly going for a handshake. She tentatively accepted his oil-soaked hand and said, "Hi, Grant. Nice to see you."

Despite the envelope of cash in her left hand, he pretended she was there to visit him. "It's pretty hot out here. How about something to drink?" he offered, trying to shield his words from his brothers, who leaned in to hear the exchange.

"Why? Are you done milking the cows?" Sarah asked, a glint in her eyes.

"Sure," said Grant, playing along. "I finished about five this morning." His brothers looked around, confused—they did not own any cows. "About the same time you usually head out to work on your dad's boat. We both have slave-driving fathers, right?"

"Whatever," said Sarah, not taking the conversational bait. She handed him the envelope and turned to leave.

Grant panicked and dropped the money. "Are you sure I can't get you anything?"

Walking away, she raised a hand to wave goodbye and snapped. "No thanks. I've got to get going. Bigger fish to fry and all that."

His fleeting opportunity evaporated in the hot sun. Lance and Brody pointed and laughed at their pathetic brother, standing alone in the driveway looking helpless. "Sarah, wait," Grant said and ran to catch up. He hoped she would turn around when he touched her shoulder, but instead, she shrugged off his hand, said, "What is it?" and kept walking.

Afraid to touch her again, he ran ahead of her and said, "I need to talk to you."

When she waited too long to answer, he instinctively knew she was about to refuse him. He bent his head to snare her eyes and asked, "How about I walk you home?"

Sarah huffed but replied, "Fine."

It was not the enthusiasm Grant had hoped for, but he would take any crumb she tossed.

On the walk back along Port Mahon Road, Grant opened his mouth a few times, but nothing came out. Sarah stopped on the road at last and said impatiently, "What do you want from me?"

The sun burned above them, and sweat poured from his forehead. He replied, "It's just—I need to sit down."

With only blacktop and field between their homes, no resting spot was available. Sarah pointed to the two chairs under the sprawling weeping willow tree next to her house and said, "You can park yourself there. Stop sweating, and tell me what's wrong with you."

Sarah marched to the tree and sat in one of the chairs. Grant followed but did not sit. He paced in front of her, looking to the sky to assist him with words.

Sarah's anxiety grew as Grant paced. She could feel what was on his mind so clearly and finally blurted out, "Are you here to apologize?"

The idea of an apology was offensive to her. It would be an opportunity for him to relieve himself of guilt, cut open her old wound, and relabel her a victim all over again.

"Yes," he said succinctly.

Feeling trapped by the arms of the chair, she squirmed. She mentally kicked herself for letting him come up her driveway. He refused to sit, and the height difference was annoying. But then he crouched to make eye contact, and that was far worse.

"Well, don't," she said, but his icy blue eyes short-circuited her brain, and her thoughts froze.

"I need to say this, Sarah." Grant was so close he could have kissed her. She smelled the mint on his breath. Her mind struggled to escape, and she was no longer listening.

But he insisted she focus on him and took her hands. His light-brown hair, with sunbaked highlights, was short above his ears and longer and thicker on top. When she managed to stop looking into his eyes, she became self-conscious, knowing he could see that she was staring at his chest. It did not take x-ray vision to see that under his blue T-shirt, he had a well-defined, muscular build and broad shoulders.

"What I did to you all those years was wrong." He forged ahead. "I hate myself for being *that* kid," he said. She wanted him to stop, but he held his palm up and said, "Please, let me finish. I apologize for every horrible thing I did to you. I don't deserve forgiveness, but I hope it helps you to know how much I regret it all."

Just looking at him made her want to forgive him, but the anger she still felt kicked in as a counterbalance. She was about to tell him to forget it, as if it never happened, but instead asked, "Why are you bringing this up now?"

"Something came over me when I saw you," he answered. "It was a fear that tomorrow would be too late. I've been a coward." Grant reduced the already too-small space between them and said, "And I've waited far too long already."

Sarah closed her eyes, wanting to turn off the empathy valve but not fully succeeding.

"Hit me, yell at me, swear at me, do *something*," he said.

In response to her silence, he groaned and sprawled backward on the grass, a wounded man.

If she had not witnessed this display of emotional surrender, she would never have believed he was capable of it. Although he was still jeans-commercial handsome, she had to admit there was something repulsive about seeing him on the verge of tears.

A crush on him, fostered since childhood, had been easy to hide within the disdain she felt toward him growing up. But she had secretly admired him—after middle school and long after the name-calling ended. That is, until he displayed this unappealing show of weakness. This was somehow worse than the teasing; she wasn't sure why.

"It doesn't matter," she said, dismissing his torment as trivial and saving herself from any further witnessing of his emotional nakedness. When he finally stood up, she addressed him as a man and said, "Forget about me and what happened before. When I'm gone, none of this will matter. And believe me, I can't be gone fast enough."

Sarah intended to say, "When I'm gone to college, none of this will matter," but her actual words hung heavily in the air, acquiring a different sort of weight.

CHAPTER THREE

DRIFT NET

Sarah thought she had successfully extinguished Grant's fire. She waited and watched, expecting him to leave. He stood his ground, and a slight smile appeared. Then she saw the embers of his eyes come aglow again, perhaps one last flare-up before fading.

"Spend time with me," he said. "Before we go."

She had underestimated him; he was determined. "Why should I?" she asked, intrigued by his boldness.

Then came the confident answer that pulled together the remnants of the man she thought she'd broken. "Because you want to."

Sarah considered his response a challenge. She was leaving Port Mahon, and nothing was going to stop her—especially not him. His arrogance in thinking he could make a difference irritated her at first; then, she considered it offensive. *He thinks I'm still the sniveling little girl he bullied*, she thought. The Captain's daughter decided she would not retreat—not with his "blood in the water." Destiny had set up the conditions for him to experience the pain he richly deserved—to watch her leave this place without granting him absolution. *Maybe I'll dish out some agony before you rush off to college*, she thought.

"So what do you intend to do—stand here for the rest of the summer?" Sarah asked.

With a big smile, he pointed to the path in the woods behind her house, giving her a little *follow-me* nod of his head.

"Wipe the grin off your face," she said. "I'm not a prize turkey."

Grant erased the smile, but it reappeared on its own. He began walking toward the path behind the house.

"And I'm not a dog who's going to follow you without any explanation."

But when he continued walking, that was exactly what she did.

They passed the rusty silos used for storing feed corn, and the driveway narrowed to a trail. Sarah moved out ahead of Grant to show him that she knew the path and to assume a sense of control. She was not dressed for woodland hiking—she was wearing shorts. She led the way toward the woods, stepping unintentionally into a patch of burr weeds. The weeds scratched her skin, but she resisted complaining and kept going. Grant saw the maze of red lines appear on her legs and held out his hand to help her navigate an easier path.

Before they stepped into the dense trees, she asked, "Are you taking me to where you bury the bodies?"

Grant smiled as if he knew something Sarah did not and said, "I'm saving that for a second date."

Sarah didn't mind holding his hand through the woods. It wasn't a romantic thing; if he knew his way around without having to fight through thorns, then fine, let him lead. The woods behind her house were shaded but not dark, and the ground had a slight rise. At the top of the wooded hill, they passed a makeshift fort, barely standing, with propped boards covered in unpainted plywood, blackened with rot—the Eriksen boys' childhood hideout.

The trees thinned to a sandy, circular clearing. Woods bordered three-quarters of the circle. A deep trench for irrigation kept the area dry. Beyond the ditch lay a recently plowed field, with young, sprouted potato plants—a few leaves per stem—lined up on mounds.

Three stool-sized rocks encircled a sandy firepit full of ashes and charred branches. Crushed, faded beer cans, crumpled strips of magazines featuring naked girls and sports cars, and old potato chip bags littered the area.

Grant sat on one of the three flat-topped rocks, making room for Sarah. She sat on one of the other rocks. "I didn't see you at prom," Grant said.

"No one asked," Sarah replied.

Grant's face turned an intriguing shade of pink.

"Who did *you* take to the prom—Jennifer?" she asked.

"No. Kim," he answered. He then said in a quieter voice, "But to be honest, I would rather have been sitting here at this firepit."

"Kim in my homeroom?" she asked.

"Yeah, yeah," he said, clearly looking for an opportunity to change the subject.

"She looks like a Jennifer, though, right?" Sarah remarked.

"I'm gonna go out on a limb and guess you don't like her."

"Why would you say that? No, I can see it now. The two of you married, with three little blond kids—two girls with pigtails and a boy with farmer overalls. Church on Sunday, Friday night fish fry."

"Exactly what I dream of," he deadpanned. "Don't forget the station wagon. Should I have asked you?"

Instead of answering, she pointed into the woods and said, "What kind of tree is that?"

Smiling to signal he was aware her distraction was intentional, he asked, "Which one?"

She pointed to a tree with dark-green fern leaves and feathery hot-pink-and-white blooms. He held out his hand to help her stand. She hesitated but then grasped it.

"That's a silk tree called a pink mimosa," he said, walking her closer to the tree.

She was struck by how beautiful, exotic, and strangely out of place the tree looked. "What's it doing here?" she asked.

"They're all over the coast in this area," he replied. "Pretty hard to miss."

"The blooms look like cotton candy. Are they sticky?" she asked.

When he turned to her to answer, she thought for a moment he wanted to kiss her. Her heart beat in double time, and she stepped back to avoid his advance. Before the moment could turn awkward, she asked, "What are we doing here?"

Just then, the wind carried mumbled voices across the field; it was Grant's brothers. Sarah turned in the direction of home and said, "It's been real, but I've got to go." Grant's easy smile agreed with Sarah's demand to leave; he appeared satisfied with the amount of time they had spent together.

As Sarah and Grant headed back together, an overcast sky darkened the woods, but he led them back to the silos without difficulty. With her house still out of sight, he stopped her and said, "Let me pick you up later."

"A second date in one day?" she asked.

He smiled. "What can I say? I like to move fast."

"I don't see the point," Sarah said. *He's not a friend and certainly not a boyfriend*, she thought. *He's nothing more than a placeholder crush awaiting a real man to replace him.*

His unbroken smile revealed her mistake: she'd left the door too generously ajar. If she'd wanted him to lose optimism, a more direct answer would have been better.

He leaned in, level with her eyes, and asked, "Will you at least let me call you later?"

The first raindrops fell, and she found herself unwilling to erase the luminous smile from his face. "Fine."

As Sarah walked away from Grant and approached her house, she saw the Captain peer through the kitchen curtains. She'd been gone for an hour on an errand that should have taken a few minutes. Grant ran past the house, trying to avoid getting soaked on his way home.

Sarah was not fully inside the door when her father said, "I see Grant Eriksen was here." Sarah walked past him, picked up her calculus book without slowing down, and headed to her room to study.

"What about the drift net?" the Captain shouted at her back.

The net! Sarah had forgotten about the drift net promised for the next day's fishing trip. Sixty more feet, one length of the Shucking House, remained to be completed on the six-hundred-foot fishing net.

The Shucking House, a community resource for all the Port Mahon fishermen, had a steady flow of operations every night except Sunday or in severe weather. Sarah had no choice but to finish the net tonight or wait another week.

"I'll finish it next weekend. I have to study," she yelled from her bedroom.

Her dad barged right into her room and said, "You had plenty of time to waste in the woods with Grant Eriksen."

She tensed with her thick book in hand, contemplating throwing it at his head.

He took his anger down a notch and said, "Drift season starts tomorrow. You saw the condition of the one we used last year. The holes are so big the fish swim right through. We'll be wasting our time out there without a new drift net. You're almost finished with it—just a couple more hours, that's all."

Sarah felt dizzy under the constant pressure and exhausted by the endless juggling of too many tasks. When she did not move from her chair fast enough, her father resorted to intimidation, pounding his fist on the wall. "I need the new net tomorrow, and I'm not waiting another week!"

In Sarah's life there was never enough time to do anything well or to recognize what had been finished. She had wire-brushed eel pots all morning so he could catch his nasty, lime-green eels again. (Mental images of eels jumping straight out of the salted barrel to avoid their doom made her skin crawl.) But all her father could ever dwell on was the unfinished, the things she had not yet done.

And he needed twenty more yards of her time before morning.

The rain fell on her window. "Get out," she said. "If you want the stupid net done, I need to change."

As she shut the door in his face, he said, "When we put it out tomorrow, it better be straight."

A commercial fishing net is constructed with exact, detailed measurements. When built properly, the net hangs flat and drifts evenly through the water. Well-made nets catch the intended species and the correct-sized fish and leave everything else undisturbed. Uneven nets, on the other hand, snag a lot of unsuspecting and unwanted sea life. Sarah was meticulous in building her nets to minimize unintended fatalities.

After changing her clothes, Sarah opened the bedroom door and asked, "Would you mind telling me how I'm supposed to study on top of doing all the jobs you need me to do?"

He did not answer her presumably rhetorical question, but as she headed toward the back door to grab her raincoat before leaving, he asked one of his own. "Who cares if you study or not? Girls don't need to go to college."

Sarah froze. Bringing Grant on the property had been a mistake. Her father was just waiting for her to pick a guy, get married, and have children. To him, walking through the woods with Grant meant she was already pregnant.

As she opened the back door to leave, a flash of lightning lit up the backyard. Any positive feelings she'd had for Grant were gone. Then she remembered the jerk was planning to call her later. She marched to the wall phone and pulled the receiver off its cradle. No need to look up the number; it was right in front of her eyes in big numbers, tacked to the wood paneling under the name Viktor.

"Is Grant there?" she asked.

A brief pause and Grant answered. With her father listening, and before Grant could say anything, Sarah said, "You can't call or come pick me up tonight. I have to go to the Shucking House and finish a drift net for my father." Sarah glared at her father, hoping he would connect the dots—that social isolation made it impossible for her to find the precious husband he wanted for her.

"I can help you," Grant offered.

Sarah skipped past the laughable idea that a farmer could be at all useful in building a drift net. She turned away from her father, signaling a need for privacy, and said into the phone in a quiet but deliberate tone, "Listen—I'm not worth your trouble. I'm leaving and never coming back. I hope you have a wonderful life." Before he could respond, she dropped the phone onto its hook.

Sarah exited, leaving the back door wide open. The Captain could damn well close it himself.

She dashed to the truck in the rain, but before she reached it, her father called out after her, “You’re not going to college!” She fired up the truck, stopped at the end of her driveway, and looked both ways. *I will no longer live on Port Mahon Road*, she silently vowed.

But instead of leaving town, she turned into the storm, in the direction of the Mahon River lighthouse—the eternal symbol of her imprisonment.

CHAPTER FOUR

LIFEBOAT

This land belongs to no one. It is part of the earth, created to feed, and be a home for, all of its people and beings. The spirit of all winged, rooted, scaled, and flightless creatures, living and unliving, have been bound to this place since the beginning of time; no person could possess such sacred ground.

Port Mahon is a rotting marsh, a recycling of everything once alive and now decomposing. The atonement of all creatures—plants and animals—is accepted back into the earth here, donating exactly what each stole to be born. This place is dense with layers. All life, all death, all hope, and all disappointment hang in its misty night air. Such a seemingly insignificant spot is the place of dreams, beauty, wonder, and horror.

For years, the guardian being protecting the earth had heard the deep suffering of the orphan spirit who'd summoned him but refused to interfere—it was not his place. But this day her shrieking spirit's cry for help started a rumble and quake inside the earth. Unable to ignore the plea any longer, he followed the orphan to the sea.

The Shucking House was empty and cold with its cement floors and cinder-block walls. When Sarah opened the front door, the wind moaned through the hollow, wide-open space built to pack the seafood delivered from the dock. The place was quiet now, but in her mind, she could still hear the roar of the conveyor belt as doomed oysters, clams, and mussels, hidden tight in their shells, were heaped into burlap bags for market.

Dampness weighted the air as Sarah passed the light switch. In the dim ambient light, she stared at the pile of rope, twine, cork, and filament mesh awaiting her handiwork. Lacking the energy to undo the tangled mess in order to tie off the last sixty feet to finish, she sat and wandered through the memories of the horrors she had witnessed on the boat. All the dead things that had stuck to the net over the years haunted her mind and populated her dreams.

The large, lifeless female loggerhead sea turtle, more than three hundred pounds, yanked into the boat the previous week was only the latest example—its copper-peaked, heart-shaped shield of armor no longer able to protect its flailing caramel-and-cream-colored neck. The crew talked about tasty turtle soup that day, while Sarah caressed its wrinkled skin, wishing it would come back to life and soar the open ocean again.

Sarah blamed herself. It was her net and her burden. The sea turtle's air-loving nose had needed to be only inches closer to the surface to breathe. But the net had stopped it. It was Sarah's anger at life that had caused her uncharacteristic sloppiness with the net. Her mistake had held the sea turtle's winglike flippers just shy of the surface.

Remembering the limp, lifeless turtle, she sobbed until her pain flowed from her gut, stung her eyes, and weakened her heart. She felt as trapped and suffocated as the turtle, as ensnared by the nets of her own making. *No college*, her dad said. Just more drift nets, more cold, more dampness, more darkness, more fish, more stink, more death. There was to be no escaping the dark and joyless life she endured on this dead-end street, under the shadow of that miserable lighthouse.

"Take me. I don't want to be here anymore," she screamed at the air, spitting tears from her mouth. She imagined that the rain pouring down outside was the life draining from all the animals that had died at her hand.

The sea called to her from the other side of the large sliding door to the dock. The heavy door's small windows, black with grime, faced the horizon, which the sun had coldly deserted. The memories of all the animals that had died alone in the nets or in the Shucking House, suffering and lost, triggered thoughts of how her mother had left her alone so long ago. She wished there had been at least a goodbye, but there had been no warning and no closure. Like a fish being yanked from the water.

Sarah's life was one served cold and brutal. A place of endings only, no beginnings.

A barrage of hail, as large as marbles, struck the sliding doors, interrupting her self-pity. She wished the ice balls would bury her, but the building protected her unworthy life. She sat silently on the floor and listened as the storm melted away any trace of desire to live another day.

Waiting for Sarah's return, Grant struggled to see the road through his northeast-facing bedroom window, but it was obscured by rain and dimmed by nightfall. When her truck had left home, he'd been ready to throw himself in front of it to prevent it from passing, but she had turned east to the lighthouse instead.

Her desire to leave Port Mahon—which he'd picked up strongly in their short time together—was a desire he identified with. He, too, wanted to escape from living a caged, predetermined life. He needed to correct her misguided theories about him.

Anticipating her return, he yearned for the opportunity to speak with her, but he was not a patient man. He paced the floor. The rainstorm worsened and reinforced the idea that he should go after her. Sarah had slipped through his fingers so many times before, but now that he had made a small connection with her, he would not let it happen again.

She's taking too long, he thought. She was alone, at the end of a treacherous road, in a storm. His thoughts spun out new dangers with every idle moment.

The bay often floods the road at high tide; she might be stranded. What if her old truck broke down? Endless dire possibilities engulfed his mind, but her words of warning kept him from acting on impulse. Sarah said she wanted nothing to do with him. And why would she? He had naively hoped an apology would fix the years of atrocities he had perpetrated on her. But he had been foolishly wrong. And he agreed with her assessment that she deserved a better man. Still, he was unable to break the bond he felt existed between them and unwilling to give up his sense that she was in danger.

Many species of birds harbored in the steel rafters of the Shucking House. The resident barn owl, with its black eyes and heart-shaped face, stirred and flapped its gray-and-gold-flecked wings, protesting Sarah's trespass. It did not approve of the interruption of its late-night dinner of scurrying floor rodents.

"I hear you," Sarah replied to the owl. "I'm going."

Sarah decided to defy her upbringing and leave the net undone, knowing full well what her father's response would be. But she could no longer profit from death and purposely end the life of any creature—with or without spinal cords. She'd already caused enough death for ten lifetimes, and she was only eighteen. She was done. Period. Decision made. Feeling trapped between her decision and her father's inevitable fury, she struggled to find a way out of the mental net she had built for herself when she was startled by a loud knocking sound on the sliding door. She tried to ignore it, but it persisted. The pounding was nerve jangling, and the sliding door rocked visibly. Just the wind, of course. No one was there, she was sure. But the banging continued.

There was a possibility, albeit slim, that someone could be stuck in the storm between the tumultuous sea and the building. Only the dock and the sea lay beyond the door, and she doubted any boats were out tonight. To be fully certain, she would have to see who was on the other side.

The unoiled, rusty metal sliders bucked and screeched when she slid the door open a couple of feet. A gust of rainy wind barged in, slapped her in the face, and drenched her body. White-tipped waves glimmered and peaked a few feet below the dock. Instead of seeing them as dangerous, she viewed them as beautifully chaotic. The wild energy of the sea was stirring something inside her, and she needed to be part of it.

When Sarah stepped out on the dock, the wind pulled her forward, and she squinted as salt water washed her eyes. The majesty of the sea compelled her to kneel, and she crawled to the edge of the dock, hugging a thick piling with her right arm. With her left hand, she grabbed a rope that was wrapped around a mooring cleat and slid forward to the edge of the decking. Her legs dangled, and the tops of the waves tickled her feet. She faced the storm and refused to turn her head. A large wave broke against the dock, soaking her. The top of the wave skidded across the deck, its foam hissing as it slipped through the cracks.

Sarah stared below into the waves, and they seemed to reach for her. The compassion for the sea turtle had opened an emotional wound. No one cared for their suffering, hers or the turtle's. Sarah lifted her chin and shouted into the wind, "Where is the love? Where the hell is it?"

The wind seemed to empathize with her plight and wrapped itself around her. She imagined her mother holding her. The wind whispered, "I love you," and pelted her with hard rain, but she did not mind the pain—it was better than no attention at all.

Sarah remembered the defiant child her mother had endured. She refused to comb her hair, drink her milk, or do anything else she was told. When she took off for hours by herself, without permission, her mother would become enraged. It did not matter how many times her mother tried to make her stay or do the right thing; she would not change. Eventually, the beatings her mother gave no longer hurt or made her cry. And when the wooden spoon, hairbrush, fist, and foot failed to change Sarah into a good girl, her mother gave up—and left.

Her father was abandoned at the same time, and his loneliness was also her fault. There was nothing she could do to fix any of it. The direction of her life was set, and there was no relief in sight, no chance to change it. All she had hoped for throughout high school was to be able to go to college, and she had done everything possible to make that happen.

But college was for the good kids whose parents loved them.

The violent storm was somehow tied to her despair; its bleak sorrow was hers. Nature spoke to her, and she listened. She was part of its family. She belonged with the sea, and it was inviting her to stay. The sea would wash her away—as if she had never existed.

She choked off her tears. Enough. Self-pity would have meant she cared for the pathetic life she was leaving. And she didn't. Her only comfort was that she had taken so little in life—and so her debt to the earth was less. A sacrifice to the sea as nourishment to the animals, after having killed so many, was an honorable death, she reasoned. Slipping quietly away would spare others any inconvenience.

The releasing of her life felt more like freedom than loss. The wind wrapped around her arms again and pulled her forward. She balanced gently on the edge of the dock. She saw the tall wave coming, the one that would take her. It rolled toward her without sentiment, and she let go of her life.

Abandoning doubt, her hands relaxed, she released the mooring—and the wave took her. The water's buoyancy momentarily held her afloat, and she rested on the shoulder of the wave, letting it carry her. She raised one hand above her head to wave goodbye.

A brilliant light flooded her as she eagerly closed her eyes.

CHAPTER FIVE

SWEPT AWAY

As the wave lifted her, a hand from heaven above grasped hers, pulling her to the next realm. But then she felt the slam of wood into her side and the crush of her hand in the strong physical grip. It was not divine intervention; it was a man.

"Sarah!" his voice screamed. She rolled onto the cold, wet wooden planks and saw the dark silhouette above her. An arch of curling ocean spray hissed over them. Sarah was breathing yet lifeless.

The figure lifted her to her feet—it was Grant—and walked her back toward the Shucking House. The door was open, and all the lights were on in the building. Still holding her with one arm, Grant slid the door behind them to shut out the storm. When the wind stopped howling, he bear-hugged her, and they shivered together, kneeling on the floor.

"I'm not letting you go, so don't even ask me," Grant said, breaking the silence. He pressed his cheek against hers as if she had just returned from a long trip.

"But I want you to," Sarah replied. She felt him pull back in shock at the implications of her words. Still, he would not loosen his hold.

"Tell me this was an accident," he pleaded.

She did not reply.

"It doesn't matter," he said, holding her steadily. "It's all right." His warm arms felt comforting. She dropped her resistance, letting his kindness fill the empty hole left by her mother, the one that had never been filled since. She sobbed against his chest. He pulled away, only enough to look into her eyes, and said, "You have no idea how special and important you are."

Sarah liked the velvet sound of his voice but ignored his words. She nestled into his chest and admitted her confusion. "How did you—"

"A gut feeling, I guess you could say. But the horrible thing is, I almost ignored it. I didn't want you to think I was a delusional, lovesick, control freak unwilling to heed a direct order to leave you alone."

"But what if those are the things I like about you?" Sarah said, half kidding, half not.

"My weakness almost killed you. I was afraid you'd laugh because I worried about you."

"You're not responsible for this. I am."

Sarah knew how Grant must be viewing her plunge into the waters: as an active suicide attempt. But she viewed it as a passive decision to let the sea take her away.

She loved the feel of his protective arms but wondered how much longer she would allow him to hold her. She wasn't ready to break away yet.

"What changed your mind to come find me?" she asked.

Grant replied, "When protecting myself stopped being as important as protecting you. I'm glad I didn't waste another minute thinking about it."

As Sarah breathed warmth into his chest, Grant's thoughts retraced the last moments before he found her. Excited to find her truck parked at the Shucking House, he thought the electricity must have been out because the building was dark. The front door was unlocked, and he called for her. He stumbled through the dark, flipping on any light switches he could find. The ice machine turned on, startling him, but he kept going. At the end of the building, he saw the open door with rain pouring in.

Grant ran out to the deck, which was dimly lit by the bright lights inside the building, and saw nothing but blackness beyond. He searched inside the door for the floodlight and switched it on and then ran back onto the dock. Sarah's illuminated hand lifted like a floating beacon above the deck. Without hesitation, he dove to the edge and grabbed it. At the same moment, he was aided by a "Good Samaritan" wave; it seemed to raise her at the same time he pulled her arm. When Sarah rolled onto the deck, the wave disappeared.

The surreal memory of the wave solidified Grant's belief that she had been saved by divine intervention. He was convinced he'd witnessed a miracle but thought the idea was too crazy to mention.

Sarah broke from her beautiful vulnerability. She released him and abruptly stood up. "I've got to go home," she said. Grant deserved some explanation, but she did not have one to give.

All she could manage to say was "Thank you" before withdrawing through the front door and hurrying out to her truck.

Grant stood in the doorway and appeared confused, while Sarah sat alone in her truck to avoid his questions.

When Grant did not leave the doorway, she rolled down her window and said, "Follow me." He hesitantly closed the Shucking House door and got into his truck. Both trucks sat idling. Sarah wanted him to leave; she needed to finish the drift net but knew he would not go without her.

She guessed he would be surveilling her driveway all night, and she would be unable to return to finish the net.

Driving on Port Mahon Road, partially blinded by Grant's headlights in her rearview mirror, Sarah felt annoyed that she was not free to stay at the Shucking House to sort out her thoughts. Her escort was ensuring a safe return to the Captain, who would be angry the drift net was not ready. She wanted to go back and finish the job she had started—which "job," she wasn't exactly sure—but there was no way Grant was going to let her do that.

Sarah drove up her driveway. All the lights were off in the house except the outside floodlight. Grant mimicked her actions from his house across the field. She got out of her truck; he got out of his. She walked to the back door; he walked to his side door, watching her the whole time. Damn, she felt imprisoned again.

Sarah lay in her bed after a long, hot shower and was unable to shut off her resentment at Grant's interference. If he had not pulled her from the waves of this world, it would already be over.

In the dark, Sarah braced for the inevitable small-town gossip. Grant would tell someone, just one person, to explain his whereabouts on a school night, and within twenty-four hours, everyone would know, including her father. Her mind drifted to the place on the dock where she had let go. Of everything. She was weary of this life and wanted it over, now more than ever.

CHAPTER SIX

HUNTED

Earth's guardian had harnessed the sea—as Storm Master. He had pushed a wave toward the orphan as she let go of her life. When earthly beings are threatened with death, a deeply rooted survival instinct is summoned. The bay rose and rolled in time to save her body but not her will to live. A different approach—drastically different—would be needed to awaken her spirit's desire to live.

A weather-beaten house sagged wearily in the darkness. A path worn around it in the soft, sweet grass. The supernatural being—now taking the form of a formidable hunter—looked up at Sarah's bedroom window as she closed her eyes.

Sarah refused to fall. Her mind was wedged between two rocks in a river: conscious and subliminal thought. She hung suspended, caught on the boundary. Life and the afterlife aligned into a point with dense gravity. Her body could not move, and her spirit drifted out into the cool night air.

Sarah awoke on the roof of her house and slid down the shingles, gently falling. Lighter, but not weightless, she stopped her slide and sat on the edge of the roof. A small dark cloud, probing, passed below her dangling feet. A dark, hulking figure crept slowly and quietly past, a black-veiled shadow following him. The flutter of his cloak created a vibrating wind that swirled, stirring loose leaves from the ground and lifting her off the roof. Her arms flailed for air resistance to control her direction as she floated softly to the ground behind him, into the darkness of his wake.

The hunter's sculpted back secreted cool mist. The cloud she had seen from above was a dense fog concealing his movement. She tilted and spun around in the breeze he created but then righted herself. She followed him closely around the house. He stopped below her east-facing window and looked up. When he stopped, the air became still. But she drifted closer anyway; her spirit was pulled with his shroud. His back was large and close, and she feared touching him.

Sarah heard his rapid heartbeat and excited breath, and the mist from his back soaked her face. She managed to remain still as he took a long step, widening the distance between them. He looked up at the house. He showed interest in her bedroom window, but it was too high. The elevated pier-and-beam foundation of the house placed her window ten feet off the ground. Her relief was fleeting, however; she remembered the tree in front of her north-facing window.

The hunter turned sideways, squarely against her house. She cowered close to the ground in his shadow, hoping he would not spot her, and accidentally snapped a small branch. The hunter scanned in all directions. His glowing eyes looked in her direction and frightened her, but he did not seem to see her. Aware of the pounding of her heart, she wondered if he could sense her presence. He shifted his stance and dashed to the corner of the house, away from her. His motion pulled her with accelerated momentum, and she swung past him into the tall grass of the front yard.

Sarah saw him clearly in the moonlight, standing against the white paint of her house. The hunter's chest was bare, and he carried an ax at his waist. He gracefully climbed the tree, and she was lifted off the ground by his wind, ascending with him. He looked in her window and searched the window frame for a way to open it. Floating upside down, she wanted him to stop but was afraid to speak to him. Righting herself, she grabbed hold of the lower part of the tree while he was distracted above her, peering through the glass.

The handle of his hatchet was raised in his right arm when she reached his feet. Sarah closed her eyes, waiting for the glass to shatter. She felt a warm breeze, and it reminded her of Grant's warm, rhythmic breathing. She allowed herself to be swept up in the sense memory.

Lost in the feeling of Grant, she felt protected, but she was actually in grave danger. When she opened her eyes, she was alongside the hunter in the tree. She looked in the window and saw herself sleeping on the bed. Her sleeping self was agitated, caught in a nightmare, and mumbling.

The hunter's massive hand grabbed her upper arm. When Sarah turned to face him, his fluorescent-yellow animal eyes, with thin, vertical pupils, stared into her soul. She struggled to get away. He pushed her out of the tree, and she fell to the ground, losing consciousness.

The scratching of a branch on the front bedroom window startled Sarah awake. The wind outside rustled the branches and shook the glass of her window. The shadows of the tree outside seemed to form a raised ax-head. Sarah froze and carefully watched. When nothing appeared to change, she was happy to dismiss the vision. *The mind plays tricks in the middle of the night*, she thought.

But something about her room felt eerily like the dream. In her periphery, a large shadow moved away from the window. With a loud bang, something struck the side of the house.

Sarah jumped from her bed and ran out of her bedroom to a brightly lit living room. But the room was all wrong—the living room no longer had furniture. No recliner, no television. The house was empty as if she did not live there at all.

I must still be dreaming, she thought.

But the danger seemed real. Each of the three windows facing the west side of the house, adjoining the porch, was missing its glass and was exposed to the night air. Sheer white curtains fluttered and spun in the breeze. The floating fabric pulled away from the window and bowed the thin metal curtain rods, which barely held on, rattling under the strain.

Sarah was trapped. The hunter chasing her would have no trouble catching her with the windows open. She imagined him easily stepping inside to kill her. *But it's pointless to run*, she thought. *I'd just be caught crossing the field.*

A cold wind pushed through the house from the back porch. She could see the back door was wide open. Sarah was sure she had closed and locked it before she went to sleep. She reminded herself she was in a nightmare and hoped she would soon awaken.

"Who are you?" she called out. The room echoed her voice, and the curtains swirled. She imagined the hunter deliberately prolonging her last moments as a thrill killing. "What do you want?"

She moved toward the window, hope diminishing with each step. She heard his soft step into the living room when the dry old wooden floor screeched to give away his position. *There he is.*

Afraid and exposed, Sarah stood in the light of the living room, ten feet from the hunter. Her toes tingled, reminding her she could run—she still had a chance to jump out the window and at least try to escape. Sarah considered her choice and remained still. Peace saturated her body. The hunter pulled his dark shadow with him as he stepped closer. The light in the room faded, drowning her slowly in the darkness. Sarah stepped back. *He intends to kill me,* she thought.

His old-fashioned hatchet made of wood and stone lifted in the deepening shadows.

Each slow step forward he took further questioned her will to live. She answered that questioning by falling to the floor in the corner of the room. Instead of showing bravery, she submitted to him, as she had submitted to the ocean wave, wanting her cold and brutal life to end.

The beast stood over her. She was disappointed in herself that she did not try to run. She hoped, one last time, that she would awaken from the nightmare and then rise in the morning to go to school. The hunter waited patiently, as if wanting her to beg for her life, but she didn't.

The hunter revealed glowing snake eyes just before the strike, and she felt his deep, heaving breath on her face—he was real. The natural bonds to life, which were supposed to kick in at moments like this, failed her. Unable to look the hunter in the eyes, she turned away and waited for the blow.

Emptiness. Then, the blunt-force instrument of death struck her head, cracking her skull—no mercy shown.

Sarah's head erupted in pain as warm liquid rushed down her face and flowed off her jaw to the floor. A loud ringing eclipsed her world. Her thoughts scrambled, and she labored to breathe. Her vision shrank to a smaller and smaller field.

Sarah's last fleeting thoughts were of Grant. He cradled her and told her it would be all right. She believed him. She mumbled a message, hoping—impossibly—that the wind would carry it west across the field to his ears: "I'm sorry."

As the blood drained from her body, Sarah struggled to breathe. For Grant, she held on a few extra seconds, knowing her death would hurt him. But this time, he could not save her. She tried to breathe once more—for him. And then she had no more thoughts. *Silence.*

CHAPTER SEVEN

REBIRTH

Sarah's spirit freed itself from her gloom. She crawled from the darkness without thought. With arms outstretched, she slid her bare belly forward, pressing against a strange, malleable fabric. The membrane of time split, and she emerged from the harsh material world of her birth into an unknown afterlife—like a butterfly emerging from its cocoon. The confining vessel of her body released her, and she fell, weightless and breathless, onto a watery surface.

Propelled by a light breeze, Sarah drifted to a shore and snagged on some tall marsh reeds. She settled upon a bank, feeling an immediate sense of belonging among the feathery blades of Kentucky bluegrass. Crisp air flooded her lungs with soothing replenishment. Breathing fully and peacefully, she lay upon the springy bed of aromatic grass.

When time disappears, the gravity of the earth lessens its burden. The ground was soft. Peace blanketed her with warmth and comfort, and she lay in tranquil anticipation of discovering the place of her rebirth. Without the weight of her former life, she smiled and relished the immense beauty awaiting her.

The familiar honking of Canada geese passed above her. She turned over effortlessly and let her eyes focus on their thin black necks, white cheeks, and plump, light-brown bodies against dark-gray wings. The blue morning sky, saturated with oxygen, lifted them in a *V* formation on their journey home. Awakened by the love surrounding her, Sarah recognized the spongy grass where she rested as a feature of her former world. But here there were no reminders of man-made imperfection. She was in the landscape of Port Mahon, but her house was absent.

The world sprang to life before her with sharper clarity than she'd ever experienced. It was as if her recollections of animals and plants were no more than dull, blurry photographs. And now the natural world was restoring itself to its rightful glory.

At first the camouflaged bunnies froze and stared as if startled by her presence. Then they resumed nibbling grass and ignored her; she posed no threat to them. A parcel of deer, with a few gangly fawns in tow, wandered in the brush nearby. Joy burst from her chest to witness the glory of the sun as it lifted in the eastern sky. It had followed her to her new home! Sarah's yearning for light rose from within her, and she reverently stood to greet the sun as her familiar friend.

Sarah looked down at her body. Without the density of the flesh, every detail was more defined. The myth that ghosts were made of gaseous, foggy vapor was false. She was sculpted from a fresh, silky fiber weave. Her desire to see herself in a mirror grew; she wanted to see what she had become. But no matter how much she tried to call forth her old possessions, man-made things—such as mirrors—refused to appear.

Sarah touched her face, her arms, her feet. Relief abounded as she felt a familiar symmetry. She decided to enthusiastically accept herself as whatever she may now be. Her decision was a pillow of comfort as she basked in the morning glow.

The sun flushed the shadows away and illuminated the landscape. She noticed a figure standing on a rolling hill facing the sun. A young man appeared to wait for her as she moved through the wild grass and walked a familiar path once paved with blacktop but now made of dirt. The man's face beamed a wide smile as he waved his arms, inviting her closer. An amber glow radiated from him, and she was captivated. As she walked the last few steps to greet him, she wondered why she did not appear to glow. She raised her hand to greet him and noticed her fingers had only a faint, shimmering luster.

"Sarah," the tall young man said as he reached for her, offering his glowing hands without hesitation. The image of her grandmother came to her unexpectedly. She recalled how crazily excited her grandmother would be, greeting her at the door on childhood visits, waving wildly for Sarah to come collect an enormous hug. Sarah hoped the man was there to help her see Grandma again.

"Yes, I'm Sarah," she said and offered her hand in return. His hands were strong, smooth, warm, but not sweaty. She figured this must be a wonderful dream because dead ghosts could not be warm with flowing blood.

Sarah's enchanting host—created by her dreams—was powerfully built. His upper arms were encircled in black tattoos, detailed with swirls and geometric shapes, resembling a map of star constellations. The inked trail of marks and figures continued up his neck and down his sides. She could not comprehend what it all meant, but she instinctively knew he was an important being.

The young man wore sparse clothing made of cotton and dyed a yellow-ochre color. His thin dark-brown hair contrasted a strong jawline and full lips. Around his neck was a string of small colorful beads and seashells. She felt a strange connection to the man, as if he were a longtime friend, though she had never met him before. Apparently amused by how long she was taking to look him over, he thanked her with a snicker.

Sarah was spellbound by his physique, and he seemed to enjoy her attention. It was almost as if he'd been conjured up from her secret list of desirable traits for a fantasy male, lifted directly from her private-thoughts diary. The young man pulled her hands toward him. He laughed wildly at her admiration and invited her in to take a closer look. Sarah felt warmth in her cheeks as she grazed his silky arms. He moved her to higher ground. As the sun climbed the sky, she wondered if he was God. As if reading her mind, he replied to her thoughts, "I am Max-ymir-he."

"Um, would it be okay if I call you … Max?"

He nodded with a smile and gestured for her to sit with him.

The bay glittered white diamonds beyond a colony of double-crested cormorants with turquoise-blue eyes and orange cheeks. The waterfowl were arguing over shoreline territory, flapping their black wings and stomping their webbed feet. Sarah recognized the shoreline as she watched the drama unfold. It was Port Mahon Road. But the dead-end road of her life had been marked with an old gutted lighthouse with a faded red-metal roof and a rusted-steel foundation, and there was no trace of such a landmark here. The lighthouse was gone, and in its place lay a natural holy land.

Together they watched the sun dominate the sky, radiating its heat. The marsh grasses swayed and rustled as the gentle, slapping waves rubbed pebbles into shiny new coins she wanted to collect.

"Am I dead?" Sarah asked.

Max seemed hesitant to provide an answer; perhaps the truth was more complicated than a yes or no. Max's amber eyes glowed faintly when he finally answered her. "I took your miserable life and brought you here."

So the cold-hearted killer who had murdered her without mercy was the friendly and charismatic young man sitting beside her amid the majesty of nature. Fully expecting anger to rise within her, as it had in her previous life whenever someone crossed her, she was surprised when all she could feel was forgiveness. Gratitude, even.

The fury of her life simply could not be summoned. It occurred to her that perhaps this world was heaven and therefore unable to channel sin.

Max interrupted her thoughts and elaborated, "I felt your suffering and wanted to share my world with you." He lifted his long arms to the sky.

When Sarah took in a deep breath to ask more questions, he placed a finger on his closed lips and pointed her to the horizon. *Be in awe of the power of this world, and do not question it*, he seemed to be saying. She surrendered to his lead and felt the heaviness of her past life disappear as the lighthouse had. The void previously created by disappointment in herself was now filled by a tide of joy.

Sarah was mortified at all the time she had wasted living in self-hate. From the context of this new realm, it was absurd to have believed she did not deserve to be born. Her lifelong preoccupation with disillusionment had robbed her of life even before Max had. Yet, sitting in this place of wonder, she could not grieve for her frivolous life any more than she could summon anger at the young man who had saved her from a never-ending cycle of misery.

Sarah walked down to the grassy shoreline and waded into the tide. Like a new baptism, the water washed away her sin and pain. She felt reborn from all the anger, and she was forgiven. Forgiven for being imperfect and for being disappointed in herself over and over. The child within her stood as a witness to the end of her suffering.

"This is such a wonderful dream," Sarah whispered to herself, stepping back onto the grass.

Max met her at the water's edge. He focused on her gaze and smiled. "You are not dreaming," he said.

She noticed the heat emanating from him as if he were absorbing the sun and radiating its energy back out. This inspired her to ask, "Is this heaven?"

He pressed his lips together and smiled with his eyes. The tilt of his head rejected her word *heaven*, and he answered, "You are home; don't you recognize it?"

"Yes, but it's missing a few things—like my house. A bed and a pillow would be nice!" Sarah laughed at her own joke.

Max appeared amused and said, "Why do you need such things?"

"Don't people *sleep* in this world?" Sarah asked.

"Of course we sleep," he replied. "When your mind is asleep, your dreams sneak out and reveal your deepest desires."

Max got up and walked away. Sarah could not help but follow, like a string tied to a balloon. He stopped at the dirt path and turned to wait for her. When she caught up to him, he was smiling again. She sensed the warmth of him inside her chest and felt her own faint heartbeat.

"Would you like to go to the beach?" Max asked and gently took her hand. She nodded, and her heart leaped with excitement to explore another familiar-yet-unfamiliar place with her fetching and friendly tour guide. After adjusting his walking speed to match her slower pace, he admitted, "I'm used to being alone." She wondered if he was bothered by her company and was relieved when he added, "But I'm happy you're here."

At their leisurely pace, they walked the narrow path between a field of olive-colored tall grass and a patch of pastel-purple-and-blue wildflowers. The hum of bees and the acrobatics of double-winged iridescent dragonflies entertained them as they approached the thick, dark woods ahead.

Max stopped at the edge of the woods and lifted her chin to ask, "Are you afraid?"

She looked away from his gaze, embarrassed to respond. Not once had she feared the woods before. But she knew something about these woods was different—even deadly—and she was afraid.

He continued to stare—in waiting—until she laughed from discomfort. But then she managed to say, "Yes. I'm very scared."

Max responded, "I will carry you."

Sarah replied, "That's not necessary." But it was too late; he lifted her over his shoulder and entered the woods. *Okay, Tarzan*, she thought. Apparently, he had not gotten the memo on how to carry a woman in a properly romantic manner. The absurdity of her position made her laugh.

The forest was dark but not dead. It was alive with the sounds of plants and animals. She heard a growl and the alarms of birds in the treetops. She and her host passed a wounded bird on the forest floor, flapping its wings and shrieking for help, but they did not stop. They swiftly and quietly advanced toward the explosion of crashing waves.

Max appeared to forget he was still holding Sarah when they arrived at the beach. He continued to carry her, stepping into the surf until they were surrounded by salt water. He stood still for a few moments before he loosened his grip, and she slipped from his shoulder. She smiled at him, and he smiled back, closing his eyes. Before her toes could touch the cool surf, he stopped her fall and held her in an embrace, content to treasure the moment.

When at last she felt his fingers loosen, she begged, "Don't stop."

With her arms still around his neck, Max's eyes remained shut.

"Can I stay here with you?" she asked.

He replied softly, "Yes."

"How long?" she asked, biting her lip.

"As long as we are connected in spirit."

Max carried her, secure in his arms, a few more steps into the bay until her feet were immersed in the surf. His loving response was unexpected and magical; it was the first time she could remember truly being happy.

"I've been alone for a very long time," he confided. "But now we have each other."

The waves tapped them below the knees, like a toddler demanding attention. As the sun sank below the forest treetops, the bright stars above them revealed cosmic causeways. And Sarah could not imagine wanting anything else.

CHAPTER EIGHT

COSMOS

Without city lights to wash it out, the night sky was almost as bright as the day. But still the moon boasted preeminence. Sarah admired its polished glow as Max gathered wood from the forest's edge and threw it into a sandpit. He tossed in some small sticks and a few fluffy tendrils of dried moss. He rubbed his palms together. A snapping charge leaped from his fingertips as if he were holding firework sparklers. The sparks ignited the moss, which lit the sticks, and soon a fire crackled. Scotch pine resin burned, and the aroma of Christmas filled the air. The mesmerizing blaze popped and echoed, its sounds unable to penetrate the thick woods behind them.

Sarah watched an ember ascend to its new home like another burning star in the heavens. Max knelt before the fire and spoke. "The stars exist to remind you that you are not really alone. We are part of an eternal family—the vast universe."

"It's so beautiful up there," Sarah said. "It looks so close."

He put one arm around her and held her hand with the other. "It's all connected. We are all part of the earth and part of the heavens."

Max put their connected hands to her chest and listened. He was careful with his words, and she waited patiently for him to speak. "You must remember, it is not the earth, this place, that hurt you," he said. "It is your living family who failed to teach you." He dropped his hand from hers.

In the firelight, his profile exposed pain, deep suffering inside his body. She could see that his amber glow had faded to a light-bluish tone. She felt him shiver as a nor'easter wind blew across the sandy shore from the sea.

"What's wrong?" Sarah asked.

Max shrugged and said, "I'm just a little cold." He pulled a warm textile blanket over them, and they huddled together in the dark. His skin slowly regained its reddish color and began to glow again softly. Soon it was too hot under the blanket. They were forced to open a flap to the outside world and welcome crisp, fresh air under the covers.

"Better?" Sarah asked. He nodded in agreement and smiled. They stuck their heads out, but their bodies remained tangled underneath. She was pinned down, unable to move, and she did not mind a bit.

Max looked up to the mysterious cosmos and said, "I didn't know."

"Didn't know what?" Sarah asked.

The comment apparently had not been intended for her. He looked at her soberly and said, "I'm pleased you are here with me."

"Me too," she replied. *I didn't expect to find more happiness* after *life than while in it*, she thought. Max's newly recharged life force soon filled her up too. She felt happy, satisfied, and warm.

"In your life, were you ever married?" she asked. He turned to her, and she had his undivided attention.

"No. Would you have wanted to marry me in life?"

"Maybe," she hedged. "But it's too late for us now. There's no one to perform a ceremony." She surprised herself by bringing it up—she'd always believed marriage was a ruse created by men to legally own and control women.

"Marriage is a decision between two people," he said. "*We* decide to be married or not."

"Did my 'maybe' bother you?"

"We have infinity to decide, don't we?" he said and grinned.

Good answer, she thought.

He crawled from the covers, reached into the sand, and extracted a smoking pipe and a suede pouch.

"Let's celebrate your arrival," he said and pulled her arms from the blanket. Sarah grabbed ahold of the blanket and moaned in protest. He let go and laughed, filled the pipe, and sat next to her.

Max dipped a twig in the fire and buried it in his herbal blend: sap of myristicacaea, dried leaves of the cherry tree, tobacco, and wild mint. Lying on her back, she peeked out from the blanket. The aromatic smoke drifted in. She waved her hands, coughing.

"Sit with me," he said, patting the sand outside her comfortable nest. She complied. He puffed, extended the pipe toward her, and exhaled slowly. At first, she refused to take it from him, but then he poked her with it, unwilling to indulge her objection.

"I've never smoked a cigarette, let alone a pipe," she said. Noticeably irritated, he took the pipe back and puffed again to keep the tobacco from burning out.

"Just breathe," he said, handing it back to her.

Sarah's hacking cough was loud enough to awaken the entire forest.

"Raised by a fish," Max huffed, letting a smile creep across his face.

He picked her up and placed her in his lap for safekeeping. He played with her red hair. She smiled. He stood up, lifting her as if she were as light as a small bird.

Sarah recognized the man who had hunted her. His animal-like eyes reflected yellow in the moonlight, but she felt only lustful desire for him. For his wisdom and his magical powers. For his wide, joyful grin. For his defined muscles, torque-loaded with power and strength. To her, he was as intoxicating as the smoke. She moved her face toward his, exploring the possibility of a kiss, but he looked down quickly and brushed sand off himself.

Max looked up at the stars, offered his chest as a pillow. Resting her head on his chest and listening to the drumming of his strong heart, Sarah fell asleep in his arms.

The entwined couple awoke to a trespassing wave. Its fingers of foam invaded their blankets and soaked their faces. They sat up quickly and watched an army of small crabs—ousted from their beds—chase the bubbling water back to the sea. The sea was rougher than it had been the day before. Max lifted his head and shook his wet, silken hair. The rest of his body was happy to remain uncooperative.

Sarah took in a deep breath and found she was unable to move. Max's arms held her in place. That was just fine with her. She kissed the arm holding her down. He moved it aside to give her space—not quite the response she had hoped for. He managed to sit up, and she reached to pull him back down. He lifted her instead and carried her down the beach, hunting for a place to hide from the burning sun.

"Max, put me down," she said, annoyance creeping into her voice. He pretended not to hear her. He stopped, placed her in the shade, and leaned comfortably against the dune. He closed his eyes.

Sarah climbed on top of him. Max smiled but kept his eyes closed, continuing to enjoy whatever private thoughts were absorbing him.

"Max, look at me," Sarah said. He ignored her. "Why won't you look at me?" she asked.

She was right; he was avoiding looking at her.

He smiled, lay down next to her, and held her hand. His eyes were still closed. His amber glow was fading again, despite being in the shade.

"Your color. It's happening again. Are you sick?" she asked.

He looked at her darkly, as if weighing his words. "You are the one who is not well," he said at last. "I don't know how much longer I can sustain you."

"Sustain me? What do you mean? I feel fine." No sooner were the words from her lips than she realized they were far from true. The elation of finding Max in this new world had been distracting her from a dire internal reality. She actually felt cold and weak inside.

"What's wrong with me?" she asked, sitting up.

He lay back with his palms upward as if trying to pull energy from the air and the sun. His color slowly returned. He put their hands side by side in the shade. "You see the glow I possess?" he said. "You do not have it."

Max placed his hand on his chest and said, "The attraction you have for me is my strong spirit energy. I carried all the living-world fulfillment with me to this place."

A burning arrow of despair shot through Sarah. She knew her life lacked any happiness, satisfaction, or fulfillment.

"Until I brought you here," he continued. "I thought my energy was endless. But now I am learning I was wrong. Sustaining *you* is exhausting *me*."

"Exhausting you? I didn't realize I was such a burd—"

"Shh," he stopped her. "Quiet your mind. I know I can help you, and we can fulfill each other." He picked her up and put her hands around his neck. "Come with me."

Max hastened to the woods, carrying her. She didn't want to enter the woods in such a fragile state. The place was threatening to her and needled at her spirit like sleet on her skin.

"I'll protect you," he said. He carried her under his chin with both arms. The creatures of the dark forest sensed weakness in the air and flaunted their razor-sharp teeth. Max hurried on and soon emerged on the other side.

He walked to the hill of their first meeting, still carrying her. The sun hung in the sky. He continued to hold Sarah in his arms and knelt before the sun. "We will journey to the sun together," he said.

Sarah was drowsy, and her limbs were numb, but she focused on the swirl of tattoos on his neck. The symbols seemed to come to life, and then Max disappeared. A blinding light turned everything to darkness, but she still felt the warmth of him holding her.

When Sarah's sight returned, they were walking on a ray of sunlight that was rolled out for them. A towering man—wearing a cloak of orbiting, electrified light—with a joyous, friendly face came walking down the sunray from above to greet them.

"This is my older brother, Elan-Purush," Max said as Elan-Purush extended his arms to welcome them. "This is Orphan," Max told his brother.

Without hesitation, Elan-Purush pulled them both into his chest for an inviting hug.

Sarah felt as if she was in the middle of two electrical transformers—their love's energy pulsed between them. The brothers held their embrace for what seemed like an eternity, and Sarah felt their warm electrical charge filling her body, mind, and spirit.

They finally separated, and Max began to talk softly in another language with his brother. The words were rhythmic, musical pulses, and the tone was serious, but the longer they stayed and talked, the better Sarah felt, until the hum of their communication soothed her to sleep.

She awoke in the night lying in Max's arms amid the grass on the hill. She did not want to disturb his rest; he was glowing with a soft, contented light. Still clutched by his arms, she snuggled under his limbs as a source of heat. She felt the healing warmth infusing her whole body.

"Don't wake me from this dream," Sarah whispered.

"This is not a dream," Max replied, awakening.

"How did you do that?" she asked him. She was referring to the whole experience—the walking on the sunray, the meeting of Elan-Purush, the healing.

"Everything is connected," he replied. He settled back to give a longer explanation, letting his hands move expressively, "In life, bodies are trapped on earth within time. After a body dies, the spirit is freed from time and travels without it."

"I don't understand how that helps you see your brother. Can you try to explain in a way that makes sense for the energy deprived?"

"Everything is connected," he repeated, "because we are all part of one universe. But each spirit is unique. It is created as a type of seed and designed to collect energy from the living world."

"Like an acorn?"

"Sort of—but not really. A spirit 'seed' grows by stealing energy from the physical, natural earth. It does this by living inside a physical body first."

"But how does it absorb the energy?" she inquired.

"How does a plant absorb the nutrients it needs from the soil? It doesn't matter how; it matters only that it does. Your spirit gathered energy throughout your physical life. When an earthly body dies, the physical shell the spirit occupies is returned to the earth, but the spirit retains the energy harvested and carries it to the afterlife."

Sarah gestured to slow down and asked, "Keeps *what* energy?"

Max held her, stroked her neck, and said, "Love and fulfillment. When the body dies, time stops, and the spirit is freed, containing all the spirit energy needed to traverse the stars."

"And how did we see your brother?"

"Cosmic pathways across the universe are built by the strongest, most fulfilled spirits and beings."

The patterns of light in the sky above them glistened. They marveled at the swirls and colors of the galaxies. Sarah glowed with a connection to the universe. Max's leaden eyelids closed, resting from their journey. She swept her hand above his chest and felt the heat he emanated and the serenity of his protection. *My radiant sleeping sun,* she thought.

CHAPTER NINE

TRANSFUSION

"Wake up," Max said, urgency in his voice.

Her eyes fluttered open to see his stern-browed face looking intently into hers. She offered a smile, but it felt weak.

Max reached into the soil and pulled out a leather bag. He placed the strap around his neck. Hovering over her chest, he listened to her heart.

"Am I dying?" she asked.

"Yes," he replied. She tried but was unable to move her arm.

"But your brother cured me," she said as he dug in the bag and found the objects he was looking for.

"No, he cured *me*," Max said. "And I revived you with my energy. But it didn't last."

Max dragged her by the arms along the hill until her body was in maximum sunlight. He positioned her arms so that her palms were facing the sun, and he spread her legs. He showed her the piece of petrified wood he had taken from his bag and placed it in her hand. "Hold this, or I'll let you die," he ordered and pressed her fingers around it. With difficulty, she held the object. In her other palm, he placed a red crystallized stone. The stone wobbled in her hand. "Do not let it fall," he commanded.

"What are you doing?"

No answer.

Max lifted a razor-sharp two-inch eagle talon and felt the hook's point. He moved it to his left hand.

He lay on his side next to her and ran his hand down her body, an inch from her skin. A swath of amber glow followed his hand across her grayish-looking skin and faded quickly.

"Please save me," she said.

"*Now* you want to live?" he asked, sounding annoyed. He used his forefinger's nail to draw a triangle around her navel. His finger burned red with heat. It scorched her, but she held in her scream. Next, he outlined an *S* and then drew a symbol of a snake with eyes and fangs. A flaming orange snake moved, alive, inside her. "I need to tell you something," he said. "The death of the spirit is forever." The snake faded away.

"What do you mean?"

"Earth death is just a transition; spirit death is permanent. If you die here, you will be extinguished forever. Do you want that to happen?"

"No!"

"Then lie still."

Max knelt beside her and laid his arm over her dying chest, now gripping the large talon in his right hand.

"I was wrong to try to kill myself," she said, watching the point of the claw move closer to her face. She pressed her head against the soil to escape. He placed his full, wet lips to her ear; his hot rapid breath was relief in the cold.

"Bringing you here was my fault," he said softly. "Saving you from yourself was temporary—I knew that. I hunted you to trigger your survival instinct. Every animal on earth runs when attacked—but not you. I took a risk—to show you the consequences of your actions—but now it's come to this. Your hungry spirit needs more from me than I offered—more than I want to give."

She closed her eyes, breathing rhythmically to the staccato of his breath, bracing for the pain.

"I could have admired you from a distance," he continued, "but you forced me to pluck my wild, lovely, purple-and-pink orchid."

He moved the talon between her eyes. Seeing the agony in her face, he set it aside. With his finger, he drew wavy lines up and down her sides. His light touch traced a yellow glow. He was giving her energy but controlling the amount he gave her, like a cosmic anesthesiologist. She needed more than he was giving, desperately more.

"Max, I'm cold," she pleaded and tried to lift her arms.

He looked at her fully and grimaced as if seeing something revolting. "My withering flower; it's so painful to watch."

"Am I that disgusting to you?" she said. He looked away to collect himself before facing her again. He placed the talon back in his right hand, fixating on the place to begin.

"This is going to hurt," he told her. He lifted the claw to her cheek and pressed down with a hard jab, digging into her flesh. He ripped her skin right down to her chin. A moist, viscous gas seeped out.

She screamed, clenching the objects in her hands. He stuck his finger inside the cut, searing her skin along the trench he'd made. The fabric of her flesh scorched and smoked.

"Stop! Please! It burns!" she pleaded, but he was not deterred.

He moved the talon to her torso and cut a curved hourglass pattern, following the contour of her side, into the edge of her stomach and out to her hips. The master artist at work, he paused to make a decision. He stabbed the point in twice, for two eyes, and rubbed them with his forefinger until they were black, melted holes.

Next, he cut a triangle, rubbing deeply, and filled the groove with his liquid-silver energy. His life venom invaded and seized her. She flailed her head from side to side, possessed by the pain.

The objects in her hands burned into her palms; she no longer needed to hold them. The crystallized stone's energy formed a current connecting the riverlike carving down her right side to the snake of her stomach.

Max straddled her torso. He tended to the deep wounds he had made to her frail, depressed spirit by ministering to her body, partially buried in the soft ground. Starting with her cheek, he blew hot breath onto her skin. She cried, "Put it out."

"I know it hurts," he said, calm as a surgeon. Her skin smoked and smelled of charred compost.

Max raised his chest and, still perched on her, looked down from high above. "Don't move, or it will be worse." He lifted the talon again and drilled a deep hole into her other cheek. She wriggled to stop him, causing a small detour of his stroke. This caused him to growl with irritation. He held her down, steadying her slightest movement, and resumed ripping deeper to make a clean cut. She fainted but awoke again to the burning of his forefinger as it traced the inside of the new gash.

"I'm almost done," he said, brushing the ash away from her skin. Sarah knew he had ripped her apart, but she lay helpless to defend herself. His last touch was lighter, across the bridge of her nose, connecting the two poked holes at her cheeks. He stared at the line until she felt the light return to her eyes.

Max stood proudly over Sarah, but her pain continued. He had branded her with his symbol—the snake. He admired his own work, and it came to life, slithering under her skin. As she looked down at her body, a reddish-orange, neon-bright current flowed through the inscribed pattern. Max peeled the objects from her hands and placed his treasures back in the pouch. He left Sarah lying in the dirt, her skin smoldering, as he went to do other things. He had implanted his life-venom energy within her—permanently—and it moved inside her like an invasive force.

Sarah sobbed without tears, alone. His doll, positioned as he wanted; she was unable to move. Carved up as he desired, then coldly left behind. Until, at last, she slept.

"Open your eyes," Max ordered her sometime later. She pretended not to hear him. The pain had faded but was not gone. "Sarah, you are better now. I promise. Open your eyes."

She opened one eye, and the stars sparkled above.

"You've been sleeping. Did you know you talk in your sleep?"

She opened the other eye to show him she was awake and refusing to speak to him.

"The sun could not stand the screaming and left hours ago," Max said, attempting humor.

His morbid joke infuriated her, and she no longer entertained the idea that she was cured of her life's anger. She regained the use of her arms first. She could see the path of light traveling along her sides, leading to a snake tattooed on her stomach. The pathway pulsed as a source of heat, circulating energy.

She rose to her feet. She felt different. "You did something to me. Something horrible."

"My energy flows within you now," he said.

He stood back to admire his design as his energy flowed within her spirit. She bent over from the pain and stumbled away. "It was the only way," he shouted after her.

Sarah wanted to escape Max, but this mysterious place was his; he was in control of all of it. He could do whatever he wanted here—especially to her. She ran toward the woods, but he somehow seized her, like a rope around her spirit, and she was unable to get away. She struggled to flee, but he easily caught up.

"Go away," she said.

"But you love me," he replied. He looked her body up and down. Where previously his eyes had been repelled by her, he was now practically salivating. He licked his lips.

"Love you? No, I don't love you. I may have thought you were lust-worthy for a brief second, but that was temporary insanity."

He smiled without concern, which only infuriated her more. She turned and stepped in the direction of the woods.

"Where do you think you're going, Orphan?"

"To the beach. Without you."

"You won't make it far without me," he said and then sat in the tall grass, smirking.

Sarah wanted to punish him, but she was defenseless. Even her spirit betrayed her in this. His energy, planted inside of her, now mingled with her own spirit and longed to be close to its original source—against her own will. She walked toward the woods alone.

Sarah peered into the forest and saw only darkness. "Max's trophy? I don't think so," she huffed, trying to manufacture some much-needed bravado. She stepped beyond the threshold of the woods. She heard Max yell for her to wait, but she did not.

It was already night, and the woods were thick with a gray fog she'd never seen during the day when they'd traveled through it. Within a couple of steps, she felt a heavy curtain close behind her, eliminating outside noise, and she felt every predator in the forest watching her.

Her spirit illuminated the trees with streaks of orange.

Watchful eyes moved closer. She heard snarls of hunger and anticipation. The creatures seemed drawn to Max's energy flowing through her. She could not control a shiver that started at her shoulder and spread through her body. She froze, then walked forward slowly, tentatively. The ground felt saturated with remnants of the dead, spirits broken and lost. She understood now. The hungry spirit predators, having lost their earthly bodies, waited in the forest to feed on any weak soul arriving from the living earth and devour its scraps of spirit energy. She retreated a step and felt a faint, cool breath on the back of her neck.

"S-S-Sarah," Max hissed into her ear. "Afraid yet?"

She turned to face him. His yellow snake eyes illuminated.

"No," she lied. He looked as wild and fierce as a predator.

He casually walked around her and said, "You should be." Max waved his hand, and the animals fled to hide. He did not offer his hand to Sarah but instead walked ahead of her. She followed, resenting her need to do so.

The night sky was lit as it had been the night before, a canvas of sparks ten times brighter than anything she'd seen in her previous life. Sarah sat on the thick blanket, sending a "Don't come near me" scowl toward Max.

"I can't believe you are angry with me. I healed you," he said, starting a new fire on top of burnt ash. "It is I who should be angry at you—for requiring so much from me."

Sarah crawled under the blanket and rolled over on her side. He dropped the blanket over her head and barked, "You're going to get hot under there." Once the fire got rolling, she crawled out of the blanket to cool off in the damp sand, as he'd predicted.

Max had located a short pipe and was rubbing tobacco leaves between his fingers to fill the bowl. The pipe was a carved hardwood snake head. Attached to the pipe with twine was a barn owl's grayish-white tail feather, with glowing golden bands fluttering in the soft breeze of the bay.

"Nice pipe. Did you make it?" she asked, resentment dripping from her voice. As angry as she was with him, he was the only company she had in this world.

He knelt in front of the new fire and smirked to himself as if he could read her thoughts. His enormous energy—what she could not see before—was overpowering her reason. Her increasing desire for him was canceling every justified negative emotion she felt for him.

"So much to learn. You see a pipe—when the feather attached to it is so much more valuable."

"I'll bite," Sarah said. "What makes it so important?"

"Because it can only be earned by an act of true bravery."

"Forgive me if I'm not holding my breath to earn one."

He lit the cherry-infused tobacco and sat next to her. "Your bravery is an illusion," he said, taking in the smoke. "Your shame hid in the shadow of your pride. Walking in the woods alone—as weak as you are—was foolish."

"Tell me something I don't know," she replied and put her hand out for the pipe. "I suppose you're going to give me a lecture about it right now. Lectures are your *thing*."

He handed the pipe to her and then moved a few feet away, studying her like a newly finished sculpture. He no longer closed his eyes or looked away as he had before. "It can wait," he said. "I must confess, I'm distracted by your light show."

"I'm so glad you no longer find me disgusting," she said. "Now you don't have to keep your eyes shut for eternity."

He continued to stare and then leaped toward her like a cougar pouncing. He grabbed her waist and kissed her the way she'd wanted him to kiss her the first day—except now everything had changed. He was no longer shy and no longer as kind and gentle as she thought. He had a hungry, animalistic look in his eye and seemed fueled by the control he had over her.

"You're so lovely," he said. He hovered over her, drinking her in with his eyes.

"That doesn't make me forgive you." She bit her lip to stop her thoughts and then poked him in the ribs with the pipe. He did not flinch. He grabbed the pipe, set it aside, and lifted her into his lap to kiss her neck.

She elbowed him away but could not deny enjoying his newfound affection. "Why wasn't it brave to walk in the forest by myself?" she asked, largely to sidetrack him—and the growing desire she felt for him, despite having witnessed his sadistic side.

Max sat up and took on a more serious posture. He pointed to a mark on his neck; it lit up like twin diamonds in the firelight. *Those are new*, she thought. "See this?" he said. "This was not bravery. It was envy. Let me try to tell this story in earthly terms. I envied my brother and entered the … er … the woods in search of glory. And found my end." He then pointed to a mark on his thigh and said, "This? This was not bravery. It was pride. This you and I have in common. I learned, too late, that avoiding shame is not bravery."

"Are you saying I entered the woods for the wrong reason?"

"Yes. Reckless is not the same as brave. But *this* mark …" He pointed to a pair of puncture wounds on his hand, surrounded by tattooed symbols. "This is a mark of true bravery, and do you know why?"

Their eyes met. He raised his fist; it trembled.

"I'll tell you. My older brother, Elan-Purush, was a great hunter and hero. I confided in a sorcerer, telling him that I was nothing, a shadow, compared to my brother's power. He sent me on a quest to capture a comet … I mean, a copperhead snake. With one condition—I had to let it bite me before I returned.

"For days I searched, afraid and unable to find the deadly snake until I fell to the ground weak from hunger and thirst. As I lay in a bed of leaves, slowly dying, a baby copperhead found me."

Max pointed to his neck again, frowned, and said, "She bit me here—the result of my search for glory." Sarah touched the smooth skin of his neck. He closed his eyes.

"The thought of returning with a tiny snake … I knew everyone would laugh. I hissed at it to make it leave. The snake recoiled and stood its ground. I kicked it away, and it struck my leg."

The two pinholes of light on his thigh sparkled in the moonlight. After a pause, he continued, eyes still closed. "It was then I heard my spirit, from within, tell me that duty to my family and myself was more important than pride. Without thinking, I grabbed the copperhead; it bit me here on the fist. I found my way back. I don't know how. As I lay dying, my mother wept, and my father could not console her. But the sorcerer whispered in my ear that no one would laugh as I thought they would. My brave spirit, he said, now had an important purpose: to protect the land, the earth itself."

When he opened his eyes, his glow returned, and he grinned, hinting he had a secret.

"We have a visitor." Max pointed in the direction of the woods. Two glowing, yellowish, elliptical eyes with fire-orange vertical pupils slithered on the ground toward them. The three-foot copper-red snake circled the fire, watching them. Max was unconcerned and puffed tobacco.

Sarah's heart hammered as she watched the snake explore the area, trying to find a place to nestle beside Max. The snake coiled up in the sand, warming itself near the fire. Sarah moved closer to Max—at least he was better than a snake. Or was he?

The snake lifted its triangular head to the sky, sensing Sarah's fear. It flicked its tail, flattened a bit. Then the snake expanded until Sarah panicked, surrendered, and fastened herself to Max for protection.

"Your point is made," Sarah said. "I'm not brave."

Max wrapped his long, muscular arms around her. She felt trapped for eternity.

"Because you are missing something you need in order to learn bravery," he said. "You must take it with you before you journey into the woods."

"Tell me what I'm missing."

"Love."

CHAPTER TEN

VIRUS

Sarah awoke to a scream. Was it rage or pain—some combination of the two? She wasn't sure, but she knew it was coming from Max.

She rose and went looking for him in a direction they had not traveled together yet: south. Another scream from him guided her to his exact location. She found him kneeling over a small pond, gazing down into the water.

"What's wrong?" she asked.

"Something terrible has happened."

"What? What can I do to help?" Sarah was alarmed by his need.

"How do I look?" he asked her, panting and holding his chest as if having a heart attack. "Tell me how I look to you."

"You look perfectly fine," she answered.

He growled in annoyance at himself and said, "I can't believe I asked you. How would you know?"

Doubled over with pain, he looked out over the pond. A huge frog leaped from a lily pad, causing an explosion of ripples. Max leaned over the water, waiting for the surface to smooth. His breathing was labored as he stared in anticipation. At last, the calm reflection showed his face. It looked perfectly handsome to Sarah—as it always had—but he gasped at what he saw.

"What's the matter?" she asked. She could not understand his distress.

"Come here," he said, patting the ground for her to kneel beside him. She did.

Now she understood his concern. In their side-by-side reflection, Sarah appeared solid and fully three-dimensional. But Max's reflection looked translucent, ghostly, as if he were not fully there. His actual body still looked dense and robust.

He groaned in distress—deep pain.

Sarah took another look at their twin reflections and realized something was off about her own reflection too. In the water she saw the likeness she remembered from being alive. She knew Max had carved lines into her face and body, but the reflection did not show them. When she looked down at her actual stomach, however, the snake outline was still there.

"Why can't I see the lines in the reflection I can plainly see with my own eyes?" Sarah asked, ignoring his groans.

He raised his voice in anger. "You are worried about how you look." He crawled away from her in disgust and muttered, "Maybe in life you were beautiful, but here you're wretched. All that matters here is spirit energy, and you have the minimum, barely enough for a twig. The only part of you that's appealing is my energy that flows through you now."

"You love yourself in me. Charming."

Ignoring her, he said, "And you are incapable of feeding and sustaining the energy I gave you. That's why my energy is drained and faded. Because it is divided between us. That's what my reflection is showing me!"

"I want to help you," Sarah replied.

"What can an orphan do to help me? You have no family, no connection, no love," he said.

"You're right," she said and walked away.

She hated him, yet she was drawn to him, *connected* to him, perhaps eternally.

As she lay on the edge of the woods, defeated by his words and defeated by her situation, she let out a cry of frustration.

Two souls in anguish, she thought, *each the cause of the other's pain. Aren't we a pair?*

After a while he approached her a bit sheepishly. "I should not have been so angry with you. It was my fault for not explaining the importance of my gift to you."

She tried to offer an olive branch in return. "Should we go to the hill today? Maybe you'll feel better closer to the sun."

"No, this drain on my energy is not one that nature's energy can replenish." He attempted a smile. "Let's not go into the woods today. We'll stay here together."

They helped each other walk to their favorite spot next to the sandpit. The sun was bright, but the air was cool. Sarah lifted the blanket over them, and they sat in silence.

Her mind began to churn. She went over their dilemma again and again: she had become the involuntary host to his transplanted energy. His decision to put part of himself, his energy, inside her without her consent had been a violation in the extreme. But his added energy *did* make her feel better, and perhaps it had saved her from eternal death—that little detail. But now she was locked in a dance of desire and repulsion for him. Wanting him and hating him.

For his part, he had implanted his life-giving energy in her, but she was incapable of replenishing and reciprocating it, so he seemed doomed to a perennial state of *less*ness. And he acted repulsed by her to boot, except for the part of himself that flowed in her now.

To continue in this way, perhaps forever, seemed like a perfect vision of hell.

The seeds of an idea began to gel in her mind.

"Max, how did you find me?" she asked. "I come from a different time."

"This place is a place without time," he replied.

"But you visited *my* time."

"I can visit any time," Max said nonchalantly.

"You mean you're a time traveler?"

Max did not seem as impressed with the term *time traveler* as she was.

"Could you take me back to a time before I died?" she asked.

He seemed to weigh the pros and cons of whether to answer her truthfully. "Yes," he replied. But before she could ask the inevitable follow-up, he added, "But I will not."

Sarah's mind raced at the mere possibility of revisiting her life, but she hid her excitement. She feared that by asking him to return her to her earthly life, he would see it as a rejection of him—a great disrespect—and would become angry. She was confident that the fury she had witnessed while he saved her spirit was the mere tip of the iceberg. She could only imagine the depth of his depravity when truly infuriated. It was terrifying to think about—being trapped with him for eternity here without a way to escape.

"Can you imagine"—he laughed—"living your miserable life all over again?"

She felt a stab of insult at this but answered with superficial cheer, "You're right. That would be horrible."

They sat quietly for a bit, and then she carefully picked up the thread again. "I'm not asking to go back to my miserable life, but I'm just wondering—do you think, if I did, I would remember you and our life here?"

"Of course. Your spirit doesn't care about time and space constraints any more than a bird cares how an earthworm feels when it eats it."

She eased into the topic again. "You said my lack of life fulfillment was what caused my spirit energy to be insufficient." She nestled down next to him as he held his heart and grimaced. "You said you are needing to sustain me, and I am draining your energy."

"Yes. But I don't know what to do. This has never happened to me before."

"Max, it's clear. I am making you sick, and your spirit is dying because of me. It's my fault."

His body stiffened. "You want to leave me, don't you?" he said.

"That's not true," she lied.

"I know I have not always been thoughtful or kind to you," he told her, "but we can find ways to make things better."

"Of course we can," she answered, perhaps a trifle overeagerly.

"I'm not taking you back to your life—so you can forget about that. Watching you suffer in life would make me feel even worse than I feel right now."

"But what if . . ." she said, dangling a possibility in the air. "What if you returned me back to my life just long enough to collect life's energy and bring it back here?"

"Life's energy comes from love, acceptance, belonging—your life had none of that."

"But maybe I could … change that."

Max shook his head and turned away. "No. We can't do this."

Sarah stood up, energized. She said, "Think of it, Max. I could come back with a full tank of energy. I would have my own life's energy, and you would not need to sustain me anymore. We could live as equals, both of us full, both of us complete."

Max looked up at her and shook his head, still rejecting her plan. *The equality message is not working*, she thought and changed her tactic. "At any point, you can come scoop me up if you don't like the way things are going. You can bring me back here, and it will be like I never left."

Sarah immediately regretted putting this escape clause on the table, but her words were having their intended effect. She could see that Max was opening to that idea, considering its possible benefits. He put his hand on his heart as if feeling for something that was missing. "Let me think on this," he said.

Max turned to tend to the fire, his default activity.

"The season is changing," he remarked after a while. "Feel that cold wind coming from the west?" As he gathered new wood and added it to the pit, Sarah thought about all she might do differently in her life if she had another chance.

At last Max sat and lit the pipe. He inhaled deeply. She noticed he smiled slyly, trying to hide it as he turned away. "Sarah …" he said.

"Yes?"

"If we do this, do you promise me you'll return?"

"Max. Look at me," Sarah said. She stared into his eyes to connect with him. But what she saw there was a repulsive neediness and hunger for control. She would rather go back to her suffering, miserable life than to stay with him, and she did not care that she was leaving him to be alone again. But she sent a different message through her eyes. "I promise to return," she said. "And when I do, I will bring back life's energy, enough to sustain us both without end."

"Do you swear on the life of your immortal spirit?" he asked without emotion.

"I swear, Max."

Something changed in Max's face; a devilish grin appeared, and a dark storm blew across his features. His eyes became the eyes of the snake—cold, possessive, deadly. Sarah was reminded, with a jolt, that she was dealing with a being far more powerful than she was.

"You had better mean what you say," he told her in a low, throaty voice. "Because you are mine. Do you understand, Orphan?"

"Yes. Yes, I understand," she said. Her voice sounded thin and reedy to her own ears. She was terrified of him.

"You are mine, and that will *never* change."

Sarah nodded fervently.

"Very well, then," he pronounced, laying the pipe formally on the ground. "I release you … for now."

Max lifted Sarah off the ground with the power of his mind and pushed her out to sea, his life venom within her. After he released her, she felt the weight of him within her and drifted toward her former life. But the imbalance of nature would not allow her to leave. She was stuck in limbo, between two worlds. A memory of the lighthouse formed in her mind, and then it appeared before her eyes. As it floated by above the water, she sacrificed a sliver of her spirit and placed it inside. The lantern tower lit and glowed, and the steel foundation settled and then buried itself deep offshore, out of his reach.

"Lighthouse, keep my spirit safe—and away from Max—until I return," she said.

ACT II

CHAPTER ELEVEN

WANDERLUST

Sarah awoke from a deep sleep but was still in the grips of the vivid dream. Her eyes took several seconds to adjust to the hard surfaces around her. It felt like an eternity since she'd been enclosed by walls and a ceiling. She was back in her house, and it was a welcome sight. Back in her miserable life!

The first sound she heard was the diesel churn of the school bus's engine. The dead-end road had only one place for the bus to turn around: the fuel-tanker storage farm entrance a mile down the road. She'd overslept—damn. She grabbed some random clothes from the floor and threw them on.

Without a truck to drive to school—the Captain had taken it—and without a second to spare, she ran for the door with her shoes and toothbrush in one hand, her backpack in the other. The door slammed shut behind her, and she sprinted to the end of the driveway just in time for the bus to pull away. She waved for it to stop—she was sure the driver saw her in the mirror—but it accelerated instead.

Down the street, at the Eriksen place, Grant stood on his porch and waved back as if she were waving at him. She threw up her arms in exasperation at having been left behind. Grant returned the gesture with a big "What can I say?" shrug and then gave her the "Wait a sec" finger as he climbed into his truck.

"Great. Grant to the rescue again," she muttered.

Grant pulled into her driveway and rolled his window down. He seemed to be making an effort to suppress a smile. Out of options, Sarah had no choice and said, "Mr. Eriksen, can you kindly give me a ride to school today?"

The ride to school was quiet and awkward. The intimacy they had shared the night before—born of a taboo event that neither wanted to discuss—weighed heavily on her mind and no doubt on his, affording little room for light banter. But in the school parking lot, before he turned off the truck, Grant said, "I have a question to ask."

"I don't want to talk about it," Sarah shot back.

"Not … that. I want to know if … you'd be my girlfriend."

What? Sarah was unprepared for this. Her head was spinning from the dream of Max, and her sense of reality was out of whack. In her heart she felt promised to another man, yet she felt she owed Grant for saving her life on the dock.

Timing provided her a convenient excuse: "We have two months to go before college. There's no point."

Grant came around to help her out of the truck—*On what planet do guys still do that?*—and said, "And we all die someday, but does that mean we shouldn't live right now?"

Sarah was reminded again of her promise to return to Max. *So why start something I'll only need to extinguish?* But she was also reminded of the mission for which she had returned to this earthly life: to gather love and fulfillment. How could she do that without getting close to anyone? What an insane bargain to have made. What an impossible position to have placed herself in. True, she'd only done it because she'd felt trapped and needed a way out, but still …

Sarah! shouted her inner voice. *Get a grip on yourself! Max was a dream. A goddamn dream. Get real.*

"We can be friends," she heard herself offering a compromise. "How's that?"

"How about exclusive friends?"

"Well … I don't have many anyway—I don't see why not."

Standing beside the truck, they faced the school's double doors across the parking lot. Bystanders geared up to spread gossip—they were already pointing at Grant and Sarah for having arrived together as a "couple." She dreaded passing through the gathering crowd at the entrance and blurted to Grant, "If you knew this was the last day of your life, what would you do today to make your whole life worth living?"

Grant didn't miss a beat. He said, "I'd ditch school and spend it with you."

"So why are we standing here?" she said without thinking.

As the school bell rang, the hovering crowd of kids watched Sarah and Grant climb into the truck. *They'll have to wait another day for their answers*, she thought. In the meantime, she knew the fiction machine would be winding into high gear.

"So," Grant asked, "what shall we do with this fine day?"

"Escape."

If he was going to help her fulfill her wish to avoid real life for another day, she was all in. Grant, apparently, was all in, too—he fired up the truck.

Sarah turned on the radio and waited to be whisked away. Grant said, "I can hear the gossip from here."

Sarah replied, "Who cares—we'll never see them again. It's the last day of our lives, remember?"

The farther they drove from the school, the lighter Sarah felt. She sang along with the radio and moved her shoulders to the beat. The weight of her burdens was lifted, if only for the moment, and she wanted him to keep driving forever.

Grant seemed to be feeding off the privilege of witnessing the joyous side of Sarah. His energy crackled; he looked ready for anything.

"Grant, do you—" Sarah said, then hesitated.

"Yes, my dear?" he responded.

She laughed. "'Dear'? Is that what you just said? Besides missing the bus this morning, did I miss a marriage proposal too?"

Grant said, "Do you want one?" He was making a joke, but a tiny part of him seemed to be testing the waters too. *He did say he likes to move fast.*

"Not today," she said. "Today I only want to be carried away."

"It shall be done."

Sarah closed her eyes and let the radio music fill her soul as they drove out of town.

Morning fog hovered above rivers, ponds, and bright-green marsh grass as they crossed several small bridges in this land of rivers and sand. Sulfur gas seeped from the ancient terrain like a pungent, unheeded warning.

Grant and Sarah continued undeterred, trespassing on marshland pregnant with the raw material of body and spirit. As for Sarah, she chose to see the fertile landscape only as an exit ramp from a ferocious, careless world. Without a destination agreed upon, Sarah pretended they were on a lifelong adventure. It was easy to put her life in the hands of the man who'd saved her, she was discovering.

When Grant suddenly drove into a lot and parked the truck, she was a little disappointed that they were less than an hour from home.

"Best I could think of on short notice," he said.

They were at the port of Lewes. Sarah saw the ferry and most of the cars already loaded on it. She hopped out of the truck, causing a dozen seagulls to flap their wings and depart early.

"You said you wanted to escape," he said, pointing to the departure sign beyond the roped-off gangway: "Lewes to Cape May."

Unable to contain her excitement, she leaned into Grant's side in a playful way and said, "So we're escaping to—"

Grant finished her sentence. "Jersey. Like I said, short notice."

Pointing to a few people in line waiting to board, he said, "We better hurry, or we'll be spending the day feeding gulls in the parking lot instead."

"I really needed this. Thanks," Sarah said, beaming a smile and grabbing his hand.

Grant squeezed her hand slowly, taking more from the gesture than Sarah perhaps intended.

Never having been on a ferry before, Sarah excitedly pulled Grant onto the ship and up the narrow stairs made of heavy steel grating. Their footsteps echoed as they ascended the vertical maze to the top platform.

The ferry engine rumbled, the great horn bellowed, and the seagulls squawked and circled as the crew made final preparations to leave port.

Passengers wandered about the decks. Plenty of benches, secured to the flooring with rusted metal bolts, were available, but Sarah leaned over the rail facing the bow. Grant took his place next to her. The ropes dropped, and the ferry left the dock. The velvet air caressed their lit-up faces as more than a hundred seagulls formed a military escort to follow them.

As the offshore wind dropped the temperature by six or seven degrees, Grant moved in close to her and draped his arm over her shoulders. For the second time in twenty-four hours, she was enjoying the warmth of his arm.

Sarah could not help but think she was taking advantage of Grant's unyielding, doting affection. It was true—she liked his attention. But she simply did not feel as strongly or as seriously—or even as romantically—as he did. And the idea that it was expected of her to reciprocate felt like a sea anchor around her neck.

"Next time I'll take you somewhere you really want to go," he said as they passed the breakwater, heading into rougher seas.

Sarah shook her head, resisting the idea of a future, but assured him, "This is great. Are you kidding? I should be in English right now." Starting an argument over a nonexistent future plan when leaving the Delaware shore—without one person knowing her whereabouts—seemed ill advised. Besides, what harm was there in pretending for a day that he was more than a neighbor who'd spent the better part of his life bullying her?

She studied the shine of his indigo-blue eyes in the morning light. She thought he wanted to say more but didn't.

Sarah wanted to explore. Dragging Grant along with her, more as a bodyguard than anything else, she roamed the deck, letting her eyes drink in the details. She pulled him to the starboard side, where the angrier-looking waves marched in formation. The ferry was steadfast in leveling the rise and fall of the bay. When Sarah stopped short at her chosen spot at the rail, Grant stumbled into her, but her unassuming strength kept them from slipping. He apologized for being clumsy, and she said, "It's all right. You're a farmer—not a sailor." Then she quickly amended, "But that's a good thing."

Grant replied, "In the early eighteen hundreds, my ancestors were sailors. They survived a shipwreck in a winter storm off the coast not far from here."

Grant blocked the wind assailing them from the open ocean, and they turned to watch the shore disappear behind them.

"I'm surprised you're chancing this," Sarah said, leaning over the rail to look down.

"Chancing what?" he asked.

"Aren't you worried I'll ... *you know.*"

His face reddened as he realized what she was implying: jump. She enjoyed watching his discomfort for a moment and then smiled. Her long hair seemed electrified by the wind, sticking out in all directions. Grant grabbed her waist and gently pulled her to him, away from the rail, without causing alarm to the people close by.

"I'm not worried about you ... doing something stupid," he said, "but why don't we—"

"Let's get a coffee," she suggested, offering a good reason to depart the rail and free herself from his grip around her waist.

He leaped on the suggestion.

As they strolled to the snack bar, the ferry quietly passed over the sunken remains of hundreds of souls and centuries' worth of ships taken by the treacherous shoals, storms, and ice of Delaware Bay. But Sarah and Grant were blissfully oblivious.

The rest of the journey to Cape May was calm, sunny, and glorious. At first, she agreed, in the spirit of cooperation, to lean against him when he offered himself as a more comfortable option than the metal wall behind the bench. But she was surprised at how quickly and easily she got used to him as a human pillow. By the time they saw the Jersey shore emerge, Sarah's comfort level with him had evolved to letting him play with her hair.

"I don't understand why you like me so much," she said. "You don't even know me."

He rested his chin on her shoulder and said, "I've admired you from a distance for a long time."

"You mean, from across the cornfield? And have I mentioned you had a funny way of showing it?"

"Your father is so proud of you. I grew up listening to his stories about you. We have more in common than you know. I feel like I already know you."

"Well, that makes one of us."

"You're a special person. I know you don't see it, but I do."

Feeling her face flush red, Sarah said, "How much does he talk about me? My dad?"

Grant moved the hair away from her cheek and said, "Talk? It's more like boasting. And the answer is a lot. Besides bragging about how smart you are—which everyone at school knows—he goes on and on about how he raised a one-of-a-kind girl, how you don't mind getting wet or dirty, how you're not afraid of anyone or anything, not even him."

"It's hard to believe he would talk that way," Sarah said. "He hardly ever has anything decent to say to my face."

"Guys like our fathers don't hand out compliments—maybe they worry we'll stop trying to be the best we can be. But everything he says about you is true. And one other thing …"

"Oh?"

"You are so beautiful it hurts to look at you."

"Now I *know* you're smoking rope. Everyone looks away from me like I'm hideous."

"That's because everyone's afraid of your father."

"Except you?" she asked.

Grant smirked and said, "Normally I would be, but I think he likes me. Besides, I'm more worried about your other admirers finding out about us. It's not safe to be the boyfriend of the 'town legend.' I'm going to need my two older brothers to protect me."

"What's this 'boyfriend' stuff?"

"Exclusive friend."

"Better."

As they talked on the bench, Sarah glanced around the deck at the people milling about. Married couples, with and without kids, cycled around the boat's perimeter to find the best panoramic view for arriving at the port of Cape May. A few, however, stared in open envy at the happy young couple sitting on the bench. The men stared in open envy at Grant.

Grant seemed to notice this, too, and became self-conscious, breaking the spell of closeness she felt.

As they arrived at the port, Sarah pulled Grant to the other side of the ferry, making room for the car-owning passengers descending to the vehicle deck. They managed to get away from the men gawking at them, but it was not long before Grant saw new gawkers.

"Maybe I should have brought my truck over," he mused.

"Why?"

"I don't know. Feels like we're a museum exhibit."

They disembarked on the long gangplank. After they passed the "Welcome to Cape May" sign, the old-fashioned red trolley waited for them and the other day-trippers outside the terminal building's gate. They climbed aboard.

The open-aired trolley's first stop was the corner of Jackson Street and Beach Avenue. The passengers were given a few minutes to step off and admire the famous array of Victorian mansions facing the Atlantic. Strolling along the sidewalk, Grant and Sarah witnessed the dazzling montage of uniquely designed masterpieces painted in colors that looked like Benjamin Moore's fever dream. The ornately detailed trim, gables, and turrets were a hoot to behold.

On the way to Cape May Point, Sarah noticed their hands together. *I see what you're doing*, she thought. Breaking free from Grant's firm grip to point out a particularly hideous color scheme on an old mansion, she left her hands dangling outside the window to avoid recapture.

When they were dropped off at the entrance of the 157-foot Cape May lighthouse, they had trouble seeing the top because of the high, blinding sun. Sarah ran to the gate and asked, "Can we go inside?"

"How about we go to the top?" he said, moving into the line for tickets.

As they ran up the two-hundred-plus cast-iron spiral steps—without stopping—they passed several visitors huddled around small window landings along the way. Near the top, they dashed through the thick, arched metal door to the red-caged observation deck outside, and Sarah raced around the circumference of the lighthouse summit a couple of times without stopping. She felt giddy standing on the very tip of New Jersey, surrounded by the ocean. "Wow!" She could barely talk, out of breath and lightheaded. They both leaned in, smashed their faces between rusty metal bars, and admired the world sprawled at their feet.

"I've never been this high in my life," Sarah said.

"You mean except in a plane," Grant corrected her.

"Nope—I mean *ever.*" She was immediately embarrassed by her tacit admission of the provincial life she had led. She'd never flown in a plane.

"It's fine," Grant assured her. "In fact, it's awesome."

It was only when the guard on deck gave them a look for having overstayed their welcome that they finally left for the beach—on foot.

"I'm starving. You?" Grant asked as they strolled along.

"I would kill for a cheeseburger," Sarah replied. A nearby food truck caught them with the smell of onions frying on a grill. By silent accord, they joined the line.

"What, no seafood?" he asked and grinned. She tensed, anticipating a "Crab Cake" joke—one of the Eriksen brothers' old names for her—but he left it at that.

"I can't do the seafood thing. I feel too sorry for them."

"But you don't feel sorry for the cow?"

"I suppose it's because I don't know any."

"I can arrange for you to meet a few," he offered.

"If you do, I won't have much left on the menu to choose from."

"You can always try the avocado."

"Can't. I used to have a pet avocado."

They walked along the beach, eating burgers and sipping on sweet tea. Eventually, they gave in to the temptation of the soft sand and sat watching colorful boats traverse the horizon.

"Time to buy swimsuits," Grant announced when they finished eating. He stood up and pulled Sarah to her feet.

"Wait. You didn't say anything about swimsuits. We're entering a whole new area of negotiations."

"I'm buying," he said. "Come on."

"You've spent enough money already."

"No amount would be too much for the privilege of seeing you—" He stopped himself as she looked at him with a hoisted brow and hands on hips. "Happy. Besides, I work, and I have savings, and we aren't coming all the way to the beach to sit on the sand."

Sarah compromised and said, "Fine. Then I'll let you pick the color."

As they headed toward a store with a sign that read, "Goin' Coastal: Beach Gear and More!" he said. "White."

Sarah objected. "White's not a color, and in case you haven't noticed, ghosts have better tans than I have. I'm going to look horrible."

Grant smiled, "You said I could pick."

"Your funeral."

They entered the store. Its wares were largely priced for impulse buyers, but one corner of the shop was dedicated to high-end designer suits. Sarah pointed to a white one-piecer on a headless mannequin with a price tag: $379. "I'll take this one," she said and watched his face to see his reaction.

He simply nodded and reached for his wallet.

"Wow," she said. "You didn't even blink. I'm impressed. I don't want a four-hundred-dollar swimsuit, goofball. I was just playing with you."

She settled for a twenty-four-dollar two-piecer from the clearance rack, feeling bad that he had to spend even *that* much. They used the changing room to get beach ready.

Walking along the beach, carrying their street clothes, Sarah caught Grant doing his best to hide his interest in her swimsuited frame. A laughing gull watched him and offered its titular commentary. Their troubles were a coast away, and the sand absorbed all concern for the future.

"Where are you going to school?" Grant asked.

"I don't think my father is going to let me go. He wants me to stay and help him." He let her avoid giving him a direct answer.

When they were chest deep in the waves, Grant asked, "What do *you* want?"

"I want to leave. That's all I care about. It's not just my body that's trapped on the dead-end road we grew up on—it's my mind too. I know there's something I'm supposed to do, but I'll never figure it out living in the shadow of my father and his dumbass boat."

"You're free right now," Grant said. He released her into the arms of the sea and watched her with a smile that disguised his apprehension. She was not unaware of the significance of his releasing her *into* a wave after having pulled her *out of* one so recently.

But Sarah was buoyant. She splashed about for a while, bobbing like a cork in the surf. Finally, she dipped her head under the water, and when she emerged, Grant was swimming to shore. When given the opportunity to be alone and free, she followed him instead.

Grant lay in the fluffy, cool sand, his eyes closed, his muscular forearm protecting his face from the hot sun, taking a moment. Sarah, dripping wet, curled up beside him, enjoying his silent attention. The two overworked neighbors shared what they had in common and what they both needed—peaceful rest.

She must have dozed. She woke to the sun dipping lazily toward the western shore, and she forgot what beach she was on, in what world. She looked around for Max, and she couldn't tell if she was relieved or disappointed when she saw a hipster bop by in a Jersey Shore T-shirt. The absence of beach chairs and playful children hinted at the late hour, as did the sun.

Grant lay next to her, sleeping. Sarah could not resist the opportunity to look him over up close. *Undeniably gorgeous—can't believe I'm on a beach in New Jersey with Grant Eriksen.*

Sarah touched his arm to wake him and asked, "What time is it?"

Grant dug his watch from his jeans pocket and stood, sand falling to his feet. "The ferry leaves at six thirty," he said. "We have over an hour."

Sarah ran out to the surf. As she played in the waves, looking back at him, she realized Grant had shared almost nothing about himself that day. She wondered why. Perhaps he was afraid she would leave him behind, along with her father, the dead-end road, and the damnable Port Mahon lighthouse.

As they stepped onto the ferry back to Lewes, a mad choreography was underway. Crewmen dashed about, load balancing the long line of cars ready to cross the bay. Sarah ran up the stairs and found the same bench they'd sat on earlier. She then felt a flush of embarrassment at her habit-based choice—she longed to be more adventurous, but her subconscious steered her to the comfortable choice that involved more of Grant's tactile attention.

He hesitated to sit down next to her, and she asked, "What's wrong?"

He knelt before her, held out his hand, and said, "I don't want to go back," in a voice that undoubtedly sounded more petulant and childlike than he intended.

But she pulled him onto the bench with her and said, "Me either."

She took a deep breath of Cape May air, wanting to hold on to it for their whole return trip. She released it at last; it belonged to Jersey.

The webbed safety net was draped and fastened behind the last car in line, committing them to the journey back to the port of Lewes. As the ferry left the dock and began motoring back to Delaware, Sarah juggled a clash of warring feelings that threatened to overwhelm her. On the one hand, she felt anxiety that time was running out and Grant was going away to college; she was already getting used to him being around. On the other, she felt desperate to leave home and never return. And then there was the whole Max dilemma, overshadowing everything.

No, she reminded herself. *That isn't real.* The thought should have brought her peace, but somehow it didn't.

"This is our bench," she said to Grant. "Promise me one day you'll ride this ferry, sit here, and remember me. Promise?"

"No."

"Why not?"

"Because the idea of not being with you kills me. I'm sorry. I know we've barely spent any time together, and I've spent most of my life trying to make you miserable—but please don't make me think of a future where we won't know each other. I don't want to wake up tomorrow and wonder if this was just a dream."

Which world was the dream for Sarah? She honestly didn't know.

"I don't suppose there's any chance you feel the same way?" he asked.

She shrugged, knowing Grant would soon find someone new in a world full of college admirers. "I feel cold," she answered, avoiding his question. A chill sea breeze was blowing in, and she felt Max's presence in the wind. Why?

Grant lifted her by the arm from their bench and escorted her to the indoor seating area. She leaned on him, wondering how she could feel so committed to a ghost in another world when such a wonderful guy—alive with passion—was walking beside her.

Outside, the wind picked up, and a light rain fell. As the boat passed over the deepest water of the bay, the Cape May lighthouse lit up behind them—a beacon calling her back to where she wished she could have stayed.

They sat together side by side in a dimly lit corner, away from prying eyes, warming themselves with each other's heat. As the Delaware coast approached, Sarah felt an inescapable doom awaiting her. She whispered to him, "If you could go anywhere right now, where would it be?"

"Hard to choose. There are so many places I want to go."

Sarah was intrigued. "Tell me."

Grant moved in closer to her and said, "Iceland."

"Iceland?" Sarah offered an animated shiver—easy to do with the temperature dropping so fast—and said, "I thought you'd prefer warmer water and fewer clothes."

"In Blue Lagoon, Iceland, the water is heated by underground volcanoes. Think of it—we could watch the glow of the northern lights as we steamed away in a mineral bath."

She blinked. Suddenly she was there with him in her mind, gazing up at the northern lights, a sight she'd seen only in pictures.

"But it doesn't matter where I go," he went on, "because I will never be happier than I am right now—right here—with you."

"You're romantic," she said. It came out sounding like an accusation.

Before he could rebut her charge, the rear thrust of the engines shook the ferry and vibrated the floor. The vessel swung wide, shifting its bow to face New Jersey. They were home—and his expression showed he wasn't any happier about it than she was.

Sarah and Grant lingered until the last minute to disembark. Dragging their feet, they silently marched to his truck. The closing of their doors behind them marked the end of their day of fairyland and their return to the marshland. Sarah looked at the floorboards of the truck and said, "Damn it!"

"What is it?"

"It's Monday. By now my dad has figured out the net was never finished, and I've messed up his whole day of fishing—the first day of drift fishing season. I'm dead."

Driving home, Sarah leaned on the passenger door with her cheek pressed against the cold glass as twilight dimmed to darkness.

CHAPTER TWELVE

SWARM

Grant drummed his fingers on the steering wheel as they passed the Killington Beach sign, impaled firmly in the mud and showing that the way home was closer than either of them wanted it to be. Spotting the town cop, Officer Smithie, hiding in the bushes, Grant slowed down to twenty-five. Sarah held the door handle, contemplating escape at any speed. Grant extended his hand to her; she refused it.

When they passed the cop, Grant lifted his hand to wave, and the officer saluted back. Only three community lights for the little town: the first was at the Creek Bridge gas station. The bugs flocked the floodlight, pitching their shadows onto the general store. The blue lights of televisions glowed from home windows as they passed the second floodlight, the one at the fire station, where teenagers huddled together sharing a cigarette.

The right-hand turn onto Port Mahon Road was at the old schoolhouse, and the softball field and basketball courts were lit.

Most of the kids of the fishing town of Slaughter Creek gathered on the playground every evening. Grant slowed down to make the turn. When Sarah saw the crowd, she ducked. Grant spotted his brother's truck and pulled to the shoulder next to the break in the fence.

The chain-link basketball hoop clanged as a ball dropped through. Grant blew his horn and interrupted a heated argument over a foul. Brody, taller than the other boys and sporting a dark tan, jogged over to the truck shirtless. His midlength light-brown hair, soaked dark with sweat, was pulled around one ear to keep it out of his eyes. Sarah peeked above the window when he went by; he'd just turned twenty and was putting on weight, and from what Sarah could see, it was all muscle. So unfair to have to pick one Eriksen, the female animal in her mused. In her mind, though, she still could not forgive any of them. Brody dangled his ripped forearms inside Grant's window and flinched—surprised to see Sarah.

"Hey, stranger," he said with a wide grin.

She raised her hand to wave, embarrassed to be caught with Grant. Brody turned to Grant and asked, "Where have you been?"

With a population of 211, Slaughter Creek was a tough place to keep secrets. Although the kids living on Port Mahon were not counted officially as part of the town, the town adopted them out of the need to add to its numbers. No one in town was a stranger; they all grew up together. Girls on the picnic tables—cheerleaders for the half-court pickup game—cupped their hands to each other's ears and whispered, gossiping about Sarah in Grant's truck.

Sarah was certain Brody had heard the news that she and his brother had not made it in the door of the school that morning. The speculation on what they had done without a chaperone had no doubt fueled a wildfire.

"We took a day off. Right, Sarah?" Grant said and turned to her and winked.

She knew Grant was trying to keep their day private. "That's right," she said, adding the thought, *Good luck with that.*

The previously arguing players, left behind on the court, yelled for Brody to throw back the basketball. Brody ignored his buddies, and Sarah caught him checking her out. Scott ran over to the truck to see what was taking so long. Scott, a perennial target of Officer Smithie—and rightfully so—lived with a cigarette in his mouth. Scott even played sports with a lit cigarette; he had a gift for shifting it around between his lips without using his hands.

Sarah didn't notice Scott creeping up to her passenger door until he comically smacked his face against the window, forgetting all about the cigarette in his mouth. Ashes flew up as he slid down out of sight and then dramatically scratched at the window, begging her silently to open it, like a dying character in a horror movie.

Sarah rolled down the window and sighed. Scott leaned in. She moved to the middle, closer to Grant—to avoid Scott, but now she appeared to be giving off the cozy-couple vibe.

"If you'd told me you were skipping school," Scott said, "I would have bailed too. We could have hung out together."

"Last-minute decision," Grant replied. He assertively put his arm around Sarah—protecting his "turf" and taking advantage of her sudden "affection."

"Lance said to thank you for not showing up," said Brody. "It was a real nice day."

A crowd formed around them; the other boys from town huddled and leaned on the truck. The admiration for the brothers was shown in the boys' solidarity, the way dogs lie all over each other when resting in a pack. The strength in their numbers, typically unsettling to any young girl, had a hierarchy. Lance was the pack-leader-in-absentia of the whole group. And since Lance's brothers now coveted Sarah, that meant she was the alpha female by default, and no one was brave enough to challenge the Eriksens in pursuit of her.

But *between* the brothers? That was a matter to be sorted out later.

Sitting next to Grant, Sarah felt unconditionally accepted for perhaps the first time in her life. Yet, as she considered each face surrounding her, the brothers included, she couldn't help seeing them as the ruthless pack of tormentors they'd always been. She refused, for good reason, to believe they had all become civilized, upstanding young men, regardless of how many years had passed.

"Grant, want in?" Scott asked, pointing to the court.

Grant seemed to feel the pressure and said, "Not tonight. I've got to get Sarah home."

The swarm of boys surrounding the truck huffed and yowled in disappointment; they were intent on having Sarah stay. Because Sarah's father monopolized so much of her time after school and on weekends, the town kids had years of unanswered questions to ask and more than a passing curiosity about her. Now Grant was providing their first opportunity to get to know the mysterious beauty who'd long eluded them. But, of course, that also meant they had to contend with Grant, who was intentionally blocking them and keeping her to himself.

The boisterous reaction of the lads wanting her to stay moved Sarah; she had never experienced her departure as being a disappointment to anyone. *Did Max drop me into an alternate universe?* she wondered.

Most of the group gave up easily and left in a huddle, discussing business that girls were not allowed to hear. A unanimous verdict about Sarah's looks, however—shouted back through the chain-link fence—was "Lord have mercy."

"Come on, Sarah," said Brody. "Stay. You need to see with your own eyes how lame Grant plays before you make up your mind." Brody was implying that Sarah had options in the suitor department, but Grant seemed unthreatened by the remark.

Scott walked around the front of the truck, lit a cigarette, and stole the basketball from Brody, who was preoccupied with Grant and Sarah. Scott bounced the ball high on the road, taunting Brody, who easily could have stolen it back but did not try.

"Come on, Sarah, hang with us," yelled someone else from the court.

Sarah leaned out the window and yelled back, "The Captain is waiting on me. I'm already in trouble." That did it; the rest of them peeled themselves from the truck and retreated to the other side of the fence. She had just reminded them, in case they'd forgotten, that her father was Captain Rex Vise—and even Lance, their alpha dog, would not cross the Captain.

Brody put his hands to his chest, feigning heartbreak. Grant put the truck in drive. Brody surrendered for now and said, "See you later, then."

On the way to dropping off Sarah, Grant told her, "They aren't that bad. You just don't know them."

She replied, "I know them all."

"Like you know me?" Grant asked.

Sarah did not want to argue with him but added, "I know enough."

"Your dad's home," Grant said as they approached the house. Sarah was panicked—the Captain should be out fishing—and said, "Keep going. I can't go home."

"Hey, I'm happy to stretch this 'date' out as long as I can, but I don't want to make things even rougher with your dad."

"Drive. Please?"

"Where?"

Sarah reached her hand out the open window into the cool night air. "Look at how clear it is tonight. The Captain should be unloading the boat right now. It's my fault he didn't go. I didn't finish the drift net, and he's going to lose it when I get home."

Grant stopped in the middle of the single-lane road and said, "It's going to be all right."

"No. It isn't. He's going to kill me."

"Then let's finish the net now," he suggested.

Sarah counteroffered. "Would you consider dropping me off at the Shucking House and picking me up later?"

"Absolutely not. We're in this together. All the way."

Headlights from behind forced them to drive on. "I don't need your help with the net," she said. "It's easier to do it alone." The truth was, she was embarrassed to be seen by Grant in her Shucking House world. In that cold, damp place, she was all the things he and his brothers had always ridiculed her for. In that cold, damp place, she was Fish Girl, forever covered in scales and stink and blood.

Grant pulled over in front of the Shucking House. Seeming to read her thoughts, he said, "I've been in there already, remember?"

"It's so disgusting. It's … I just want to do it myself," she pleaded.

"It's not going to change how I feel about you." He was adamant.

Sarah was trapped by his chivalry. He got out of the truck, and she buried her face in her hands as if to disappear. He patiently circled the truck to retrieve her. She remained anchored to her seat. He leaned in her window and said, "Listen, Sarah, I have brought pigs to slaughter. I have had to put down dying cows. And believe me, there is nothing worse than the smell of 'organic' fertilizer and chicken coops. Trust me. I can handle this."

She sighed, giving in, and let him coax her from the truck. They walked through the front door. She muttered, "Still stinks," and fumbled for the light switch. "Ta-da. Welcome to my world," she said. "And you wonder why I want to get out of here."

Sarah kicked the neglected pile of net. It caught her toe, and she tripped and stumbled to the floor, her hand catching on the sharp corner of a crate.

"Are you all right?" Grant asked, grabbing her arms to lift her. Her palm was bleeding, and he wiped it off with his shirt. Cuts were an everyday part of life to Sarah, no biggie. She reached into the net pile and commenced her instruction.

"This is the top line," she said to him, holding up a yellow rope. "It floats. This is the bottom line, the lead line, and it's weighted to sink. They have to line up when the net drifts in the water." Sarah picked up both ropes and walked them, with Grant in tow, to the far wall. "One complete length of the building to finish the net, twenty more yards."

She tied the bottom line to a long metal post angled into the wall. She pulled until all the slack was out of the rope, reversed a loop, and tied a double half hitch to keep the rope tight across the building. Then she counted small white corks and threaded them on before pulling the slack and then tied the top line.

With both ropes tied nicely to the wall, she retrieved a thin white cord with black marks on it and tied it between the two yellow ropes. "This is the guide to make sure the net is hung equally between the two ropes," she told him. Sarah slipped her fingers along the smooth polyester rope, pushing the corks along to line up with each black mark on the guide. "I can't believe he lied to me," she said, plucking a six-inch plastic tool called a needle, already threaded with twine, from a bucket.

"Who?" Grant asked, walking up behind her.

"The Captain. He made me think there was something wrong with the net, but it's fine."

Sarah pulled the first loop of the mesh net up in her left hand. Grant stood behind her, very close, and watched over her shoulder. He lightly stroked her upper arm and said, "You're deceptive too. You're way stronger than you look."

She counted to eight and wrapped the twine over the rope, threading a loop. She repeated the loop and pulled hard to make the knot stay in place. "You're distracting me—pay attention," she said, squirming under his touch.

"I'm watching. I'm learning," he said but continued to tease her with his fingers.

The truth was she liked his touch, and for a moment, she wondered what it would be like to kiss him, but she needed to finish the net.

"Count to eight, create the knot, double it, and pull it tight," he recited, showing her he was paying attention.

After inspecting the bottom rope, she found a problem and carried a bucket of lead weights a quarter of the way down the length of the floor. *So my father didn't lie*, she thought.

"Everything all right?" he asked.

"It's missing lead." She showed him a small torpedo-shaped weight she'd taken from a bucket.

"You mean like real lead, as in lead paint?" he asked.

"Lead," she affirmed, her voice as weighty as the metal itself.

"Shouldn't you wear gloves? I thought lead damaged your brain cells or something."

Sarah shrugged and pressed the small weight inside the hollow middle of the wrapped polyester fibers of the rope. "This job can't be done with gloves; I've tried. Besides, it's too late for me—I must already be brain impaired to be building these nets in the first place."

"*Over* the rope, Grant," she corrected when his hand traveled in the wrong direction.

"Sorry," he said. He reversed and backed out the knot. Sarah pulled and tied off the anchor rope to the wall again. Grant appeared to be catching on with his part. Sarah faced him from the other side of the two hanging ropes—safe from Grant's wandering hands—and threaded the ends of the mesh loops and tied them to the rope. She overtook him quickly and finished the task at hand before Grant was halfway done with the top line. "You're fast," he marveled.

"Almost done. I really appreciate you helping me," she said.

"It's all yours," he said, handing her the twine. He examined his hand for new blisters.

Sarah finished the rope Grant was working on and untied the ropes from both walls. They walked the net back and piled it against the wall closest to the dock, the mesh fluttering along the floor. They left it there for the Captain to use on his next fishing trip.

At the doorway of the Shucking House, they stood under the bright moonlight as it illuminated the old lantern tower of the square lighthouse. Grant held her, and she blushed.

"Still standing after all this time," he said.

"I want to leave here so much … until I think about leaving her all alone," she said, pointing to the lighthouse. The sudden change of heart surprised her. The lighthouse had always stood as a quintessential symbol of loneliness to her, but now she realized it was also a symbol of home—one that dwelled inside her, for better or worse.

"You know it's haunted, right?" he asked. The unpainted wooden shell and black empty doorways hovered above the tide.

"Are you going to tell me ghost stories now?" she asked him. He reached for her as if to sweep her up in his arms. She scurried away from him, toward the truck.

"Only if you want to hear them," he said, catching up to her. They climbed into the truck and shut their doors.

She said, "I bet mine are scarier than yours."

They drove away from the Shucking House. After they passed the lighthouse, Sarah said, "I'm scared, Grant."

"Of your father?"

"Something else," she said. Except for her doze on the beach, Sarah had not slept since she'd awoken from the dream of the spirit world.

"Love can be scary," he said, smiling to show he meant it as a joke.

When she did not laugh, he pulled over, sensing her concern.

"Do you know that prayer," she said, "that goes, 'If I die before I wake, I pray the Lord my soul to take'?" She pressed her face against the passenger-side window and looked up to the cosmos.

"Of course."

"Have you ever thought about what it means?"

"Can't say I've thought about it very much."

"I have," Sarah said. "It means someone can steal your soul when you sleep, and you won't go to heaven—you'll go someplace else, maybe be trapped for eternity there."

Grant placed his hand on her leg and said, "It's been a very long day."

Sarah folded her arms and shivered. After a moment of silence, she said, "I'm afraid when I go to sleep, all of this will be gone, and

I'll lose you forever. I think this may be the dream I will wake up from and that I'm really dead already."

He pulled her close and hugged her, even as she resisted. "Here's what I think: you're dog tired. Last night ..." He seemed reluctant to bring up her jump into the waves. "You lived; you didn't die. This is real, and I'm not going anywhere."

"Listen to me, Grant. Last night, after ... you brought me home, I had a nightmare that I was killed in my sleep. I know it was just a dream, but it felt real. *Really* real."

"If I could stay with you all night to keep you safe, I would," he said.

"Come on; let's go. I have to face my father." She shifted away from him.

"Just leave him a note. I bet he'll get over it, knowing the net is finished."

She agreed—he was probably right.

They sat in silence for a while. The windows of the truck were fogged, and Sarah could barely see beyond the condensation. Grant's breathing was heavy, and she unconsciously mimicked his pattern.

"Ask me," he said, moving toward her again. Their lips almost touched.

Sarah said, "Ask what?"

"Ask me for anything, and I will—"

"More time, right here," she said.

"It's yours." He leaned back in his seat, and she did the same. They sat apart but holding hands as the warm ground met the cold air from the sea and a ground fog seeped into the truck, adding density to the mist created by their breath.

"What are you going to say tomorrow at school?" she asked to break the silence.

"About us?" he asked reluctantly. "What do you want me to say?"

"That I'm ... your girlfriend."

Instead of replying, he squeezed her hand for a long time. It was a stronger "yes" than words could convey.

"Hearts will be broken—like your prom queen, Jennifer's," she said.

He didn't bother to correct her. "You mean the hearts of all the guys in love with you."

She rolled her eyes. "In your warped brain, everyone wants me."

"I'm serious. I hear the crap they say. Some of it's pretty disturbing. You need to be more careful."

The windows dripped condensation and began to defog on their own. She said, "Isn't that what boyfriends are for?"

Grant moved closer to kiss her, and Sarah thought she glimpsed a shadow in the rear window of the cab. She whipped her head around to see the outline of a dark face hanging upside down from the truck's roof. She blinked, unsure whether her eyes were playing tricks, but when the silhouette moved, she whispered, "Someone's out there."

It can't be who I think it is. It can't be; it can't be.

Grant tensed as the truck shook. Someone jumped off, bouncing the suspension, and landed softly in the sand.

Sarah checked her door lock as Grant flipped on the headlights. The fog had grown thick as they sat. With the defrost on high, he wiped the dripping condensation from the inside of the windows. As the windows cleared, he reached under the seat and came up with a handgun. *Whoa!* Sarah thought. *What's this?* He racked the slide and slipped out of the truck.

"Grant, no!"

She scanned the landscape for movement, as Grant did a 360 scope of the area, using the truck for cover. After a few minutes of searching but not finding anyone, he got back in the truck and locked the door. "It's probably someone from town screwing with us," he said.

"I've worked at night by myself at the Shucking House for years, and no one ever bothered me before."

"Remind me to tell you about the history of this place sometime. You're not as safe as you think. You should not be on this road at night by yourself."

Grant put the truck in gear and drove slowly toward home. The road, visible only in patches where the wind disrupted the fog, was difficult to see, but they both knew it well enough to avoid the ditches on both sides.

Before they arrived at her house, he stopped the truck and kissed her hand. "You don't have to go in there," he offered. "You can stay at my house, and we can call your father when he wakes up."

"I can handle my father."

Grant gave her a squeeze and said, "The good news is, your house is safe because no one messes with your father." When Sarah moved to get out, he said, "Let me at least walk you to the door."

"No, I don't want to wake him. Besides, *you're* the one in danger coming around my house in the middle of the night."

Two o'clock in the morning—all the lights were off, except the floodlight on the willow tree. Fog obscured the driveway and lawn. Sarah dashed up the drive, carving her way through the ground cloud, as Grant sat at the end of her driveway with the headlights off. She climbed the front porch, out of his sight. She finally heard his truck drive off.

Sarah lifted the right-side window on the front porch to crawl through it. She wrestled with the curtain as she slipped her leg over the heavy wooden sill. The house was dark when she landed one foot inside the living room.

Click. The sound of a gun hammer ratcheting.

She gasped and lifted her head—smashing it into the bottom of the raised pane. "Oww!"

"Damn it, Sarah. I almost killed you," the Captain barked, lowering his gun in the dark. He turned on the table lamp and rubbed his eyes.

Her head hummed with pain, and her father said, "That was really dumb, Sarah. What possessed you to climb in here like a criminal?"

She pulled her whole body in the window and said, "I'm sorry. I didn't want to wake you. I know you have to get up early."

With a penetrating squint in his eye, he asked, "Where have you been?"

"The drift net is finished."

"Viktor said you and Grant were late coming back from school. Real late."

"Can we discuss this later? I'm exhausted." She knew she could not lie to her father and get away with it, so she didn't even want to try. "I'm sorry I messed up the fishing trip," she added, facing him. "I know you were counting on the net today."

But Grant was right: now that the Captain knew the net was finished, he was no longer angry. He stumbled back to his room, saying over his shoulder, "We didn't go. The bilge pump broke, and I had to order a part."

Just before shutting his bedroom door, her father said, "Grant Eriksen, huh? I suppose you could do worse."

As she stepped from the shower, the foggy mirror reminded her of the face she'd seen in the truck window. She shuddered at the implications. The scenario her fears were whispering about was not possible.

She hoped she could sleep peacefully. She said to the foggy mirror, "If you are real, Max, please give me one more day."

Unable to keep her eyes open a minute longer, she headed to her room and recited the prayer—"As I lay me down to sleep, I pray the Lord my soul to keep …"—just in case.

CHAPTER THIRTEEN

WARNING

Sarah exited her house to find Grant waiting for her in the driveway. Her heart quickened, but she also felt a flash of annoyance at his presumption. Was she required to ride with him to school every day now?

He seemed to read her mind. He rolled his window down, held up his hands in surrender, and said, "I was in the neighborhood, so I thought ..."

She shot him a smile of mock suspiciousness and climbed into the truck.

"You look like you've had more sleep than I have," he remarked. "Is everything all right?"

"I got lucky," she answered. "The boat was broken yesterday."

"Whew. I was worried your dad might ..." There was no need to finish.

"He caught me coming in and almost shot my head off, though," she said.

"That's not funny."

"Who's joking? I heard the click of his .45, and I thought it was game over."

Grant shook his head, muttering, "I knew you should have stayed at my house," and backed out of the driveway.

As the truck approached the Eriksen house, Brody was standing at the edge of the property, flagging them down. He leaned in the window and said, "The weather is supposed to be good for a couple of days. Lance wants to know if you're going to the farm after school."

Lance walked up behind Brody, and they huddled at the window. "Rex thought she was an intruder last night and almost shot her," Grant told his brothers, excited to have a story to share.

"Were you scared?" Brody asked.

"I'm still breathing," she said.

Brody turned to his older brother and said, "See, Lance? I told you she's a badass."

Lance shoved Brody aside, stuck his face in the window, grinning, and said, "I mean, it's not like she was chased by a guy with a chainsaw."

Grant looked down at his feet and mumbled, "I haven't told her about that. Yet."

Sarah scrunched her face in confusion.

"Ocean City graduation party," Lance said. "You're invited."

"Is that supposed to clear up the chainsaw reference?" Sarah asked.

"It's a long story," Brody started to explain. "Lance is planning a—"

Grant cut him off, answering for Sarah, "She'll let you know. She might be busy."

"Well, anyway, what about the farm?" Lance demanded of Grant. "You gonna be there?"

"It's my job, isn't it?" Grant said. "I'll be there. Always am."

Sarah turned on the radio as Grant sped off toward school.

In the school parking lot, Sarah embraced Grant, trying to summon the desire to enter the building. When they passed through the double doors, a crowd was gathered—the crowd they'd avoided yesterday by skipping town. It was already common knowledge that they had arrived at school the day before but had never made it to class.

With graduation fast approaching, the senior hallway noise level was at a solid eight on the volume scale. Kim, the blond girl Grant took to the prom, slammed her locker door, registering a ten. Heads turned.

Grant defended himself to Sarah. "I've been busy—no time to break up. Not that there was anything to break up. Besides, she's harmless. I've got bigger worries—like being jumped by the football team in gym class today—when they find out you're 'off the market.'"

They stopped short of Sarah's homeroom and let Grant's now-ex-girlfriend walk by. Grant seemed amused by her hostile strut and leaned in to kiss Sarah as others watched.

"It's not funny," Sarah said, poking his chest. "Is that the way you're going to treat me when you're done with me?"

"Kim and I went to prom; that's all. Anything more than that is in her mind only."

Grant pressed against Sarah until she felt the cold cinder-block wall behind her. She turned her head to avoid his kiss.

"What's the matter?" he said, smiling. "Can't you see we're completely alone?" He kissed the cheek she brusquely offered.

The first bell rang—the warning. The onlookers in the hallway dispersed. Grant stepped back and said, "See you at lunch?"

She hurried off. Kim was lingering next to Sarah's homeroom door, surrounded by her support group, waiting for Sarah.

"I'm sorry, Kim," Sarah said and looked down. She meant it.

Kim spat out, "Skank," and walked off with her gang.

Sarah's best, and only, girlfriend, Renee, sat in front of her in homeroom and was excited to see her today, but Sarah was exhausted and rested her head in her arms on the desk. Renee punched her shoulder and said, "So?"

"So … what?"

"Don't even. Spill it."

Sarah lifted her head and said, "All right, I'll tell you, but you can't tell anyone." Sarah was stalling. She knew Renee could not keep a secret and would cave under the pressure.

Renee turned the imaginary key in her lips and threw it over her shoulder. Others were already listening in but pretending not to. Luckily, the bell rang and saved Sarah temporarily from giving up her secret.

"Listen, everyone!" the teacher said, interrupting the chatter as an announcement came on the PA to remind everyone to pick up yearbooks from the school spirit store. The room burst to full volume, and the excitement flowed to the hallway.

Sarah and Renee stuck together in the moving crowd. Renee was a dark-haired girl with a medium complexion who had moved to Delaware from Puerto Rico before high school. Voted Most Likely to Succeed, she was smart and pretty. She was also a social butterfly—a foil to Sarah's antisocial tendencies. But the girls had a common purpose that brought them together: making sure they got better grades than all the boys in the advanced classes. Renee often lamented the fact that she needed a scholarship to afford college, while her brother received full support from her family.

Dragging Sarah to first period arm in arm, Renee demanded to hear the gossip firsthand, but Sarah held out. When they arrived in class, Sarah pulled her English term paper from her backpack. The assigned topic was the ecological impact of nuclear power. She left it on the teacher's desk.

The girls sat down together. Sarah could not keep her secret any longer and whispered, "We went to Cape May." Renee beamed and began peppering her with questions, but the teacher, Ms. Catalano, kicked off class, silencing the gab.

"Miss Vise," she said, "since you were 'out sick' yesterday, we missed your topic for our classroom discussion. Tell us about your paper."

Sarah stood up and felt the usual flush she experienced whenever group attention landed on her. She imagined her classmates as flounders in human clothes—her usual technique for handling performance anxiety—and said, "The Oyster Shoal Nuclear Power Plant in New Jersey has been operating over twenty years, superheating Delaware Bay water to cool its reactor. The commercial fishermen are being blamed for the impacts to the fish supply, while the power plant uses a filtration system that traps and kills the biological soup necessary to sustain new generations of sea life, including microscopic bacteria, fish eggs, and plankton. The food chain of the bay is being disrupted by the loss of these tiny life forms—these near-invisible organisms—and all the regulators can think to do is concentrate on mature, fully grown fish. But my argument is that one fish egg weighing almost nothing is equal to a future fish weighing as much as fifty pounds, and we are overlooking the true cause of the dwindling supply of fish in the bay."

The teacher seemed to rankle at Sarah's theory and said, "Miss Vise, your issue with the nuclear power is hot filtered water, not the disposal of contaminated nuclear waste?"

Sarah replied, "I take offense at everything a nuclear power plant represents, but if I have to write a paper about it, I choose to argue that even its smaller, more overlooked impacts are extremely detrimental. To some of us more than others."

"What about all the good the nuclear plant provides by replacing unclean energy sources with a clean and plentiful supply?" Ms. Catalano queried.

"Does having an abundance of anything give us an incentive to limit what we use? I don't agree with that premise. The best option is to learn to live with less."

Ms. Catalano smiled and said, "I may not agree with you, Sarah, but at least you gave us food for thought in our discussion. Now who would like to offer a counterargument?"

Sarah knew she would not be called upon again, and Grant was the first thought she had once her mind was freed.

She daydreamed through three periods until lunch.

Grant was hip deep in a conversation about the Sixers' playoff run with Paul, his buddy on the varsity basketball team, when he saw Sarah enter the lunchroom. He stopped the conversation midsentence and reached for Sarah as she passed. He and Sarah walked away from Paul for privacy, and Grant said, "I cannot remember one word from classes this morning."

Sarah grinned. "Me either."

"I mean, usually I can remember *one*."

"I think someone might have said 'the.' Not sure, though."

The noise level in the lunchroom suddenly dropped, and Sarah had the feeling the crowd was trying to eavesdrop on them. Or maybe she was just being paranoid. Sarah pulled Grant through the back doors of the lunchroom and into the warm outdoor air.

"You're not hungry?" Grant asked.

"Not for the chipped beef open face."

Sarah leaned against the red brick wall next to the designated smoking area and pulled him close. He leaned in to kiss her, but Sarah stopped him and said, "I wish we could leave."

"There's no escape for you today, Miss Vise," answered Grant. "Not after yesterday."

"Are we going to be in trouble for that, do you think? No one's said anything to me."

"Nah, we're in the senior home stretch. We could probably murder someone right now, and no one would give a crap. But we better not push our luck."

Sarah made a theatrical pout face and lowered her chin. She buried her head in his chest, and he hugged her. The smokers gossiped among themselves and did not pay attention to the couple—except one, a junior named Eddie. Called Sketch by almost everyone, Eddie was a permanent resident of high school's Island of Misfit Toys. He wore a khaki army jacket—even in the summer—and his short black hair was spiked stiff with gel.

Eddie stared at the couple from a distance with darkly hooded eyes.

Scott, the boy from town with a cigarette always in his mouth, bopped onto the scene to interrupt Eddie's stare fest. "What's the big secret?" he asked, horning in on Grant and Sarah.

Sarah dislodged herself from between the two boys and said, "I'm trying to convince Grant to ditch the rest of the day."

"But we're staying," Grant said, resolute on the matter.

Scott argued on Sarah's behalf as she stepped back to give him room. She sensed Eddie's stare and turned toward him.

Caught looking, Eddie flicked his cigarette away and approached Sarah as if he had something on his mind. "You been practicing for the typing test?"

Sarah shrugged, uninterested in making small talk. Eddie lit a new cigarette and stood awkwardly beside her. When the bell sounded, Scott dashed off, unable to sway Grant.

Grant reached for Sarah's hand and said, "See you after last period?" She shrugged a yes, showing her disappointment, and he smiled.

Paul and Grant headed for the gym together. Eddie followed Sarah to class.

"You didn't show up yesterday," Eddie said. "You promised you'd help me with the geometry final in study hall yesterday."

"Oh, crap—sorry about that," Sarah said as they sat down next to each other in typing.

"And here I was thinking I was your boyfriend," Eddie said. He snorted a little laugh.

Sarah gave him an affectionate punch and said, "Aw. Nothing's changed. We're still friends. Please be happy for me."

Eddie smiled, patted her shoulder, and said, "I'm just giving you a hard time, Sarah. I like seeing you happy."

After typing, Sarah and Eddie walked to study hall together. "I wish you weren't graduating," he said. "It's going to be boring without a worthy opponent to help save the world from my demon's wrath."

In study hall they played a long-standing fantasy role-playing game called DarkRealm. Sarah's character was a crusader, a warrior against evil, named Joanna. The main character Eddie played was a demonic force for evil named Sketch—thus the reason for his nickname. Two other kids in class, Ryan and Matt, also had characters in the game, and every day the foursome adventured strange worlds, rolled dice, wielded powerful weapons, and battled for the soul of DarkRealm.

"Without your mad skills throwing dice, the world will be doomed," Eddie said as they entered the classroom. He headed for the game group.

"I thought you wanted help in geometry," Sarah reminded him.

"Let's finish the game instead," he answered.

Sarah shrugged a *no*. She sat between two occupied chairs, blocking Eddie from sitting next to her, and said, "I told you last week—Joanna's retired. She got accepted at DarkRealm State, and she needs to move on and get ready."

Eddie huffed and went to join the others.

Sitting in study hall, her nose in her calculus book, Sarah's mind was running around on top of the Cape May lighthouse with Grant. When she glanced at her empty place next to Eddie, Ryan, and Matt, she saw they were whispering among themselves and shooting disparaging glances in her direction. Sarah, glad when the bell rang, left the room in a hurry without saying goodbye and headed for calculus.

Eddie followed her. "How about helping me with geometry tomorrow?" he asked.

Before Sarah could answer, Renee came charging up from the rear and elbowed Eddie aside, hungry for tidbits about Sarah's previous day.

"So what did you two do in Cape May?"

Sarah stopped, and Renee and Eddie rear-ended her. She stared at Renee, arms folded. Renee was supposed to be keeping her trip a secret, and now she had let Eddie, of all people, in on it. Realizing her mistake, Renee said to Eddie, "This is none of your business, loser."

About to apologize for Renee's insult, Sarah looked toward Eddie. He was gone.

Cold stares greeted Sarah when she entered the calculus classroom; she felt encircled by sharks. Renee noticed it also.

"What's his problem?" Renee asked, pointing at Sarah's ex-chemistry-lab partner, Jon, exuding a serial killer stare.

"Grant warned me about this. He said a few guys would be upset at the news that he and I were together, but I thought he was exaggerating."

The girls sat down. "This is your fault," said Renee. "I've told you before; you're too nice to them. They think you like them when you don't."

"I'm hardly a prize worth fighting over," Sarah stated. "I'll be lucky to even go to college."

"Grant thinks you're a prize, and every scowl in here agrees with him."

"It's not just the boys," Sarah said, pointing subtly at a couple of death-staring girls who seemed equally angry at the news. "You must be the only girl in this school that's not 'into' Grant."

Renee said, "Oh, I'm on that list too. But I'm not dumb enough to stand in a line that never moves."

When class was over, Sarah felt exhausted by the endless questions she'd fielded all day. She met Grant in the parking lot, and he helped her into his truck. She slumped back in the warm seat.

"Do you have time for a side trip?" Grant asked.

"Anything to get away from people for a while," she said.

"It'll get easier," he promised.

They drove to the Eriksen family's farmhouse and commercial agriculture operation less than five miles southwest of Slaughter Creek. Grant shut the truck off and said, "This is my grandfather's place. My uncle runs it now. When my brothers and I talk about 'the farm,' this is the place we mean, not our house on Mahon."

They stepped out of the truck, and a man who resembled Grant's father walked up and said, "Hey, Grant."

Grant shook his hand and said, "Uncle Harald, this is my girlfriend, Sarah."

Harald beamed, tipped his hat, and said, "It's nice to meet you, little lady." Then he turned to Grant. "Do you have time for a quick pass over the south field? It needs copper—all the rain, you know. The field needs better drainage before we plant again, but we should try to save the crop."

"Where's Brody?" Grant inquired.

"Mixing chemicals in the back. Lance is in Wilmington picking up seed."

Grant said to Sarah, "I have a job to do, but it won't take long. Do you need to go home?"

"*Need* is a strong word," she said. "I'll wait."

Brody ran up to them, clothes covered in white powder, as Harald stepped back and said, "I'll leave you to it, then. I'll be at the house if you need anything."

Grant and Brody walked toward the outbuildings in the back, and Sarah followed. Grant said to his brother, "Sarah wants to wait here for me."

Brody's face lit up. "I'll wait with you," he said to her. "It should be quick—like everything Grant does."

Grant shot him a baleful look. He then unlatched the sliding door to a large barn and said, "Fastest tractor we've got."

Sarah drew in a breath as Grant pulled the tire chocks from the wheels of a 1970s yellow-and-silver Grumman G-164 Ag-Cat biplane. Brody pulled the plane out of the building and onto the mowed grass. Grant walked around the single-propeller plane with the thirty-five-foot wingspan, giving it a visual inspection, and then climbed inside and began going through a printed preflight checklist.

While Brody fueled the plane, Sarah walked over to Grant and said, "You're a pilot?"

Grant grinned sheepishly, knowing he'd had plenty of opportunities to mention it.

"Since when?" she asked.

Grant smiled and said, "That depends on when you start counting—a few years."

"You didn't think this was a detail worth mentioning?"

"I'm mentioning it now."

"I'll take her to the field if you want," Brody "generously" offered.

"That depends."

"On what?" said Sarah.

"Whether you want to watch." Grant smiled. "You decide. I'll be right back." He stored the checklist in the seat pocket and fired the ignition. Brody pulled Sarah off to the side just before the engine started, and the propeller torqued and spun.

With only a moment's hesitation, the plane went racing across the grass strip and lifted up above the field. Brody and Sarah sped off in his truck to go observe Grant's field-spraying flight.

Brody drove without apparent regard for any life form, human or otherwise. Chickens scattered in every direction, and a cat caught off guard scurried up a tree. Sarah struggled to click her seat belt in the bouncing cab. The silver-and-yellow biplane followed above and then passed them on Sarah's side of the truck.

Brody turned onto a rough dirt road, and Sarah implored, "Can we slow down?"

"I've seen you blow past our house faster than this," Brody said.

"That's when I'm driving."

Brody laughed but did not limit his speed. Above the trees, the plane banked sharply toward the ground, and Sarah's heart sank with it. When Brody stopped the truck, they had a good view of the field from the side. Sarah and Brody jumped out. Grant was already at the far end when Brody unlatched the tailgate. They sat on it for a front-row seat.

The low-flying biplane passed, spraying a dusty mist on the leaves. "That's copper sulfate for the mold," Brody explained.

"Is it healthy?" she asked.

"Now you sound like Grant. It won't hurt you—unless you're mold."

"Maybe I am," she said, "because this stuff tastes like death." Sarah licked her lips, tasted metallic pennies, and spit on the ground. Brody smiled at her unladylike display.

The plane neared the trees at the far end of the field and soared high, turning 180 degrees, and dove back to the ground. Sarah gasped and put her hand over her mouth. She was certain Grant would crash.

The plane lifted and straightened as it passed, and Brody waved at it.

"Don't distract him!" Sarah yelled.

"You have nothing to worry about," Brody assured her. "He's good at this."

At the end of the row, the plane ascended toward the fluffy white cumulus clouds. Then, with no trees and power lines to the south, the plane flew toward them, straight and level. The wings wobbled when he went by.

"We call that a wing wave. I think he's showing off a little," Brody said.

Sarah gasped at the passing plane and asked, "Are you a pilot too?"

"Uncle Harald was a military pilot and taught all three of us. Lance is a good pilot, but the maneuvers are harder than they look—Grant is more of a natural at this kind of flying. I think calling Grant a farmer is a stretch; he'd rather be doing this."

"What about you?"

"I know how to get from point A to point B, but I like my feet on the ground." She nodded in agreement.

Brody squinted into the sun to see Grant's progress. The plane passed them again, approached the trees, climbed fast, and looped back around. Sarah covered her eyes and said, "It's hard to watch."

Brody laughed and said, "You'll get used to it."

When she heard the buzz of the plane grow closer, she peeked through her fingers and breathed a sigh of relief.

"So I had an ulterior motive for stealing you away in my truck," said Brody.

Sarah glanced at him suspiciously. She wasn't sure she wanted to hear what he was going to say next.

"Can you keep a secret?"

"I can, but I'm not keeping anything from Grant." *Well, nothing* you *tell me, anyway,* she thought.

"Fair enough." Brody seemed aware that the conversation felt more intimate than he intended. He jumped off the tailgate and placed a bit of distance between them. "Lance and I need your help."

"My help? With what?"

"On graduation night, we have something special planned after hours on the boardwalk in Ocean City. But Grant won't go without you."

"Who else is going?"

"Just us four—if you say yes," he said.

"I thought you guys had a lot of friends."

"Not for this."

"Not sure I like the sound of that. How important is this to you?"

"Let's just say, it won't be long before Lance comes crawling to you himself, on his hands and knees, to beg."

"Well, in that case," Sarah said with a grin, "tell him I'll think about it."

Brody walked around to the driver's side of the truck. "Sarah, there's something else before we drive back." He stuck his hands in the pockets of his jeans, sparing another look at Grant sweeping by in the plane. "Lance and I want you to know, all that stuff we said as kids—"

Sarah interrupted, bracing herself for another awkward round of apologies. "Look. Don't worry about—"

Brody grinned and continued, "We meant every word of it." He opened the passenger door for her. "However, we do sincerely apologize for all the things we failed to mention."

"Such as?" Sarah asked with a twinkle in her eye. She jumped off the tailgate and got into the truck.

"Such as … Miss Sarah, you are looking mighty fine today."

"For the record," she said on the way back to the farm, "Grant never asked me to go to Ocean City."

"He's probably scared he'll chicken out."

"I can't imagine him being scared of anything," she said.

"He's got a few weaknesses—and I'm looking at one right now. Can I tell Lance you're in?"

"Lance can sweat it out."

Behind the big farmhouse, the plane's engine shut down, and the propeller stopped, but the buzz continued to ring in Sarah's ears. High on adrenaline, Grant ran to greet Sarah, lifting her high in the air, ignoring Brody standing next to her.

"No problem," Brody said. "I'll put the plane away since you asked so nicely."

"Did you miss me?" Grant said to Sarah.

She replied, "What if I did?" He went in for a kiss, but she sidestepped it. "Why didn't you tell me you could fly an airplane?"

Ignoring the question, he asked, "Do you have to go home?"

"I do," she replied, "but I want to talk about this."

"I'm all ears."

She felt his confidence surging as he took her hand on the way back to the truck. "The way you were flying," she said, "it's dangerous."

"It is—if you don't know what you're doing. But that condition doesn't apply to me."

"Modest in addition to being moderately okay looking." Sarah liked his cocky display. She enjoyed his quiet, confident demeanor on the drive home—until they turned onto Port Mahon Road. The road brought out her bitter side. "Are you also the guy who crop-dusts the pesticides for mosquitoes?" she asked Grant in a suddenly accusatory tone.

"My job is mostly seed and fertilizer. This year we've had a mold problem because of all the rain. We only use natural pesticides, and the fungicide we spray is safe—I make sure."

"Way to dodge the question," she said. "Are you the one who flies over my house and sprays for mosquitoes, yes or no?"

He attempted a smile. "Why? Are you, like, a Save the Mosquitoes activist?" He grinned in amusement, but this only sparked her fury—he was dismissing her concerns as trivial.

"Not particularly," she said, "but the stuff that's sprayed in the air to kill them is even worse. It's toxic for wildlife and for people."

"I didn't know how strongly you felt about it. No, I don't spray for mosquitoes."

She detected the retreat of his confidence as he turned into his driveway. "Would you like to stay for dinner?" he asked.

Nice try, she thought. She threw her backpack over her shoulder, exited the truck, and said, "No thanks. I have to study."

She struck off down the road toward her house, leaving Grant with his head spinning.

Grant followed her, driving slowly with the passenger window down. "Please don't be mad at me," he said. "The pilots the state sends here don't care if it's too windy or if they don't get close enough to the ground, so it's better when I do it. I don't like spraying chemicals any more than you like killing fish …"

She was surprised he knew her feelings about that.

"But these are family obligations we are born with. Just like you—I have no choice right now, and that's why I'm leaving. I'm breaking over a hundred years of family farming tradition to become a commercial pilot, but in the meantime, I do what I have to do."

"You can't just keep talking *at* me until I feel better—it's exhausting. When I'm upset, you have to trust me enough to let me sort it out on my own."

"Okay, but to be fair … the last time I left you alone, you tried to … forgive me if I worry about leaving you alone in your house when you're upset."

Sarah kept walking and said in a voice approaching a shout, "Well, you better get used to it because I like being alone. I have to study for finals, and you have to start packing for pilot school. By the way—your plan to become a commercial pilot, that would have been nice to know too. Those are the kinds of things people tell each other when they're in a relationship!"

As they reached her driveway, he stopped and called out, "Please call me later."

Sarah was grateful her northeast corner bedroom window was not visible from Grant's house. After processing all the new information she'd just learned, she had no choice but to break up with him. The feeling of being left behind once was already bad enough; she couldn't imagine being left over and over again as he went off to fly around the world.

The main reason, of course, that she was compelled to break it off: he knew her secret. He had witnessed her suicide attempt, and now he could bring it up anytime he saw fit, forevermore. If she wanted to wash herself of the filth of that mistake, there was really no choice but to break up with him.

Flipping the pages of her English lit book, unable to concentrate, she knew she was wasting her time and learning nothing. Laying her head on the pillow, dreading having to break up with Grant, she rested her eyes. *I believed you were a family farmer*, she thought, *but now I know you aren't coming back after college.*

As Sarah slipped into a dream on this warm summer night, her bedroom door opened. A shadow entered, and the door clicked quietly closed. A young man lifted her sheet and slid in beside her.

"Grant?" she whispered in her sleep.

"It's me, Max-ymir-he," the man answered.

"Max?" She turned away from him, trembled, and waited helplessly for him to steal her soul.

Lying on her side, she felt the smooth comfort of his bare skin under the blanket. His hand traced her shoulder, along her arm, to her fingers. It tickled. "I miss you," he said. His warm kiss stirred her awake, and she touched the silky skin of his forearm. He kissed her with full lips on the back of her shoulder and said, "Sarah, I have to tell you something—you're in danger."

"Is this a dream?" she asked.

"You're not dreaming. And I have to take you back with me now before you're murdered."

Sarah mumbled sleepily, "No. It's too soon."

"I've seen it—your death," Max said. "If you die, here in this place, before I bring you back, your spirit will be lost. I will never be able to bring you back with me."

"Then come back just before it happens," she said groggily.

The warm pattern of kisses up her arm meant he wanted to stay longer. She bit her lip, dying to turn around—knowing what facing and surrendering to him would mean—an end of her earthly life.

"You don't understand," he said. "I can't come here anytime I want. I must find … entry points in time's fabric. This is the closest I've been able to get to the time it happens. Each time I return at a later point, you are already gone. I cannot pinpoint the exact moment of your death, but I know it is coming soon."

"Max, leaving now makes no sense. Nothing has changed in my life yet. If I go now, I won't have enough spirit energy."

"You aren't listening. We assumed you would have a long life, and I could steal you back anytime I wanted as if you never left, but this is the closest time I can get to you before you die. I've come back so many times to the painful aftermath of your murder; please don't make me try again. I've watched the dreams of your murder haunting your killer after your death. I cannot chance losing you forever."

"Everything can change now that you've told me," she said. "I'll be careful, and you'll have more opportunities. I'm not going to die."

Max moved the hair from her ear and paused until she needed him to kiss her. She felt his light breath warming the spot where he would kiss next. She couldn't think of anything else.

"I miss you so much," he said. "It took your leaving to make me realize I'm in love with you. And I'm begging you to come back with me. If your spirit is lost, mine will be also."

"Your energy is not enough to sustain us both in your world, remember. I promise I will fight for my life. I won't be murdered. If you love me, you'll give me a chance to fulfill my life's journey the way you were trusted to fulfill yours."

Max groaned and slumped over dramatically, giving up much more easily than she imagined. "You are right, I hate to say. You must be given the chance to save your life now that you have received this warning." *This is too easy—he's up to something, but at least I'm safe for now*, she thought.

"Hold me," she said, liking his attention when it came without deathly consequences. "Tell me how you've been."

"I've been lonely, Sarah. It's been cold. I've been sitting alone on the hill and remembering your smile—and your beautiful spirit light."

She didn't want to remind him that the beautiful spirit light he admired in her was his own. Rather, she let him bury his face in her chest and grasp her tightly as she held his head of silky brown hair. Her dubious "protector" had come back to rescue her once again from her miserable life.

After a while, Sarah peeked out of the blanket and saw the moon glowing—they were no longer in her room but on the hidden beach next to the forbidding woods. She felt his sultry breath deepen as he fell asleep, using her spirit as his pillow.

Sarah held Max until she was unable to stay awake. She traveled among the stars with him for an indefinite time and then awoke, alone, to the blare of her alarm clock. A faint impression of his body hinted that he had been with her in bed, but she knew it was just a dream.

CHAPTER FOURTEEN

ICE

The visit from Max, the "warning," felt almost like cheating on Grant when Sarah replayed the vivid dream in her mind as she got ready for school. The guilt sharpened—for good reason. This—*what?* This phantasm?—slips into her bed and tells her she has to hurry up with her life because she's going to die soon? How could she complete her mission to collect life's energy while feeling doomed and guilty?

Sarah felt as if two trains were heading directly toward each other on a single track. She feared a jealous reaction from both men—and for good reason—but she worried that Max's fury, in particular, could be deadly for both her and Grant … *if Max doesn't get what he wants.*

When leaving her house that morning, she could not face Grant. The truth was, she was hooked by the lure of a supernatural man, making it impossible for Grant to compete. Yes, Max was scary and unpredictable, but he had his moments; he had his qualities. Even if he was a ghost. The warm kiss on the back of her exposed shoulder—

he was real enough. Even his hungry, animalistic nature felt magnetic to her. *Must be why girls choose the bad boys*, she thought.

Dreaming about a "bad boy" with mystical power was not winning any points for Grant, the Shakespearean "good man." When comparing the two men, the mere mortal naturally held a lesser hand of cards. But still, she could not deny her deep, growing attraction to Grant. Not only was she wildly tempted by his looks, but she was also addicted to being the recipient of his generous attention, loyalty, and kindness.

I am certifiable, she thought.

A journey toward her life's true purpose appeared impossible now that Max had warned her of impending death and professed his love. He had sent Sarah back to this life to collect life's energy—which flowed from earthly love—but now it felt like she would be carjacking the soul of any man unlucky enough to cross her path. The love she was supposed to collect was for Max, not herself, and she was now on short notice.

Traversing her driveway, she looked across the field and saw the Eriksen boys in their usual place on the porch. This time she stood at her mailbox and let the bus pick her up. *Grant will easily find someone else.*

But what if I never get over him? she thought as she passed him on the bus, looking down. Suddenly it seemed easier to collect fulfillment from anyone except Grant—because she realized that every new moment with Grant would follow her to Max's world. The definition of hell would be an infinity of having to be with Max while remembering Grant and wishing she could be with him.

If she could avoid Grant, she reasoned, and be with someone else she cared less about, she would not pine for her lost life on Port Mahon Road when in Max's world. Sarah found solace in this idea of finding someone she liked less than Grant. Surprisingly, in this scenario, Eddie was a more appealing option. Between Max and Eddie, there was no competition—she would never miss Eddie for eternity in the company of Max.

Sarah waited outside her homeroom, knowing Grant would find her. "Are you mad I didn't ride with you today?" she asked when she saw him.

"Mad? No, I'm worried about you."

"You don't need to worry about me; that's not in your permanent job description. Everything is fine. But I need a break. I'm not used to all this attention."

"I understand. It's completely fine," he said. "Don't answer now, and it's all right if you say no, but I wanted to offer you a ride home after school."

She shook her head no. He was stoic in response to her refusal and asked, "Can I call you later?"

She agreed it would be all right, and he nodded, biting his lip. When he walked away, she felt enveloped in a cold storm cloud.

In homeroom, Renee asked, "What's going on?"

"I'm exhausted by the attention from him and everyone else," Sarah replied. "I asked him for a break."

"Fire one day, ice the next," Renee said.

"You mean I'm the ice?"

"He's definitely the fire."

"Well, his fire has been melting my ice into a deep puddle," said Sarah, "and I'm drowning. I've got to end it if I want to breathe."

"I can definitely see why after a whole two days together, you would need a break from this nonstop relationship avalanche."

Sarah shot her a sheepish grin.

"Has anyone ever told you," Renee continued, "you give up too easily? You have no idea how lucky you are. I wish someone felt about me the way he does about you. Hope you don't take too long to figure it out, Sarah, or you are going to lose him."

At lunch, Sarah stayed outside with the smokers to avoid Grant—he noticed and gave her the space she wanted.

"Where's your boyfriend?" Eddie asked her.

"I thought you were my boyfriend," she said.

Eddie hesitated to smile but seemed to enjoy the boyfriend idea as he smoked his cigarette.

"Grant's inside," she said, putting her hand out for his cigarette.

Eddie handed it to her, a look of surprise on his face. "Why are you out here, then? Did you break up with him?"

Sarah sat on the step with Eddie. The quiet, awkward, chain-smoking social reject was somehow familiar and comforting to her today. She inhaled the smoke, unafraid, but her lungs rebelled with a furious cough.

"Take it easy there, Joanna."

Her eyes teared up in reaction to the smoke, and she jumped up to escape the fumes.

"Let's go," Sarah said, waving her arms to clear the smoke clinging to her body. Eddie sacrificed his cigarette and followed Sarah inside. He slowed to get a nice view of her backside and then sped up to walk next to her, making a squeezing motion with his hand in the air behind her butt.

Grant appeared out of nowhere and pulled Eddie's head down by the neck, bending him over in the center of the crowded hallway. Eddie tried to get away, and Grant shoved him into a wall of lockers. Eddie fell to the floor. From there he tossed an obscene gesture in Grant's direction.

Grant yanked him off the floor and punched him in the face, letting him fall again. On the floor, Eddie put his hands up in self-defense, and Grant descended on him, intending to hit him again. Before he could take another swing, Sarah rushed to Eddie's aid, forcing Grant to hold back. Blood flowed from Eddie's nose as Sarah pushed Grant aside and yelled, "What are you doing to him?"

Grant looked ready to explode, not only at Eddie but at Sarah. But he somehow managed to back down. Bleeding from the nose and mouth, Eddie cursed Grant and then got up and ran. Sarah chased Eddie and tugged on his jacket so she could get him some help. To escape from her, he grabbed her hand and swung it away from him with violent force. Her hand smashed into the cinder-block wall, and he ran off. Sarah's wrist felt broken. When Grant reached out to her to assess the damage, she shrieked, "What is wrong with you?"

Grant tried to explain. "You didn't see him. He was—"

"Grant! Sarah!" interrupted the voice of Mr. Williams, the upper-class chemistry teacher. He stood three feet away from them, stern-faced, hands on his hips. "Principal's office, *now*!"

Sarah slapped Grant's hand away as they walked to the principal's office. When they arrived, she sat on the opposite side of the waiting room from him. She was called into the principal's office first.

After giving her account of Grant's seemingly unprovoked attack on Eddie, she marched out to find Grant's eyes glued to the floor, avoiding contact with her.

Sarah went to the nurse's office, where she found Eddie holding a towel full of ice to his face.

"I'm sorry Grant did this to you," she said.

"How can you like that stupid jerk?"

"I never thought he would—"

"Whatever. You two are meant for each other."

Eddie was sent home. Sarah returned to class with an ice pack for her wrist.

Renee sat next to Sarah in calculus and said, "Grant's suspended for the rest of the week but not for finals and graduation."

"Wow, that's fair. He gets the last two days of school off, and I have to clean up his mess with Eddie."

Renee said, "You have no idea what Sketch did, do you?"

"I don't care what he did," Sarah said, wincing at the pain in her wrist.

"He was doing the ass-grabbing gesture behind your back. Everyone saw it."

"Big deal," Sarah said.

"He got what he deserved."

"Gestures are harmless. They don't hurt anyone."

"Oh, really?" said Renee. "Eddie got thrown off the bus last fall for doing skeevy things with the girls on the bus. I told you, but you never listen."

Sarah acted unimpressed, so Renee added more detail. "He sat in an aisle seat using a dentist's mirror to look up girl's skirts as they walked by. You think that was a harmless gesture?"

"Rumors," Sarah said.

"He's disgusting and perverted. You're the only girl in school who even talks to him. Look what he did to your hand."

"He was mad. Grant punched him in the face."

"You're dating the most admired guy in the school, and you insist on keeping a friendship with a freakin' loser. What's wrong with you? How much more BS do you think Grant's going to put up with before he moves on?"

Sarah realized the room had gone quiet with listening ears. She glanced around the room, and people pretended to busy themselves.

"I'm telling you straight up," Renee said, "you're wrong to be mad at Grant, and you need to apologize as soon as you see him—before it's too late."

Grant's truck was not in the parking lot at the end of the day. As she rode in the front seat of the bus, her mind turned to Max's warning. Murder? Her? Really? No, in the cold light of day, it seemed impossible. Was Max an illusion, or was he real? That was the burning question. If he was real—alive in some other dimension—then he might have become jealous of her flesh-and-blood boyfriend, Grant. This might have caused him to visit her dreams and press the timetable—by inventing the lie of a murder. He didn't reveal the identity of the other person whose dreams he had supposedly visited—the alleged murderer. Why not?

Because it was a bunch of crap, that's why. A lie told by an illusion.

The most likely explanation for Max's appearance in her life was that her subconscious invented him the night she tried to kill herself. He then reappeared in another dream, warning her about her impending death, only when she thought seriously about leaving Grant to rid herself of reminders of her suicide attempt. *Max is a defense mechanism—when I'm afraid to live, he appears in my sleep, ready to take me away from the pain.*

Sarah reflected that she was swiftly ruining her relationship with Grant. And if she succeeded, all that would be left was an imaginary ghost of a boyfriend in some crazy afterworld—and that did not seem particularly fulfilling.

Maybe Eddie deserved it, her mind spat out.

Sarah looked at her wrist—swollen and purplish-blue, but not broken. She was happy to see Grant's truck parked at his house when she stepped off the bus. Just knowing that his feet were on the ground, that he wasn't flying around somewhere in the sky, made her feel grounded. But she could not bring herself to visit him; she was too embarrassed. She kicked stones all the way up the driveway to her house.

"We lost a guy today," said the Captain from his armchair the moment she stepped in the door. "Sorry excuse for a man. He fell off the boat and then yelled he couldn't swim. What kind of idiot takes a job on a fishing boat not knowing how to swim?"

"Someone died?"

"No: quit." His eyes flashed to her wrist as she crossed the room. "What the hell happened to you?"

"Grant got into a fight—"

"Grant Eriksen did this?" he said, rising from his seat. "Well, he'd better damn well—"

"Not Grant." She cut him off. "Grant would never hurt a woman. I'm surprised you would even—"

"Well, then, spit it out," the Captain said, setting his jaw. "Who? Why is it that women can never give a straight answer to any damn thing?"

Sarah took a brief moment to indulge her hope that his use of the term *women* signaled a grudging acceptance of her blossoming adulthood. "On the way to class, I was walking with—"

"I don't need ten minutes of *why*; I just need the *who*. Whoever did this better be half dead already, or he will be soon."

"Well, you don't have to worry because Grant beat the guy senseless until I stopped him."

The Captain rolled his eyes. "You mean to tell me some guy almost broke your wrist, and you stopped Grant from beating the hell out of him?"

Now Sarah was confused because the story was coming out backward. Grant slugged Eddie before Eddie hurt her wrist.

"I stopped him because I didn't want Grant to kill him."

"Are you sure you're feeling all right? My Sarah would have beat the crap out of the poor bastard herself."

Sarah headed for her bedroom, recognizing that any further conversation would only muddle things even more.

"Where are you going?" the Captain yelled. "I need you to pick up a block of ice from Dover before we go fishing."

"My wrist hurts," she said.

"You'll be fine. Put some salt water on it. It'll heal in no time."

Sarah sighed. She didn't bother to argue about the ice-fetching task; she knew the guys at the ice plant would put the three-hundred-pound block on the truck for her. But as she opened the door to exit, she saw a rope across the back of the bed of the truck.

"Where's the tailgate?" she asked.

The Captain chuckled. "The reason the guy quit was not because he couldn't swim. He was thrashing in the water. I pulled him by the hair and put him back in the boat—and he was fine. But later, when he stood on the tailgate, the rusty hinges gave way, and he broke his foot. The bastard flipped me off and quit. After I saved his life—no good deed goes unpunished."

"I'm not getting a block of ice in a truck without a tailgate."

"Then get your boyfriend to drive you."

She slapped her hands to her sides, immediately regretting the move because of the shooting pain. "Damn it!" she screamed at her wrist. Or perhaps at her father. Or perhaps at her life. She was resolved not to ask Grant for help after how she had treated him.

Grant and Lance sat on the porch as Sarah drove past without a tailgate. She felt embarrassed, conditioned as she was to drawing ridicule from the boys because of the duct-taped and roped-together life she lived with her father.

The truck with the yellow rope across the back sped through town, and she hoped no one noticed. Three lights in Dover, and she was at the ice plant.

The guys at the icehouse were always nice to Sarah. They would jump up right away to score the block of ice for her. She'd waited in line plenty of times and had seen how others were treated—not as well. Sarah's regular ice guy—twenties, thick beard, plaid long-sleeve shirt—walked out on the loading dock as she backed the truck up. "Sarah, did you know you're missing a tailgate?" he said, carrying a big set of tongs.

"Um, yeah," she replied out the truck window, "that would explain the presence of the rope." The guy nodded slowly as if digesting a complex point of philosophy. Usually, Sarah hung around and chatted with him, taking advantage of the cool mist in the middle of summer, but today she only wanted to escape her embarrassment.

"You should get that fixed," he offered. Another priceless pearl of wisdom.

"I'm in a hurry today, Earl," she said without getting out of the truck.

He pulled the block and slid it off the landing onto the bed. The truck shook under the weight. The ice slid forward onto the plywood board near the cab, and the young man said, "Always nice seeing you, Sarah. Take it easy without that tailgate, now."

She raised her hand and turned onto the street, heading home.

At the first light, she stopped slowly and looked back. The block of ice had not moved. She never recalled the ice leaving the plywood or touching the tailgate. *The tailgate isn't necessary—I'm worrying for nothing*, she thought. The light turned green, and she smoothly drove to the next intersection. The next light was already green, so she kept going. As she neared the last light before crossing the highway, it turned yellow, and she sped up to make the light.

When she turned to look in the back of the truck a minute later, the block of ice was gone. She rose in the seat to see if it was against the cab—it was not. She surveyed the road behind the truck; the block of ice was not on the ground. Instead of going straight home, she stopped at the gas station on the corner and paced around the truck. *What if I hurt someone or caused a car accident?* she thought. She was worried the police would be looking for her.

Sarah sat on the back of the truck, with her back against the rope and her face in her hands. She looked up at the sound of a vehicle parking nearby. Grant stepped from his truck and approached her. Mr. Everywhere. He said, "Sarah, I'm sorry. I didn't mean to—"

"This is not about you," she said. "I'm over that already. I realize now—Eddie had it coming."

"What's wrong, then?"

"I lost a three-hundred-pound block of ice."

CHAPTER FIFTEEN

MIMOSA

Grant offered to pick up another block of ice before the ice plant closed and to meet Sarah and her dad at the dock.

"Grant's a good man; you're too hard on him," the Captain said as he drove the familiar stretch from the house to the dock. Sarah held her swollen wrist up within his peripheral vision and hoped for a speck of mercy from her father, but he did not comment. She decided to go in for the kill instead, knowing she had him cornered for the moment.

"We agreed I was going to college in the fall, and you said I could go."

He looked as uncomfortable as she intended him to be. "I need you here," he said after a pause. "All the guys out here are idiots. They whine like babies. They can't cull or tie a knot to save their lives." It was rare for her dad to admit he needed anyone, and he was squirming as he did so. "You can go to the college in Dover and work here," he said.

"I didn't apply to any schools in Dover. The choice is University of Delaware or Penn State."

"Why didn't you apply at places we can afford?"

"I got a scholarship to Delaware, remember?"

"It won't pay for all of it. You'll need transportation, and all we have is this truck." She listened to the rattles and squeaks around them, knowing that college might depend on this old truck holding together—if she was not able to afford to live on campus. Sarah imagined having to hitchhike to school in Newark every morning. Yeah, no.

"I can get a job—one that pays actual money—and buy a car. I'm eighteen now."

His face turned red, and Sarah knew enough to stop talking. Too late. "You're a pretty girl," he said. "You don't need college. Be nice to Grant, get married, have kids, and forget about wasting time and money on college."

"Grant's going away to college."

He took a long, deep breath and said, "Plenty of fish in the sea."

When they pulled up at the dock, the Captain saw the crew was not at the boat yet and said, "See what I mean? Sorry son of a bitches are late. They better show up."

Sarah hoped she was off the hook for hard labor because of her wrist, but no such luck without the men showing up. "The gas cans are inside the door," the Captain barked. "I'm going to the other docks to see if I can get more crew."

Sarah used her left hand to lift the sharp-edged handle of the red-metal five-gallon gas can. Together, the steel and fuel weighed almost fifty pounds. She took a step, and the can swung too much—gas escaped from the uncapped spout and splattered on the dock. A residual trail of expanding rainbow spots marked her steps to the boat.

She lifted the gas can to the gunnel rail of the *Outlaw*, and it teetered with the rocking of the boat, dangerously close to falling in the water. Unable to control the can or to pour its contents into the gas tank with her injured hand, she set it back on the dock. As she did so, the edge of the can caught the plank and tipped over. She stopped the fuel spill, but the dock reeked.

Sarah hurried back inside the building; only nine more gas cans to lug to the boat. She carried the next one in a staggered fashion—lifting it, walking one step, and carefully putting it down—but the fuel still splashed out. Now an uncontestable trail of gas led to the *Outlaw*. Angry with herself, she thought, *Grant's not the only one spreading toxic chemicals.*

She let her right hand assist, but her wrist failed her, and the can slipped and fell over. The Captain walked up, crewless and alone, just as the gasoline gushed between the planks into the bay.

"What the hell are you doing?" he growled, grabbing the handle.

"Sorry, it slipped," she said. "I only have one working hand!"

He shoved her aside. The Captain picked up the gas can easily with his right hand, held a funnel with his left, and smoothly poured gas into the fuel tank.

Sarah watched the results of her oil spill floating by on the surface of the water.

The Captain said in a gentler voice, his way of apologizing for barking at her, "Don't worry about it; it'll evaporate."

"Whatever was wrong with my wrist before," she said, "I just made it worse."

"The first aid kit is in the bow," he snapped.

Sarah and her dad boarded the boat, ready for fishing. The culling box had been replaced by the new drift net. Dave showed up—this time he was the one arriving late—at the dock, and the

Captain started the engine. The ropes were already dropped before Dave climbed aboard.

The Captain mumbled, "My crew—one man and a lame woman. Those sorry son of a guns will pay for this."

"What about Grant?" Sarah said. "We need to wait for him. He doesn't know what to do with the block of ice."

The Captain put the boat in gear and said, "He'll figure it out." *Of course he will—because he's a man*, she thought.

"He's doing us a favor. The least we can do is—"

Too late. The boat lunged forward, and the floorboards vibrated with a deep rumble that massaged Sarah's feet. The compass spun, and they headed for Killington. Sarah handed her father a bandage roll and stuck her arm in his face. He gave her wrist a hasty wrap.

"We'll finally get to see how your drift net does," he said, his attention returning to what was important.

The net glistened perfectly white on the stern floor, the cork line on the starboard side, the anchor line on the port side. The bay was smooth, and the air was crisp but not cold.

When they reached the spot the Captain had in mind, he shifted the boat into neutral and then walked to the stern and threw the flag off. With the engine in idle, the ropes pulled evenly off the deck as the boat skated east. The net trickled off the back, uniform and straight.

"See that—how the corks skim the surface, letting the branches float past," he said. "This is going to be a good one. You have a gift, Sarah." He smiled proudly at his daughter.

Sarah would take the praise wherever she could get it, but she was not looking forward to what would happen next.

Dave threw the flag marking the end, and the Captain cut the engine. They sat for a while with only the slap of the waves against the boat, and for the first time, it seemed like they were on a leisure fishing trip. The sun, low to the west, still had enough heat to warm them.

Rex let out a contented sigh, pulled a soda from the cooler, and asked the others, "Want a water or something?" The boat rocked from side to side as the waves passed.

"You know they used to fish this beach using horses or mules onshore," he said after quenching his thirst. "The people who write the rules think modern technology makes it too easy to catch fish, so they regulate the boats, but you don't even need a boat to catch fish. These waters were fished from schooners and the shore with huge nets for over two hundred years without changes to the fishing population. The fish only disappeared *after* the regulations—not before—because they protect the biggest, meanest, most predatory fish in the bay. *Those* are the ones they won't let us catch."

The Captain tended to repeat himself when venting his frustrations over being regulated by scientists and lawmakers. "What do you think a fifty-pound fish is doing all day swimming around in the bay?"

Sarah rolled her eyes. It was hard to tune him out with the engine off. She mentally hummed as loud as she could, but after listening to him beat the same horse to death, she knew his forthcoming diatribe by heart.

The Captain answered his own question. "They eat the smaller fish. Do you think they have a moral compass? No, they eat anything slow enough to catch. If they'd leave us alone, we'd catch the largest fish, feed the people, make a little money, and the fish population would come back. But they've convinced everyone the situation is our fault. Once they've driven us all out of business, they'll probably blame the weather. That's why you can't get a fishing license anymore. Except you, Sarah. When I die, you'll get my license—and all the contempt they have for fishermen like me—will pass to you because you're 'grandfathered in.' And that's how this commercial fishing boat license will sink to the bottom of the sea."

Well then, let it sink now, she thought. *Spare us both a lot of time and energy.* She was relieved the spiel was over. There was no stopping it in the middle, but once it was finished, it usually took a few days before it came up again.

The Captain kept an eye on his "new baby"—the net drifting on the bay. "Time to see how good a job you did," he said, rubbing his hands together. He walked back to the wheel to turn the engine on again. Sarah was nervous anytime he turned off the *Outlaw* at sea—there was no guarantee it would start again. She said a little prayer each time he cranked the engine and was thankful whenever the boat started.

Sarah was given the top line to pull. It was easier than pulling the bottom rope with the lead weights. The bottom line would sometimes pull up horseshoe crabs from the sea floor and tangle into the mesh. Without a good working wrist, she hoped to avoid horseshoe crabs today. The Captain stood in the middle of the stern, wearing a black beanie and rubber suspenders, and pulling the net with cotton gloves.

As they hauled the ropes in, the Captain dropped the empty net around him at his feet and was soon stuck in place, buried in the net. At first nothing came up in the net, and Sarah's stomach sank at the idea of having wasted all that time and effort. Drift nets were tricky; they tangled easily. Anchor nets, on the other hand, were held in place with wooden stakes and were tended daily, weather permitting. She built those over the winter months—for three hundred each. When the bay froze over, that was how she and her father got by.

The sea trout, also called weakfish, began showing up in the net. They had freckles and slim, purple-and-white reflective bodies that reminded Sarah of the color of a fuel spill. The fish flopped and heaved violently as the Captain banished them to a confinement area in the middle of the deck. Most of them gave up pretty readily, but some had a reserve of fight when they realized the sea was gone for good. In the end, they all resigned with open mouths.

Sarah used her left hand to pull, sitting on the cork line to mark the progress. The Captain and Dave stayed ahead, providing slack to make it easier for her. Each pull of the rope brought fresh trout on deck. The Captain was a fast picker; he handily pulled the fish from the grips of the net without tearing holes. "No horseshoes tangling up the net so far," he said. "My daughter, the master net builder!" He was downright giddy at the haul.

Bluefish and shad appeared in the net, and an occasional juvenile sandbar shark, but the net had snatched up a veritable school of sea trout in the process. "Oh, doggie!" the Captain howled. The fish plugged every other hole, and the Captain finally slowed progress to a crawl.

The fish caught at the beginning of the night provided the soft, bloody bed for those caught later. An occasional flip of the tail marked a final breath. Sarah could not look at the pile; she turned her head to escape the sight of death.

"Great job, Sarah," the Captain proclaimed. Sarah grimaced.

The Captain pulled the flag from the water and drove the boat. Not enough fish to fill the boat and too early to quit. The flag was thrown again to repeat the drift.

The Captain got on the radio and bragged that the *Outlaw* was loaded down after one pass. Soon a second boat arrived, and the ring of occasional laughter echoed from the other boat, farther offshore. *Talking about girls or the marine police*, Sarah surmised, *as always*. Dave had nothing to say this trip. He touched the rope burn on his neck from time to time, stared at her like *he knew*, and stayed to his side of the transom.

The two boats floated in harmony. The fish blood on the deck mirrored the red of the clouds at sunset. Sarah felt the guilt of being the executioner who had extracted the water from their gills; the Captain had merely piled up the corpses.

Unable to wait any longer for the drifting nets to lure their catches, both captains started their boats. Over the rumbling engines, excited hollering started on the other boat within minutes. Sarah felt the illness of success when she saw that the second drift was better than the first. A bluefish snapped, chewing at the mesh to free itself. The Captain slammed it against the rail; it went limp, and he threw it on the floor.

"Damn bluefish tearing holes in the net," he mumbled.

Darkness was descending. The Captain flipped on the work lights. The doomed and dying fish waited to be freed from the net, their bodies bent, but they did not stir mercy in the fishermen, their mortal enemies. Their mouths gasped, and the Captain ignored them as he continued to pick the bones of the net clean to make room for the next night's drift.

The Captain danced a quick jig when the flag was pulled. The two boats headed for the docks of Mahon River, their running lights on.

When they arrived at the dock, Sarah climbed from the boat, as disgusted as the Captain was elated. Sarah hauled herself up the ladder of the dock to get the ice crushed for boxing the fish. That was when she remembered: they'd left the ice-fetching responsibilities to an eighteen-year-old farmer named Grant Eriksen.

She entered the Shucking House, dragging her feet. That was where the big block of ice, prescored into six fifty-pound blocks, was fed to the ice crusher to finish breaking it down. Sarah held her soaking, bandaged wrist, scouting around for the block of ice. She opened the latch of the walk-in freezer, and all the ice was already crushed and stacked in boxes. She stood in the doorway in disbelief that her job was already done. *You are incredibly sweet, Grant.*

With difficulty, the Captain and Dave unloaded the heavy boxes of fish from the boat. Sarah ran out onto the dock. "All the ice is crushed in boxes in the freezer," she yelled. "I'm leaving. I've got school tomorrow."

"All right. I'll be home late," the Captain said, still brimming with glee. "We must have over a thousand pounds here."

Sarah was free! She wasted no time leaving. With a heavy heart, knowing the net she'd built had been lethally successful, she went home to an empty house.

The lights were off at the Eriksens'. It was too late to call and thank Grant for taking care of the ice for her.

Unable to shake the images of death she had witnessed, she removed the slimy bandages from her wrist. Why was she no longer able to shut her emotions off when killing fish? Why had her sensitivity to death become so heightened lately?

The hot water steamed the small bathroom mirror, and she hoped she would not see Max's face in the foggy mirror. The steam did, however, remind her of her heated exchange with Max that morning.

Instead of sleeping, Sarah suffered. In the dark, she put the pillow over her face to block out the images of fish unable to breathe. She held her breath in remembrance of their final moments. And then she began to drift. She found herself swimming the oxygenated waters of the bay, surrounded by glowing, energy-filled fish tails dancing in the strong current.

Her conscience finally found peace, knowing the fish of this world were free, strong spirits in the afterlife.

In the morning, Sarah stretched her arms, feeling as if she were reaching beyond the ceiling into the sky. The sun, already about its business of warming the coastal marsh, woke the birds, which called to each other in celebration of a magnificent morning.

Sarah looked out the window. The front "lawn" was unruly and tall, nesting all the insects and small animals that welcomed ground cover. She opened the window and let in the glorious scent of onion, mint, lavender, thyme, and basil from her lawn garden—plants the mosquitoes naturally avoided. The Captain's ongoing order to cut the grass came to mind. It was only a matter of time before she would have to run the bunnies out of the field. *A free lawn is beautiful and should grow however it wants—cutting lawns was invented by control freaks*, she thought.

A surprise awaited Sarah out her east-facing window. Pulling a yellow sundress over her head, she noticed dark-green fernlike leaves where none typically stood. She ran to the window and opened the pane to see a new pink mimosa silk tree, like the one she'd pointed out to Grant in the woods behind her house. The pink blooms were withering from the shock of being moved, but she could see the soaked, freshly dug ground where the tree had been transplanted.

Sarah hurried to Grant's house. The boys were not outside yet. She tiptoed to the northeast corner window and peeked inside. She saw movement and jumped to the side. Another peek caught Grant getting dressed. She lightly rapped on his window, looking away reluctantly. He came over, opened the window with a smile, and poked his head out.

"You gave me a tree."

"Uh-huh," he said, extending his arms. She pulled him forward and kissed him—their first real kiss, sweet and warm, right there at his window—and he tried to lift and steal her into his room.

"What's going on in there?" his mother said on the other side of his closed door.

"Step aside," Grant warned Sarah.

He climbed out the window, inadvertently stomping on a daffodil, and fell back against the house. Sarah approached him from the front and leaned on him with all the burden he could hold.

They embraced against the house, uninterested in engaging in the conversation of mere mortals. Footsteps sounded in the gravel behind them.

"I need a hug too," said Lance. He scooped his long arms around them both and pulled them away from the wall. Sarah would never admit, in a million years, she loved that split second they were all glued together—before Grant dug his thumb into Lance's arm, forcing him to retreat.

"You just sniffed my hair," Sarah said to Lance. "I caught you."

"Coconut. Nice." He grinned.

Grant repositioned himself on the other side of Sarah so they could fend off further attacks from his brothers.

"Get a room," Lance advised and walked back into the house. The smell of cooking bacon drifted out the door.

"I thought everyone would be sleeping," she said to Grant.

"We're farmers. We're allergic to sleeping in. And good luck sneaking in my room with my mom on high alert."

"I was not trying to sneak in your room," she protested. She reached back to slap him in defense of her honor, but her wrist sang out in pain, reminding her to proceed with caution.

"You almost caught me with my pants off. A man can dream, can't he?" He inspected her wrist and said, "It's not swollen anymore. I can't believe your father made you work yesterday. I thought *my* father was bad."

"The Captain said the cold salt water would help. I guess he was right."

"Still." Grant led her to the chairs on the porch, asking, "Are you hungry?"

"Not really," she replied.

Unconvinced, Grant went in the porch door and came out with a plate of buttered toast and bacon, which he placed in her lap. "Orange juice, milk, or water?"

"Juice, please."

He came back with a tall glass of orange juice as his mother held the door open for him, saying to Sarah, "If you want anything at all, don't be shy." Sarah smiled her thanks, and Mrs. Eriksen disappeared back to the kitchen.

"You gave me a really big tree. Wow," Sarah remarked, chewing crispy bacon. "That couldn't have been easy."

"I had help from some farm equipment laying around."

"And from me," said Brody, bounding up the steps, taking off a pair of work gloves.

"Oh yeah," Grant said, "and Brody and Lance helped."

"Whatever he's saying about me is not true," Lance said, stepping out onto the porch.

"He was saying you helped," Brody replied, "but I agree. It was not significant enough to earn a mention."

"I thought you liked your orange juice with champagne," Lance said with a laugh to Sarah, ignoring Brody.

"Oh, I get it," she said. "Mimosa. Like the tree. Did you stay up late thinking of that one?"

Lance sat next to her, and she was once again sandwiched by the two brothers. "I prefer my trees sturdy and strong, but I guess, being a girl, you prefer yours pink and fluffy." He smiled and looked into her eyes until she felt he was intruding on her private thoughts.

She broke eye contact and said, "I do love the tree. For real. I can't believe you guys went to all that trouble."

"It's the least we could do," Lance said. "Considering our track record."

"Don't believe the 'we' part," said Grant. "Brody and I did all the work. Lance came in at the end and watered it."

"You moved a fully grown tree in the summer. Unless you want it to die, watering is the most important part."

The bus passed the Eriksens' in the direction of Sarah's house and the dead end. It would be back in a minute after turning around. Sarah stood up.

"Leave it," Grant said, referring to her dishes. She rushed off the porch to retrieve her backpack outside Grant's window. Grant followed her.

"Remind me to show my thanks for the tree later," she said, putting a flirty twinkle in her eye.

He put his hands on her waist and said, "Thank me now."

She looked around, searching for his brothers' prying eyes and those of the approaching bus riders. "Later." She scurried toward the street.

"I can take you to school," he said, stopping her in her tracks.

"Aren't you banned from school property?"

"The terms of my probation were not that specific. I can plead ignorance."

The bus was on its way back. He took her hand and said, "Let me drive you." She hesitated and then stepped back from the street and waved the bus to keep going. She turned around to see his brothers laughing; they seemed to know Grant and Sarah were grasping at the fleeting time they had left, holding on to it as tightly as possible. Neither she nor Grant could slow it down, but they were trying.

"Lance, we're borrowing your truck," Grant announced. "I don't want mine to be seen at school."

"Take Brody's," Lance objected.

They got in Lance's heavy-duty double-cab truck. Grant started it and spun the tires in reverse without moving, and the rocks flew.

"You better not disappear with it all day," Lance warned.

Grant smiled and backed out on the blacktop without turning to see if cars were coming. Lance threw his arms up and yelled, "You didn't even look!"

"I looked," Grant said to Sarah. "I just wanted him to think I didn't."

Sarah laughed.

"So …" he said as they headed up Port Mahon Road, "are we naming the tree?"

"Is that customary?"

"I think this one deserves a name, don't you?"

"Are we now naming trees as if they're children?"

He looked at her with playful hope in his eyes. "I like George."

"I have enough men in my life."

"Georgia, then."

"Georgia works."

CHAPTER SIXTEEN

REDLINE

The cool morning air howled through the truck on the country road. They were finally alone. Sarah dodged arrows of wind until Grant rolled up the glass. No longer preoccupied with wrangling her hair, she embarked on an exploration of Grant's weakness for her attention. With one knee on the seat, she nestled up to him and wrapped both arms around his neck. She brushed his fine hair back and exposed his ear. With gentle lips, she explored the uncharted territory.

As if to cool himself down, he cracked the window. She paused momentarily and then continued crawling along the precipice of his mental fortitude.

The steering wheel was in danger of being crushed by his white-knuckled grip. The breeze tangled their hair together. Tensing in anticipation of the placement of her next kiss, he seemed unaware that she had unfastened the top two buttons of his shirt. She trespassed freely within the cotton fabric. Then she knocked on the door of his heart, literally and figuratively, and asked, "Do you love me?"

Grant swallowed, freed one hand from the safety of the wheel, and found her warm palm resting on his chest. She gazed at his eyes and waited for whatever response was forthcoming.

His eyes did not retreat from the question, but neither did his lips offer an answer. Clearly, he was aware of the magnitude of the question; clearly, he knew—as she did—that they had strayed beyond the realm of childish flirtation. She needed his answer to be certain. And she could see in his eyes that he needed his answer to be *law*, a place upon which the decisions of a lifetime would be built.

She was surprised to find herself okay with his silence. She didn't need an answer now. The question had been planted. That was enough. It was putting down roots.

Approaching the city ahead, Grant slowed down long before the twenty-five-mile-per-hour speed limit sign. Instead of repeating her question, Sarah resumed kissing him on his neck. Grant pulled over to the side of the road to breathe. With the truck still in drive and his foot planted firmly on the brake pedal, he turned his face to capture her next kiss. His soft lips met hers.

"At this rate, you'll never make it to school," he warned. She ignored his words, looking to his eyes to give away his thoughts.

In lieu of pressing for a profession of eternal love, Sarah settled for exploring something far more earthbound and physical. Looking at the truck's tachometer, she noticed the maximum engine revolutions per minute to be about seven thousand. That was its redline, its danger-of-blowing-up point. The question was: What was Grant's? What was that discrete point at which his thought process broke down, and he surrendered to pure emotion?

He kissed her. She was fueled to press him further, slowly accelerating toward his redline. He put the truck in park, released the brake, and freed his mind of the road and their destination.

Now that she had his full attention, she resisted his desire to take control. Locking eyes with him, she pressed herself against the door and then dove into the back seat, laughing, knowing he would pursue her there. Cars rushed by and shook the truck. Without waiting for a safe moment, Grant climbed out his door and plunged through the backseat door on the driver's side. He paused to take in her beauty and then knelt beside her and raised the back of her hands to his lips. Uninterested in sensitivity, she pulled him toward her until his lips pressed against hers. She kissed him back with a passion equal to his.

The blare of a semi-tractor-trailer's horn caught their attention momentarily. From what Sarah could see in the mirror, the semi was being squeezed between a car crowding the center line and Lance's truck, which was parked in a decidedly dangerous location.

The indisposed couple in the back seat ignored the honking, but soon the sound became continuous as the semi loomed over them. As it blared past, way too close for comfort, she had that disoriented feeling of not knowing which vehicle was moving. For a moment, Sarah was unsure whether Grant had really put his truck in park. He embraced her, anticipating impact. She continued to kiss him, unconcerned about the laws of physics; she could think of no more perfect way to die.

With a loud bang, the side mirror flew from the truck. The semi hadn't quite cleared it. The cab shook violently. The kissers awoke back into the world, their spirits juddered too. Grant, confused at first, looked around for damage, noticed the mirror gone, and waved indifferently at the loss as if bidding the part good riddance. "Not the safest place to park," he admitted.

"Ya think?" said Sarah. "Oh well, at least this is Lance's truck."

Grant seemed to consider the disturbance insignificant and resumed a full embrace. "Serves him right," he said, searching out the exact place under her chin he last kissed. "Karma is a—"

Another car beeped as it swerved to dodge the glass and debris in the road.

"Maybe we're tempting fate by staying here," Sarah said.

Grant was not listening. Instead, he kissed her on her neck. Her hand blocked a subsequent kiss. "What about the old saying that lightning never strikes in the same place twice?" he said, apparently less concerned about the danger than about stopping what Sarah had started.

Redline achieved and exceeded, she noted to herself. Mission accomplished. For now.

"I don't think that applies to Mack trucks," she said, unable to lift his weight off her. "Come on. We have to go."

"You're already late for school," he replied, holding her to keep her from moving. "What's the harm in being a little later?"

Just a little spark and lizard brain takes over, she noted, feeling the heat of his passion. "You have a side mirror to replace before you go home," she said.

When he saw she was no longer participating, he backed away, releasing her. "I wish I could see you later today," he said, "but I work this afternoon, so I can't pick you up. Tomorrow I've got a job flying for a Maryland farm just over the border. I'll be gone before you leave for school, but I'll be finished by early afternoon. I can pick you up after school tomorrow. Will you go out with me tomorrow night?"

"I work Friday nights, remember?" she said.

"After work?"

"I won't be back from fishing until, like, a million o'clock," she said, climbing into the front seat. "Then Saturday at dawn, I have crabbing."

He came around and sat behind the wheel again, his brow crunched in thought. Yet another car honked, snagging his attention. He stepped out of the truck and collected the largest chunks of the broken mirror from the road, clearing the way for traffic. The responsible Grant Eriksen was back at the helm. At least partially.

He shook his head as if clearing his mind of Sarah enough to drive. Sarah, without the burden of driving, was busy adding the last several minutes to her memory bank to replay later.

Grant looked to the side mirror, no longer there, and smiled. If it was bothering him at all that he had messed up his brother's truck, he wasn't letting it show.

When traffic cleared, they drove off. Sarah was confident that if she touched him in any way, she would not make it to school. Instead of complaining about their busy schedules, he held her hand and kept driving. If he was unhappy, it was imperceptible. That suited Sarah fine. She was like her father: she had no use for whiny men. She admired Grant's quiet resolve.

She also liked knowing where his redline was.

The school parking lot was full, and they were the only ones outside. Thirty minutes late, Grant stopped near the door to drop Sarah off. He chased her across the bench seat and kissed her against the passenger-side door, giving her one last chance to change her mind.

Sarah's reddish-brown hair caught in the wind and blew out of the truck, drawing the attention of administrative staff whose windows faced the front drop-off area. Sarah noticed them staring, aware she was going to be in trouble—not just for being late, but for being late with the handsome young man who was currently suspended.

Grant got out of the truck and pulled Sarah's hand just enough so that she fell back into his arms. She pressed herself against him and looked up into his ridiculously blue eyes, unable to summon a care about who might be watching. At last, she swung away from him, taking a step toward the school door. He clasped her arm, stopping her advance. Dizzy on her feet, she took another step closer toward the school, and he finally let go. An intolerable space expanded between them as she contemplated the unthinkable; it would be more than a day before she would see him again. And then it would be a whole weekend without him.

The show was over. Sarah slunk through the office door to retrieve her late pass. As she stepped up to the counter, she found a slip already waiting for her. She did not have to say anything. The slip was marked "Excused," and the ladies smiled when Sarah waved goodbye.

Perhaps the office ladies had been young and in love once. Who knew?

Sarah searched for Eddie between classes, but she was rushed by a crowd of classmates who'd rarely had words for her before that day, seeking her comments for their yearbooks. Her relationship with Grant had elevated her to celebrity status. By third period, she had collected a nine-inch stack of yearbooks and had writer's cramp before lunch period was over. Sarah struggled with what to write in the books and resorted to general good wishes. After all, she knew these people by name only.

"There you are. I need to talk to you," Sarah said, chasing Eddie up the hallway on the way to their after-lunch class together.

"What do you want?" he seethed at her with a cracked voice. His cheeks were swollen, his eyes bloodshot; she could feel the disdain in his stare. She was certain the thought of striking her crossed his mind. His demeanor yelled she'd better not touch him or else.

"I was wondering if you still want help with—"

"I'm busy," he snapped, turning his face to hide it from her. Sarah wanted to console him and cry with him, but he smashed his fist into a locker as a warning for her to stay back.

"I'm sorry," she called after him. "How can I make it up to you?"

"Break up with your pig farmer," he barked.

"Don't call him that," she said, reflexively rising to Grant's defense.

Eddie stopped and turned to her, shaking with fury. Tears escaped his eyes as a small crowd formed around them, pointing and laughing. Sarah shouted at them, "Leave him alone."

Shamed to nothingness, Eddie surrendered all pride as the laughter mounted. He fell to his knees on the floor and said to Sarah, "Just go."

She stood defiantly in front of him and said, "I won't."

He looked up at her with the eyes of a broken child and said, "I love you."

She cast her eyes around, embarrassed for him. "Come on, Eddie," she said, holding out her hand to help him up. He rejected it, pulled himself up by a locker handle, and sprinted away.

Sarah refused more yearbooks to sign and hastened to study hall, hoping to see Eddie there. She knew he was suffering, and when he did not show up to study hall, she figured he'd left the school grounds, unable to face her any longer.

Entering calculus, Sarah saw Renee smiling, eager to hear the latest gossip firsthand. Sarah's mood improved, knowing the topic would be her favorite one: Grant.

"Why were you late this morning?" Renee asked in a suggestive singsong voice.

In lieu of an answer, Sarah held up a folder and pointedly fanned herself with it. Renee grinned as the two friends found their seats.

"He is so hot, Renee," Sarah whispered, flashing an eye toward Kim, who sat on the other side of the class firing bullets from her eyes, as usual.

"Tell me something I don't know," Renee said.

"Well … did you know he's a freaking pilot?" Sarah asked.

"What?"

"I thought the same thing—how did he keep that a secret in this town?" Sarah looked around to see who was watching. Eyes lowered to books. "You should see the crazy stunts he does. His brother Brody took me to a field to watch. It's insane."

"Brody—remember the crush I had on him?" Renee said.

"I thought your crush was on Lance," Sarah replied with a laugh.

"Lance too. That boy was one fine senior varsity quarterback. Do you remember?"

"Half the girls in school fantasized about being his 'wide receiver.' Try living next door to all three of them—such a burden."

"Gone downhill since high school, have they?"

"Oh, terribly so. They'll be at the graduation next Friday, and you can see for yourself," Sarah said.

"You have to help me get a picture of them with me in the middle."

"Take a number in *that* line," Sarah joked. Because it was so close to graduation, she decided there was no harm in confiding with Renee and went on. "Seriously, Renee. All three together are a *lot.* This morning I was at their house, on the porch, and when they were all paying attention to me at the same time, I felt like I was going to pass out. Lance walks around without a shirt, showing off; he knows he's gorgeous. You have no idea how hard it is to not reach over and touch him. And Brody, remember how skinny he used to be? Well, no more. Whatever their parents are feeding them, Brody is going to be as ripped as Lance soon—and he's so much easier to get along with. Now Grant, the gentleman of the three, is as tall as Lance. But he's the modest one. You never see him in public with his shirt off, so you have no idea what's under there, but I do. Don't get me started." Sarah paused, bumping up against an internal boundary line.

"Start already," Renee begged, her eyes lighting up. "Start, start, start."

Sarah immediately regretted mentioning Grant. There was something special, even privileged, about seeing him in a way so few others had. Sure, his brothers were gorgeous, but when she imagined Renee dating either of them, she did not mind at all. But Grant was another story. Sarah caught Kim looking in her direction and felt a stab of jealousy at the idea that he had paid her any attention at all—ever.

"You better not let that one go," Renee said, "or I will get his number and ask him out myself."

"Over my very cold and very dead body."

Renee giggled, pulled out her yearbook, and said, "Last-minute Sarah—if you don't sign now, you will forget forever." Sarah reluctantly accepted Renee's yearbook to sign. "And while you're at it, put Grant's phone number in there."

Sarah squinted a nonverbal threat.

"It's a good thing he has two brothers I can call," said Renee, "before you have to kill me."

Sarah flipped through Renee's book, and it was full of comments. She reached into her bag and offered her own yearbook for Renee to sign. The book still looked fresh off the press. Renee flipped through the pristine pages and said, "This is majorly pathetic, sister."

"I'm just selective. Feel free to take up a whole page. Use two if you need 'em."

It was difficult for Sarah to write in the yearbook of her only true friend, the one who had suffered with her through all the hard classes. She knew she was unlikely to ever see Renee again after graduation, and she was not ready to let her friend go. Holding back tears, she wrote, "Only a lucky few of us get to experience a love that changes us in a way we will never forget. You will always be remembered. Thank you for all the immortal memories, Renee. Love, Sarah."

Renee handed Sarah her yearbook back just before class was over. Unlike Sarah, who stored her book away without looking at it, Renee immediately flipped through the pages, searching for the new entry. When the bell rang, Renee stood up and grabbed Sarah's arm.

"I'm going to miss you," she said, placing her head on Sarah's shoulder.

"I'm going to miss you too," Sarah said, holding back what she did not want to feel.

"Thanks for what you wrote. I think that's what I worry about the most—being forgotten." *You're not the one I wish I could forget*, Sarah thought.

Sarah felt her shoulder getting moist from tears. "I could never forget you," she told Renee. "You've been my only real friend." As they walked out of class together, she added, "At least we still have finals and graduation."

"Don't forget, you promised me a picture with the Eriksen brothers," Renee said.

"Hmm. I thought I said, 'Take a number,' but yeah, I promise. I promise I'll try."

Counting the hours till Grant picked her up from school the next day—Friday—she wrote off the whole Max thing to an overactive imagination and told herself she no longer required the services of a make-believe boyfriend. And since every thought she had was now of Grant, there was no room for Max to haunt anyway.

The next day, Friday, at three o'clock, seniors were freed from the chains of high school for the last full day. Kids ran from the doors of school but lingered in groups outside, relishing the time they all knew was ending.

In the student parking lot, Grant leaned on the hood of his truck, waiting for Sarah to emerge. A crowd hovered around him, and Grant took the time to shake the hands of all his longtime friends. A new level of respect had emerged for Grant in the final days of high school. Unlike his brother Lance, who had attracted the spotlight because of playing football, Grant was well liked but was not the kind of guy who grabbed for glory. So he was surprised by his newly raised profile. What Grant knew (but Sarah didn't) was that much of his recent boost in status was because he had performed the unattainable feat of dating Sarah Vise.

As he awaited Sarah's arrival, he reflected on his fortune. The guys in school felt Sarah was as untouchable as a girl in a fashion magazine. During junior year, on a road trip to a basketball game, Grant had mentioned to his teammates for the first time that Sarah was his neighbor. He was upset with his brother Lance and told them what had happened.

A tall, military-looking guy with dark hair had picked Sarah up at her house. As the brothers watched, Lance said, "She's looking for me in all the wrong places."

Grant, outraged by his brother's comment, emptied the air in all of Lance's truck tires in the middle of the night. Grant was upset that Sarah would date a guy who closely resembled his oldest brother. More disconcerting to Grant, Lance had figured it out about the same time.

For years, Lance had so many girlfriends he was unable to keep their names straight and resorted to using generic pet names to avoid messing up. Since his graduation, he'd been frequenting the beach towns within an hour's drive and telling his brothers he preferred to keep his girlfriends at the beach, in bikinis, where they belonged.

But since Sarah had turned eighteen, a few months earlier, Lance had started spending more time at home—a stone's throw from her house. Grant was sure his brother intended to pursue Sarah.

Grant figured Lance was waiting for him to leave for college, find an away girlfriend, and forget about Sarah. But leave it to Sarah to shake things up on Port Mahon Road. A month before Grant apologized under the willow tree, the three brothers watched a tall, dark-haired, private-college kid pick Sarah up in a newer-model black Porsche 928. They blinked at the strange occurrence, sure that no car of its kind had ever anointed Mahon. Sarah's date (only the second one they'd ever seen her go on) compressed the timetable for taking action, and Grant knew Lance would not wait much longer.

After seeing her drive off with Porsche guy, the three brothers sat around the circle at the Boulders, over too many beers, and Lance brought up the topic of settling down with the right girl. "I love Mom," he said, "but the girl I marry will sit right here, drink beers, laugh, and tell stories like one of us. She'll want to be outdoors more than indoors, and you'll all love her as much as I do—except you'll keep your hands off because you're my brothers. I mean, without that kind of love and relationship, why get married at all?"

The only girl Grant knew fitting that description: Sarah. He would not risk losing her to his unpredictable, arrogant brother. And that was why he jumped the line and bravely asked her out first. And that was why, in his mind, he deserved to be with her. His friends, certain that Lance would end up with Sarah, were shocked to see that Grant had triumphed. He enjoyed upsetting everyone's expectations in that regard.

At last, he spotted Sarah coming out the door. She ran to him. "I missed you," he said and kissed her in front of anyone who wanted to watch. Her lips, stuck to his, were exactly where he wanted them to be.

Confetti struck Sarah in the back of the head. Kim had thrown slivers of a dozen prom pictures at her as she walked by. Grant laughed—the seriousness of high school girls—and buried his face in Sarah's flowing hair.

"You are so mean to her," Sarah said.

"It was a dance, not a marriage proposal," he replied. "And all I did was laugh." He leaned in, hungry for more attention from Sarah, but she leaned back to argue on Kim's behalf.

"I know, but what's wrong with being nice to her—even if you don't want to see her anymore?"

"She just threw trash at your head."

"Still."

"You really want me to talk to her?" he asked. "Sure, let's invite her over. Maybe Brody will take a shine to her, and we can all be friends. While we're at it, let's invite your friend Sketch into the mix, and we can have a fivesome. On second thought, let's ..."

He continued in this vein until she kissed him, effectively shutting him up. "You win," she said. "I admit, I don't like sharing Brody with anyone."

"Brody?" He cocked his head like a confused dog's. *She's joking,* he realized and discarded the idea without a second thought.

Sarah smiled as if she'd given him something to worry about. "I have to get home," she said.

"Ah—no, you don't, it turns out."

"Yes, I do. I have to work. We've been over this."

"Nope, I took care of it. You have the night off." Disbelief shot from her eyes. "I asked your dad, and he said it was fine—no problem whatsoever."

Sarah looked bewildered. "You must be using voodoo. I can't get him to agree to anything."

"Voodoo? Nah, he was happy to give you the night off."

"Then you must have mentioned that your family owns half of the farmland in Kent County."

Grant opened the truck door for her, and she climbed inside. "No, that didn't come up, but I might have volunteered to cut three acres of grass tomorrow."

"You know my dad better than I thought," she said, settling into her seat.

"No big mystery. He's like my dad; everything is negotiated in labor hours." He put the truck in gear, waving to a few friends who were still standing around, and drove off. "I have a surprise for our first date."

"I count Cape May as the first date."

Grant chuckled until she playfully punched his shoulder.

"I loved going to Cape May with you," he said. "I did. But as I recall, we fled town to avoid your father, and you dodged kissing me for more than twelve hours straight."

"True," Sarah admitted and then giggled and laughed until she accidentally snorted.

"What's so funny?" he asked, failing to see the humor.

"No offense, but it was honestly the best day of my life. What's wrong? Did you have to tell your brothers the truth—that after an entire day and night, we only held hands?"

"It would be nice if—this time—we could manage a detail worth keeping secret."

Sarah put her arms around his neck and kissed him on the cheek.

"Our odds are better already," he said.

Passing through the town of Dover. he asked, "Are you all right to hang out at the Eriksen Farm for a while?"

"With you, right?"

"No, I'm leaving you with Brody all night. Of course with me. My family is having a cookout, but we can leave anytime you want."

"Promise?"

"Promise."

CHAPTER SEVENTEEN

SKY

They arrived at Eriksen Farm and parked behind the two-story farmhouse with a wraparound porch, a manicured lawn, and a large variety of blooming flowers. Several new outbuildings behind the home stood in prominent contrast to the smaller old farming barns. The shadow of the metal Quonset hut that housed the combine fell crudely across the hand-carved moldings of an old red Dutch barn with a rounded foundation and white gambrel roof. Several old stone buildings and grain silos were still in use. Old and new, side by side.

In the area where they parked, workers were busy loading and unloading trucks using tractors. Brody's truck was parked there, but not Lance's.

"I forgot to ask," said Sarah. "What happened when Lance saw his truck?"

"I thought about bringing it back to him damaged, but I took it to the dealer instead. Just a few scratches, really, after the mirror was replaced."

"Did he go ballistic?"

"No way—he laughed and wanted to know why you and I were parked on the side of the road. He wanted details."

Brothers: Sarah would never understand them as long as she lived. "He wasn't pissed? Not even a little bit?"

"Nah, we've all broken things. No big deal. One time Lance backed a tractor into his truck and totaled it. He laughed so hard he couldn't stand up. Why would he care about a mirror?"

"I guess I assumed he would have a temper."

"That's because your only male role model is your father."

Pretty astute observation for a farm boy who still hasn't graduated from high school, Sarah noted.

"*No one* has a temper like your father," Grant continued. "Anyway, what's with all the questions about Lance? An interest I should know about?"

"Is he available?" Sarah answered, teasing. When he didn't smile, she said, "Just kidding, doofus."

They held hands on the way to the front of the house. Two little girls ran out, yelling for Grant. He lifted the smallest one, Shelly, a seven-year-old wearing pink shorts, cowboy boots, a T-shirt covered with hearts, and a French braid in her hair. "How's my sweetheart?" he asked.

"We want a ride on the pony," Shelly demanded. "Now!"

The other little girl, the older of the two, pulled his pant leg and pointed to the red barn, where, presumably, the pony awaited. He knelt to hug her with his free arm. "Don't you want to meet my girlfriend first?" he asked.

As the older girl looked up at Sarah, tears welled in her eyes, and her face crunched into a frown. "But, Grant, I thought *I* was your girlfriend," she said.

"Anne, you're my cousin, and that's a really special thing. This is Sarah."

Anne pressed her face into his chest, "hiding" from Sarah and leaving wet tears on his T-shirt. Shelly wiggled until he let her go and then ran off, yelling, "Mommy, Grant has a girlfriend!"

The older sister, her cheeks still hitching with sobs, followed her little sister off.

Grant looked at Sarah with his arms wide in incomprehension as if hoping for an explanation of the inner workings of girls. "Is it the first thing you learn—how to make a man feel guilty for breathing?"

"It's in our DNA: everything wrong with the world is a man's fault."

"I hope you're joking," he said.

She cupped her hand around his ear and said, "But think how awesome you must be for us to still want you desperately in spite of how evil you are."

"Desperately?"

She winked.

Grant walked up the stairs into the kitchen, and Sarah followed. He filled two glasses with iced tea. His aunt passed through the kitchen, looking for Grant. "I told Shelly and Anne they have to wait until after dinner for the ponies."

"Aunt Elin, this is Sarah," Grant said. They exchanged the usual introduction pleasantries. The girls ran through the kitchen, giggling, their grief temporarily forgotten.

"Your girls are so cute," Sarah remarked.

"I guess they are—sometimes," Elin said and chased her girls out to the porch.

Grant and Sarah followed them out and sat on a couple of wooden rockers. More people arrived for the cookout. "You have a lot of family," Sarah observed.

Uncle Harald sat in the rocker next to them and said to Sarah, "I bet you're excited; high school is almost over."

Before she could answer, the little girls ran over and said, "Sarah, would you please play horseshoes with us?"

Sarah had the distinct feeling they'd been put up to this request by a grown-up trying to make her feel welcome, but she accepted their invitation anyway. As she walked away, she saw Grant and Uncle Harald diving into a serious-looking conversation, and she wondered what it was about.

When Grant approached Sarah a few minutes later, she was chasing rusty horseshoes that had been flung nowhere near the posts.

"Are you going to marry Grant?" Anne asked her.

"Uh ..." Sarah groaned, hoping Grant hadn't heard the question.

Anne pursed her lips and threw a horseshoe overhand, coming much closer to Sarah than to the post.

"Good throw," Sarah said, ignoring the obvious attempt on her life.

Grant announced, "Girls, your mom said it's time to eat."

Anne ran up to Grant and said, "I don't like Sarah. Marry me instead," sticking out her bottom lip. Grant grinned and shrugged at Sarah.

Shelly said, "Shut up, Anne. I like Sarah."

Aunt Elin yelled for the girls, and they ran off to find their mother.

"Sorry about that," Grant said and led Sarah toward the food, fetching a plate for her.

Brody walked up behind them in a line that had formed in front of the grilled chicken and cheeseburgers. After loading their plates, the three headed for the picnic table farthest from the crowd.

"Want a beer?" Brody asked.

"I'm good," Grant said.

Brody chuckled as they sat and said, "So let me get this straight: you guys had a fender bender—*while parked?*"

Sarah blushed without comment and waited for Grant to field the question. Grant rubbed her knee below the table and kept eating, refusing to take his brother's bait.

Brody shifted gears, leveling his gaze at his brother. "Sarah tells me you haven't asked her to the Ocean City party after graduation."

"Because it's ridiculous," Grant said between bites, "and she doesn't want to go."

"Hmm, that's funny. Because when you were flying around having your World War I fighter pilot fantasies, she told me she *wanted* to go."

Brody winked at Sarah, and she smiled.

"That's because you didn't tell her what we're doing," Grant said.

"What *are* we doing?" Sarah asked. "I can't seem to get a straight answer on that."

Grant put an arm around Sarah and said, "Tell her, Brody."

Brody burst out laughing, lowering his head to the table. "I don't even know where to start."

Grant glanced at him, unamused.

"Guess I'll start at the beginning," said Brody, composing himself. "Lance wants us all to drive together to graduation on Friday. And when the ceremony's over, we'll drive down to Ocean City and stay overnight on the beach. Sarah, you're going to love it. We'll light a big bonfire. Lance really knows how to throw a party."

"I think you're forgetting the part I classified as ridiculous," said Grant.

"That part is Lance's deal, not mine. It's not like he's going to force anything on you."

Grant huffed and glanced at Sarah. "The only way I'm going," he said, "is if you tell Sarah everything and she still wants to go."

Brody laughed again, and Grant could not help but join in this time.

"Stop laughing, you two, and just tell me," Sarah demanded.

"Ever been to the haunted house on the boardwalk?" Grant asked her.

"No."

"There is no way Sarah is scared of a stupid amusement park attraction," said Brody. "Ask her."

"I know she's not afraid of amusement park rides," Grant shot back, "but that doesn't mean she wants to hang out in one as part of a lame graduation stunt."

"What's the big deal?" said Sarah. "I'll do it. Next topic."

"Brody, damn it, you're not telling her everything."

"Grant is worried he'll embarrass himself in front of you. Lance, you see, has challenged him to a fight, of sorts, in the haunted house after hours."

"I'm not worried about embarrassing myself," Grant protested. "But I am embarrassed about the whole plan."

"Lance said Sarah is welcome to take your place. He says she'd probably do a better job of beating his ass. He might even volunteer another part of his anatomy—"

"Watch it, Brody," said Grant, flashing a serious warning with his eyes.

Sarah slapped the table to break up the alpha-dog moment. "Well, *I* think it sounds like fun. So ... just talk my dad into letting me go, chaperone-free, with you three to an overnight beach party in Maryland, and I'll go—but good luck with that."

Brody smirked at his kid brother. "I told you she wants to go."

"Only because I haven't had a chance to offer her a nicer alternative."

Sarah knew they were still not telling her everything but said, "Grant, please talk my dad into this. I do not want to miss whatever it is you guys are plotting."

Grant stood up and said to Brody, "Okay, tell Lance he got his way—again." He turned to Sarah and said, "Take a walk with me."

He started off in the direction of the outbuildings, and she took his hand to join him. "Are you mad at me?" she asked. "Did I do something wrong?"

"Of course not. Lance won't drop this anyway. It's better to just get it behind us."

"That fight you're going to have with Lance has nothing to do with me, right?" she asked.

"No, it's an old tradition."

"There's an old tradition to fight after hours in a haunted house?"

"The fight is the tradition. The place is Lance's extremely dumb idea."

They stopped near the hangar barn where the ag-cat biplane resided. "How'd you like to fly with me?" he asked.

"That plane has only one seat, as I recall."

He marched past the building storing the ag-cat and turned the corner to another building facing the south field. He slid open the door, revealing a different plane.

"You've got to be kidding me," she said.

A Grumman American AA-5B Tiger rested on the cement floor, its low-profile wingspan spread across the whole enclosed building.

"Hmm, I'm not so sure this is a great idea."

"You'll be completely safe," Grant promised. "Come on. Fly with me."

"Do I have to be the copilot?"

"No, I'll take care of everything."

"Why does my stomach feel like I just swallowed a tank of live minnows?" she asked.

"That's the feeling that tells you—you're alive!"

When both doors were opened, the plane's red detail glistened in the sun. Its white-and-blue diagonal paint, with a galloping orange-and-black-striped tiger decal displayed on the side, stood out against the empty space. Grant attached the tow bar to the nose wheel of its triangular landing gear and easily rolled the light plane from its platform. He turned the plane wide onto the grass path. In the late-afternoon sun, he opened the gliding bubble canopy, uncovering two white-leather seats (the rear seats were folded forward for light cargo).

"Step up," he said, showing her where to stand on the wing root.

She hesitated and looked inside. The plane was roomier than she had anticipated. He lifted her hand, providing balance, and said, "Climb in."

He brushed the hair from her eyes and said, "There is one thing—if you want to kiss me like you did yesterday morning, do it now and not in the plane at a thousand feet. Or at least not when I'm taking off or landing."

She smiled back and said, "I can't promise anything."

He paused for brief reflection and said, "Oh, well. What's life without a few risks?"

Grant inspected the outside of the plane using the handbook's preflight checklist. He opened the cowling and checked the oil. Then he checked the frame, landing gear, and tires. After circling the plane, he climbed in next to her and handed her a green headset, leaned over her and plugged in the jack, and then tugged the straps of her seat belt. Satisfied she was safe, he buckled himself in. When he put on his headset, she imagined they were preparing to go on a mission to Saturn.

There was something about the way he double-checked her seat belt and took care of things for her that put her completely at ease about the flight. He was calm, confident, and kind.

Grant set the brake after pressing on the pedals to test them. He turned the wheel to make sure the wing's ailerons were free and checked that the fuel tank was on full. He flipped to another checklist and meticulously followed each instruction: fuel mixture set to rich, one-eighth throttle, carburetor heat off, master switch turned on.

Grant took a moment to scan the area around the plane from the pilot's seat. When he was certain the propeller was clear, he turned the key. The engine cranked, and the propeller swung into an uneven buzz, and then, within a few seconds, the propeller disappeared, leaving only the outline of a white circle formed by the tips of the blade's paint. The plane pulled forward against the parking brake, and freshly cut grass sprayed in the air.

Grant flicked the oil gauge; the oil pressure was good. He turned to another page, preparing for a soft-field takeoff. He set the flaps to zero, released the parking brake, pressed the top of the pedals with his toes, and changed pages.

Sarah watched him check page after page of lists. It was so much more complicated than she'd ever imagined. She sat in awe as he flipped buttons and changed settings.

Grant turned the transponder to "Standby" and pressed the avionics power switch. The radio came on. He glanced over at Sarah and said, "How are you doing?" His voice was intimately close, amplified in her ears, and the engine noise muffled.

"Can everyone hear me talk?" she asked, concerned she was on a speaker channel like on the boat.

He pointed to his left thumb and said, "I press this button to make a radio call. Otherwise, you're only talking to me."

The Tiger taxied along the bumpy south field, passed the corner of the last of the buildings, and turned onto the middle of a long, grassy airstrip. Grant slid the glass canopy shut. He said, as if whispering in her ears, "I'm ready. Are you ready?"

Sarah bit her bottom lip, no idea what to expect, and said, "Let's go."

Grant called Dover Air Force Base for clearance through their airspace. "Dover tower, Grumman Tiger, five, five, x-ray, request traverse your airspace northbound over coastline to Port Mahon at one thousand feet."

Dover Air Force Base tower responded, "Roger, Grumman Tiger, squawk five, three, two, six, maintain one thousand feet. Cleared through Dover airspace along coastline." Grant repeated the information back and set the small knobs on the transponder to five-three-two-six.

Standing on the brakes, nose aimed north, ready to take off, Grant pressed the throttle all the way, and the engine's rpms accelerated. The plane shook, dipped forward, and tugged against the constraints of the brakes. When Grant released the brakes, the plane sprang forward, hopping lightly along the grass airstrip for the length of the cornfield adjoining the property.

The plane increased its speed, and the bumps smoothed as the wings provided lift and rendered the wheels superfluous. The unobstructed glass-canopy view, full of medium-blue sky, pitched up toward heaven. The quiet drone of the engine carried them as if weightless. The smooth air lifted the wings, and the plane soared toward a few white, fluffy clouds painting the sky above them. With the starboard wing angled below the horizon, the heading indicator spun to north by northeast, and they continued a gentle climb.

Before long, they were looking down from amid the clouds. The tan strip of coast blocked the dark-green land's escape to the deep-blue bay. Grant pulled to three-quarter power. They leveled out at one thousand feet, following the coastline.

A mix of adrenaline and elation rushed through Sarah, and she quietly took it all in. For the first time, she felt she was part of something bigger than herself.

"Remember the Cape May lighthouse?" he asked, interrupting her fascination with the sky.

"How could I forget?"

He pointed ahead and said, "Well, there's *our* lighthouse." The Mahon River lighthouse, its hallowed square structure floating on an invisible frame of steel, had defied over eighty years of bay storms and erosion so it could stand as the silent witness to their childhood, which they were now leaving behind.

They passed over the abandoned lighthouse and flew above the road they both had shared, without being together, most of their lives.

"Doesn't look like a dead-end road from here," Sarah said. She recognized Leipsic, the fishing-town port, winding beneath them. All the places they could never walk or drive to lay before and below them, revealing themselves as pristine habitat for wildlife.

Looking down at the landscape, Sarah had a stunning realization: the lines Max had scratched into her skin represented the river's tributaries. She touched her cheek, tracing the beginning of the long, now-invisible curve. Where the Mahon River now ended by erosion, the river continued along her skin as it would have flowed in Max's time. Following the path with her fingers, she felt the flowing river spirit he had infused deep within her.

Grant could not have known that by showing her what she could not see from the ground, he had poured fresh life into her connection with Max—just when she thought the ghost haunting her was gone. No longer spellbound by the spectacular views, she searched within for a sign of a spirit hiding in her.

The sun was low on the horizon as they approached the Saint Georges Bridge. Grant said, "It's time to go back." He called for clearance, and the tower responded. Grant again repeated back the instructions and added power to climb.

The plane lifted higher, turning with a thirty-degree bank until they were heading due south.

"Are you allowed to fly at night?" she asked, watching the last of the sun's red fire dip below the curved horizon.

"Yes, ma'am. I can fly on just instruments, but there's still plenty of light."

As they flew southward, Sarah felt she was sailing into a crossroads. Above her lay the universe, and below her lay the dark-green marsh of home. To the east lay the vast blue sea, ready to sweep her away, and to the west, the sun skipped ahead into its destiny without her. They were headed home. Grant followed a new checklist and reduced power until they tipped toward the earth, losing altitude.

Streetlights perpendicular to their flight path were lit from Slaughter Creek to Dover. Headlights of cars crisscrossed ahead of them. Sarah searched inside the dark cabin for something to hold on to as they continued to lose lift, drifting quietly down toward the farmhouse, aiming for the thin grass strip used as a runway. They passed just above the trees surrounding the farm, and the wind bled off the wings. She felt a sense of slow motion until the ground rushed beneath them just before landing. The plane bounced a little, and they slowed before reaching the end, the south field.

The sun's descent had coincided with the plane's. With landing lights on, they turned onto the dark path back to the hangar, stopping where they'd started. Grant opened the canopy and used a flashlight to review yet another checklist. He recorded time and information from the gauges into a book and then turned off the avionics, lights, ignition, and master switch. He unbuckled and pulled off his headset, and she did the same. He took in a big breath and climbed out to help her. She wobbled on the wing but stepped firmly onto the soft grass and scurried to the hangar.

Grant walked up to her, and they hugged in the dark doorway of the metal building.

"That was mind blowing," Sarah said. She was overwhelmed with joy, yet a trickle of disquiet flowed through her. She had never seen Delaware from above. If Max were an illusion, how could his handiwork on her body have matched the real riverscape so perfectly?

Grant took her hand, snapping her back to the present moment, and they walked inside the building. He found the light switch, and the interior lights flashed on, blinding their night vision. Sarah stayed by the door while Grant pulled the plane back inside. With the two big sliding doors pulled together, except for a small space in the middle, Sarah sat down in the opening between them, listening to the wind move in the south field's crop. Grant put the chocks on the wheels and shut off the light. He sat down on the cement behind her and pulled her into his lap.

Sarah said, "Can we stay here for a few more minutes?"

"Is everything all right?"

The crickets were raucously loud, and she thought they would help her remember this moment. She was not sure how some memories became long lasting, and others faded with the passage of time. All she knew was that she planned to keep this particular memory with her forever—no matter what happened.

As if reading her mind, Grant said, "I have everything I want, right now, with you. Please help me stop the clock because this is where I want to stay."

"This is a pretty good place to be," she agreed.

They stood up and dusted each other off, but she continued to block the exit, preventing their return to the farmhouse. He spun her around and lifted her off the ground. She wanted him to kiss her without hesitation—and he did. She wanted him to keep that tight grip around her and not let go.

"We don't have to leave this second, do we?" she asked. One hand abandoned her and found the handle. It slid the door closed. The same hand raised the flashlight, led the way in the darkness back to the plane, and unlocked the cargo door. Letting go of her long enough to show the way inside, Grant climbed in ahead of her. They crawled forward until they touched the back of the pilot's seat. When the flashlight turned off, the rest of the world turned off too. In the small space, they clung together and blanketed each other.

After a long silence, Grant said in the blackness, "I love you."

Time no longer existed in that sacred space. "I love you," she said. The actuality of their love could not be given or taken; it could not be lost, forgotten, or borrowed. It simply *was*.

A fleeting thought about a promise made to Max intruded on her happiness. *It was only a dream*, her mind insisted.

And even so, a promise was revokable; her love for Grant was not.

His hand swiped across her bare stomach, making her dizzy with desire for his touch. He found her mouth in the darkness, kissed her, and said, "Leave with me." When she did not answer, he said, "I will not leave without you."

Before she could respond, they heard the hangar door open. Brody yelled from inside, "Are you guys in here?" As Brody's footsteps approached the plane, they held in laughter to the point of torture. Inside the compartment, they tried not to move or breathe. They knew what kind of talk the brothers would start if they were caught together in a cargo hold. Just as their resolve was about to break, Brody abruptly left.

Brody was off checking another building by the time Grant slid the hangar door open softly for Sarah to exit. Grant spotted him on his way back to the farmhouse, sneaked up behind him in the dark, and grabbed his sides.

"Damn!" Brody yelled. Grant and Sarah laughed at his blood-drained face.

"I think we know who's going to be running out of the haunted house screaming like a schoolgirl," Grant said.

"It's Lance you need to be worried about," said Brody, "and I'm not the one he's coming after with a chainsaw."

"Wait. What?" Sarah asked with genuine concern.

"He's just kidding," Grant said.

"Then why do chainsaws keep coming up?" she pressed.

The brothers looked at one another. "It's just part of the stupid joke—nothing to worry about," said Grant.

The farmhouse lights were off now. Brody fished around in a tub of half-melted ice that had been left outside. "Want a beer?" he said and lobbed one for Grant to catch.

Grant caught the beer and lifted his hand to catch another to give to Sarah. Under the stars, the three of them sat in the bed of the truck, drinking wordlessly. Brody shot occasional glances at his brother as if wondering why he was so quiet. "Time to call it a night," Brody finally announced, stretching his arms. "I've got to be back here in six hours."

When he drove away, Grant pointed to the metal building, a silent invitation to return to the cargo hold.

"I don't recall you saying you got me out of work in six hours," she said with a yawn.

"I didn't plan that far ahead," he admitted, "but I will next time."

She opened the door of his truck, yawned, and crawled inside to sleep. "Tell him you'll cut the grass next week, too, so I can sleep in."

She put her head on his lap, and he lay his flannel jacket over her. "You've been drinking," she reminded him when he started the truck.

"One beer. But I do know all the bumpy dirt roads home if you want me to take those to avoid the cops."

She didn't answer. She was already asleep.

"No more sneaking in windows," he announced as he drove up her driveway and parked. Still asleep, she mumbled something about breaking a promise. He helped her to the back door. She kissed him good night and said, "Sleep well."

As he walked back to the truck, she heard him say, "Not much chance of that."

CHAPTER EIGHTEEN

SIREN

After their flight together and their time in the cargo hold, Grant was consumed by obsession, unable to sleep. In his thoughts, Sarah's eyes were glowing emeralds, stars of light, inviting him to pursue her. And he knew he would freely do so—to the end of the world. The eyes and hands of his imagination explored every curve and bend of her. He was powerless to stop.

He had no real incentive to sleep; no dream could compare to her enchantment. It was as if his mind were no longer his own. Finally, in the small hours, seeking an explanation for her hypnotic control over him, he rose from his bed and began to search for answers in the dusty encyclopedias in his room. With a flashlight, he perused pages of Greek mythology and settled on an image of Urania, one of nine daughters of Zeus and Mnemosyne. With her cloak embroidered with stars, Urania was a goddess and the Muse of cosmic heaven. She was a lure to many a godly and earthly heart.

He also read of the infamous sirens. Born of a union between a Muse and the river god Achelous, these beings were gifted with harmonic, oscillating voices. The sirens moved the oceans with their powerful and alluring chorus and could also bind the soul to heaven—or hell.

Odysseus, defenseless against the song of sirens and bound to the mast of the ship: That was an image Grant could identify with. He knew the torture of Sarah's siren call and knew the immense restraints that would be required to separate him from her. Although the Greek tales were mythical, just knowing that other men had felt the suffering of a beautiful woman festering in their minds made him feel less clinically insane.

Grant stood at the window. Her house was still dark at four o'clock in the morning. Although he had never been in her room, he could see her sleeping in his mind's eye, covered in a thin, silky sheet. His love for her was pure and infinite, but it was tightly wrapped in a desire he was unable to strip away.

Sleep deprivation was new to the hearty sleeper. The effects were beginning to kick in; his muscles begged for rest even as his mind continued to burn. Hoping for a miracle, he lay in bed and closed his eyes. The thought of her lips kissing him flipped him to his side.

His mind embarked on a journey across the dangerous waters between their bedrooms. He counted the steps it would take to visit her; the counting served not to lull him but rather inflame him. The only cure, the only relief from his restlessness, was to be with her. He settled in the comfort that she would, one day soon, lie beside him in his arms, and he could sleep again.

Hot-pink firework blooms of the silk tree filled Sarah's view to the rising sun. She opened the window and caressed Georgia's friendly leaves. The trip with Grant into the clouds had irrevocably changed her life. Her mind no longer dwelled in the particulars of drudgery. Instead, it soared toward the sun.

Sarah resisted the urge to visit Grant; she wanted him to rest. By the time he awoke, she knew she would be sailing on the bay, her hands sunk in vile rubber gloves.

Sarah returned from crabbing in the afternoon to three acres of freshly mowed and trimmed grass. The perfectly straight lines, carved by an expert, would no doubt impress the Captain. She looked to Grant's house, and his truck was not there.

Sarah drove into the backyard, hoping to find Grant there, but he was gone. The time he spent on the neglected lawn had no doubt taken away from another chore. Before she could thank him, he had already moved on and was now sweating somewhere in a field in the hot sun.

Suddenly, the two new lovers had become like separate moons locked in their own orbits, passing near each other but unable to touch. Their lists of responsibilities kept them close enough to almost catch passing glimpses of each other but unable to converge. The thing they had most in common—besides the road they had shared for most of their lives—was the constant work that called to them.

On Saturday afternoon, Sarah waited until the absolute last minute for Grant to return. When she left, late, for drift fishing, his brothers were home, but Grant was not. He was still navigating his sea of green; she would soon be navigating her sea of blue.

When Grant returned, Sarah was gone, and Lance was leaving for the beach. Brody drank beers, and Grant joined him, but his sense of taste had deserted him, as had the lure of alcohol. Sarah was all the intoxication he craved. Grant waited for her return, and the present rolled into the past. The vigil willow guarded Sarah's home as the Eriksen family retired.

In bed, Grant listened for her truck and said, "Good night, Sarah."

Grant's sleep pattern was upside down. Instead of synching with the night, as his body should, his mind stirred him awake. Sarah was home, and he was glad, except he found himself in the tortured position of being unable to see her—it was the middle of the night.

He smelled smoke in the breeze, and from his window, he saw a small orange blaze—the size of a campfire—in the woods behind Sarah's house. Lance was not home, and Brody was sleeping. The fire was not coming from the Boulders, the Eriksen boys' campsite; it was closer.

The clock reminded Grant of how little time remained before his morning flight to fertilize the recently plowed field for his uncle. Knowing he would need whatever sleep his brain would allow, Grant resisted the urge to find out who was out there behind Sarah's house.

"Let it burn," he muttered about the fire and stumbled back to bed.

The C-5 military cargo plane flew over Sarah's house, heading north on Sunday. It was almost eleven o'clock in the morning when she woke, famished, to the smell of cooked eggs and toast.

Must be my birthday, she thought as she stretched. She ran out to the living room and looked across the cornfield. The growing corn crop was beginning to obstruct the view to Grant's house, but she could see that the only truck there was Lance's.

She huffed and walked to the kitchen. Rex sat at the kitchen table with his coffee, already finished with breakfast, and said, "Good morning, Sunshine."

Sarah made a comical display of looking over her shoulder to see whom he was talking to and then walked over behind her father, hugged him, and gave him a kiss on the cheek.

"I left you scrambled eggs," he said.

"Yummy," she replied and floated to the stove, smiling. "What did you do with my dad after you killed him and took over his body?"

"What did you do with my daughter?" he said, and they both laughed. "Grant did a terrific job on the lawn yesterday."

"I saw that," she said, sitting down and pulling up her knee to rest her head on.

"I guess your date went pretty good."

"It was all right," she said, not wanting to share any details.

"Yes, sir. Grant knows how to impress a father. He's all right in my book." Rex got up and moved to his recliner to watch television. She wondered if he were aware that Grant could fly an airplane and whether that would change his opinion of him, but she was unwilling to find out—in case it opened a whole new area of resistance.

"Before I forget," Rex said over his shoulder, "tonight, we're repairing all the crab pots we brought to the dock yesterday, and we need to tar the eel pots. But don't worry; I'll dip them. I just need you to hand them to me."

Sarah sat on the back porch, facing the field toward Grant's house, and studied a history book for finals. She looked up every time she heard a car on the road.

A small plane flew over, heading east. The unfamiliar plane flew close to the ground toward the air-force-base fuel tankers off Port Mahon Road. A gray cloud spilled from under its wings and drifted toward Sarah, chasing her inside. She closed all the windows, but the chemical fog seeped through the cracks. Sarah begged her father to leave for the fresh air of the dock to get away from the toxic pesticide cloud, and he was happy to accommodate her willingness to go to work early.

The leaden baton was passed to Grant, who came home early, hoping he would find Sarah home, but she was still gone. Grant frowned and stirred the food on his plate, lost in thought, and his mother's look of concern for her youngest son deepened.

Later, Grant sat on the porch and looked at the empty house across the field, thinking of all the opportunities he'd lost growing up. If only he had more time to convince Sarah to leave with him. But time was running out, and neither of them was staying in one place long enough—thanks to their many obligations—to find the other available. It was the same cruel trick a shadow plays: always moving just before capture. He longed to chain her wrist to his for a while—but even if such behavior were an option, it would have to wait until morning.

"Where are you going?" Brody asked, interrupting a beer-driven discussion he and Lance were having about some girl Lance was going to introduce to Brody at the bonfire on Friday.

Without giving an answer, Grant wandered out into the cornfield.

Grant followed the floodlight in Sarah's willow tree. He stepped out of the cornfield and into the Captain's twilit yard. Remembering the strange campfire he'd seen the night before, he snooped around in the trees behind her house. Something on the ground grabbed his eye: a blackened patch of earth with a pile of ashes and some burnt branch ends in the middle. No beer cans or other signs of kids partying. A lone vagrant? A passing backpacker? Why wouldn't they pick a spot deeper in the woods, farther away from the house? Odd.

On the way back, he spotted an old grayish-white wooden ladder lying in the deep grass that rimmed the corn silos. Acting on impulse, he carried it to the empty house. Between the thick leaves of the silk tree, under Sarah's window, he leaned the ladder against the house. He moved the branches in front of it until he was satisfied no one would notice it there, and then he left.

He made his way back through the field quickly. His brothers were still on the porch, beating the same conversational topic to death. He reached into Lance's cooler for a beer.

"Not home yet?" Lance asked, and his brothers laughed.

Grant didn't answer; he just leaned back in his seat.

"We're still trying to figure out," Brody said, "how you two managed to get in an accident while parked."

"Move on from it," Grant said.

"Has it occurred to you, little brother," said Lance, "that your new girlfriend might be—well, let's just say—trouble?"

"What do you mean?" Grant asked, lifting a brow.

"It's only been what—a week? And so far, you've been suspended from school, sideswiped by a semi, drafted into mowing her lawn … neither of us knew you were taking the Tiger the other night. Poor Brody saw you take off with her and got down on his knees to say the Lord's Prayer for your safe return."

"Whatever," Grant said and stood up, unwilling to have a discussion about Sarah, especially with Lance.

Lance stood up and blocked him from leaving.

"What are you doing?" Grant asked.

He looked at Lance's hand on his shoulder until Lance lowered it, saying, "Listen. We know you like her. We like her too."

"And that's the real problem here, isn't it?" said Grant, staring into his oldest brother's eyes. "You like her, Lance. Admit it."

Brody jumped up and interceded before things took an ugly turn. "That's enough. It's none of our business what you do with Sarah."

Grant huffed in concession, sat down, and said, "You're right about that."

"So … my guess," said Brody, "is that you're not in the mood to talk about this coming Friday night."

"You're right about that too." Grant folded his arms sullenly.

"Sorry, bro, we'll cut you some slack," Lance said and held out his hand. Grant slapped it away, and they laughed.

"Anyway," Brody said, "I can't speak for Lance, but I'd say Sarah is hot enough to risk a little bad luck."

"I'll drink to that," Lance agreed.

"Well, you better get used to having her around because she's with me, and she's taken. And I hope she tortures you as much as she does me. You both deserve it."

The clock in the kitchen chimed ten o'clock, and Sarah was still not home.

Grant retreated to his bedroom. Everyone was sleeping by the time he finished taking a shower to pass the time. He lay in his bed and saw Sarah's headlights flash against his bookshelf when she returned to her house.

He waited until all the lights had been out at the Vise house for an hour and then crept from the house. He stole silently through the corn, crossing the gulf between him and Sarah like the ferry doing a night run to Cape May.

A light mist hung in the air. He took his time walking around the house. He was certain everyone was asleep when he climbed the ladder to Sarah's room. Her window was partially open. The ladder sank in the soft mud as he lifted the pane higher and climbed inside. He knelt on the floor as the heavy pane fell with a thud—*broken sash cord, damn*. She stirred under the blanket but did not wake. He had forgotten how beautiful she was until he saw her sleeping.

"Sarah," Grant whispered.

She was in a dream, far away. She heard Grant's voice call her, interrupting the wish she was whispering into a wood fire. Max was seated next to her.

The sand bubbled and swelled. A hand sprang out from it. Grant emerged from the ground and rolled out in front of Sarah—bleeding from a gaping wound.

Max explained sternly to Sarah, "You promised me."

Grant reached for her—seemingly mortally wounded—and Sarah wept. To console her, Grant said, "I have a secret." She got closer, and he said, "My body is made from the land. Max is the Spirit of Death, but he cannot hurt me because I'm the Spirit of Life."

Sarah opened her eyes. Grant thought she was awake. She stepped to the window, opened it wide, and muttered what sounded like, "Come in, Spirit of Life," and then fell back to bed. Grant climbed in next to her and realized she was still asleep.

"Sarah, wake up," he said, moving her hair away from her closed eyes.

"Watch out!" she said. He whipped his head around, looking for movement at the bedroom door. But the door remained closed—she was still dreaming—and he spoke her name again.

"Sarah."

"Grant?"

"Yes. It's me," he whispered. "Wake up."

"I love this music," she said softly, though no music was playing.

He tried not to laugh. "Sarah, wake up, there's no—"

She interrupted him in a harshly serious tone. "I made a promise."

"What promise was that?"

"To return to Max after stealing love from you."

"Who is Max?"

"You told me he is the Spirit of Death," she said, "but he does not look like a spirit of death to me."

"What does he look like to you?"

"He's handsome," she answered with a smile. "A young man with swirly tattoos all over his body—lots of muscles. He's big … strong … powerful. A magic man."

Grant was stung by her words and regretted asking, but it was too late. He knew she was dreaming, but the tone in her voice seemed to be saying she was in love with someone else. The idea stabbed at his heart.

Grant slipped down to the floor and waited awhile longer to see if she would wake up, hoping she would not talk again. More details about "Max" would only make him feel worse. The window yawned openly, inviting him to leave. He climbed down the ladder.

His hope for a stolen private moment they could laugh about later had devolved into something he could not understand. Just knowing that another man was in her thoughts and dreams made him burn with jealousy.

When he climbed into his own bed, he remembered the words more clearly. Sarah said she was stealing his love and giving it to some person named Max. At first this did not make sense, but then he understood it better. His love for her did feel like it was being pulled from him, drained away like blood. For the first time, he felt it; yes, his love was being stolen.

Grant longed to ask her about it, but to do so, he would have to admit he had climbed into her bedroom in the middle of the night without an invitation.

CHAPTER NINETEEN

FLANKED

Fifty-five hours had passed since they'd last been together—except for the midnight visit Sarah was not aware had even happened. Grant watched from his bedroom window as Rex hung his elbow out the gold pickup's window, driving down the potholed driveway. The pickup turned and headed for the dock. The Captain would never be deterred by rain; Grant wanted to hug him for being so beautifully predictable.

Grant waited a few minutes in case Rex returned for a forgotten item. The mist was thick out there. Grant yanked an all-weather jacket from the coatrack and quietly stalked through the kitchen toward the side door.

"But you haven't eaten breakfast," his mom said to him, pointing to an unused plate.

"Say hi to Sarah for me," said Lance, and he and Brody grinned at each other.

Viktor snapped the newspaper he was reading to get the boys' attention back to things that mattered. "Mold is going to kill us this year."

A light wind pushed the storm door open wide. Grant was gone before the door shut.

It was nearly impossible to surprise Sarah using a vehicle with tires; her driveway was six years overdue for a grading. The silver truck wobbled its way through the same water-filled holes Rex's truck tires had just navigated, making a gravelly, grinding sound. His dutiful vehicle tolerated the beating each hole imposed, but not without the brakes screaming for mercy when he stopped at her back door.

The calendar had inched forward as if made of stone. Their Friday night flight to nowhere felt less real every moment they were apart; he needed to replant the memory firmly back in the soil of reality. Two half days of school for final exams remained, and then—at least in theory—Sarah would be free from her father's continuous monitoring.

Grant skipped up the worn, broken, whitewashed porch steps. When he looked up, she was already waiting for him in the open door with a smile.

The beautiful Sarah made his feet stumble on the uneven boards of the porch, and she laughed at his awkward entrance.

"Those steps are dangerous," he said, moving toward the door to escape the rain.

Her auburn hair fell around her glistening-green eyes in long, loose, wavy curls. A long white-satin ribbon fluttered down the side of her face and landed gently in front of her right shoulder. Slipping inside the door, he closed in on the small space between them and gently pressed against her. She did not move.

Sarah's smile erased anything on his mind that was not her. "Can I come in?" he asked.

He stepped forward into the house, and she shifted her weight back to let him in. He dropped his jacket to the floor.

Grant's inability to control himself in her presence was an energy Sarah seemed to feed on. Internally, he tossed another shovelful of coal on the blaze that was already burning in him. As he moved toward her, she pushed against him, displaying strength against his advance—confirming his suspicion that she had been hiding a powerful force within her affected frailty. When she proved herself unmovable, he stopped pushing and kissed her open mouth. The two forces stood at rest.

Now that he had acknowledged her dominion, she led him with a step backward. He moved with her deeper into her house.

Their desire felt like a tidal force; the sea and the land needed to agree on who would win now and who would win later. Sarah stood on his toes and kissed him. All sense of boundary dividing them disappeared. He lifted her. Her resistance gave way, and they fell through her bedroom door and onto her bed.

As the sun pushed past the leaves and lit Georgia's pink blooms, Sarah lay beside the same window she was unaware he had breached only hours before. He stripped off his shirt. Her fixation on his bare chest fueled his hunger for her to touch him. Then, one by one, he opened the tiny pearl buttons of her white top.

He needed her like his lungs needed air.

He stopped for a moment, savoring her beauty, and then continued his methodical advance. His fingers slipped inside the opening of her blouse, stirring her conscience awake. But she slithered out from under him and jumped from the bed. She stood before him in the dappled morning light, blushing pink and looking achingly disheveled, the locks of her blouse open and her wild red hair tousled.

"We're going to be late," she said, no playfulness in her tone.

In Grant's mind she was a goddess of love, demanding he stand as a soldier to battle her puritan demons. He decided Julius Caesar would not take orders from Queen Cleopatra, so he lay on his side, shirtless, looking up at his temptress, and beckoned her back to bed. School be damned—it was the enemy of his desire.

"Finals," she reminded him.

After a defeated sigh, he reached his hand out for her, needing strength to get up. She hesitated and then pulled him from the bed, exercising enough willpower for both of them.

With his shirt and jacket in hand, he made an abrupt exit. In the pouring rain, he pulled the shirt over his soaked head. "You had your chance," he told her with a wry grin after they climbed into his truck and shut the doors.

"My one and only opportunity, and I blew it."

Grant turned on the truck and saw they had less than fifteen minutes to make it to homeroom. Calculating the time to drive eight miles, he was thankful no checklists were needed.

"Your porch is going to kill someone," he said, trying to think of something that would douse the embers still burning in his lower body. "I'll fix it."

"You've already done enough for me," she said, lacing her words with suggestiveness as she rebuttoned her top.

The truck's tires spun and grabbed for traction. Once past the minefield of her driveway, he turned wide left, causing Sarah to slide across the seat, stopped only by the locked passenger door. The truck skidded on the wet pavement of Port Mahon Road.

"Remind me to order shocks," he commented. "The tenants have really let the property go."

She punched his upper arm. It hurt, but he would rather have died by shark attack than admit it. He turned on the wipers, unable to see much of the road. She crept up close to him and kissed his neck, and he struggled to drive between the lines.

"You like torturing me," he observed but did not stop her.

Sarah walked in slow motion to homeroom, her feet buried in imaginary feathers, deep and fluffy. She kicked them into the air until she was coated.

Sarah stopped just before entering homeroom, snapping out of her daydream. She remembered something she'd forgotten—her backpack. She turned and ran to her locker. The yearbook left behind at home did not matter to her; she didn't need any more last-minute entries from people she barely knew. But a pencil—that she did need. With her head deep inside the locker, feeling around on the bottom, she searched for a stray one.

No luck. The bell rang; she was late. Cursing quietly, she accelerated her search.

An explosive force struck Sarah's bent back like a battering ram. Her head cracked against the rear of the metal locker, backed by a wall of concrete. She yelled in pain, her cry largely swallowed by the enclosed space, and then stumbled backward out of the locker. The hallway was sparsely populated, but she saw Eddie turning the corner.

When Sarah staggered into homeroom late, she was holding the side of her neck and caressing her shoulder. The sharp metal door of the locker had cut her neck. The teacher said nothing as she took her seat.

"What happened to you?" whispered Renee in shock. She handed Sarah a tissue.

Sarah dabbed the tissue on her neck and said, "Eddie. That's what happened."

"Are you telling Grant?" asked Renee.

"I'll take care of it myself," Sarah answered.

When the bell rang, ending homeroom, Sarah forgot all about her need for a pencil. Instead of going straight to her exam, she ran out to find Eddie in junior hall. The hallway was flooded with a river of faces. She spotted him downstream and yelled, "Eddie, get over here!"

He scurried ahead to avoid her. Unable to make progress, she grabbed an open locker and slammed it in frustration.

Sarah babied her shoulder through the history exam, answering the short-essay questions with the ease born of her natural intelligence. When the period ended, she turned in her test and hurried off through the gabbing crowd. She found a few basketball team members huddled in the senior hall.

"Have you seen Grant?" she asked Paul, the tallest boy.

"What happened to you?" he asked, noticing her neck.

"Remember the guy Grant beat up last week?" she said.

"Hey, you gotta see this!" Paul yelled to Grant, waving over the shorter crowd between them. Grant was just leaving his class at the other end of the hall, which was now teeming with clusters of kids relishing their last hours of high school.

"Is that him?" one of the players asked, pointing behind Sarah. "The one who did it?" She turned to see Eddie galloping the short distance toward her. The crowd reflexively parted as he charged. His hands grasped her neck, and he crashed to the floor on top of her. Growling like a rabid animal, he began to squeeze the life from her body.

Sarah lay still on the glassy tile as Eddie choked her. A crowd quickly gathered but formed a perimeter ring around them rather than rushing in to help.

Grant's line of sight was blocked by the mass of bodies rushing in for a closer look. He fought his way through them, using his farm-conditioned strength. Most of the onlookers were cowards, only willing to observe, not help. Some, however, perhaps harbored the same jealousy that was fueling Eddie's attack.

By the time Grant wedged his way through most of the throng, some of his player friends had recovered from the shock and were striking Eddie about the face and ears. Eddie's grip did not weaken in the least. Alarmed by his resistance, several more kids joined in to hit him, and he shook under the strain. He tucked his head close to Sarah's to avoid further blows. Now, with his body flat against hers, the boys feared they would hurt her if they hit him too hard.

Thick, dark-red blood drained from Eddie's nose. He yelled defiantly to the crowd, "I'm not letting go until she's dead!"

Eddie's bloody slobber dripped into Sarah's mouth as he kissed her goodbye for all the crowd to witness. They gasped in disgust, and a few dispersed to gag and heave.

Their disgust left an opportunity for Grant to push in closer. He pressed his way past the final wall of backpacks.

As he broke through the perimeter, he saw Sarah motionless on the floor and Eddie kissing her bleeding lips. The football coach, also the senior health teacher, came rushing in from the opposite side, yelling for everyone to move out of the way. With his momentum already built up, the coach hit Eddie broadside with the same tackle he taught his linebackers to execute. It was enough to loosen Eddie's hands and tumble him away from her.

Freed from the worry of harming Sarah, the basketball players piled on Eddie without mercy. They pulled him to his feet, restraining his arms. Eddie spit blood and cursed at them to let him finish her.

Everyone's attention was on Eddie except Grant's. He dove to Sarah's side. Her pink blush from earlier was gone; she was white with bluish lips, her face smeared in blood.

"Call 9-1-1!" Grant shouted as the players dragged Eddie away toward the principal's office, one of them punching him in the head for good measure.

Grant sat at Sarah's side, holding his breath. The football coach pressed her wrist and felt for a pulse. He put his ear to her mouth, straining to hear for breathing above the cacophony of the crowd.

"She's got a pulse," he pronounced, "and she's breathing."

Grant lifted her hand; there was no resistance.

"Don't move her. It may be her neck," the teacher warned.

Grant gently released her hand. Horror at the possibility of Sarah being paralyzed washed through him like scalding water.

The teacher snapped his fingers and clapped his hands. "Sarah, wake up!" he barked.

Grant lay on the hard floor beside her, unable to touch her, and softly begged, "Sarah, please wake up. Please. Please. Come back to me."

Her eyes stayed closed, but her skin began to return to a pinkish shade. She labored to breathe, seemingly forgetting how to exhale, and then hyperventilated.

The nurse appeared on the scene, pleading for a paper bag, and the crowd rummaged through their backpacks. An anonymous rescuer, who had happened to forget that lunchtime was not included in half days, volunteered his packed lunch. He hadn't inscribed an entry in Sarah's yearbook; they hardly knew each other, but he helped save her life.

Sarah pulled at Grant, trying to sit up, but she was still unable to breathe.

"The ambulance is on the way," the nurse said into Sarah's glazed eyes. The nurse gave her the brown paper bag to breathe into and motioned to Grant to have her lie back. The bag expanded and crushed as she struggled to find air.

The EMTs arrived through the main corridor. Kids scattered to make way for the gurney.

"I'm going with her to the hospital," Grant announced.

"Absolutely not. I'm calling her mother," the nurse responded.

"Calling her mother?" Grant echoed in disbelief. "She doesn't have a mother. And unless you have a ship-to-shore radio, good luck calling her father, who's in the middle of the Delaware Bay right now. She has no brothers or sisters, no aunts or uncles, no grandparents. If it says differently on her emergency forms, ignore them. I'm the only one who can help her."

The nurse looked stunned by this revelation. There were several stunned faces among the senior-class crowd as well. They had all grown up with her, and she had been nice to them, but who knew she was so alone in the world? Many of them, along with the Eriksens, had called her names and flicked rude comments at her since kindergarten. Grant included himself on the list of monsters in the room. Shame painted the senior hallway as the EMTs lifted her off the floor and placed her on the gurney.

"Grant, I'm not going to stop you," the nurse said, apparently sharing in the shame. He ran down the hallway after the EMTs and held the front doors open for them.

"Are you her brother?" they asked.

"Uh, yes. Stepbrother," he replied and unconsciously turned his face away. They welcomed him inside the ambulance and raced to the hospital.

Grant listened to Sarah's heartbeat and counted.

"You're the Captain's daughter," he said, holding her hand, "and you're tough as nails."

"Please God, let that be so," he whispered beneath his breath.

CHAPTER TWENTY

BROTHER

In the dimly lit hospital room, the processed air chilled her exposed skin. A constant stream of oxygen supplied nourishment to her brain. Sarah's unencumbered spirit, no longer enamored with the world, journeyed to find home. Her spirit knew the way to the afterworld; she no longer needed Max's help.

Sarah's spirit traveled through the darkened mist, following the Mahon River. A light-gray sky urged her spirit to hurry as the wind accelerated too. Sarah squinted as frigid, horizontal rain stung her cheeks; she was unable to control her speed. Swirling gusts of wind fueled by the sea carried her along, and she lowered her head just before impact with the water. She struck the surface headfirst and tumbled in the surf, the salt water filling her nostrils. Soaked and battered, she strode out onto the land, directly into the wind. Unable to retreat and without anything else to grasp, she wrapped her arms around herself.

She seemed to be walking into a small but powerful hurricane. The storm pounded at her ears as she pushed toward the hurricane's center, where Max stood on the hill, appearing electrified. His long arms raised, he summoned the wave tips to break away from the surface. He pivoted slowly counterclockwise, and the wind and seawater swirled and mixed at his silent command. Giant swells jumped up and clashed as if excited to be chosen next by the Storm Master. If this really was Max, then he certainly wasn't suffering from any kind of weakening—spiritual, physical, or otherwise. In fact, she'd never seen such a raw display of power from him.

"Max?" Sarah asked as she ventured closer. He continued summoning the storm without responding. As she drew near him, the wind died. He was the eye of the storm, she realized. She hesitated to speak again. She wondered if he might be someone else until she recognized the raised, moving tattoos on his back. His earlier amber glow had now become pearl white. His skin sizzled and popped as water reacts to hot grease. Unable to control her curiosity, she lifted her finger and reached out slowly to touch him.

The storm's speed quickened and clawed at her back.

Although she was afraid his skin would burn her, she continued to extend her finger as she struggled to remain standing. An electric bolt leaped from her finger to his back with a *snap*. With white, hollow eyes, Max wheeled and looked upon her without speaking. She felt a burn circulating within her, his charging spirit thickening and moving in her blood. She doubled over in pain and backed away. The storm whistled behind her head, its fierce current pebbling her back with sand and rocks. Without words, he reached for her, demanding she return to him.

Instinctively, she withdrew.

With an amplified, inhuman voice, Max bellowed, "You cannot escape me."

As she inched away, she lost her balance and tumbled out of the hurricane's calm eye. A gust of wind ripped her away into the gray darkness of the storm.

Velcro straps restrained Sarah. She awoke and saw Grant sleeping a few feet away on a narrow bench without a pillow or blanket. She called for him, but her voice was garbled and cracked from her injury and from hours of inhaling dry air through a mask. She struggled to free herself from the thin straps. Grant awoke, got his bearings, and moved in to help her.

"How are you feeling?" he asked, touching her cheek.

"I only hurt in every single place," she answered, removing the mask. "What happened?"

"Don't you remember? You were attacked—by Eddie." He seemed panicked at her confused silence and said, "Do you know who I am?"

She rolled her eyes and answered right away, "Of course I do, Lance." His eyes widened, and she laughed. "I'm kidding. You're that pilot guy who's not a bad kisser."

"Sorry," he explained. "They told me you may not remember things."

"You might want to try a more challenging question; I've known you my whole life."

"Okay," he said, doing a fake straight face, "do you remember our trip to that little wedding chapel in Vegas? An Elvis impersonator presided over our ceremony."

"That's right," she said, playing along. "Your brothers wore Elton John sunglasses, pimp hats, and blue-polyester suits. Your mother fainted with happiness. Who could forget?"

She reached for him, and he gently held her. "We actually could use a couple of days away together after graduation," he said.

"That would be heaven," she agreed. "Imagine shutting the curtains and sleeping till noon." Thinking about the clock made her sit up and look around with a feeling of missing something.

"Your dad's out fishing," Grant said, seeming to sense the source of her anxiety.

"Fishing? How long was I sleeping?"

"It's nine at night," he informed her.

"We have exams tomorrow," she said, her knees crashing into the rolling table over the bed.

A nurse bustled in with a pitcher, and Sarah said, "Excuse me, I need to see a doctor. I want to leave now."

"Relax," the nurse said, filling a pink plastic mug with ice water. "You're not going anywhere yet. Drink your water. I'll be back."

She shuffled out the door. Sarah sipped the water, feeling its blessed hydration.

"Before I forget," Grant said. "I'm your brother. I mean step-brother. It was the only way they'd let me stay with you."

"There's something I've been wanting to tell you," Sarah said, patting the bed and motioning him to sit next to her. "There's a reason I haven't … given myself to you yet. My dad adopted me. I'm an orphan."

Grant stood up from the bed, not sure where this was going.

"You never heard about the scandal involving your father and a young girl from town?"

Grant's lips parted. Sarah said, "I came with the house." When she could not hold a straight face any longer, she laughed, spraying water across the bed.

He bent over in disgust at the implication that they were related. "Don't even joke about something like that," he said.

A doctor appeared in the doorframe. He had barely set foot in the room when Sarah said, "I need to be discharged, right away."

He moved in to examine her. "You have quite the goose egg on the back of your head, Miss Vise," he said, waving a flashlight and pointing his finger for her eyes to follow in different directions. "Not to mention the bruises on your neck."

"I cannot afford to be here, and I have finals in the morning."

"But your brother said he talked to the school. You have a couple of extra days, and so you should rest."

Sarah looked to Grant. He shrugged behind the doctor.

"I want to leave now," Sarah persisted. "I feel fine."

"You've had a concussion," the doctor explained. He turned around, looking for support from Grant, but Grant only smiled for appearance's sake and refused to intervene.

"I don't care," said Sarah. "I'm leaving!"

After the doctor left, the nurse came in with pills and insisted Sarah take them immediately.

"Did my dad come here?" she asked Grant when they were alone again.

"He was only here long enough to ask me for Eddie's address."

"Oh no. You've got to tell him I'll handle Eddie. The last thing I need is a father up on murder charges."

"Actually, Eddie's here," said Grant.

"What?"

"Under mental evaluation, on the third floor."

"He should be in prison."

"Don't worry; I'm not letting you out of my sight. I won't give him another chance to hurt you."

"Grant, if you want to help me, you need to get me out of here."

Grant's eyes focused on her neck, causing him to wince at what he saw. But he sighed at the pointlessness of arguing with her. He sat in the chair and used the room phone to call home. "Mom. Please ask Brody to meet us at the hospital. We're coming home." After a pause, he said, "Yes, I told her she needs to stay and rest."

He looked a bit surprised when the nurse came in and removed the needle from Sarah's arm. "The doctor's releasing you," she said, "but you cannot drive. If you feel dizzy or faint, you need to come back to the hospital immediately. Take two pills at two and six to keep the swelling down."

When the nurse left, Grant returned to the phone. "She can stay in my room." A loud objection followed. Grant tried to cover the receiver. "Let me talk to Lance," he said, but Sarah could still hear his mom's voice on the phone. "Of course not, Mom. That goes without saying." He listened again for over a minute without saying anything. "Fine. I love you too." He hung up.

"I want to go home to my own place, Grant."

"No way. We don't trust your father will be able to check in on you the way you need. My mother insisted—it's better if you stay with us in case you need help."

Sarah rolled her eyes and sighed.

Brody's blue pickup rounded the ER unit's curb. The brothers helped her into the truck. Seated between them, she leaned on Grant all the way home. Her eyelids were heavy, and she muttered, "My brother—sure," before falling asleep. Brody looked at Grant, and Grant waved off the question before he asked it. As she slept, Brody told him that Lance had snagged his truck from the school parking lot and that Lance was hot on seeking vengeance on Eddie.

When they arrived home, Grant carried Sarah to Lance's room. In the dark, he took her shorts off, lifted the freshly laundered sheets, and rolled her under them. He lay a soft blanket over her and kissed her forehead. He contemplated crawling in beside her but knew that was against the agreement he'd made with his mother.

Grant checked his own room. Lance was snoring in his bed. Grant gently closed the door behind him and went to the kitchen.

"I cannot believe that woman," said Clare Eriksen.

Grant looked at his mother in confusion.

"Rebecca Vise. Sarah's mother. Leaving a little girl defenseless in a world of wolves."

Grant was not interested in his mom's judgments; he was too busy huffing over the game of musical beds playing out in his house. Sarah was not allowed to sleep in Grant's bed—as if he would take advantage of his battered girlfriend. He wanted to argue, but he knew his morally traditional parents were not going to let two eighteen-year-old adults sleep in the same room without rings on their fingers—even if one of them was unconscious and medicated.

Viktor entered the kitchen, and Clare brought him decaf coffee. "What's this?" she asked, pointing to a plastic grocery bag on the table.

"Clothes Rex brought to the hospital," Grant answered.

The sight of a girl's clothes stuffed into a bag by a man's clumsy hand fired Clare up again. "How could she leave her daughter like that?"

"Ancient history," Grant's father grumbled.

"And Grant, how could you let this happen to her?" she went on. "Why weren't you there to stop him?" In his mother's world, the men protected the women, and there was not one excuse or exception to the rule. Grant's inner turntable, spinning at 33 1/3 rpm, was already playing the same record within himself.

"It's not his fault," his father said. "He can't be everywhere. He already gave the kid a black eye or two."

"I'm sorry," said Clare. "Your father is right. I didn't mean it like an accusation. It's not your fault."

She reached for Grant's hand across the table. Grant held it and said, "I know," but he felt it was his fault. A kid like Eddie ... Grant should have seen it coming.

"Still, I don't understand," continued Clare, unwilling to move on. "What kind of school are they running where a young girl is safer on a darn fishing boat?"

Lance casually strolled into the kitchen, clad only in his underwear. He scratched his belly and yawned dramatically to indicate that his slumber had been disturbed by all the commotion. It was typical of Lance to flaunt the fact that his body had filled out ahead of his brothers'. Unable to pass up an opportunity to show them he was bigger and stronger than both, he grabbed the milk from the refrigerator and stood in the fridge light's flattering glow.

"Lance, we have company," Clare said, looking away from her eldest in embarrassment.

"Mom, I know. She's in my room. And by the way—I keep telling Grant she's trouble, but he doesn't listen." He filled a large glass to the brim with milk. "Everywhere she goes, disaster follows."

"Lance, go back to bed," Grant said in a tone that reeked of diminishing patience.

"I would, baby brother. But your damsel in distress is in my room, slobbering all over my pillow."

"Boys!" Clare raised her voice.

"I'd be happy to move her back to my room right now," said Grant, standing up.

"Sit down, Grant," his father ordered quietly.

Grant slumped into the kitchen chair and sighed. "It's not my decision, Lance. Mom told me to put her in there."

"Every day with that girl, it's some new piece of drama," Lance replied. "Why can't you see it? You're going to college in Indiana in two months; you don't need this."

"Mom, please make him shut up before I do," Grant said.

Brody walked in and injected a lighter tone. "What's going on in here—late-night family WWF?"

"Brody, tell him he's lost his mind," said Lance. "She's nothing but trouble. What's it going to be tomorrow, Mafia hit men? Killer clowns? I don't know what he sees in her."

"I do," Brody said, moving his eyebrows up and down.

"Looks aren't everything, Brody."

"Luckily for you, Lance."

Lance sat at the opposite end of the table from Grant, leaving Brody and the parents in the middle to try to maintain the peace. Lance pushed on. "I know you like her, but come on. You missed a final today. What if she's hit by a bus tomorrow? Are you going to—"

"That's enough!" Grant said, rising from the table.

"Lance, stop it!" snapped Mrs. Eriksen. "And Grant, go to bed. You're exhausted."

"I'm fine," Grant answered reflexively.

"You're not fine," she said. "That's what we're telling you. You're exhausted. By her. You aren't eating or sleeping."

"It's true," Lance agreed. "She's driving you crazier every day. And I, for one, am not going to stand by and watch you fly a plane when you're in this kind of shape."

Silence reigned around the table as everyone chewed on this undeniable concern.

"He's right," said Clare at last, happy to use any excuse to keep her youngest son safely on the ground. "I don't think you should be flying right now."

"I hate to say this, but I agree," Viktor chimed in. "No flying until things settle down. Until you're eating and sleeping normally again."

"Half asleep, I fly better than you, Lance," muttered Grant. "You're the one who shouldn't be flying—ever. Stick to digging ditches."

"Looks like you don't dig enough of them," Lance said, reaching across the table to feel Grant's muscle. Grant slapped his hand away and stood up.

"That's enough," Viktor said.

"I cannot believe this is my family," Grant said, disgusted. "Sarah was attacked by a jealous, psycho maniac today. And you talk about her like she's bad luck. What happened today was not her fault. Her mother leaving was not her fault, and her father—"

"But this relationship is making you crazy, Grant," Clare interrupted. "Can't you see that?"

His brothers nodded in agreement. Viktor lifted his hands in a *calm down* gesture and said, "Now wait a minute, everyone. Grant, your mother used to drive me crazy too. I married her to stop the madness, and it worked." Viktor put his arm around Clare and kissed her forehead.

Grant was happy to have his father as an ally.

"I like Sarah," Viktor continued. "We've watched her grow up. She works hard, and she's a good kid. You could do much worse. You want my advice?"

Grant nodded.

"If you love her, be with her. All of us will support you because we are your family." He gave stern looks to Lance and Brody. "But if this is something else, Grant, something more selfish than love, your mother and I are asking you to let her go now. It wouldn't be right for you to prey upon her at this confusing time. She doesn't have family to support her like you do."

"Dad, I love her," Grant said, putting his hand on his heart. A silence settled around the table.

At last, Viktor said, "It's decided, then. Support your brother, and no more talk about people being bad luck or any such superstitious nonsense."

Grant was relieved to have told his family his feelings, and it turned out better than he might have expected, all things considered. Mr. Eriksen got up from the table and said, "But Grant … she stays in Lance's room. Try to get some sleep—on the couch." The senior Eriksens retired happily to their room.

Brody slapped Grant across the back to acknowledge his bravery. Lance muttered as he walked past, "Never going to work. She's a ticking time bomb."

"A hot ticking time bomb, though," Brody added. Grant punched Brody in the shoulder, returning him to his bedroom.

On the couch, Grant twisted and kicked, unable to sleep. He waited for two o'clock and then opened the door of Lance's room, holding Sarah's medication.

"Grant?" Sarah asked.

"Yes. Time to take your pills." He handed them to her with a glass of water.

"I feel bad about taking Lance's room," she said.

"Don't worry about Lance. He's fine."

"I wish I had a family like yours. They love you enough to tell you the truth."

"You heard that?" He tried to remember everything that had been said. "How much did you hear?"

"Enough."

"You can't listen to everything my brothers say. Or my mother. They run their mouths, but then they come to their senses eventually." He paused for a moment. "Are you on their side about the flying too?"

"I'm on your side, goofball, but we better get to sleep. We have exams tomorrow."

"My family is yours for the taking, by the way. I only ask one favor in return."

She liked the idea she could one day claim a family as her own. "What is it?"

"Can we stay out of trouble until graduation? If I don't graduate on time, my family is going to send me to Siberia just to break us up."

Sarah pulled his hand to her cheek and said, "Deal." She kissed his forearm and fell asleep.

Grant sat in the chair next to her. A sense of quiet elation settled over him, having confessed his love for Sarah to his family. He imagined it was the unlucky, unhappy ones—those who were unable to find love early in life—who had created the ridiculous myth that real love is found only later in life. *There are no prerequisites for love,* he thought. *It happens when it happens.*

"Say hello to Max for me," he whispered into Sarah's sleeping ear. "Tell him you have a boyfriend now. He'll have to find someone else to haunt because he's not taking you away from me." Grant tiptoed to the door.

Before he opened it, she said, without awakening, "I'll let him know."

CHAPTER TWENTY-ONE

ENVY

Bacon stirred Sarah from paradise. In her sleep, she wandered a field of pink clover and gold-and-white dandelions that spread for miles. In search of a four-leaf clover, she hunted among the reddish-purple flowers for the elusive fourth heart petal. Time after time, she lifted a stem with seeming promise, only to find that three hearts were all it could muster. Undeterred, she continued to search, fueled with the hope that a four-leafer awaited, just out of reach.

A strong southerly breeze blew up, liberating a million dandelion seeds from their translucent white spheres. All her wishes were released along with them. They lifted and fluttered joyfully above the lime-green clover leaves.

The parade of fluffy parachutes marked a secret path, and she followed it. There it was: alone in the dry sand, a single four-leaf clover, cowering in hiding as her shadow approached. Instead of plucking the lucky clover from its roots, she stepped aside to give it light—and told it to enjoy the sun. Witnessing its existence was infinitely more rewarding than possessing it.

Sarah's nose tickled as the smell of bacon reached it again. She lifted her arms for a long, deep stretch. The smooth sheets and soft blanket felt too delicious to abandon. She pulled up the covers and reburied her head in the down pillow.

"Don't get too comfortable," Grant said, sitting on the chair next to the bed.

She opened one eye and then flipped her head in the other direction. When the sunlight found her face, she placed the feather pillow over her head and said, "Go away."

Grant tapped her on the shoulder with a glass of water and two pills and said, "You must be feeling better."

"How does anyone get out of a bed this comfortable every morning?" she asked, clutching the blankets to protect her turf. "Time?"

He peeked below the blanket and said, "Plenty." He pawed at the blanket for a break in the perimeter, but she held firm.

"Then come back in a few hours," she commanded.

"Not *that* much time," he said.

She moaned, but pleasantly. Night was losing its grip on her.

"Breakfast is a good reason to get out of bed," he said.

Sarah finally paid attention to her snarling stomach and agreed breakfast was an incredibly good reason to leave Lance's room. She wiggled her toes off the side of the bed to test the temperature.

"Breakfast is getting cold," called Grant's mother from the kitchen.

Sarah demonstrated the mechanics of a pirouette with her fingers and said, "Turn around." The gentleman faced the north field from the bedroom window so the lady could change. She pulled on a black metal-band T-shirt and cutoff jean shorts and dashed, without warning, ahead of Grant to the breakfast table.

"Ah, looks like you feel better," Clare said.

"Much. I'm feeling good—almost like it never happened," Sarah answered.

Clare poured Sarah milk. "No, thank you, Mrs. Eriksen."

"Please call me Clare," Grant's mom said and put the milk in front of Grant. "Orange juice?"

Sarah nodded and smiled.

The center of the kitchen table was piled high with scrambled eggs, pancakes, bacon, sausage, and scrapple. "Don't be shy, Sarah. You must be starving." Clare pushed a jar of Amish strawberry preserves in front of her and offered a plate of toast. Sarah grabbed a slice of toast, and Grant did the same. Clare said, "Thank God, Viktor. He's eating again."

Within a few minutes, the other two seats at the table filled up with Eriksen brothers.

"Lance, I'm sorry I took your room last night," Sarah said.

He shrugged. "Hey, we're neighbors, right?"

"You recover fast," Brody commented, seemingly happy to see the female addition to the family breakfast table. They all studiously ignored her yellowish-green bruises, which only made Sarah more aware of them.

"You forgot these," Grant said, sliding her pills next to her juice.

"I slept great. I don't need them."

"The best medicine is a good night's sleep," Clare opined, shooting a meaningful look at Grant. He looked like he hadn't slept again.

Viktor closed the *Farmer's Almanac* he was reading, slapped it down on the table, and looked at his sons. *Here comes the farm talk,* thought Sarah. She was right. "We finished the drainage ditch on the south field yesterday," he said. "Hope it dries out soon."

"Didn't the copper work?" Grant inquired.

"Doesn't look like it. Dew and mist, besides the rain."

"What about doing it again this afternoon?"

"Rain's in the forecast tomorrow," Viktor replied.

"Damn," Lance said, stamping his foot.

"So," Grant said, "are we going to have to start over?"

"Hard to say," Viktor replied. "At least the property isn't flooding anymore." He closed the subject by snapping open the morning newspaper in front of his face.

"Thanks for helping me out yesterday," Grant said, turning to Lance.

"Sarah's welcome to stay in my room anytime," Lance replied. He lifted his eyebrows a couple of times.

"I meant with the ditch," Grant said with a *knock it off* in his voice.

"How do you think I got these?" Lance said, contracting his biceps. "The reward for hard work." He grinned at Sarah.

Clare was reading a magazine by now, so both parents were tuning out the boys, a habit they seemed quite practiced at. Without the eyes of his parents on him, Lance continued to flirt openly with Sarah. Grant glared at his brother but failed to curb Lance's behavior.

Each time Lance laughed, Sarah was powerless to resist the contagion—not because his jokes were funny, but because she viewed him as absurdly full of himself. And each time Sarah laughed, Lance took it as further encouragement, if for the wrong reasons.

Just when Sarah had finally recomposed herself, Lance did a full Schwarzenegger muscle flex, and she almost fell out of her chair laughing. She was unaware that she had chosen the wrong side in a civil war and that, to Grant, her laughter was equal to sitting in Lance's lap.

Brody seemed to sense the mounting tension and strained to hold back any enjoyment, but it was a struggle, what with Lance and Sarah laughing so hard.

Lance waited until Sarah had a mouthful of orange juice and said, "My down pillows are awesome, aren't they? So downright downy and downful."

Burning orange juice escaped from her nose as she laughed and answered, "I'm down with them."

Grant handed her a napkin sullenly and said, "I'll take you home so you can get ready for school." Sarah suddenly felt she was being awkwardly rushed.

"Thanks for breakfast," she said, addressing the whole family. Goodbyes were exchanged, and Sarah left by the side door with Grant.

"I'm sorry," she said preemptively to lessen whatever trouble she knew she was in.

Grant did not reply.

The Captain was already gone when they parked at her house.

She needed to seize control of this situation. Instead of exiting the truck, Sarah crawled across the seat and wedged herself between Grant and the steering wheel. He was about to speak when she stopped him and said, "Kiss me, stupid."

Without permission, she trespassed on his wounded terrain. His blue shirt, coming alive in the morning sun, accentuated the blue of his eyes, giving him added soulfulness. The moisture of her lips grazed his. Reluctant to surrender to her reckless, uncommitted soul, he mustered the strength to remain still. He seemed determined not to take another solitary step emotionally.

"Do you like my brother?" he finally blurted out.

The love she was holding open for him instantly retreated. "No way," she said, making a sour face. He observed her as if she were a lying child and leaned back until his head touched the rear window.

"Wait a minute," she said. "You're not asking—you're accusing. You're actually accusing me of being in love with your brother."

She felt trapped, from a self-defense angle. If she were to point out Lance's flaws, Grant would defend him from attack; if she said anything nice, or even neutral, it would appear she indeed had a thing for him. She decided she had nothing to say to convince Grant one way or the other. And she suddenly lost her ability to care. Grant had become unappealing in his immaturity and insecurity.

"I mean, I get it," Grant went on. "You like older, and he's older."

Too smart to chase a bone, she ignored his remark.

"I need to get dressed for school," she said. "I'll be right back." She freed herself from the cramped confinement of the truck and made her exit. Grant closed the door behind her and listened to mosquitoes stabbing at the windows, searching for a way inside.

The obvious had eluded him, and it stung to think about. Both of his brothers teased her—they loved to prove how little they liked the beautiful girl next door, but it was Lance who was the most weakened by her. Lance had been in love with her the whole time. Why hadn't he seen it? With that revelation accepted, Grant did some quick analysis and decided he could live with his brother's envy. Lance would not betray him and break their brothers' bond.

As long as Grant was on the scene, that was.

However ... Grant's plans to go to Indiana for a bachelor's in aeronautical science—assuming Sarah stayed behind—would leave her alone with his brothers. Lance, who never had plans to do anything but carry on the legacy of the family farm, would now be in an enviable position. With Grant away, it would be so easy for Sarah to turn to Lance. And because Grant's romantic relationship with Sarah was still unconsummated, Lance would not feel duty bound to stay away from her. Grant felt ill imagining what the consequences of his leaving would be. He thought about coming home for holidays and how that would feel. *Ugh.*

Unable to sit still, he got out of the truck and paced, swatting away the small swarm of mosquitoes that seemed intent on having him for breakfast.

"They're attacking you preemptively," Sarah shouted from inside the house. "They must recognize you as the spray guy. They want you dead. Come inside, for crying out loud."

Grant entered the house reluctantly and sat at the kitchen table, sulking. Sarah walked up and stood provocatively in front of him. She wore a rose-colored miniskirt and tan wedge sandals. The thin blue sleeveless turtleneck tank top was cropped, showing off her flat stomach. The finger-shaped bruises on her neck were hidden under the high collar.

"Skirt," he pointed out.

"Correct," she said, crossing one of her long legs in front of the other. "A-plus for vocabulary."

"Are you sure you want to go to school?" he asked, a hopeful tone creeping involuntarily into his voice. He wanted to stay angry, but if she was proposing a "peace offering," he was incapable of passing up the opportunity.

"Yup, I do," she said and stood behind his chair.

"You could have fooled me," he said and walked out, returning to his truck. She joined him there a few moments later.

"Is there something on your mind?" she said.

Grant held back from pounding the dashboard with his fist. "Stop acting so damn innocent. You know what's wrong." He slumped over the steering wheel and groaned, a new level of frustration reached. For the first time since the day he walked her home, he felt he could not go on with this; his heart couldn't take it. After everything, Lance was going to win. Grant wanted to cry but refused to do so in front of her. She reached out to console him, and he held his hand up in a *stop* gesture.

Sarah slid closer to him, but not too close, and said, "Wild guess: You're angry with me."

He rolled down the window to relieve the pressure in his head as the truck rocked from side to side down the driveway. She cozied up to him—again. The seemingly innocent affection, the nonstop flirtation, the endless teasing. "Siren," he muttered as they sped off down Port Mahon Road, his window open.

"What did you call me?" she asked, yelling over the wind. Her bitter voice, carried by the wind, seemed to follow them down the empty road. Grant rolled up the window.

"I think I understand him," he said.

"Who?"

"The guy who tried to strangle you." The moment the awful words were out of his mouth, he wished he could rewind his mouth. He knew it was an epic betrayal for him to align, in any way, with Eddie.

"You what?" she said, her voice now so quiet it was almost inaudible. He vastly preferred her yelling. Her silent affliction filled the cab of the truck like smoke. He pulled over and jumped out. The weight of having said such a thing to her made him breathless, and he walked into the cornfield.

Bending over to catch his breath, he heard the long, hard leaves rustle as she came up behind him.

To his surprise, she addressed him as if he'd said nothing to hurt her. "Can we discuss this back in the truck?" Her tone indicated she'd made some kind of decision. She swatted at starved bugs, which, like Grant, could not control their hunger in her presence. With a big sigh, he followed her back to the truck, through the muddy earth.

Once he resumed driving, she announced, "If you want to break up with me, I understand. But it's important we finish exams today."

"I didn't say I wanted to break—"

She cut him off with, "I know you can have any girl you want, and I want you to be happy."

"If you really loved me," he said, "you wouldn't give up so easily. So I guess I know where you stand."

"That's so unfair," she said. "I do love you, but you're only with me because you feel sorry for me—not because you really want to be with me. I'm the poor little motherless girl next door who needs you taking care of her."

The idea that Sarah might end up with his brother still sickened him, but he knew the situation was reversed: *she* was the one who deserved better, and he was no longer sure he was the better man. Lance would never have told her he agreed with Eddie.

Late for school, they faced the principal together to take their makeup exams. The principal sent them to the library, separating them from the rest of the students to make sure no further incidents happened on school property. "Good luck," he told them, giving them a look that suggested he understood the turbulence of young love.

"All finished?" the monitor asked Grant three hours later when he turned in his papers.

"Yes, ma'am," he said. He stood at the door, looked back at Sarah, and left.

Sarah turned in her exams and was waylaid by questions from the monitor, who wanted to absorb as much gossip as possible before the long hibernation of summer break.

"We know you'll do great in college," she finally said. "Don't forget to come back to visit." Sarah walked out, knowing she would never see her again.

Sarah looked for Grant's truck in the parking lot, and it was gone. No surprise. She'd fully expected him to abandon her as her mother had, but she had not expected it so soon. She took off her sandals and walked barefoot to the stoplight. Home was eight miles away, but she was glad there was a breeze along with the sun.

Grant drove up alongside her and stopped. "What are you doing?" he asked.

"I thought you left," she said.

"I pulled around to the front to wait for you there," he said.

She resumed walking on the curb and replied, "I can walk." She had already decided this was a perfect place and time to end it—she would no longer have to wait for him to leave her.

Grant stopped in the middle of the road, put the truck in park with the hazards on, and ran over to her on the sidewalk. He lifted her into the air and carried her back to the truck, not like Max had—over the shoulder—but the way she wanted, cradled in a romantic way. The light turned green, and cars honked, but he took his time, showing her she was the most important person in his life.

The light turned red again. He placed her in the driver's seat and held her, standing with the door wide open, unconcerned about who was watching. "What I said was horrible and unforgivable," he told her. "You deserve better, and there are better men out there than me. Lance would never have said that to you. But there's something you need to know and remember for the rest of your life because it will never change."

"What's that?"

"I will never love another woman, ever, as much as I love you."

"I love *you*, Grant—not your brother," she answered. The light turned green, and they kissed in the intersection, ignoring the hurried world full of complaints.

"Are you ready to have some fun, then?" he asked as he climbed in next to her and gently pushed her toward the passenger side.

"Does that mean you're not breaking up with me?"

"I'm still thinking about it." He grinned.

Sarah flipped the visor down and studied her bruises in the mirror.

"We'll tell everyone you battled a legendary beast," he said. The reference to a beast reminded her of Max and how he had appeared the last time she saw him—and the threat he had issued to her. She was still undecided whether Max was real or an imaginary character conjured from the trauma of suicide. *If he's real*, she thought, *I'm screwed.*

"Does this fun involve sleep?" she asked.

"I think it's about time you stop asking questions and start enjoying the ride."

"No, I'll tell you what it's time for: drift fishing."

"Not today," he said.

"What do you mean? Are you going to deal with my dad if I don't show up?" *One pact with the devil at a time, please*, she thought.

"Yes. But only if you do something for me in return."

"Anything to avoid facing my father on the subject of missing work. Well, *almost* anything."

"Okay, here's what I need from you: no more questions for the rest of the night."

"What are you talking about?"

"That was a question." He laughed. "And you're not allowed to ask any. For one night."

"I still don't get it."

"You, Sarah Vise, are not permitted to pose any further interrogatives of me, Grant Eriksen, for the remainder of the day."

Wow, this was going to be hard. "I'm not sure I *can* stop asking questions," she said.

"Just try. For me. For one night."

"Oka-a-ay." *I get it—look pretty and be quiet.* Sarah stared out the window, a bit disgusted.

Grant traveled the long way to the coast, enjoying the drive without Sarah's questions, and parked on a dirt farm road behind Brody's truck. Brody was rummaging in the truck bed as a tractor idled alongside. He turned as Grant pulled up. "You got any gloves?" he asked. Grant reached across Sarah for a pair and handed them to his brother.

"Sarah, you're looking good this afternoon," Brody commented, taking the gloves. He stared overtly at her short skirt, hunting for all the real estate the skirt failed to cover.

"Thanks, Brody," she said, wondering if his attention was going to cause a brawl with Grant.

Brody pressed on. "You know, Sarah, I'm thinking it should be illegal for you to wear a skirt without some kind of hazardous warning label."

Grant said nothing. Sarah didn't get it—her laughing at Lance's dumb pillow joke was somehow more offensive to Grant than Brody's trying to undress her with his eyes.

"These are dangerous weapons," Grant said to her, covering her knees with his jacket.

Enough already—I'd rather be called Crab Cakes than endure one more sexually loaded compliment, she thought.

"So … are you going to hang out here and make me jealous while I plow this field?" Brody asked.

"When you're done, we'll be at the Pit. Bring beer," Grant said.

Brody saluted, and they drove off, leaving him alone.

"You are aware," Sarah said and kissed Grant, "that it's after exams now. You know what that means."

"Whoa, slow down," he said. "I've got to drive."

But she did not slow down.

"I didn't explain all the rules of my deal," Grant told her, attempting to salvage his sanity so he could drive without crashing. "I can still ask *you* questions, but you can't ask me any."

"That's not fair!"

"That's the rules. And I'll deal with your dad, and I'll mow as much grass as it takes to make him happy."

"Fine," she said, folding her arms playfully and moving to her side of the seat.

"Okay, here goes. Who's Max?"

"Why?" she fired back reflexively. "Damn it. Not asking questions is harder than I thought."

"I'll give you a mulligan on that one. The reason I ask is because you talk about him in your sleep."

She was horrified and wanted to know what he knew. "This no-question thing is really unfair because I've got a whole bunch I want to ask you right now. You set me up so you could grill me without consequence!"

"No. All I've done is liberate you for one night," he said and kissed her. "So come on. Max, who is he?"

When she did not volunteer an answer, he asked, "Is he an ex-boyfriend? Current boyfriend? The guy with the Porsche—was that Max?"

She wanted to ask, *What guy with the Porsche?* But she was forbidden from questioning. Then she remembered. "Ah, you must mean the University of Delaware Porsche guy. Want to know about him? Oops, that was a question. When I sent in my application, I attached a paper I wrote about growing and harnessing biofuel. They sent an 'ambassador' grad student down with an internship offer, thinking that would convince me to turn to the dark side. We had coffee, and I sent him packing when he told me what company funded their research."

"*That's* who Porsche guy was?" Grant asked with a look of surprise. "Then who is Max? Can you please just answer that question?"

"Max is no one."

"Well, he must be someone because you can't stop talking about him. Come on, Sarah, be honest with me."

"Grant. He's not real. He's made up." If Grant had asked the day before, that answer would have been more purely truthful. The day before, she was still hoping Max was a figment of her imagination, a dream. But since the attack from Eddie that almost killed her, she feared Max might be much more real, and much more dangerous, than she originally thought.

"His name is Max something unpronounceable. He's some kind of ghost haunting Mahon. I had a dream he killed me, but he sent me back to my life. He made me promise I would return to the afterlife after collecting life's fulfillment. But it was just a dream."

Grant shook his head in disbelief.

"Grant, don't. Don't laugh at me. Don't dismiss me. It's true. I had a weird dream, and it was so real and powerful. I haven't been able to shake his memory."

"Let me get this straight. In addition to my brothers, who are unable to control themselves around you—and a maniac who would rather go to prison than let you be with me—you also have a ghost man who pursues you in your sleep? But I have nothing to worry about because the man you dream of every night is imaginary?"

"Not every night," she said, cracking a smile.

"Does that about sum it up, or is there anything else I should know?"

"That about covers it," she said, hoping more than ever that Max was not real.

CHAPTER TWENTY-TWO

THE PIT

The ancient river crushed quartz rock into fragments, and the naturally formed gravel deposit was mined at a depth of fifteen feet—two hundred feet wide and nine hundred feet in length. The excavated material, piled behind a flat stone ledge, formed a loose mountain of rock.

On the ledge, to each side, sat two dormant backhoes, rusted with age, silently guarding the man-made pond filled with rain-fed swamp water—and snakes. At least five species of legless reptile, three black and two tan, considered the recently formed body of water home. All could swim, all were aggressive, and one was venomous.

The quarry hole full of snakes—lovingly referred to as the Pit—was a swimming hole for the recklessly brave. The black eastern king snake—named the king of snakes for a good reason—hunted with its head at a forty-five-degree angle above the water's surface. Its long black body with yellow chain-link bands constricted its prey. The northern water snake, tan like the copperhead (which was also a resident, and venomous), swam below the surface.

Brush and trees claimed the other side of the pond. Deep marsh mud, sprouting thick green grass, formed the far edge. The black racer snakes weaved and climbed trees on the other bank, while the eastern rat snake, also scaled in black, lay in wet ground, raising its head high above the grass whenever noise was present.

Grant drove slowly on the long dirt road to the Pit. The area was private property, originally owned by Grant's grandfather, Harald Sr., who sold the property to a lifelong friend. They passed a large Criminal Trespass sign, with its warning about poisonous snakes, but kept going. The warning sign—generally interpreted as a welcome sign—marked the preferred destination spot for the local teens, especially the boys. The brothers had permission to enter at will and frequently opened the chained gate for impromptu parties.

The Pit had only one rule: jump in on the first visit, or never return. Interference with this rule in any way resulted in a permanent ban. Girls were exempted from the barbaric ritual. The enforcer of the rule was Lance, who was a firm believer in the old way of doing things. He was intolerant of cowardice and insisted his tight inner circle prove themselves at the Pit.

Peer pressure around the Pit was tremendous for the local males. A surefire way to become a town legend was to run and jump off the ledge without looking first. Lifelong respect was bestowed upon the blind jumper, even if that respect had to come by way of a hospital room.

The rules also stated that everyone had a choice to walk away—except when they really didn't.

The silver pickup parked on the far side of the rock ridge. Grant and Sarah were alone. He turned off the truck, took in a deep breath, and moved closer to her.

"Come with me," Grant said.

Sarah looked in the direction of the snake-infested water and said, "Lead the way, dummy."

"I don't mean that. I mean when I leave for college."

Sarah did not answer.

Grant stared at the floor of the truck. "Marry me," he said at last.

"Were you born this serious?"

Grant held up a reprimanding finger. "You just asked a question."

"It was rhetorical."

He put his head in her lap, looked up into her eyes, and said, "Say yes."

"It's only been two weeks. What if you change your mind? And before you point it out—yes, that was also rhetorical."

"Time won't change how I feel."

"Yeah, but if you throw some time into the mix, I'll have a chance to catch up."

Grant kissed her. The absolute certainty of his lips was a place where she could rest her worried mind. This man—her childhood tormentor—invigorated a desire to want everything he could offer. She felt entitled to his familiar passion without the need for making promises.

"I love you," he said.

She soaked in the sound of it, even as it weakened her resolve. She slipped down and faced him, lying across the seat. "Please don't leave me," she said. "Even if ... it takes me a while to be ready."

"Never," he answered.

She played with his light-brown hair and said, "You are my rock."

"And you are my sea." He traced the scattered freckles on her cheeks with his finger. "Please marry me, Miss Vise?" he asked again and kissed her hand.

"I may still be accepting offers," she said with a smile.

"You mean like the 'magic man,' Max?"

She thought, *I never referred to Max as a "magic man."*

She felt herself withdrawing as she remembered her vow to return to Max. She remembered his hollow eyes and inhuman voice. A chill in the air gave way to cold fear in her body.

"Hey, I was just kidding," Grant said, touching her nose.

"So was I."

"What's wrong?"

She brushed her arms up and down to warm them. Grant assisted with his warm hands.

Maybe the time had come to be more honest with him. But what would the cost be? "Don't think I'm crazy," she said with a shiver. "But I'm afraid."

"You don't have to be," he said. He pulled his jacket from behind the seat and draped it over her.

"When I go to sleep, I'm scared I'll never wake up, and I'll lose you forever."

"You've been through a lot, Sarah. Everything is going to be fine."

"You don't know that. There is more to this than you understand. When I almost died, my spirit … went somewhere. And I had to make a bargain to come back here. I'm in love with you, and my time is running out." She desperately wanted him to fix her problem and undo the promise she made to Max.

"Your time is not running out," he said. "I promise. That thing with Eddie just freaked you out, and understandably so."

She nodded, knowing in her heart it would not be long before Max would steal her soul. She had witnessed his white-hot power firsthand, and she knew he no longer needed her to collect life's energy. He was acquiring that energy on his own somehow. The reason he wanted her back was more selfish and elemental: because part of him dwelled within her. Soon he would pluck his orchid, by the roots again, from this world. "I'm going to miss you," she said. The salty tears flowed at the thought of telling Grant goodbye for eternity. He hugged her, and she cried even more.

"You don't have to miss me. You're coming with me, or I'm staying here with you."

She let her mind go where it was pulling her. She imagined being trapped in the afterlife with Max, knowing she would spend eternity longing for Grant, her lover from another time. This day—right here, right now, at the Pit—might offer the last memories she would be able to make with him. And the more she wanted to be with him, the more painful these memories would be in a world without him. She cried, holding on to him, fearing what Max would really be like once she became his captured possession, and he no longer had to even pretend to be gentle and caring. She lingered in the private suffering Grant could not understand.

She heard two trucks park alongside Grant's. She knew whom it must be. She felt touched when she heard the brothers closing their doors quietly so as not to disturb her and Grant.

She sat upright and rubbed her face. Grant moved out of the way, into the window, and Lance placed a cold, dripping beer on the back of his neck.

"I know you like my brother, but you have to stop letting him beat the hell out of you," Lance said, pointing to her now-brownish bruises. He leaned across Grant, handing Sarah a beer—making sure it dripped on her bare thighs.

"Are you going in, little brother?" Lance asked, pointing to the quarry pond.

"Not today," Grant said. Lance moaned his disappointment. "The glory is all yours, gentlemen."

Brody walked around to the other side and stuck his head in the truck. "If she's crying, you aren't doing it right." He winked at Sarah. She smiled to let him know she was fine.

"You really did pick the most boring one of us," Lance said to her.

Lance and Brody stripped their shirts off, ran to the ledge, and jumped without surveying for what might be awaiting them below. Grant pulled blankets out of his truck and helped Sarah climb the steep gravel hill. His brothers whooped and laughed as they climbed out and sat on the landing. "Check out the size of that king snake," Lance yelled up to Grant.

Grant descended the side facing the water—with boyish curiosity—and spotted the long *S*-turn on the surface. Sarah, still refraining from questions, waited for him to volunteer a description when he climbed back to the top.

"Let's just say it's big enough that Lance will find excuses not to go back in the water for the rest of the night."

The brothers fetched blankets, coolers, and dry branches, systematically filling in the real estate around Sarah and transforming it into a site for a campfire cookout and beer party. They lit the wood and stood around cracking open beer cans. With a good idea of where the smoke was headed, they opened metal folding chairs and placed them upstream from the smoke. Sarah sat between Grant and Brody, and Lance sat closest to the trucks.

"We're going to make that scumbag sorry he ever laid a hand on you," Brody said.

"That's right," agreed Lance. "No one messes with our little sister."

"How about you just find him and bring him to me?" Sarah suggested.

The three brothers sat on the ridge at dusk, kings of their terrain. "Rumor has it you can lift a hundred pounds of fish over your head," Lance said to her, apropos of nothing.

"I'd ask how much you thought that cooler weighs, but Grant told me I ask too many questions," she said, smiling at having outwitted the embargo on questions.

"What the hell, Grant?" Lance said. "What kind of BS is that? Sarah, you can ask me all the questions you want. And my answer will always be the same—yes, you can have my body."

Grant groaned, lifted his hands in surrender, and said, "All right, you win. Questions allowed." He turned to Sarah. "I'll still talk to your dad; don't worry."

Brody lifted one of the coolers and said, "That's at least fifty pounds."

"Come on, guys," said Grant. "She was in the hospital just yesterday."

"So we'll give her a fifty-pound handicap," Lance said.

"Generous," Sarah said. The slender girl of not more than 120 pounds stood over the cooler. "At least sixty pounds," she said, testing the weight and dropping it.

"We know rumors are always exaggerated," Lance said. "You don't have to prove anything to us."

Sarah smiled and tipped the cooler to grip one side at the bottom. Without trouble, she lifted it to her shoulders.

The beers rolled, the water sloshed, and the cooler rocked in her hands. "Don't drop the beer," Brody begged.

"I won't," she said, moving her other hand to support the bottom of the cooler. "Try doing this in a storm on a boat," she said and hoisted the cooler high over her head.

Lance, duly awed, stood up, walked over, and took it from her—all his muscles contracted.

"Our Mahon little sister is awesome," Brody said.

"Legendary," Lance agreed and shook Grant's hand.

Sarah smiled widely at the idea that she had a couple of older protective brothers. The three Eriksen hearts, plus a fourth—her own—suddenly became the elusive, four-leaf clover of her dream.

"How 'bout we drop the little-sister stuff now?" Grant suggested.

"Don't listen to him," Sarah said. "You're both officially adopted as my big bros."

The now-blazing fire was beginning to attract the attention of the local lads. Truck headlights bobbed on the road toward them as Lance and Brody collected firewood.

Scott's truck arrived first, and he brought two girls. More headlights cautiously turned onto the road to the Pit, and pretty soon a small crowd had gathered in the lower area. Lance was in charge and greeted them all to ensure he knew and trusted everyone in attendance at the impromptu party.

As Sarah was climbing the hill toward the cooler, Lance caught up with her and said, "You're going with us on Friday night to the graduation party in Ocean City."

Sarah answered, "Unless I'm in prison for killing Eddie Kasik." Her dark humor resonated with the brothers' typical banter. She and the Eriksens had more than the road in common—none of them had had an easy life, and none of them had much tolerance for weakness.

"If you want something done right, do it yourself," Lance said. Sarah saw Grant bristle; evidently, he'd heard an insult in Lance's comment she had not. Perhaps he thought Lance was implying that she was forced to take care of Eddie herself because Grant had not taken care of him for her.

"If he showed up here right now," Lance asked Sarah, "what would you do?"

"It would be hard to choose," she said. The beer freed her imagination, though, and she treated the campfire audience to a glimpse of the wickedness of her mind.

"I'd unpack my Remington .30-06 rifle and walk him down, backward, to the ledge of the Pit. He'd see the barrel staring into his eyes, and I'd ask him if he'd ever seen the damage this rifle inflicts on a watermelon at short range. I'd tell him in great detail how his brains would blow apart, but I'd give him a choice: a bullet or the snake pit."

The topic of how to kill Eddie turned into a drinking game. The Eriksen brothers were no longer just the kings of the ridge; they now shared a deadly queen to tighten their bond.

"Got any more?" Lance asked, mesmerized.

"You said you like digging ditches," said Sarah. "If you would dig me one on Killington Beach at low tide, I'd gag him, tie his hands, and bury him in the wet sand on a full moon. We could watch the female horseshoe crabs climb on his face as the tide came in to drown him."

The sinister tone of the conversation troubled Grant. He imagined Lance and Brody carrying out murder for Sarah. "You're cut off, sweetie," he said to Sarah, taking her beer.

Lance bellowed, "Let my little sister speak her mind."

Grant stared into Lance's eyes and didn't like what he saw there.

"She needs to talk about it—it's therapeutic," Lance continued, delivering an intentionally evil laugh. Sarah joined in. Infused with bloodlust, she was no longer as lovely to Grant.

Lance noticed the lonely girls still sitting in Scott's truck and said, "Hold that thought, Sarah. I'll be right back." Brody followed Lance down the hill.

"Alone at last," Grant said, hoping to lighten her mood.

"I think I scared them away," she slurred.

"They love it. And you deserve to be angry after what Eddie did to you, but don't you think you've killed him off enough times for one night?"

"You're right," she said as Grant laid a blanket over them. The anger she had bottled up was barely noticeable now that she'd vented it, but Grant anticipated her anger would return.

Sarah stared into the fire and saw Max. Then the mental image changed to Eddie. Blood dripped from his mouth, and he tried to kiss her. She winced at the thought.

Scott arrived at the fire from the trucks, and cars parked below, accompanied by two blond girls Sarah didn't recognize. One seemed to be with Scott; the other was in the unenviable "third-wheel" position and looking eager to change that.

"I'm Yvonne," said the latter, a slender, tanned girl with long, straight blond hair and high, sculpted cheekbones. She waved cheerfully at the others around the fire.

"I'm Lance," said Grant's brother instantly, his face lighting up.

When the second girl stepped fully into the firelight, Lance said, "Annette," in a notably more tepid tone. Clearly, Lance and Annette had a history of some kind, and Lance was not thrilled Scott had brought her.

"Yvonne is my cousin," said Annette to everyone. "She just moved here from Virginia Beach."

"You're seeing Scott now," Lance said to Annette, manufacturing a passable smile. Annette nodded, moderately embarrassed, and Lance said loudly enough for Scott to hear, "Scott better treat you right. Tell me if he doesn't, and I'll straighten him out for you."

Yvonne sat on a spare cooler, and Lance gave her his full and undivided attention. "Where do you live?" he inquired.

"Rehoboth. My parents have a beach house."

"Nice," Lance said. "Want to go to Ocean City with us on Friday night?" Yvonne looked shocked by the sudden invitation but covered it with a smile. Lance added, "My brother Grant and his girlfriend, Sarah, are graduating on Friday, and we're having a party on the beach for them."

She looked over to the couple, happily sharing a blanket, and they seemed to provide a layer of comfort for her. "Sounds like fun." She shrugged.

"Want a beer?" Brody asked, handing her one without waiting for an answer.

"Wait a minute," Lance said, stopping her hands from making the exchange. "How old are you?"

"Seventeen."

"Brody, you got any of that nonalcoholic beer?"

Brody paused, only for effect, and said, "Nope."

Lance put on a show of being a conflicted man and then grinned and handed her the beer back. "Well, maybe just one."

A guy from the crowd down below ascended the hill but stopped short of the top and said, "Lance, have you got a second?"

Bothered by the interruption, Lance turned to Brody and said, "I'll be right back." He headed down the hill.

Sarah could see, between the beams of headlights, Lance making the rounds and shaking hands.

"I'm Brody, by the way," said the middle Eriksen, extending his hand. Yvonne flipped her hair and shook his hand but did not let go.

Brody began plying Yvonne with questions, and the answers grew quieter—more intimate—each time. Grant shifted and leaned forward as if also interested in the answers, and Sarah took note.

Sarah could tell Yvonne liked Brody better than Lance, but Grant's continued attention to Yvonne made her want to punch him. Instead of following up on that impulse—which she thought was "the Eddie" in her—she squeezed his hand to get his attention. Grant briefly looked at Sarah but went right back to staring at the beautiful girl.

Lance returned to the fire, and Yvonne said to him, "My sister's nineteen. Can she come to the party on Friday?"

"Is your sister as pretty as you?"

"Everyone thinks so," she said and looked away. Brody lightly touched her hand in empathy. He knew what it was like to be a sibling of a major looker.

"She can definitely come, but this is more of a private party, so no one else is invited," Lance said, rolling his eyes toward Annette and Scott, who were deep in conversation, smoking cigarettes. Yvonne nodded and understood that meant she should not mention it to them.

"What's your sister's name?" Lance asked.

"Monika."

"Does Monika have a boyfriend?"

"They broke up when we moved to Rehoboth."

"Sounds like a heartbreaker," said Lance.

"I think she can handle you, if that's what you mean."

"Is that right?" Lance said and smirked. He already seemed to be conceding Yvonne to Brody in favor of the sister behind mystery door number two. "How about I take you home, and you can introduce us?"

"Smithie's out there waiting for us to leave," Grant said, reminding him about the local cop who loved to bag drink-and-drivers.

"I'll let a few beers wear off first," Lance said and then ran off to join up with a couple of town guys who were discussing dragging someone's reluctant little brother to the Pit.

"Don't feel you need to take that ride with Lance," Grant said to Yvonne, freeing himself from the blanket.

Yvonne said to Brody, "If you come along—as a buffer and a little added protection—I wouldn't mind."

Sarah huffed and rolled her eyes, knowing Brody was no match for Lance. Brody was the safer choice, the better choice, but the two brothers together in the same car? Sarah did not offer any assurances.

Lance called for his brothers; he needed them for something. Grant stood up, and Sarah waved for him to please go.

Yvonne sat next to Sarah, her eyes taking in the scratches and bruises on Sarah's face.

"Brody is a good guy," Sarah offered.

"How long have you known them?" Yvonne asked.

"My whole life."

"What do you think of Lance? I mean, he *is* pretty hot," she said, fanning herself with her hand. Sarah was about to answer, but Yvonne continued. "He's in charge around here, isn't he?"

Sarah nodded. "Good catch, but I cannot imagine dating that ego for more than a day. He played football in high school, and every girl—I mean *every* girl—was in love with him. A new girl every week, but yet he was always available—buyer beware."

"Oh, my sister is going to like Lance. She'll have him wrapped around her finger so tight; he'll be howling like an abandoned puppy."

"I'd pay to see that."

Yvonne looked over at the three brothers congregating around Grant's truck at the foot of the hill. "Damn, girl," she said to Sarah. "I can't imagine having those three for neighbors. I would never leave my street. How'd you pick one?"

Sarah stood up to look down the hill and said, "That's easy. Just look at him."

The guys were roaring at some joke Lance was telling. Yvonne said, "I can see that."

Noting Yvonne's eyes lingering on Grant, Sarah said calmly, as if talking about the weather, "Yvonne, you seem like a nice girl, but if you even think about *thinking* about paying attention to Grant, I will break you like a breadstick and throw you in that snake pit."

"Oh no. Trust me—I'm fine with Brody. Besides, you look like you can scrap."

The girls exchanged smiles.

"Were you in a fight over him?" Yvonne asked. "Is that how you got those bruises?"

"Something like that," Sarah said, stretching the truth but not exactly lying.

"Want anything, Yvonne?" Brody called out when he returned to the fire to check on her. "We have soda, water, beer …"

"You are so sweet," Yvonne responded, "just like Sarah said."

Brody stirred the fire, adding a branch, and said, "Sarah, you're ruining my reputation."

Lance came up the hill; Grant followed him. "Are you ready to go home, senorita?" Lance said to Yvonne.

"I think so," Yvonne said and waved goodbye to Sarah.

Lance stumbled on the way down the hill to the truck. Grant followed Lance back to the truck, and Sarah could hear the two arguing about Lance driving drunk. Lance seemed a bit belligerent.

She got up and walked closer to the trucks. Lance pushed Grant aside, and Grant grabbed the keys from the seat of the truck. Lance grabbed his younger brother's forearm with his massive hand. Grant didn't back down. He stood in Lance's face and said, "You're not driving."

Brody tapped Grant on the shoulder and said, "I'm fine to drive."

Grant gave the keys to Brody and walked away.

"Can't wait for Friday, little brother," Lance said in a deliberately menacing tone as he climbed in the passenger side of his own truck.

Sarah watched the headlights of Lance's truck, with Yvonne in the middle, head toward the main road.

"She'll be fine," Grant said, sitting down next to Sarah.

"Well, I'm so relieved," Sarah said, unable to keep the sarcasm out of her voice.

"Damn, Sarah. You can be so cold sometimes," he said.

Sarah felt a flush of shame. She knew she was feeling jealous because she was no longer the center of attention of the three doting brothers. "I really am relieved Brody is driving," she said, an attempt to redeem herself. "Yvonne seems nice. And Brody deserves someone nice."

An exodus of cars followed Lance's truck; when Lance left, the party was over.

"Are we staying?" Grant asked.

"Let's, for a bit."

"You must be feeling better, my dear."

"Actually, I'm feeling kind of hot," she said. She got up, sat next to him, and cuddled up to her favorite of the three brothers.

"I'm trying to be good, and you're not making it easy," he said and piled more wood on the fire.

"What do you think of Yvonne?" she asked. Grant didn't answer. "Admit it. You were staring. I could see how much you liked her."

"Now you're worried about competition."

"I'm not *not* worried about it."

He sat down, placed Sarah on his lap, and said, "I cannot wait for the day you trust me. I've asked you to marry me and begged you to go away to college with me because I love you."

"But it's obvious, even if you don't want to admit it to yourself. You were staring."

"She reminded me of someone. She didn't remind you of anyone?"

"Who, Kim?" she said, referring to his prom date.

"Uh, no, not even close. Yvonne is much more beautiful than Kim."

"I swear, if you compliment her one more time, I'm going to want to hurt you."

"You really don't know who I'm talking about, do you? Do you not remember? Your mother—she reminded me of your mother."

ACT III

CHAPTER TWENTY-THREE

SECRET

The Captain traded his salty scowl for the prideful beam of a doting father when Sarah stepped out of the rusty pickup to join the pregraduation crowd at Grant's house.

"Big smile. That's what I like to see, Sarah." He twirled her around, lifting her without effort. When her feet landed, he said, "You're so grown up now."

He turned away from her, pretending he had something stuck in his eye that needed to be removed right away. In a pinched voice, he said to the man behind him, "Isn't she beautiful?"

Lance stood first in line to greet Sarah in the unofficial receiving line. He was clean shaven, his dark-brown hair was cut shorter, and he looked particularly handsome in his pressed collared shirt and tie. He took a step forward. Still the biggest guy in the family, he looked down at her and said, "More than beautiful. She's an angel."

Sarah was touched. He bent his knees and gave her a gentle hug and his congratulations.

Brody tapped Lance on the shoulder for his turn, and Lance stepped aside. Brody, his wet hair combed and tucked behind his ears, bowed and lifted her hand. "Wait until Grant sees you. He's going to pass out." Brody did a little dance move with her, without music. Grant leaned against the post of the elevated porch, watching them dance together.

Sarah wore a cream chiffon dress that drifted and rolled above her knees, with a wide gold sash at the waist. A gold laurel-leaf headband kept the curls of her auburn hair under a measure of control as mother-of-pearl earrings dangled like wind chimes in the warm southerly breeze. The ribbon trailing from the sash hung to her side, drawing eyes down to her matching open-toe sandals. Grant waited for Brody to finish with her so he could grab a minute.

Lance put his arm around Grant and said, "I've changed my mind—you're going to have to fight me for her."

Brody heard Lance, turned around, and said, "Me too, bro."

Grant reached for Sarah's hand, which was wrapped around Brody's lower back, touching her fingers until her hand fell into his. With a gentle tug, he pulled her away. She pressed into his chest and looked up.

"Wow," Grant said and turned her around once and then twice. Her dress gently lifted, and he admired every inch of her.

Clare walked up, holding a camera. "Would you three let Sarah breathe long enough for a picture?" Sarah smiled wide, soaking up the attention. Grant, in a fitted blue suit, kissed Sarah's cheek for a picture. "Look at you—such a gorgeous couple." Clare snapped a photograph.

Grant pulled Sarah far away from his lovesick brothers and said, "You are the most beautiful girl I've ever seen. Literally. Anytime, anywhere."

She smiled so much her cheeks hurt. Her father caught her rubbing them and said, "You're out of practice with that."

"Dad, you look handsome," she said, struck by how all the men around her had been sculpted by hard work. Behind her back, Grant touched her fingers. She turned, and Grant forgot himself; he kissed Sarah. Grant's parents turned away to give them privacy. The Captain cleared his throat, but Grant was slow to back down.

"Grant, do I have to remind you I own firearms?" the Captain said.

Grant unlatched from Sarah's lips and said, "No, sir." Lance handed the Captain a beer to distract him while Brody walked Grant away.

Clare seized the opportunity to introduce Sarah to the whole family. Sarah shook hands with Cousin Finn; his wife, Elsa; their two-year-old daughter, Ivy …

"We've got everything packed in the truck, including Sarah's overnight bag," Brody said to Grant.

"If you guys really cared about me, you would have booked a private room on the beach," Grant said, looking back at the lovely Sarah.

"We're not making it easy on you," Brody said.

Grant grumbled, "Lance and his rite-of-passage nonsense."

"It's tradition. You know this goes all the way back to when our family first settled here."

"I don't want her to be in the middle of it, that's all."

"Lance insists she's the perfect witness. She's always been a part of our lives, and she grew up on this land. Girlfriend or not—ready or not—it's time for your trial. Besides, we both know you aren't afraid of anything except her. So that settles it."

"Speaking of girlfriends," Grant said, "are they going? The sisters? Yvonne and Monika?"

"We're picking them up on the way down."

"That'll be cozy," Grant muttered, unhappy with the plan of driving to the beach together.

"That Monika is something else," said Brody. "Wait till you see her. Lance actually stutters when he looks at her. Swear to God. I think there is such a thing as too good looking."

"There is," said Lance, striding up to join them, "and she's my girl."

Sarah heard him from a distance and shouted, "Lance, it's so nice to see you're finally in love."

"Nah, but she'll do for right now," Lance said.

"Are you always this honest?" asked Sarah.

"Only in the presence of family, little sister."

Grant went back to get Sarah, but the Captain stopped him and said, "Let me drive her to school one last time." Grant could not remember ever seeing the Captain drive her to school.

As the boys watched Sarah walk away with her dad, Lance shook his head and said, "I don't know, bro. Maybe we should change the rules for tonight's rite of passage. Maybe it should include taking that young lady's virginity."

"Knock it off, Lance," said Grant. "Besides, who says she still has it?"

"What?"

"Her virginity," Grant replied.

"I say," replied Lance, walking away.

Rows of white chairs waited on the unmarked grass of the football field for the senior class to fill them. The metal bleachers were still sparsely filled, and the outdoor concert stage and podium stood empty.

Out in the parking lot, family members clustered near the decorative purple, blue, and gold entrance to the outdoor stadium, hoping to seize one last flurry of kisses, hugs, and handshakes with their young graduates before the ceremony.

The brothers arrived after the rest of their family and parked the farthest away. Unbeknownst to their parents, the boys had stopped for supplies and alcohol and were in no hurry. On the long walk across the parking lot, they unrolled shirtsleeves and tightened neckties. Grant took a deep breath and gave his suit jacket to Brody to hold, exchanging it for a blue graduation robe. "Another stupid tradition," he muttered as Brody handed him a square cap and tassel to put on.

Eighty-two degrees in the late afternoon. Grant was already starting to sweat before he saw Sarah approaching the gate. She was glowing in her white robe with blue-and-gold ribbons. The brothers shared the same image of her. Grant said, "I'd cross a war zone for her if one was in my way."

"You aren't looking hard enough," said Lance. "A war zone is exactly what I see. You're not the only one who has eyes on her." Lance casually pointed out several male faces whose sole attention was on Sarah.

Before Grant had an opportunity to catch up with Sarah, the crowd buoyed her through the gates and to her seat.

Their last names forced them to sit apart. Grant was closer to the front, so he had to resort to stealing occasional backward glances at her. She was happily preoccupied.

Shade from newly arrived clouds lowered the temperature a few degrees, but still Grant had to open his robe to stop from overheating. The announcements and speeches began. Grant didn't hear a word of it; he heard only what was going on in his heart.

The dark storm at the dock came to his mind. He heard the splash and saw Sarah return to the surface—her hand reached for him. This time, in his mind, he was too far away to touch her. He dove into the salt water, not to save her but to save himself from losing her. The waves and current dragged them out to sea together. He told her it was all right, and he knew it would be. Their minds searched for meaning in their short lives—which had been spent in obligation and formality—but found only unnamed emotions. He closed his eyes, lifted her to the air, and asked God to take her before he no longer had the strength, or air, to survive.

When the crowd erupted in laughter from a joke in a speech, Grant stirred from his daydream and pulled in a breath. Realization dawned that by catching her hand at the dock that day—in real life—every minute with her since that moment had been a gift.

The first rows stood in front of him, and each name was called to collect the symbolic blank scroll.

When Grant's row was called, he put his robe back together and stood. "Grant Eriksen" was amplified, and he skipped up the short stairs. He walked across the stage to shake hands with the principal. His friends and extended family filled the air with hoots and praises. His brothers were loudest and rowdiest, easy to distinguish from the others.

Grant could not help but smile. The crowd favored him as a small-town celebrity—not for his athletic ability, like Lance, but for his good nature. Grant had followed his own path and had never felt the cold of being in Lance's shadow. He took a moment to appreciate himself for this fact. Alas, it was not a quiet moment. Lance and Brody did not stop clapping and yelling until Grant stepped off the stage.

The last rows were finally called to stand. "Sarah Vise" was announced. Grant saw her shyness at being called in front of a crowd—he knew she viewed them all as strangers. Grant's stomach tightened, knowing how few people really knew her or had managed to make a connection with her. She climbed the stairs to a round of silence, but when she stepped on the stage, Lance stood and hollered for her. Grant and Brody and the whole Eriksen family joined in, along with Rex Vise. Then the whole crowd, including the students, cheered for Sarah. Grant felt a lump in his chest from the ocean of support that poured out for her. She froze in the middle of the stage alone, in her white robe and gold honor ribbons, and waved a thank-you to the crowd.

After she collected her scroll, a whistle followed, acknowledging her beauty. It was a whistle that mimicked the boatswain pipe on a naval ship, the one sailors used to bring attention to a pretty girl at the harbor. The shores of the Delaware Bay, with its long maritime history, overflowed with the descendants of military sailors, civilian mariners, and even pirates. Sarah, also a sailor, was spared no mercy as other men in the audience joined the call.

Grant made eye contact with Lance; he knew his brothers would not disrespect her like that—at least not in front of Grant and Rex and the whole Eriksen family.

Rather than being bothered by the whistles, Sarah blushed at her newfound fame and did a funny little curtsy in response to the admiration. She gave her audience a big smile and a goodbye kiss before she stepped off the stage.

Grant remained standing until she spotted him in the crowd. She mouthed the words "Thank you," and he collapsed into his seat. He was completely in love with her.

The prepared speeches droned on, and Grant looked for family and friends in the crowd. Along the top bleachers, he spotted Eddie's wild black hair and saw his arm held down below the steps, hiding a lit cigarette. Eddie was not graduating, and Grant doubted he had any reason to be there except to see Sarah.

The Captain had mentioned he'd received a letter about an upcoming mediation with the school regarding the Eddie incident. He asked Grant to attend because he knew he would try to kill the kid if he saw him. Eddie had been discharged from the hospital with no charges brought against him, and he was free to go wherever he pleased.

Grant empathized, in a small way, with Eddie's obsession but could not fathom how he could want to hurt Sarah—even if she rejected him. Thankfully, the privacy of his skull shielded the world from knowing that his obsession rivaled Eddie's. He thought about her constantly during the day; all attempts to distract himself failed. And at night she was the steady object of his lustful dreams—when he managed to sleep at all. There was no escape from her.

The thrill of acrobatic flying was the dopamine he usually soaked in. But now flying had become a cheap substitute for the rush she gave him. *At least I have control over the airplane*, he thought.

Eddie moved to the top bleacher, leaning against the wall like a vulture. Unable to shake the feeling Eddie was stalking Sarah to attack her again, Grant code-signaled his brothers for their attention. Grant pointed above them, and the boys scanned the crowd. The brothers' ancient sign language allowed them to home in on Eddie quickly. With a nod, Grant confirmed that his brothers had the right guy in their sights. Lance and Brody hurried off, splitting apart like pack wolves on a hunt. From opposite sides of the bleachers, the two slowly ascended the steps.

Finally, the caps were thrown, and Grant slipped away from the smiling, hugging crowd. His brothers had captured Eddie swiftly and held him captive in the shadows below the bleachers. Grant ducked under the metal slats.

"Is this the guy?" Lance asked. His face was red, waiting for confirmation.

"What are you doing here?" Grant demanded of Eddie.

Eddie struggled to free himself from the brothers. He spat in Grant's face, but Grant calmly wiped it off and flicked it back in Eddie's eyes.

"Maggot," Brody said.

Lance bore down on Eddie with his mass, making Eddie kneel before Grant.

"Sarah's father told me he was going to hack you up into eel bait," Grant informed Eddie. "He said the pots are ready to go as soon as he finds you. He's here now. Should we go get him?"

"Fine," said Eddie. "I don't care. She's ruined my life. I bet you know how she can do that, Grant. She told me she loved me, and when she got pregnant, she said she wanted to have a family with me."

"Take it back, liar," Brody said and punched him in the same ear that was still black from the previous attack. Eddie's face was pouring tears.

"I'm telling the truth," Eddie said. "It was last fall. A few weeks later, she changed her mind. She said she was afraid to be a mother because her mother abandoned her. I begged her not to get an abortion, but when she finished making one of those fish nets, she had the money to get it done. She broke up with me because I refused to take her to the doctor. She killed our baby—that selfish bitch."

Grant took a step closer to look him in the eyes. Eddie cowered.

"Grant, he's full of it," Lance said, and Grant's legs trembled.

"What would you do if you were me?" said Eddie. "I lost it. How could she do something like that? How could she be so cold? She killed my baby."

Eddie collapsed to the floor, broken down by his own words. Lance and Brody grabbed him under the shoulders to lift him up.

"Let him go," Grant said. Grant walked away—he needed air—and his brothers followed, reluctantly leaving Eddie behind. Eddie called after them, "Hope you don't want kids with her. You can't say I didn't warn you."

Grant turned, intent on killing Eddie with his bare hands. His brothers blocked him. They turned him around, marched him away, and tucked their shirts back in.

The implications of Eddie's words poured over Grant as he emerged from below the bleachers. He kicked at the grass and was slow to return to Sarah, who was encircled by his family. Brody went back for Grant's jacket, and Lance held his brother up with one arm.

"All I can say is I hope you're right," Grant said to Lance, referring to Lance's theory about Sarah's virginity.

"Me, too, brother," Lance said, patting Grant on the back. He knew what Grant was referring to.

"Where have you boys been?" said Viktor Eriksen. "We've been looking all over for you." Brody came back with Grant's jacket, and Grant put it on. Clare peered through her camera lens and took a picture.

Sarah pulled Renee onto the scene. She had been patiently waiting for the boys to return. "Renee wants a picture." Sarah took Renee's camera and snapped the shot. Renee was smiling, but the boys were not. Sarah cast a look of concern at them, but none of them met her eyes.

Clare studied her usually boisterous boys and said, "What's wrong?"

"Mom. Nothing. We're tired of all the talking," Grant said. He could barely stand. He leaned on Brody for support. Sarah shot him another worried glance.

Lance put a hand on Grant's shoulder, walked him away from the crowd, and said, "Let's get out of here. It's time to make a man out of you."

Grant said, "I'm not in the mood."

"A man does not retreat, little brother."

"It's going to have to wait," Grant told him, raising his voice. "I'm not kidding." Grant looked at Sarah and said, "I've got to talk to you right now."

Lance grabbed Grant by the shoulders and shook him. "Not now, Grant."

"Damn it, Lance. Lay off." Grant's voice was trembling.

Brody stood between the two brothers. Trying to defuse the tension, he looked at both of them and said, "Now I'm pissed. When did Grant get taller than me?"

Their mother seemed to sense the tension in the air and said, "It's graduation, boys."

The Captain walked over, curious about the mounting conflict over Sarah.

"Eddie is here," Grant said, hoping those three words would explain the disruption to everyone, even if they didn't tell the whole story.

"Where?" asked the Captain.

The brothers glanced about, but they were not interested in finding Eddie; they'd heard and seen enough from him for one night.

"He must have left," Brody said.

"That's because he knows my sons will protect her," Clare said and hugged Lance, turning him into a big, squishy teddy bear.

None of them noticed Eddie, who was close enough to hear their conversation and was dialing it in like a radio tuner.

"Miss Vise." Lance addressed Sarah formally in front of the Captain. "Are you ready for an adventure watching Grant cower like a toddler at the haunted house on the boardwalk?"

Sarah looked at her father, who had agreed to the trip earlier in exchange for Grant's promise to grade his driveway.

"Get out of here and away from that lunatic," said the Captain. "Go have some fun; you kids earned it."

"Thanks, Daddy," Sarah said and hugged him.

"Grant, you are going to keep Sarah safe, do you hear me?" the Captain said. It wasn't a question. "Not one scratch. I mean it. I will hold you personally responsible. No excuses."

"Yes, sir," Grant answered.

All four nodded as if they were already in trouble for something they hadn't done yet.

The Captain hugged Sarah and said, "Stay out of trouble." Then he pointed his iron-strong forefinger at Grant and said, "Sarah, don't let this one get away. He's a good man."

"Not a man yet," said Lance, as the foursome walked past the exit gate, "but he will be before this night is over."

Crossing the parking lot, the brothers were already unbuttoning their shirts and stripping down to the T-shirts beneath. Unconcerned about the crowd in the parking lot, the brothers took their shoes and pants off, pulling shorts over their boxers.

Brody put his arms out the passenger window and beat the sides of the truck, the signal they were ready to go. Lance turned on the radio, and Grant sat, lost in his unsettled soul.

"I know you can't be scared at what these boneheads are planning," Sarah said to Grant, "so what's the matter?"

Grant stewed silently, visions of Eddie's death playing in his mind.

"Let it go," Sarah said. "I'm over it."

"You're over it? How is that even possible after what he did to you? Why does it always seem like you're protecting him? Maybe there was some truth to what he—"

"Grant!" Brody said, cutting him off. Then he turned to Sarah and said, "Ignore him. He just needs a beer on the beach."

"After we pick up the girls," Lance reminded him.

Sarah rolled her eyes.

They drove up and parked at a Rehoboth Beach house on stilts. The house was in a prime location with an unobstructed view of the beach. The two girls were waiting on the porch when they saw Lance pull in. They were all smiles to greet their new beaux.

Brody and Lance hopped out of the truck, and Sarah and Grant got a good look at Monika, the new man-killer. Lance lifted her up as if they had known each other for a lifetime, smiling at her with enough energy to blind her. Brody helped Yvonne into the back seat and decided to join her there.

"You can sit on my lap," Brody said, and they switched places, forcing Sarah to move onto Grant's lap.

Sarah gritted her teeth and said, "We're going to have so much fun. Are you excited?"

"Hey, girl. Oh, wow, you're a fast healer," Yvonne said, noting Sarah's clear complexion. The bruises from only a few days before had almost entirely disappeared. *Wondering about that myself,* Sarah thought. She shook her head, dismissing all notions of spirit energy.

Yvonne introduced her sister to everyone, and the expected round of pleasantries and congratulations ensued. Monika was every bit the looker Lance and Brody had boasted about.

Grant was not having fun, but he pretended to be, hoping the over-the-top beauty would make Lance move on from Sarah. Worries were piling up for him; he needed something to eject from the list.

"I'm giving you fair warning," Grant said to Monika. "You have your hands full with this guy."

She replied, "Don't worry about me. I can handle him."

"Are you sure?" Lance said and squeezed above her knee. She jumped away from him and pressed herself against the passenger door in a theatrical overreaction. Everyone watched the performance from the rear. Within a couple of traffic lights, her ploy had worked; Lance was begging her to sit closer.

"Promise you'll behave yourself?" Monika said teasingly.

"I promise."

She pulled the visor down and fixed her lipstick in the mirror, saying, "I'm not convinced."

The brothers in the back looked at each other and laughed. When Lance saw she was not readily returning to his side, he waited for a stoplight, unbuckled his seat belt, and grabbed her playfully. She screamed and laughed, and the dance continued.

On the north side of Ocean City, with their windows rolled down, they drove past the crowds that formed at every corner across the main drag. Sarah's unruly dress, captured by the wind, required constant attention to control. What had happened under the bleachers became less of a concern to Grant the longer the dress fluttered. He forgot about his brothers, and all he could think about was Sarah's floating dress. And her lips, of course.

"What's the plan?" Grant asked Lance.

"After hours at the haunted house. I told you already. I know a kid who works there, and he's in on it. Everything is all set."

"You're just wasting your time; you won't scare me."

"We'll see," Lance said, adding a maniacal laugh.

Lance knew exactly where to park the truck. The pier had a large Ferris wheel and a host of other carnival rides. The haunted house stood near the end closest to the beach. The day crowd was packing it in and exiting the parking lot.

The brothers excitedly hauled supplies to a predetermined spot on the beach that Lance had chosen for their campsite.

While the boys busily set up the campsite, the girls gave Sarah lessons on how to expect royal treatment.

Monika was checking herself in the truck's side mirror when she saw Sarah lift a chair out of the bed of the truck. "What are you doing?" she asked.

Sarah shrugged and dropped the chair.

"You've got a lot to learn, girl," Yvonne said.

"I'm all ears."

"Let them do their thing," Monika said. "They've got this; they don't want any help from us, or they would have asked."

Sarah felt guilty and lazy just standing there as the guys walked up to the truck and hauled things away.

"What if they do ask?" Sarah said.

"They won't," Monika replied. "And if you help them, they'll think of you as another guy. Guys like guys, but they like girls even more. Trust us."

When the truck was empty, Lance ran up to Monika and tried to carry her off to the beach. She screamed and ran away, and he chased her down to the waves.

Brody and Grant walked Yvonne and Sarah to the site together. Sarah could see that Grant was only putting on a show of being party ready. His eyes told a different story.

The campsite the brothers had set up was a beautiful thing. Coolers, chairs, blankets, towels, tents, a boombox, and propane lanterns were arranged in an inviting layout. A fire was already burning in the firepit, and it wasn't even dark yet.

Sarah rested her head on a pile of towels and soaked in the music of the tumbling waves as Grant—lost in thought—drank a beer in silence. And then another. *What are you hiding?* she wondered. While his brothers and their dates were laughing and telling stories, Grant remained grim and ruminative—a side to him she had not witnessed before.

Sarah captured his attention only when she stepped out of the glow of the firelight and began fumbling with her clothes. The crashing waves were too tempting to pass up. She tugged at her dress and lifted it over her head. Temporarily tangled in the fabric, she was startled by a gentle pull from above. "My imagination has already undressed you a hundred times," Grant admitted as he freed her from the unruly dress.

"Then why so standoffish?" Sarah smiled. The white swimsuit from Cape May, revealed in the absence of the dress, reflected the full moon's light. Without an answer, Grant carried her to the water. There, forces of nature converged; the surf pushed them together. He kissed her. The tide clawed the sand under their toes. They clung to each other—and fell to the sand like lovers in an old-time Hollywood movie.

Wrapped in his arms, she forgot about everything but his lips and his skin. But then, out of nowhere, the idea that he would eventually abandon her invaded her thoughts. At precisely the same moment, a similarly derailing thought seemed to strike Grant. They stopped midkiss and pulled back from each other, embarrassed by the sudden disconnect. "The moment" had been lost somehow, and it wasn't coming back. Grant stood awkwardly and returned to the campsite and his beer. Sarah followed, sitting near him but not with him.

The other two couples remained uncomfortably wordless for a few moments. Then Lance broke the silence. "I don't know how much longer I can watch my little brother act so pathetic," he slurred. The big man had finally reached an intoxication level Sarah had not witnessed before. "I swear, Sarah, if my brother is still a virgin by tomorrow morning, I'll adopt you as my real sister and cancel the whole thing."

Grant turned his face away from her. She was horrified for him.

"I'll do you a favor," Lance said to Sarah and sprang to his feet. "I'll set him up myself. Get him broken in for you."

He swayed slightly as he stood. "Ladies," he yelled over at two girls in beach chairs next to their own fire. They looked at him expectantly. Even in his worst shape, Lance got the benefit of interested attention from females. "Would either of you beauteous beauties be interested in helping out my very handsome virgin brother over there?" Before they could answer, he added, "It will only take a few minutes of your time."

Their answer was muffled, their faces buried in their hands. "What's the matter? Boyfriends?" he asked. They nodded and pointed at two guys on their way back from the boardwalk.

"We'll talk after they leave," he said, loudly enough for the men to hear, and stumbled back toward the campfire. All eyes were on the two girls as the men returned. Brody stood up, ready to bail Lance out of the mess he had created. Monika and Yvonne almost knocked their heads together laughing so hard, and Sarah mentally searched for her jaw that had figuratively dropped to the sand. Grant opened another beer, ignoring the whole show.

Lance motioned for the sisters to be quiet; he was listening for the boyfriends' reactions. One raised his voice toward Lance. Lance stood up and yelled, "All I did was ask my lovely neighbors for a cup of sugar." The men shook their heads, urging the girls to fold up the chairs to leave, and Lance fell to the sand and laughed until he was unable to catch his breath.

When the laughter died down, Lance stood up again, without a wobble, grinned, and said to Monika, Yvonne, and Sarah, "Look at the time—see you at midnight, ladies." He grabbed a large duffel bag and strode off in the direction of the haunted house on the boardwalk in his bare feet.

Grant walked toward the surf without words, and Sarah watched as he threw himself into the merciless hands of the Atlantic Ocean.

"Did you know?" Monika asked Sarah, smiling and scanning for Grant in the dark surf. "That he was a ..."

"Sure," Sarah answered untruthfully. "So what?"

Brody locked eyes with Sarah. He winked and kept her secret.

CHAPTER TWENTY-FOUR

BLOOD

Carnival games of chance crowded the Fun City boardwalk on the way to the haunted house. The Eriksen beach party, absent Lance, walked past long lines of beachgoers waiting for greasy pizza and peanut-oil-soaked french fries. The smell of powdered funnel cake sweetened the air, and a crowd of teenagers, quarters in hand, swarmed the pinball arcade.

An old man waving a long, crooked stick stepped from the shadows, stopping Monika in her tracks at the ring-toss game. "Three rings for a dollar," he propositioned, a roll of bills peeking from his fist. The necks of green glass bottles lined up in an open, military formation, but as the plastic rings were flung, all bottles evaded capture.

"Lance is waiting for us," Brody said, nudging Monika along.

Sarah relied on Grant's steady hand as they dodged a seemingly endless tide of hurried people flowing from the opposite direction. It was nearly midnight. When the Ferris wheel loomed above them, Sarah stopped and leaned back to observe the gentle swing of the top cars. Sneakers dangled, and loose flip-flops threatened to fall. She pointed to show Grant her interest, but he urged her onward, through the neon lights and thumping music of the ground-level rides. Important matters awaited.

Ahead, the Haunted Manor sign flickered in neon oxblood red below a flat-topped mansard roof. The Second Empire Victorian–style building was the main attraction on the boardwalk, mainly because of its live actors who hid in corners and under floors, waiting for unlucky guests to pass. Its main distinguishing visual feature: The tail of a plane jutting from a second-story window.

Monika, the currently unattached fifth wheel, sprinted to the entrance ahead of the others, searching for Lance. A group was gathered outside holding tickets, waiting for the last walk-through of the night. Brody curled his arm around Yvonne's waist and headed for the exit door rather than the entrance. He called for Monika.

Grant stopped on the right side of the large exit door, leaned against the wall, and pulled Sarah close, offering her the first—and much-needed—warm hug they'd had since tangling on the beach. She smiled; his troubles appeared to have lightened. He returned the smile.

"Glad when it's over," he said and exhaled.

Brody and Yvonne claimed the narrow real estate on the left side of the door and huddled together. Sarah heard banging and muffled screams on the other side of the wall.

Monika walked up to them and stood directly in front of the exit door, her palms lifted in confusion.

"Where's Lance?" she asked.

Neither brother answered—they were both distracted by their dates. *No idea and don't care*, Sarah thought as Grant's lips brushed hers. From within the building, Sarah heard the chuff and whir of a pull cord starting a two-stroke lawn mower. The sound died. Then she heard it again, followed immediately by a sputtering. Just before conking out again, the motor caught and quickened to a throaty growl. *No, that's a chainsaw!*

The exit door flew open. The chainsaw was lifted high in the air, sputtering in the dark doorway. Its thick exhaust poured out around a hulking masked man, his white butcher overcoat spattered in blood. *Za-zing!* A pull of the throttle caused an earsplitting mechanical scream. The shocked crowd formed a semicircle around the scene, all eyes on the butcher and the unlucky blond girl—Monika—who had fallen to the ground in front of him.

Monika picked herself up and marched toward the butcher, waving away the smoke as the exit door slammed shut.

"There he is," Grant offered anticlimactically.

"What the hell!" Monika yelled. She clenched her fists and stamped her right foot once, twice, three times. *A raging bull about to attack*, Sarah thought. Then Monika did just that—she charged at Lance. He needed both hands to control the chainsaw but refused to put it down. Rather, he held it up over his head and ran in a circle in front of the exit door to avoid her fists. The crowd stepped back, giving Lance room to run around, but it did not retreat.

Lance was blocked from escape by the crowd. Monika chased him as he dashed past his brothers—his mask still in place—and said to them, "You were supposed to tell her."

"It's my fault! I forgot to warn you—I swear," Brody told Monika as she ran by. He held his stomach, laughing, and dropped to his knees. The stench of the oil-rich fuel mixture traced Lance's erratic path, and the stiff ocean breeze ushered the smoke offshore.

"Oh jeez," Grant said. Tears of laughter fell from his eyes, and he leaned on Sarah for strength.

The chainsaw butcher stopped suddenly and addressed the crowd. "What are you looking at? Never seen a chainsaw before?" Monika would not give up the chase. She plowed into his back—his solid stance unshaken—and bounced off. The movie-star blonde had finally caught up with the bloody, chainsaw-wielding butcher guy, and the audience howled at the "show."

Lance revved the motor above his head while she punched him several times in the back. He absorbed the blows as if they were insect bites. With every punch she dished out, the crowd's laughter increased. She finally gave up and stormed back to confront his brothers. The crowd cheered.

"Show's over," Lance yelled to the crowd and shut off the chainsaw. It dangled from his left-handed grip, and the crowd dispersed quickly.

Monika pulled Yvonne away from Brody and said to her, "I'm ready to go home."

Brody inserted himself between the two sisters. "Monika, it's my fault. I was supposed to warn you, but I forgot. Every Friday night Lance puts on this midnight show for the crowd. Please don't be mad. He really likes you."

When Monika folded her arms and rejected his plea, Brody appeared to panic and said, "Please forgive him, Monika. If you don't, he's going to kill me."

Yvonne held Monika's hands and nodded in agreement with Brody, vouching for his innocence. Grant grinned at the exchange. Sarah stared into his eyes, light headed from laughing, and quietly asked, "Did you and Brody *really* forget to tell Monika?"

Grant put his finger to his lips and said, "Shh." Whatever the answer, Sarah was relieved she hadn't been the target of their chainsaw prank.

Lance raised his mask and laid the chainsaw down. He pulled his yellow gloves off. He held out a hand for Monika, but her arms were still tightly folded. Lance just stood and waited. Sarah watched in disbelief as his unyielding confidence magically unfolded her arms and pulled a smile from her. *Who's howling like a puppy now?* Sarah thought and rolled her eyes.

A man dressed in black poked his head out of the exit door and said, "Lance, you ready?" Lance nodded, and the guy disappeared behind the door.

"Let's go," Lance said, staring at Grant. He led the group to the front entrance, holding Monika's hand, and tapped a few times on the door. The door creaked open. Lance and Monika entered; then Grant urged Sarah inside. Brody and Yvonne followed, grasping for each other's hands.

"Monika?" Yvonne whispered.

"She'll be waiting for you—on the other side," Lance replied. He offered a maniacal laugh just before the door shut. Sarah felt the final rush of outside air touch her behind the ears. Grant pulled her close in the darkness. With her free hand, she reached back and tugged at his T-shirt.

"You didn't answer my question," Sarah whispered. "Did you and Brody really forget to tell Monika?"

"Are you kidding? We were under strict orders *not* to tell her," Grant whispered back.

Brody and Yvonne snickered in the dark. "You really know how to keep a secret," Brody said to Yvonne.

"In front of all those people, seeing my sister chasing him all over … I just about peed my pants," Yvonne said.

Siblings, Sarah thought. *One minute they're thick as thieves, and the next they're throwing each other to the wolves.* Lance had humiliated

Grant, telling everyone his virgin secret. Grant could have ruined his brother's plans by telling Monika, but he didn't. Sarah wanted to be angry with him, but he was kissing the back of her neck.

An audio system popped on and crackled over their heads. Ominous horror-movie music began to play.

"So?" Grant said and then kissed her neck again. It tickled. "Thanks to Lance, we know where things stand with my … romantic history. What about yours?"

She twisted to avoid his lips. "What about mine?"

"Have you ever … you know?"

"You, Grant, are not allowed to ask me, Sarah, any more questions," she answered. "I'm liberating you for just one night."

An orange glow dimly lit the floor. The ominous music ended. It was followed by a series of short snatches of news broadcasts and '80s songs, interrupted by slivers of static—as if someone were searching for a frequency on a radio dial. And then …

A trained baritone voice: "I see you there—hiding in the séance room. I locked all the doors and nailed the windows shut. Hide if you like, but you will never escape me."

A flash of bright white light flooded the room, temporarily blinding Sarah. Then the door to the next room sprang open. Its strobe lighting forced her to close her eyes, but the ghostly white images still flashed behind her eyelids. Sarah pulled her hand up to her eyes and said, "I can't see."

"I'm good; I was looking down," Grant said. "Close your eyes. I've got you." He gripped her hand and pulled her through the doorway to the adjoining room. Sarah felt the effects of vertigo and then became aware that the floor was twisting and moving. She reached out, palms extended, feeling for a wall. Grant held her waist, and she leaned into him.

"Step up," he said. She floated, almost weightless, up the short steps to the next room. "How are your eyes?" he asked.

"Better," she answered, trying to blink away the few floaters still hanging on. The end of a dark, thin hallway stopped them short, and they crushed together against a wall. They had missed their turn. Groping about, they quickly found an unobstructed path. This time they felt along the walls to avoid hitting another roadblock.

As they crept along the hallway, hand in hand, Grant said, "I don't trust Brody behind us." To quicken their progress through the black maze, they let go of each other and felt the walls with four hands instead of two. Ahead, a glowing exit sign marked a door but also illuminated the stairs to another floor. Sarah pointed to the door, but Grant ignored her and climbed, two steps at a time, to the top level. She followed.

A dim light outlined wooden rafters above and revealed the way forward. This passageway was wider than the one below, with short walls. A cool breeze provided relief from the stuffy lower level. Grant turned the corner ahead of Sarah, and she followed. She heard water dripping into buckets—or into puddles?—and the floor turned soft and squished under her feet. She froze as they approached a wall of mist. She pinched herself to stop her mind from slipping away to another place of marshland mud—a place with crooked branches that guarded a demonic forest.

"Grant," she called as the mist rolled past her. She felt a cool touch on the back of her neck and heard the soft *S* of her name up close. It lingered in her ear. She turned and swung her hand outward but met only air. Which way was forward? She took a step, reaching out, bending her knees, worried she would fall down a hole or a staircase.

That's when she felt it—the sense of snakes crawling up both legs. But she was afraid to check with her hands.

"My wild orchid, did you forget your promise?" whispered a voice. She froze with fear as a light touch of fingertips dug into both sides of her waist. "You can't escape—me."

"You're not real."

"You hear me, don't you? You feel me, don't—"

A rush of wind blew toward her.

A hand grabbed her arm, and she gasped.

"Max?"

"Sarah, it's me," Grant said.

She pressed up against him and said, "Sorry … the mist … I thought for a minute … "

"It's dry ice, and people are hiding up here to spook you. Let's go," he said. As he pulled her along, a gloved hand reached out from a corner and brushed her shoulder. She squirmed, rolled her shoulders up and down, and sped up; no way was she going to scream.

When they reached the end of a hallway, Grant led her behind a false wall, pulling a black cloth in front of them, concealing their location. "A creeper usually stands here—get down," he said. They faced each other in the dark, waiting for Brody and Yvonne to pass.

"Here's where we split up," Grant whispered. "Lance is waiting for me near the exit. Whatever happens, don't be afraid. I'll be all right."

Brody and Yvonne were laughing, not a care in the world, as they stumbled past the black curtain. "Time for the test of bravery, brother," Brody yelled into the corridor, thinking Grant was still ahead of him. Without a word, Grant kissed Sarah with electrically charged lips and left. Knowing the danger ahead, Grant left Sarah—alone in the dark—to go take care of his stupid big brothers.

Sarah hesitated and listened for Max. After counting to three, she hoped the coast was clear. Then she decided to run after Grant, away from Max, whether he was real or not.

Sarah found the stairs to the lower level and followed the path in the direction of Brody's and Yvonne's laughter. She plowed into a person dressed in black. "Umph—watch it, lady," he yelled in her ear as he stepped aside. She was sure Max was right behind her—stalking her.

She spotted Grant in a corridor illuminated by black light; he was stalking Brody and ready to pounce. *Brothers—it never stops.* Grant grabbed Brody from behind without warning. Brody turned and tripped, falling to the floor and dragging Grant with him. They struggled on the floor. "It's me," Grant yelled after pinning Brody down.

"No kidding," Brody said, pretending he knew all along.

Sarah heard the chainsaw start. She saw Yvonne pass through the lit doorway ahead. *Must be the last room before the exit*, she thought. The chainsaw revved. Lance was alone with Yvonne. The chainsaw sounded like it was cutting wood—the ticking of small wood chips sprayed the walls.

When the brothers rose from the floor, Sarah squeezed between them. Tentatively, Brody, Grant, and Sarah looked into the next room from the doorway. Lance was no longer in his butcher's overcoat and mask. He wore goggles and was slicing a short stack of muddy wood; sawdust sprayed the air. Even with the exit door propped open, the room smelled like a mixture of the Port Mahon marsh and engine grease; apparently, that was the effect Lance was going for. Sarah covered her nose; Grant pulled up his T-shirt to cover his face.

Lance stopped cutting wood and brought the chainsaw to the middle of the room. He laid it slowly on the ground and shut it off. "Brody, your girlfriend fainted—not sure if it was the chainsaw or the smell that got her," he said, grinning. Brody helped Yvonne to her feet and whisked her out the door, apologizing for his brother.

Lance stood over the chainsaw in a wrestler-ready stance. He beckoned to Grant. "Come on, little brother." Grant stepped forward and stood on the opposite side of the machine. The two faced each other, eye to eye. Grant turned to Sarah and sighed. Lance said to Grant, "You know the rules of engagement."

"Let Sarah leave first," Grant said. Lance did not answer.

Sarah approached Lance, looked up at the older Eriksen, and said, "If you hurt him, you'll answer to me." Lance smiled, seemingly unconcerned—but perhaps his smile did falter a little. Sarah walked out.

The chainsaw started again, and Sarah turned. As the door slammed behind her, she saw Lance with the chainsaw in his hand and immediately regretted leaving Grant alone with him. She clawed at the handleless door to get back in. Brody pressed his ear to the door and listened. "Step away from the door," she yelled at him. He stood back as she got her nails under the wood and began to pry. Almost open now. Then she heard the click of the door latch from the other side—it was locked. Now she and Brody both pressed their ears to the door.

Meanwhile, Monika brought Yvonne a chair, and the two sat chatting as if nothing was happening.

"Are you a man or not?" Lance asked from within the room.

"Man enough," Grant answered. Sarah heard the brothers' bodies collide like football linemen and slam into a wooden wall. The two men wrestled their way around the perimeter of the room until they reached the other side of the door—the chainsaw moving and knocking around—and Sarah and Brody had to step back to avoid the harsh pounding. The fight was right there, inches away, but there was nothing she could do to stop it.

After a few moments, the scuffle moved away from the door and into the middle of the room again. Brody and Sarah tentatively leaned in to listen.

The chainsaw revved and continued to move. Sarah looked to Brody, her eyes wide as coasters. "They're fighting over control of the chainsaw," he said.

"What?" Sarah cried in horror.

"That's the tradition. That's the rite of passage."

"Why didn't you tell me? Are you people *insane*?"

Grunts, a collision, and another wall crash issued from the room. And then the pop of glass. The light under the door went out. They were fighting in the dark now with a live chainsaw! The motor continued to sputter until there was a loud *za-zing!* Someone new had control of the machine.

Brody looked at Sarah in panic and pulled at the door but couldn't pry it open. The chainsaw revved again in the dark. Yelling and pounding rang out from the inner room; someone was looking for the door from the inside. A clink of metal—the latch opening.

Sarah and Brody stood back, the door flew open, and Lance ran out in a panic. He looked for a light in the outer room and flipped it on. Sarah saw Grant on his knees, hands on the chainsaw, blood dripping down his face, as the door swung closed again. He'd won the tussle, but at a cost.

"He's hurt!" Sarah screamed in Brody's ear. She tried the door, but it was stuck again. When Lance rushed over to help, Sarah punched him with a right hook to the face.

Lance barely flinched. Brody saved Lance from another blow by successfully prying the door open. Sarah ran through the door to Grant.

"You're hurt," she said, holding out her hand to him. "We've got to get you to a doctor."

"No, I'm all right," he said with a grimace, pretending he was not hurt.

"You're not all right. You're bleeding," she said.

Lance rushed in and elbowed his way to his younger brother. "Let me see where you're cut!" he demanded. He reached out and pressed his index finger to Grant's forehead, where the wound appeared to be. He probed around a bit and studied the blood on his finger and then proceeded to stick his bloody finger in his mouth. "Yum," he said.

Sarah shrieked in horror.

The three boys burst out laughing.

"Ketchup," explained Lance.

The boys laughed even louder.

Sarah glared at the three of them with eyes that were flamethrowers, trying to decide which of them to immolate first.

Brody held his hands up in surrender. "It was Lance's idea. Grant and I told you a thousand times it was a prank—and still you fell for it?"

Sarah's focus narrowed to seeing only Lance. "Grant, she's going to beat the crap out of me," Lance said with genuine alarm. "Please put a leash on your girlfriend."

"Why would I do that? She's your adopted little sister, remember?" Grant answered.

"Lance, take me to the beach, or I'm going home," Monika yelled in a bored voice from the sideline. Without hesitation, Lance ran to Monika—saved by the belle—and left Grant to smooth things out with Sarah.

Sarah turned to Grant and said, "The whole thing was an elaborate hoax to trick me? You should have told me."

"I did tell you, about fifty times. I also told you the fight was real," he said, pointing to a scrape and bruise on his knee. "And it was."

"That chainsaw was real too. You could have been killed over a joke, stupid."

"It was real, but I wasn't in any danger of being killed, Sarah."

"But the light was out, and the blade was spinning."

"Trust me. I wasn't in danger."

Grant grinned and headed out of the building. The others followed.

As the three couples walked toward the beach, Lance ran up to a limping Grant and said, "You're not hurt, are you, little buddy?"

"Of course not," Grant shot back. "I'm just limping so that Sarah realizes how much she loves me." He made a show of leaning on Sarah a little bit more.

"All of you are a bunch of pansies," Lance said, moving to the front of the pack to lead them back to their campsite. "Except Sarah—she's the Tasmanian Devil."

Sarah surprised herself at how quickly she forgave Grant. She was thankful Grant wasn't really hurt and could not help but be grateful to be alive, collecting memories as souvenirs. Again, she felt that terrifying certainty that time was running out for her. She was sure Max had been present, in some form or another, in that haunted house. *This will be one of those memories I'll hang on to forever. I'm going to miss Grant and his big, dumb, beautiful bully brothers so much*. The thought caused a few silent tears to fall, and she kept walking.

Brody offered support to Grant so he could walk more easily on the thick sand of the beach. Sarah could see Grant preferred the able help of his muscular brother and let go of him. After a few minutes of reflection, she only had one question left: "And why were you never in danger from a spinning chainsaw blade in the dark? Who are you, Ironman?"

"Sarah, we're farmers," Brody chimed in. "We have more than one chainsaw."

"And …"

Grant chuckled. Brody answered, "They started the second chainsaw—the one *without* the blade—the second you left the room."

Sarah fell asleep, covered in towels by the fire, to the laughter of Lance telling stories around the campfire to his brothers. Sometime later Grant woke her with a gentle shake.

"Sarah, I need your help with something," he said.

"Okay," she replied, struggling to remember where she was.

Grant knelt beside her and said, "I need to ask you to be my witness."

"Witness? To what?"

"You'll see. The fight at the haunted house—that was just a male ego thing. There's a more important ritual we have to conduct. It's called the bravery blood oath."

"The what?"

"It's been passed down in my family for generations—always between brothers. Lance says the ancient way requires a witness from the land, and, well, you grew up on Mahon just like we did. So … you're our tribe."

Without further questioning, she followed the brothers down the beach. At a location they seemed to have prechosen, they knelt in the sand. Lance and Brody positioned themselves side by side as Grant knelt, facing them. Lance pulled an object from a sheath and handed it to Grant. Sarah watched with wide eyes as the full moon illuminated the white handle of a double-sided dagger.

With none of his customary goofiness, Lance said, "Grant, you are our brother. What kind of bravery do you choose to bind us with?"

"Lance, Brody," said Grant with matching intensity, "you are my brothers. I choose 'fist' as the form of bravery that will bind our spirits for eternity." Grant turned his hand upward and raised the sharp point of the blade. He made a tight fist and buried the tip of the dagger in the soft flesh that stretched between the thumb and forefinger.

Blood dripped from his hand. Lance took the knife.

"I also choose 'fist' as the form of bravery that will bind our spirits for eternity." Lance stabbed his fist in the same place. Brody took the knife, repeated the words, and cut his fist as his brothers had. With solemn deliberateness, they brought their palms together and clenched them in a three-way fist. They stood up in unison, still linked together by hand, and Sarah felt something move within her—a longing she could not explain.

"Brothers forever—in life and in death," Lance said. He pulled his brothers up into a group hug and noticed Sarah standing to the side. "Sarah, get over here," he said, and they made room for her in the huddle. Sarah felt part of something vital, as never before—she had a tribe.

As they walked back to the pup tents along the Atlantic, Sarah said to Grant, "You chose fist. What were your options?"

"Neck, thigh, and fist," Grant answered. "It comes from a rite of passage that was handed down in my family as a brother's ritual. We swore an oath to true bravery by choosing a wound of the fist."

"And the other two options?" Sarah asked, crawling through the triangular opening of the small tent.

Grant followed her and squeezed in, lying next to her. "The other two represent false bravery: seeking glory or avoiding shame because of pride."

"Copperhead," she mumbled.

"What?"

"Bring me the knife," Sarah said.

Appearing confused but going along without question, Grant tipped his head out of the tent and yelled, "Lance, Sarah wants the knife."

A few moments later, Lance dropped the double-sided bootstrap dagger outside their tent opening. As he walked away, he said with a grin in his voice, "Hope to see you in the morning, brother."

Sarah crawled to the front of the tent and grabbed the polished blade from the sand; it reflected bluish in the bright moonlight. She needed to be forever connected to Grant. Sitting in the tent opening, she made a fist and aimed the blade at the soft spot between her thumb and her forefinger. Grant intervened, placing his hand over hers. "No."

"Don't stop me," she said. "Blood is one of the few things I have to give."

"You don't have to do this," Grant said. "In fact, I don't want you to."

"In Cape May, you asked me what *I* wanted. Well, here's my answer. I want you"—she stared into the shadowy outline of his eyes—"to stop trying to save me."

Grant nodded slowly and released her hand. The knife tip effortlessly broke her skin. When blood dripped from the wound, Grant placed his bloody palm against hers and tightened his grip. She released the knife, which stabbed, point down, into the sand.

"We have a blood bond now," she said. "So tell me your secret."

"You already know it, thanks to Lance."

"Not that one. I don't care about that one. I mean the one you've been keeping from me all night. What happened at graduation?"

Grant hesitated for a few seconds and then spoke. "Eddie said he lost it because ..." He paused. "You got pregnant with his baby and had an abortion."

"What?" Sarah said, floored by the accusation.

"We didn't believe him but—"

"But what?"

Grant paused. "He seemed to know you … pretty intimately."

"How so?"

"He knew about your mother leaving. He said you sold a net to pay for the abortion." Grant appeared restless and uncomfortable with the topic but forged ahead, still gripping Sarah's hand. "Look, I know how hard you've had it in life. I'm not going to judge you. Whatever happened between you and Eddie, it doesn't matter—as long as it's over."

"What happened between me and Eddie was a year of playing DarkRealm together in study hall. That's all. We chatted sometimes, the four of us; he picked up some details about my life from that."

Sarah grimaced at the thought of doing the deed with Eddie and then burst out laughing.

"What's funny?" he asked.

"Have you ever seen Sketch without his army-green jacket? Because I haven't. I don't think it actually comes off." She laughed again. "Just speculating here—I don't have any firsthand knowledge—but isn't it kinda tricky to make a baby with all your clothes on?"

Grant smiled and then focused on their hands, still locked together in an oath of bravery. He said, "I hate to admit this, Sarah. But when Eddie said those things, I … well, I didn't exactly believe him, but I didn't exactly *not* believe him either. It was Lance who had your back, a hundred percent. He knew it wasn't true."

"Grant, who am I in the tent with?"

"Me."

"I'm only going to tell you this once, so listen carefully. I like Lance. I like his weird mix of self-absorbed humor and flair for the macabre—he makes me laugh. I get why the guys admire him and the girls swoon, but I don't love Lance that way. I don't have any romantic feelings for him at all, and I never will—not ever."

Grant pressed his forehead into Sarah's, closed his eyes and hugged her with his free arm.

"Do you understand, Grant? I don't easily love, but I do love you."

"You love me," he said as if letting the idea sink in for the first time. She nodded, and he pulled her to the blanket. "You love me," he stated again, as fact, and softly kissed her lips.

"For God's sake, yes."

"Sarah," he said but then could not marshal a single rational thought.

Outside their tent, the turbulent surf resculpted the sand. The wind whipped the sides of the tent, threatening to steal the fabric protecting their privacy, but Grant held on to it, ensuring he would win the Battle of the Wind.

Sitting in the triangular opening of the tent, they suspended their hands over the blade—the tool that bound them. Its oiled scrimshaw handle, she now saw, was carved with the same symbol she had stumbled upon in the forest between Port Mahon and Killington Beach: two concentric circles enclosed by a diamond shape split into two triangles. Now, as then, it marked the place where she ventured beyond the bindings of worldly consciousness.

They unlocked their hands—now free to explore and touch each other. Ignoring the blood, which was starting to dry, they put those free hands to work.

"That day I brought the rent to your house," Sarah said in response to his daring explorations, "you told me all you wanted to do was to apologize."

"Did I say that? What I meant to say was—all I wanted was to apologize—and undress you."

"Is that all?" she asked.

"Definitely not. Definitely not all."

"What else? Never mind. Why don't you just show me?"

CHAPTER TWENTY-FIVE

LIGHTHOUSE

Several versions of the Mahon River lighthouse had been built, but each had succumbed to the Delaware Bay's relentless tides, frigid winds, and merciless ice storms. The first lighthouse, built in 1831, was a guide for the Mahon River oystermen to safely return home. But the vengefulness of the sea wrecked it quickly; its plaster crumbled into Mahon's Ditch. The bay won the first round; the wind now skipped across the bald landscape whistling a sailor's tune.

But the land dwellers were stubborn and not easily deterred. On the same mud, they rebuilt the lighthouse and added eleven spherical reflectors in its lantern room—a prideful attempt to rival the sun. The bay heaved, slathered, and spat on man's atrocity. Within twenty years, the second lighthouse was leveled.

The industrious men dared to rebuild. They deflected the rain with gutters, and when the structure crumbled again, they finally retreated a quarter mile. The bay charged ahead, consuming the quarter mile of marsh, captured its prey, and destroyed the fourth lighthouse.

Another retreat, a quarter mile inland, north by northwest, and the fifth Mahon River lighthouse was constructed. This time the men prayed for the sea's mercy.

Mahon River lighthouse number five's foundation, sixteen screw-pile columns, was anchored over thirty feet deep in the soft marsh. The keepers and their families who lived there kept the lamp burning for those who wandered up the Delaware Bay in search of a new life or safety from the rough seas. The raging bay unleashed fury, but the defiant number five did not budge—much like the lightkeeper's wife who, after her husband died, insisted she could do the job, a role given only to men.

Sarah, who had spent her childhood wishing the bay would demolish the remains of the lighthouse, changed her mind after she promised to move to Indiana with Grant. It was now two months after graduation and two weeks before leaving. As Grant made plans to leave, she suddenly found herself unable to drive past the abandoned lighthouse without stopping for a social call. She ignored the building's squat ugliness and saw only its connection with her—the bay had lifted the lighthouse from the water, as Grant had lifted Sarah, saving it from death.

It's a romance, she thought.

From the rain-wet hood of Sarah's truck, she consoled lighthouse number five. "I can't leave you—you're stuck with me like your stilts buried in the mud."

Sarah had always carried on one-way conversations with the lighthouse, but lately, she thought she heard responses. Fully expecting the lighthouse to understand her words, she shared her latest news. "You should have seen him—he's so happy. A farm out there in Indiana, not far from the school, called him yesterday about a job."

Whenever she was in Grant's arms, she honestly wanted to leave Port Mahon Road, but when he went to work, she felt the emptiness in leaving. She changed her mind at least twice a day, like the tide. For two months she hid the truth, telling Grant she could not wait to leave the miserable road, and he built pilasters upon that foundation of mud.

"But I know I can't leave you behind," she told the lighthouse, "and I can't take you with me."

She heard the lighthouse's reply—it told her she should leave with Grant.

"But I'll miss you too much," she said.

Love is lonely, she thought. The more love she felt for Grant, the more she missed him when they were apart. The more love he gave her in return, the more she felt the connectedness to everything here—the Bay, the Road, the Wind, the Sun, and the Lighthouse; they were her extended family, and she did not want to leave them.

Grant found Sarah on the hood of her truck in front of the lighthouse. When she saw him, she groaned at the feeling of butterflies in her stomach that he unfailingly caused. He ran to the front of her truck, held out his arms, and asked, "How's my girl?"

Sarah, soaking wet, simply said, "The rain just stopped."

"There's a new invention—it's called an umbrella."

"I like the rain," she said, unmoved.

She slipped from the hood. He caught her fall and said, "Me too."

"You're early."

"Only got half done before the storm clouds showed up. I was going to keep flying, but your voice in my head said don't risk it. I had to see you. I have news." She was still preoccupied with the lighthouse behind him, but he didn't seem to notice or care. "I called the Indiana farm. The grain embargo on overseas exports is crushing them, but they need an ag pilot. They aren't offering much—a rent-free place to live and a small wage for extra fieldwork. I didn't think they'd agree to us living there unmarried, but they're 'over a barrel,' so they said okay."

Sarah continued to stare at the suffering lighthouse with no shutters or doors.

"Not excited about the news?" he asked. "Didn't you miss me?"

"Too much," she said, coming out of her fog. He hugged her.

"What's the matter?"

"I have news too," she said. "The Captain. He won't let me go anywhere without being married. He said you can come visit on holidays." What she was saying about the Captain was true, but it was also a handy excuse for not going to Indiana.

"If you stay, he will run your life. I know how you feel about marriage—a piece of paper designed to own you—but we don't have to be married to leave together." Sarah frowned, and he asked, "We are going, right?"

"Yes, we're going."

Grant raised his fist to the lighthouse and yelled, "Did you hear that? Sarah is leaving with me."

There was no reply.

Grant drove Sarah to their favorite hiding place, near the public boat ramp—a thin grassy "road" obscured by thick, tall reeds, out of view of the parking lot. They would often steal away there—out of sight from family members watching their every move—and just be together. Sometimes they would hold each other for hours—but usually kissing led to sweating and cracking the windows open.

He backed the truck into the dried golden seagrass that bent and covered the trail. He draped her still-wet body in a warm plaid blanket and pulled her close.

With the engine cut, the grass—objecting to their uninvited intrusion—tapped the truck with tiny electrostatic pulses. Grant searched under the blanket for bare skin. She helped him find some. The boy she had watched from across the field had turned into a man she was proud to love.

"When you're flying alone, what do you think about?" she asked, pointing to the sky.

"All the places we'll go," he said, lifting her chin. "What do you think about when you're alone?"

"How what little time I have is slipping through my fingers."

"But you'll always have me," he said.

Sarah heard the voice of Max from deep within her say, *Not always and definitely not forever.* "I'm not so sure about that."

"What do you mean? Is something on your mind, Sarah? Whatever it is, you can tell me."

Sarah broke down crying before she had the courage to tell him the truth. Grant held his hand out for her, but she pulled away from him and leaned against the passenger door, facing him from a distance.

"I'm not going," she said. The truth uncorked.

Grant smiled, which Sarah found an odd response. "I knew you would say that," he explained. "It's scary to leave, but this will always be home, and we'll be back."

"I know I promised to go, but I can't. I didn't want to say anything until I was certain."

Grant continued to smile but a bit sadly. He shrugged and said, "I thought you might say that too. It's settled, then—we're staying."

"Grant, no, you're going. Without me. You're meant to be a pilot, not a farmer. I won't let you give it up for me."

"I'm not going without you."

Sarah pressed herself against the door, afraid if he so much as touched her, she would give in to him. "When you followed me home that day," she said, "you wanted to apologize, but I could not forgive you. You've spent two months proving you're a good man. But all this time, even though I loved you, I still thought you deserved the torment. My mother never offered a path for absolution, so why should I give one to you? But I was wrong."

"Sarah, no. Don't do this," he implored.

Sarah continued to make her case. "I love you. I do. That's why I can let you go—because you'll have a better, happier life without me. You and I both know I belong here."

"There's nothing for you here," he objected.

"You saved my life that first day. I'm sorry it took this long to forgive you. The burden you feel you took on—leave it here. Go. Fulfill yourself. I want what's best for you."

"Name one thing so important to you here that you cannot leave it behind."

The answer came easily. "I know this sounds ridiculous, but I cannot leave the lighthouse behind."

"You'd rather stay here for a broken-down lighthouse than be with me? I'm taking you to the hospital to see if you've really healed from that concussion."

"That sounds like the bully you've tried hard to overcome. But he's still in there, isn't he? The bully?" She took a deep breath and continued, "I know you love me, but there's another part of you that wants to possess me—and that's not love. If I truly wanted to be with you, don't you think I'd be finding it easier to leave an old lighthouse on a dead-end street and a controlling father?"

"Oh, come on, you're just scared. So am I; I'll admit it. Change is scary."

"I'm not afraid of change. I'm not even afraid of death—as you well know. But I am afraid of you. You want to own me like my father."

"Afraid of me?" Grant fired back in shock. "Are you aware that all you ever give me are impossible choices? And this is the best one yet. You want me to 'let you go' to prove myself. By that logic, your mother has really proven her love—by not visiting you for a decade. I want to marry you because I love you, not because I want to own you."

Grant turned the ignition key as if preparing to move on, literally and figuratively. "But forget all that," he said. "I have one question before you ruin our relationship over a lighthouse. You made a promise to the man in your dream, Max, right? You said you would take love from me and bring it back to him. Am I right?" Seeing her confused expression, he explained, "You really do talk a lot in your sleep. All I want to know is—are you breaking your promise with me to keep a promise to him?"

"He's not real," she insisted.

"Oh, I think we both know he's real to you."

"What if he is real? And what if I am keeping … do you think you own me because you saved my life?"

Grant paused and winced. "You lied to me this whole time? You said you loved me."

Knowing she was saying this for his own good—but not thinking about the consequences—she forced the words out: "I can't lie to you anymore. I don't love you."

Grant looked at her, stunned. "Every time I show you how much I care, you hurt me."

Instantly hating herself for lying, she screamed, "Stop caring, then. Because it's over." She slammed the door and ran, unable to escape herself.

Grant rested his burning red face in his palms, unwilling to chase her. Her words had paralyzed him, and he waited for hope to return.

When it finally did, he drove to the dark lighthouse to find her truck gone. *She chose the ghost instead of me*, he thought.

Grant skidded to a stop in front of the lighthouse. He got out of the truck and stood throwing rocks at the old building from shore. "Damn you! You're nothing but a beacon for dead ends and broken dreams."

Sarah immediately regretted the decision to break up with Grant but knew it was the right thing to do, the *only* thing to do. And now she lay in bed, living with the misery of her decision. She crawled under the blanket to bury herself, covering her face with the pillow and bending its ends over her ears. But she could not drown out the voices from her past …

"Mommy, can I stay with you?" the young Sarah asked her mother, Rebecca, on the phone. The Captain stood over her.

"Is your father there?" her mother asked. "Are you all right?"

"Mommy, come home. I don't want to stay here anymore. I'm scared."

"What happened? What's wrong? Did he hurt you?" Rebecca asked.

The young girl looked up at her father with his menacing black eyes and could not answer.

Rebecca said softly, "Listen, Sarah—I'll come get you tomorrow when he's out fishing. You need to miss the bus to school."

"No, Mommy, come get me now, please," Sarah cried.

Click, and a dial tone.

The Captain snatched the receiver from her hand, grabbed her tiny shoulders, and said, "What did she say?"

Sarah looked him in the eyes, mustering a warrior's strength from within, and said, "She's coming tomorrow to take me away forever. I hate it here, and I'm never coming back."

The Captain slapped the defiance off her face and knocked her thin frame to the kitchen floor. "The hell she is! She will never leave here—ever—with anything that's mine. I dare her to come back here and try. It'll be the last thing she ever does."

And her mother never showed. She hadn't heard from her since.

The memory replayed in her mind until she fell asleep, and then it continued.

That night, in her dream, a young Sarah noticed Max hiding in the shadows under a table. As she bent to get a better look at him, he disappeared. The dreamworld quaked, and she felt the imbalance.

She wandered, as a child, looking for Max.

Sarah slowly approached a corner of a building, sensing he was waiting on the other side. She backed away, and he stepped out of hiding, towering over her. Bending down, he said softly into her ear, "Orphan, you will keep your promise. No excuses. Life is not easy for anyone."

Grant ached from the wounds Sarah had inflicted. Everything he'd planned for, trashed. Hours earlier, he was the happiest he'd ever been, and now he felt lost. In his mind he replayed, over and over, fantasies that refused to die. His unrealistic hopes were now his torture. He banged his fist on the wall next to his bed and rolled over, unable to sleep. His thoughts burned for her, but now the red flames of her hair brought intolerable pain.

A bitterness born of deep betrayal mounted in his gut. His mind flipped, at intervals, between intense love for her and intense hatred. The two sides of him battled in a sleepless war. As much as he knew he loved her, he also wanted her to share in his misery. A curdled liquid death formed within him and circulated in his blood.

He opened his bedroom window and left to go wherever his feet would carry him, feeling a need to walk off the resentment and hate.

"All journeys must end," said Max, next to her in bed. "Besides, your spirit is too irresistible to wait any longer." An eastern king snake weaved back and forth, slowly climbing the rungs of the ladder to Sarah's room. Its glossy black scales dulled as it reached for Sarah from the window ledge. It silently slid and dipped under her pillow, poking its head out from among her curls. The feel of a gentle, cool, gliding sensation pleased the skin of her neck, and the touch brought a dream—more vivid than a memory …

A little girl with freckles and light-brown hair ran to Sarah, and Sarah picked the girl up and put her on a merry-go-round. The child giggled with delight, holding the metal handles and battling centrifugal force. "Mommy, make it go faster!" she screamed.

Dream-Sarah pushed the carousel for a couple more turns and then stepped away. Unhappy with the slowing effects of friction, the girl complained, and Sarah smiled. Before the ride fully stopped, the little girl jumped off and ran for the swings. She chose the lowest-hanging one, next to an older boy who was testing the limits of the rusty chains. Grant sat nearby at a picnic table, and Sarah waved to him.

Max sucked in a deep breath and exhaled at the intrusion of Grant. The snake heaved, its grip tightened, and another coil wrapped around Sarah's neck. Max said, "I promise I will make it painless this time." The snake slowly applied constriction.

A kiss on her ear was followed by the whisper of her name, and she awoke.

Her eyes shot open, and she found knees pressed into her chest, hands wrapped tightly around her neck. Gasping for breath, she struggled to get away. No luck. She threw her fists at the attacker and fought for her life. A new strength of spirit possessed her—a desire to live. Her body and spirit joined forces as never before to fend off the would-be murderer. The bed slammed against the wall. She scratched at his face, and he yelled, "I love you!"

Sarah managed to lift him. His sweaty fingers lost their grip on her neck. He tried to surge forward, but she held her arms outstretched, locking her elbows and keeping his hands away. His fingers curled and groped, inches from her neck.

The door crashed open, and he turned to look. A brief silence ensued, and then the deafening boom of gunfire. Hot blood and tissue sprayed into Sarah's eyes. The man's head—what was left of it—lolled on his shoulders, and his limp body slumped onto her mattress.

An electric switch clicked, and blinding light stung her wet face. The walls of her room, she saw, were painted in a bright explosion of red. The Captain held a .45 caliber revolver. He dropped the gun and ran to his daughter. He pulled the male body off the bed, and it slid to the floor.

Sarah screamed and jumped from the bloody bed toward the doorway. "You killed him!" she shouted. "You killed Grant!" She rubbed her eyes, smearing the slimy matter into her skin.

The Captain ran from the room and returned with towels. As he helped her wipe her face, he said, "That's not Grant. I don't know who it is."

Sarah's heart felt a rush of relief as her mind felt the grip of terror. If it was not Grant who had died in her bed, there was only one other man it could have been.

But that was not possible. Max wasn't part of this world.

Twin sirens howled, waking the sleepy town's volunteer firemen: one at the firehouse in Slaughter Creek and one close to Sarah's house. She continued to wipe the blood off—pretending it was fish blood to maintain her sanity—as a siren blared down Port Mahon Road. The Captain grimaced at the body and said, "No need for an ambulance." But the siren blew past the house, headed for the docks. A moment later, another siren went by. The Captain turned the lights off, looked out the window, and said, "The lighthouse is on fire."

Sarah stood up and bore witness to the final dawn of the lighthouse, its red blaze and black smoke rising to the sky like a signal for help. Within a few minutes, there was nothing left to see; Mahon River lighthouse number five's ashes ascended to heaven.

Sarah looked away, feeling a part of herself die, and moaned, "Not her. Not her."

CHAPTER TWENTY-SIX

DEATH

The Delaware State Police brought more lights and sirens to Port Mahon Road, trying to sort out the tangled mess of events that had happened on the same night. Outside her house, in the driveway, Sarah pushed away medics and refused to be taken to the hospital. She was haunted by flashes of waking up breathless at the hands of two different men: Grant and Max. She thought she saw each of them strangle her in his own way.

But the dead perpetrator turned out to be neither one.

"He parked his car at the old schoolhouse on the corner," the officer told Sarah. "Do you know him?"

"He attacked me at school a couple of months ago. His name is—was—Eddie Kasik."

She was unable to feel anything whatsoever for Eddie's fate. Eddie no longer had a face—the Captain's gun had taken care of that—and she hadn't recognized him without his jacket and gel-spiked hair. She was thankful the sun had not been shining in the room; the shadows spared her a terrible memory. The last thing she remembered, clearly, was Grant being there. The Captain had to reassure her many times before the police arrived that he did not shoot Grant, but she had difficulty ignoring what she knew was true.

"Do you know anything about the lighthouse fire?" the officer asked her.

"I was asleep; then I was busy being strangled," she replied, annoyed by the question.

"I understand that, but do you know anyone around here who may have wanted to set it on fire? One of the local kids, maybe?"

Sarah shrugged.

Heavy boots echoed on the uninsulated wooden floor. A man with a camera took photographs of the northeast bedroom of the single-story rental home as detectives with flashlights walked the perimeter to investigate the scene. The Captain made a pot of coffee, and a conversation convened among the brotherhood of men at the kitchen table.

"I received a letter from the state about a mediation," the Captain told the other men. "It was coming up next week. Stupid kid put her in the hospital a couple of months back. They let him out like nothing happened." The Captain's hands gestured passionately as he spoke. The three officers in the room—two from the state police along with the local town cop, Officer Smithie—shook their heads in disgust at the failed court system.

Officer Ward, the ranking Delaware State Police officer, said, "We contacted them, Rex. The city police did their part, but the district attorney didn't pursue criminal charges. The kid's lawyer convinced the DA it was a momentary lapse in judgment, an isolated incident caused by a breakup, and the judge agreed to supervised mental health treatment instead."

"Looks like you can skip the mediation," Officer Smithie said, and the other officers chuckled darkly under their breath. "We think the kid might have been stalking her. That car parked at the old schoolhouse? It belonged to his dad. It's been there, off and on, for months, but we checked it out, and nothing came up. No reason to be suspicious. We just found the kid's backpack, stashed in some bushes, near a campfire site out back that was probably his."

"It's a shame," said Rex. "I opened the door and saw she was struggling to get away from him. He was trying to kill my daughter. I didn't know who it was. When you see something like that—I don't know—you just react."

"You did the right thing, Rex," Officer Ward replied. "Any of us would have done the same thing."

One of the detectives came in holding a flashlight and asked the Captain to go outside to look at something he had found.

"He came in through her window this way," the Detective said, lighting the steps of the ladder, hidden by the leaves of the mimosa tree. "Is this your ladder?" he asked.

The Captain froze at the sight of the old ladder and said, "Uh, yes—it's mine. He must have found it and put it there."

Sarah found her father and said, "Tell them I don't have to go to the hospital. I'm fine." The illuminated steps leading to her window distracted her plea; she knew who had put the ladder there. The gift of the tree had been a Trojan horse, hiding an ulterior motive.

"Let them check you out, sweetheart," the Captain said, rushing her away from the area.

"I don't want to leave, Daddy."

"Is there any way she can skip the hospital?" the Captain asked Officer Ward. "She's been through enough, hasn't she?"

"I don't see any reason why not," Ward replied. "We've got the man who attacked her—and I use the term 'man' loosely. We'll document her injuries here. The court didn't bother to issue a protective order, so why should we force her to go to the hospital if she doesn't want to go?"

"Slow down. What's your name?" an officer said, stopping the young man running up the driveway.

"I'm Grant Eriksen. I live next door."

"We have an investigation going on here. You'll have to come back later."

"Is she all right?" Grant asked. His eyes were puffy, his face red from running.

"She's going to be fine," said the officer. "Hey, listen. We're also investigating the lighthouse fire. It looks like it may have been arson. Did you see anyone walking or driving on this road before sunrise?"

"No, sir. We were all sleeping when the sirens went off."

"Rex, we're not arresting you," Officer Ward told the Captain, "but we have to take you to the station to fill out paperwork and get your formal statement. We'll also need to take the gun as evidence. It will be released back to you after the case is closed."

"But he came into my house and tried to kill my daughter," Rex objected.

"It's just a formality. You know you're protected under the castle doctrine, but we need to file the paperwork. I'm sure you'll be free to go about your life by later today or tomorrow morning."

"Damn kid. I'm going to miss a day's work." His cavalier comment about Eddie's death raised the eyebrows of a couple of the officers.

As they escorted the Captain to a trooper's car, Sarah ran up to hug him.

"I'll be fine, Sarah," Rex said. "Home before dinnertime. Stay with Viktor and Clare until I get back."

The coroner took the body, and then the police cars thinned out. On the back porch, Sarah sat on the top step with her arms folded. "Are you going to be all right staying here by yourself?" the last officer inquired as he was about to leave.

"I've got neighbors," she said.

"Right. That guy Grant came by asking about you."

"He lives right there," she said, pointing to the house across the cornfield.

"Do you want a ride over there?" he asked. She shook her head. The thought occurred to her that he might actually be flirting. At a time like this. She looked away to avoid eye contact.

"No thanks," she said.

"You just went through a pretty traumatic experience."

"Please. Just leave," she said, having grown weary of all men—including the ones who appeared nice and helpful.

A minute after everyone had left, Grant approached from where he had been waiting in the cornfield, a few rows back.

"Are you all right?" he asked.

"He's dead. Eddie's dead," she answered. "I hate him, but I didn't want him dead." She lifted her hand to stop Grant's advance. A voice inside reminded her of all the horrible things she had said at the Pit.

"I'm sorry you had to go through that," he said.

"Do you know how he got into my room, Grant? I'll tell you how—a ladder. Any idea how that got there?"

Grant's skin paled, and his breath grew shallow. Under the weight of the implication, he put his hands together to pray for forgiveness and said, "You're right. I put the ladder there a long time ago. It was stupid for me to leave it there. I wasn't thinking."

"What were you doing all this time? Stalking me in the middle of the night? Watching me sleep? Spying on my dreams? Is that how you know so much about Max?" She stared at him in stark accusation, revulsion curling her lips.

"I know how it looks, but I used it once—I swear. I tried to wake you but gave up and left."

"Why don't you do that now?" she said. "Leave."

"After what happened, I don't want you to be alone."

"I said it yesterday, and I'm saying it now. I want you to leave for college. Alone. I don't love you." Tears streaked her face, sparkling incongruously in the new morning sun.

"But you said you did, and I believed you," he said.

Sarah walked to her back door, opened it, and said, "I meant it when I said it. At least I think I did. But now, I hate you." Her piercing stare showed him her disdain. "I know it was you who burned down the lighthouse. Why did you save me from being swept out to sea, only to burn me down to the ground? I can't even look at you anymore."

"I didn't burn down the lighthouse," he said.

"It wasn't Eddie—he was busy trying to kill me! Only you knew what it meant to me. And you hated it for that. How could you destroy what little I have left?"

"I promise you, Sarah. I didn't do it. I'm begging you to believe me." She retreated, closed the door behind her, and locked it with a firm decision never to speak to him again.

He pounded on the door, on the porch he had never fixed, and said, "Please, Sarah. Don't do this to me. Please …"

Sarah sat at the kitchen table, alone. The energy of her spirit was strong, and it reached for Max, saying, "I'm ready to leave and keep my promise." She knew she would never escape death anyway. Max was the victor against his weak, flesh-bearing mortal competitor.

"It won't be long now, my love," she heard Max tell her. A northeasterly wind blew across the sea in his world, traversed time, rose from the Delaware Bay, and touched Sarah's cheek, drying her eyes. A peacefulness lifted her mood, and her worries departed on the winged Spirit of the Wind. She was spared the pain of the loss of the brief love she'd had for Grant.

"Don't leave me, Sarah," Grant said aloud, walking, lost and alone, in the tall corn. The shrieking pain of Grant's spirit vibrated through the land. To save himself, he needed to escape the ground and find the only solace he knew. He ran to his truck and drove it away so fast the dust appeared to be a menacing storm following him.

Grant's innocence was lost—the life he dreamed of had evaporated. His fear of the ground was greater than his fear of the air, and all he wanted to do was fly away and leave his home, the place inhabited by everything that tortured him, especially inescapable Sarah.

Without thinking—on autopilot, so to speak—he arrived at Eriksen Farm and stopped at the barn doors. He passed Lance's truck on the way to the outbuildings but didn't see him.

After fueling up, Grant sat in the cockpit, struggling to concentrate on checklists he knew by heart. The radio call for clearance confirmed that the southerly direction was all blue sky. Dark rain clouds formed to the north, mirroring the dark clouds in his heart, but he was in search of the sun. Taking off into the wind heading north, he saw his family's farmland pass below, and then he turned southeast—away from the storm—for a trip down the coast, as far from the memory of Sarah as he could fly.

Grant's thoughts betrayed him. A magnetic connection with Sarah called to him. He imagined her beside him, her lively red hair with its white-satin ribbon fluttering across her bare, pale-white shoulder. He wanted her and refused to let her go. The fear of losing her forced him to turn around.

Sarah left the suffocating house of bad dreams and grisly memories; she couldn't bear to stay there any longer. She walked around the outside of the house and leaned on Georgia, the mimosa tree outside her window. The ladder was unmoved, and the window was still open.

She sat on the wet ground against the tree Grant had planted for her and looked up through the fernlike leaves and pink blooms. The life she imagined was empty without him. All the elements were still there, but putting them together now seemed elusive.

She resented him for having inserted himself in her life and becoming indispensable to her. *But that's what men do*, she thought. Her life right now was completely defined by male-dominated, possessive behavior. Yet she could not deny they all loved her in their own way. Her spirit did not care what kind of love they unsheathed—to the spirit, all love was energy, and so it was up to her to decide what love she wanted her spirit to feed upon.

It was *her* decision. Hers.

The Captain's fatherly, controlling love was like the men who'd arrived by ship and wanted to own the land—as if anyone could truly own the earth. She could no longer be the land her father dominated. As she stared up into the open window, her body decided for her spirit: free yourself, and never return to that room.

Eddie Kasik, the man who sought revenge against another man out of envy, wanted to be the one to decide her fate—but Eddie did not realize how many other men wanted to control her life—and her death. Eddie was picked off by a more ruthless version of himself. He had proven no match for the Captain, who knew blood sport as a way of life and who protected his limited possessions without mercy.

Max had taught her, in death, a sobering truth—that life is the last opportunity to fortify one's weapons for an infinite journey. To believe she could commit suicide to escape a difficult life felt silly now, knowing the truth: self-destruction only weakened the spirit. And a weak spirit entering the realm of the afterlife was gobbled up as ferociously as prey by a predator.

Max, in his own way, loved her too. She could feel that love circulating inside her. It was familiar, and it moved under her skin. He was a mentor, a healer, and a friend, but his motivation was selfish. She was his spirit possession.

But a decision to walk away from Max was impossible—she was forever tied to him.

Thoughts of Lance, another dominant male, came to her out of nowhere. Why was she thinking of him—the oversized, overconfident bully of her childhood, who as a man led everyone around him down a natural path to strengthen their spirits? All his actions, however ridiculous, felt purposeful in retrospect. His thoughts were a stream of joyous energy. At that moment she felt strangely connected to him, as if their spirits were communicating as they'd never done before. His spirit asked her to take care of his brother on his journey to college. The loving older brother was worried for his young brother, leaving the safe harbor of home and going to places where he could not protect him.

Grant. Back to him again. Grant loved her, but his love, too, was tainted with hints of control and obsession. Was that the most important thing, though? No. What mattered more was that she wanted to be with him. That was the choice her heart and spirit were making. That choice was not controlled by anyone. She felt, for the first time, that her purpose was to be strong for him, like family. She suddenly felt horrible for the way she had treated him. Ever since the day of his awkward apology, he had been nothing but kind and patient, despite all her mistakes and miscues.

She realized something else for the first time: that the flow of energy that alternately drained and filled her spirit was entirely dependent on how *she* felt; it was independent of what others said or did. She had always thought that life's energy was absorbed from others, but now she understood—it was the love within her that either filled or vacated her spirit. She was at the helm.

Love was something you radiated from within, not something you looked for out there.

Leaving a ladder under her window had been reckless, no doubt—but how could Grant have known what Eddie would do?

A lightning flash lit the sky—and then an explosion. From within, Sarah felt a violent shaking. She turned to the road and saw a plane caught in the power lines leading to the fuel storage tankers. The heavy engine and propeller dangled diagonally, suspended and trapped by the landing gear holding the plane above the ground.

The plane's cowling smoked. Sarah ran toward the plane, and then she saw the bright-orange flames burst from the engine. Smoke and fire engulfed the cockpit.

Sarah dropped to her knees in the freshly cut front yard. She heard the screams from the Eriksen driveway.

Crack! The tail of the plane broke off and fell into the roadside ditch, and the rest of the plane sprang upward slightly on the wires.

The flames were gone within minutes, but the black smoke continued.

Sirens blared for the second time. The volunteer firemen, already exhausted from the lighthouse fire, redonned their still-wet gear and piled into the fire truck. These were local boys who'd braved the Pit and were loyal to the Eriksen brothers—now they were being called to witness the destruction of one of their own. By the time the fire truck arrived on the scene, rescue was no longer an option; it was a recovery operation at best. The men helplessly watched as their friend's ashes fell to the ground with the rain.

When the siren finally stopped, the remains of the plane crashed to the ground. Sarah screamed, repeating, "No. No. No." She remembered the last words she had said to him, and she turned away, unable to absorb any more of the horror.

She stumbled through the rain to her father's gold pickup, drunk with grief, and lifted the door handle. Opening the door, she felt gutted, as if her entrails were unraveling to the ground. She climbed into the truck, shaking uncontrollably as her spirit bled out.

From her mailbox, Sarah could see that the fire truck was blocking the road to town, but Sarah had no intention of going in that direction. She did not want to go near the black wreckage heaped on the ground, smelling of burnt fuel and plastic. She saw Brody, his hands on his head, screaming in disbelief, unable to save his brother.

Her epiphany about her life's purpose had been rendered instantly obsolete. Without a reason to live any longer, she vowed to take the love and memories of Grant to the afterlife.

Sarah turned east without anyone noticing. The last thing she saw was Clare, her hands over her mouth, bent over in pain. She knew her own mother would not have the same reaction to her end. In the rearview mirror, the pink mimosa tree, receding in the distance, drank the ashes diluted with rain.

As Sarah drove slowly down the road that had paved her life's path, she carefully cataloged the memories of Grant, knowing there would be no more. "This is my fault, Grant," she muttered. "I'm so sorry."

She was unprepared to confront the burnt remains of the lighthouse. The structure still stood but was without a face. Her feet were numb as she tripped out of the truck, unable to find her footing. The iron pylons rose from the marshland without purpose. Sarah splashed through a foot of seawater and silt to hug the pillars. Blackened debris bobbed around her ankles.

"I'm going to miss you, old girl," Sarah said. "Where I'm going, you can't come with me, but the bay will keep you company. I won't forget you. I promise." The pillars dripped in silence. No reply. The truck—with its door still wide open—invited her back inside to take shelter from the rain, but Sarah stumbled past the truck, making her way to the Shucking House.

The Shucking House was mile marker zero: the place of endings and last chances. She was reminded of the night of the last big storm, but she knew Grant would not intervene this time. As she plodded along, events replayed themselves in her mind's eye, allowing her to witness how horribly she had treated him. She relived every missed opportunity to leave with him, to say yes instead of no, to love. Each time she had assumed there would be another chance, never considering the possibility that her chances would run out so soon.

Sarah passed the place where they had hugged after he saved her life and said, "You knew the right moment to leave home to rescue me, but I waited too long to save you." She sat beside the memory of him until the air, too thin to hold his image, released him, and he disappeared. She visited the place where she had landed on the dock after he pulled her to safety. She remembered him hovering over her, saying her name.

As daylight departed, a black storm spun from the sea, echoing the storm of that previous night. Fierce waves slapped the dock, breaking over her body, drenching her as before. A mist lifted from the sea's surface. Max was coming for her.

"You win," Sarah said softly, lying down on the wet planks and waiting for Max to steal her soul. The loneliness, the loss of Grant, was more than grief. It was soul pain. Each memory of him, encapsulated by a tear, fell to the sea. It felt sacrificial. She pressed her eyes shut to think of something—anything—to keep his memory from leaving her.

The familiar cool mist, emanating from Max, touched her cheek. "Open your eyes," Max said. She turned away from him and wanted it to be over. Nothing happened.

"What are you waiting for?" she asked. She heard the thunder but no words from Max. She turned and saw that he was now floating in a wave out in the water. He smiled and gestured for her to join him. Sarah reached out for him, but he was too far away.

Tired of his games, she yelled, "Max, take my hand. I want to leave."

"Free yourself," he said. "Don't look to me to do it." She stepped to the edge of the dock but moved no farther.

"Not brave enough to jump?" he asked.

"I've done it before. I can do it again."

"Go ahead, then."

"Take me like before," she begged. Max raised one palm into the air, and her body lifted. The dock seemed to lift into the air along with her, and she felt the power of gravity's pull, unwilling to let her go. A sudden stop caused her to lose her footing, and her feet dropped off the dock's edge. Below the planks, she caught hold of the slippery, barnacle-laden wooden ladder.

She managed to anchor her feet on the bottom rung, and the ladder gently swung—under the planks and then back out again. Rusty nails in the deck above groaned as she balanced and lifted her foot to the next step. The water rose below her, devouring the exposed wooden posts, pressing her to climb higher. The old ladder creaked and wobbled as she reached the top—then it broke off and fell away as she landed facedown on the deck.

She grabbed onto a deck board and straddled the horizontal wall of planks. Beneath her, the monstrous, thrashing waves peaked, pounding the wood under her belly and rocking her. Turning her head to the side, she saw Max's bare feet. He was sitting next to her on the deck.

The sea dropped to a safer level and paused as if waiting for her decision. Max sighed. "This is the ledge between two worlds—life and death. Which do you choose, Orphan?"

"I can't," was all she could think to say, unable to make a choice.

"You fear life. You fear death. Here we sit."

She reached for him, and he stood; he would not take the hand she offered. "Tell me—do you have anything left to live for?" he asked.

Sarah quickly replied, "No."

"Let's go, then," he said and dove from the dock, but she did not follow. She spotted him in the water, just below the surface. A tall wave rolled toward her and lifted him out of the water again.

Max emerged from the water—changed—and stepped back onto the boards. His long, dark, wet hair dripped, and his eyes glowed an electrified Caribbean blue. He appeared to have aged, and his face bore a coarse, full beard. He was less muscular but somehow more perfect than before. Mesmerizing. The salt water on his skin quickly dried, turning to vapor like water poured over smoldering rock. His skin was a granite-whitish gray, like polished solid stone, with a bluish glow and silver veins. Now showing himself more honestly, he stood over her and said in a voice that sounded amplified, "Are you sure you don't have anything else to live for, Orphan?"

"I lost what I had to live for."

"But you'll always have me," he said, echoing Grant's words from the day before, and he held out his dripping hand. With difficulty, she resisted the temptation of his offer. She fought her muscles in order to remain still.

Sarah searched her chaotic mind for a reason to live, but she could think of nothing. He leaned in close and bathed her face with his warmth. His beard grazed her neck. The storm muted, and he turned his ear to her chest and listened. Sarah's heart raced, filling the void with its pounding. Max grinned at her natural, impulsive reaction to his full attention and then said, "Everyone has someone to live for."

"What do you mean?" she asked.

He would not tell her.

"Sarah, if you want to decide whether to live or not, you must stop looking for reasons outside yourself. Your spirit has a voice. What does it say? Shh. Quiet your mind."

She closed her eyes, held her breath, and felt a warm vibration welling up from within her.

The vibration was making a sound, a soft electrical hum, a faint ringing—but not in her ears; rather, it was in the very nerves and cells of her body. "It sounds like—I don't know—like *ah-um*," she said. Max nodded and placed his smooth finger gently on her lips.

There was a faint, almost imperceptible rush of static, and she thought he heard the words from deep within: "Don't be afraid." She looked to Max for confirmation that she wasn't imagining things, and then the words came again, more clearly this time: "Don't be afraid—to love yourself." He nodded in silent agreement.

"Can you forgive me for breaking my promise?" she said.

He did not respond verbally, but a white feather magically appeared in his hand, and he gave it to her. It looked just like the one attached to the carved, snake-shaped pipe Max had lit on the night he gave her back her life. "This belongs to you for choosing the path of bravery—to stand and fight for your life instead of retreating and escaping. You can't journey into dangerous and difficult woods without love—for yourself."

Sarah took the grayish-white feather with gold-buff bands and twirled it with her fingers. She brought its soft hairlike tip to her chin. It tickled.

Max said, "This feather contains part of your mother's spirit. She told me that when I found you, she wanted you to have it."

"My mother? But she's not dead," Sarah said, confused.

"I'm afraid she is, Orphan. She died some years ago, by your world's reckoning. When you were a child."

"What? Tell me that isn't true."

"It is true. But remember, death of the body is not also death of the spirit. I assure you—her spirit is alive." Sarah knew by his face that he was hiding something.

"How did she die?" Sarah asked, struggling to find peace amid all the horrible news she would now have to live with.

Max shrugged and said, "I can't say, but every thought she has is of saving you."

"You did all this to save me?" Sarah asked.

"Not exactly," Max said as she felt the tug of energy leaving her. The storm had subsided, and Max stood. He reached out to help her up, saw the wound on her hand, and asked, "What's this?"

"Your story—it's been passed down through history all the way to my time. Grant and his brothers—and I—took the oath to be truly brave."

Max leaned in to study her hand. He smirked—exactly like the boys did after pranking her at the haunted house. He let go of her and said, "One of my favorite earth-dweller stories. Copperheads are my favorite."

Sarah frowned and asked, "What's going to happen to Grant?"

Max said with a hint of disdain, "Yes, you're connected in spirit, but you are not strong enough to protect him."

"Protect him from you." When he turned away, she said, "This is not over. Is it?"

Max turned away, looking into the distance, where the remains of the lighthouse lay, and said, "Your lighthouse—it still stands. In my world, not yours. The moment you left to return here, it appeared there. I don't know why. It's a man-made monstrosity. So I tried to destroy it with lightning—twice. Each time, it fell into the sea, but when I woke up—there it was again. I was sure destroying it here would work."

"It was you who burned the lighthouse?" *Not Grant.*

"But there it sits in my world—useless and ugly. All day and all night—it shines and blocks my view of the sun."

Sarah smiled an inner smile, thinking about the lighthouse glowing endlessly in Max's world, containing a part of her spirit. In a way, she had never left his world. So in a way, the deal she'd made with Max was null and void.

A fog began to form behind Max, and he slowly stepped back into it. Her desire for him, still alive in her body, if not her mind, welled up one last time.

"Max, I thought you were going to at least try to take me back to your world." She taunted him, figuring he would have done so already if that was his intention.

Max stepped forward, grabbed her, and said with a tight, powerful squeeze, "Don't tempt me—I want to."

He lifted and swirled her as a dense fog formed around her and said in her ear, "Like you said … I can steal you back anytime, and it will be like you never left." As he put her down, he said, "But not both of you at once." Then he added, darkly, "And no, he cannot come with you." When her toes touched the dock, Max was gone, and the fog thinned.

His final words illuminated the path—her life's purpose. She needed to learn to collect powerful spirit energy like Max. The eternal life of her spirit, and Grant's, depended on it.

CHAPTER TWENTY-SEVEN

AFTERLIFE

Sarah shut the door on the darkness of the Shucking House and refused to look back. She decided she would keep every promise, no matter how difficult, and her first would be a monumental task. *Grant, I promise you—I will become strong enough to find your spirit and protect you from Max.* Through a lingering haze, she returned to her truck, the door still wide open. As she was about to climb in, she noticed something odd: Grant's truck, parked beside hers in the shadowy fog.

She ran to look inside, but no one was there—it was empty and cold. Who had driven it here? A brief hope that she had imagined the airplane crash faded as she entered her own truck and closed the door. She cranked the ignition, and the headlights flickered. The battery—drained from having left the door open—was unable to start the engine. She tried it again. The ignition made a clicking sound, and the dim headlights briefly illuminated a man standing in the tide, in the fog, in front of the collapsed lighthouse.

She bounded over stones and glass to reach him. She paused at the edge of the shore and looked out at his familiar silhouette, wandering in the water. Grant.

She called out, "You're alive. How?"

He turned, looking as shocked as she was, and stumbled from the mud toward her. When she saw his face up close, she was afraid to touch him. She thought he might be a figment of her imagination—a mirage. Or a ghost.

She pulled in a breath when he grabbed her hand. He was freezing cold. "You're soaked," she said. His body shivered as he hugged her warmth.

"I thought I had lost both of you," Grant said without loosening his hold.

"I don't understand," Sarah replied.

"You and Lance. I saw your truck with the door open, and I knew I had lost you to the sea." He took a breath to tell her more, but no words came out.

Sarah understood, at that moment, it had been Lance flying the plane. She envisioned life without him and closed her eyes to hold back the rush of hot tears.

"It's my fault," he said at last. "I was supposed to finish the north field this morning because I quit early yesterday, remember? When we heard the news about you, Lance probably worried I would be tempted to finish the job. He knew I'd be in no condition to fly, so he took the duster plane. Why didn't he tell me? If he had just said something, anything, I would have stopped him. And then the storm blew in, out of nowhere. Dover Tower reported wind shear, but it was too late …"

"It not your fault," Sarah said. She pulled him from the mud, and he leaned on her all the way to the truck. He opened her truck door, and she got in the driver's seat.

"I thought you … left without me," he said. "I figured I was too late this time. After the crash, I wished you had taken me with you. It was so hard not to dive in after you. But as much as I was tempted to die with you, I could not do that to my family. Or to myself."

"I'm here for you now. You'll always have me."

"All I wanted, Sarah, was for you to love me back. But I understand if you don't. Really—"

"I do love you." She cut him off. "I admit it—I was scared. But I'm not anymore. I'm sorry. I didn't mean to put you through so much pain. I thought you would be better off without me, but I don't think that anymore. When you're ready to leave, I'm going with you."

"I can't leave now. I have to be with my family. In fact, they're probably worried sick about me right this minute."

"I understand," she said and shut the door, her mind flooding with grief for Lance, the brother she'd never had. "You'd better go see them. They need you." She put her hand on the key and remembered the battery was dead. *I'll wait till he leaves and then walk home*, she thought. *I can't bear to have him rescue me again, not now.*

But Grant didn't budge from where he stood. He tapped her window.

She rolled it down, and Grant said, "You're my family too." When Sarah didn't reply, he opened her door and said, "Get out."

As he lifted her from the truck and carried her to his, she asked, "What about the truck?" Grant didn't reply. "It's family too."

"You don't need your father's truck. Let it keep the lighthouse company until your dad finds it."

The fourth heart of the lucky four-leaf clover had been plucked away from the stem of the Eriksen family, ripping deep wounds in the remaining three. Lance's noble death, motivated by love of his brother, returned his elements back to nature, but his spirit would not be contained by this world.

The closed-casket ceremony was for the living, not for him. But those left behind could find no words to express their grief. Brody, Grant, and Sarah agreed he would have liked more laughter and less crying. He had never been fond of whining about the unfairness of the world.

Sarah took her place among the two brothers and three other strong men to carry his casket to its resting place on the land upon which he lived large. It lay buried alongside great men and women whose names and stories had been lost by the ravages of Western colonialism.

After the exhausted parents turned off the lights to attempt sleep, Lance's siblings—along with Sarah, who was staying in the Eriksen house—crept outside. They made their way to the Boulders in the woods behind Sarah's house and built a ceremonial fire for him. Brody took his place on his designated rock, and Grant sat on his rock with Sarah on his lap. An empty rock rested between them. At first the only sound was the crackling of oak and maple kindling that filled the void of their loss.

At last Sarah said, "I promise we will see him again. I'm sure of it."

Brody added branches to the fire and opened a beer. He offered one to Sarah, but she refused. "He'll still be talking about the look on everyone's faces," Brody said, "when they saw you as a pallbearer."

Sarah turned her face from the warmth of the fire to shed a tear. Grant brushed it from her cheek and said, "He wouldn't want you to cry. He used to tell us all the time that he was born with all he could ever want in life—family and people he loved."

"I would have liked more time with him," she said. "It's me I'm feeling sorry for."

Grant opened a beer and said, "Yeah. Damn, I miss him."

"Max is real," Sarah said, seemingly out of left field.

The two brothers looked appropriately confused.

"Who's Max?" Brody asked.

"Sarah has an imaginary boyfriend she dreams about," Grant said with a smile.

"Brody, don't listen to him. Max is real. He's a ... being who protects this land. He told me a story behind your brother's blood oath."

"You sound just like Lance," said Brody. "He spent a lot of time out here with our great-grandfather. He had a gift for remembering every detail of those old stories. He told us the Norse myths and the local legends."

"Take a seat, and tell us a story, Sarah," Brody said, pointing to Lance's rock. "But in honor of Lance, it's got to be a scary story."

Grant nudged her to take up Brody's offer, and she moved to Lance's rock. "Let's see what you've got, Miss Vise," Grant said. "Come on, give us a scare for Lance."

"The blood oath of bravery has a story behind it," Sarah began. "A boy journeyed into the woods to capture a copperhead but was required to allow himself to be bitten first before bringing the snake back. The boy received three bites. The first two were a result of false bravery, but the third was the mark of true bravery." Sarah lifted her fist and pointed to her cut.

"Your ghost boyfriend taught you that one?" Brody asked and laughed.

"No appetite for ancient wisdom?" said Sarah. "Maybe I'll summon the copperhead snake, and you won't be laughing."

"Come on, Brody," Grant said. "I want to hear the whole story."

"We don't want a lesson," Brody protested. "We want a scary story."

Grant stood up and walked behind Sarah, "sneaking up" on her in plain sight, and Sarah smiled.

Sarah took a deep breath, preparing herself for the meat of the story. She stared into the fire and whispered the prayer: "As I lay me down to sleep, I pray the Lord my soul to keep. If I die before I wake, I pray the Lord my soul to take." She continued the story. "When you sleep on the land of Port Mahon, your soul is not safe. Max can steal your spirit in a dream, and you won't go to heaven. You'll be trapped in his spirit world for eternity, or he can feed you to the wolves of the woods, who devour weak spirits. He said real death only happens when your spirit dies there—in the afterworld."

The brothers grinned.

"I can see you're not convinced of his power," Sarah said. "I experienced it. He killed me in my sleep with a hatchet and brought me to the afterworld."

"But you're here," Grant pointed out.

"He let me go," she said. The fire reflected in her eyes.

"Probably because he figured out that trouble follows you everywhere," Brody said. "No offense, Sarah, but the afterlife is not safe with you in it."

"Sounds like you're channeling Lance," Grant told his brother, to which Brody raised his beer in salute.

Sarah smiled. *It's true. Max probably threw me out because I was killing him*, she thought.

Grant kissed her cheek, and she turned her lips toward his. "Get a room," Brody said.

"Speaking of which," Grant said, "the couch is *really* uncomfortable, Sarah. Marry me so I can go back to my own bed."

After everything Sarah had been through, Grant's big, loving family insisted she stay with them. The Captain disapproved and pushed back at first, but Sarah continued peppering him with questions about her mother, Rebecca, until he gave in and agreed to let her go.

"I volunteered to take Lance's room," she said. "But you wouldn't let me."

"Wouldn't you be creeped out to take his room so soon?" Grant asked.

"No. He's on a journey—that's all. He's not really gone."

"Maybe she wants a ghostly midnight visit," Brody suggested.

"That's not funny," said Grant.

"Lance did say she was welcome in his bed anytime," Brody said, raising his beer again in honor of Lance's humor. He finished it and opened another.

"The word was 'room,' not 'bed,' and that's not happening," Grant said. "She can stay in my room, and I'll stay on the couch."

Time to change the subject, Sarah thought. "Max could have stolen my spirit, but he said he could not take us both. What do you think he meant by that?"

"You and Lance?" Grant mused. He then asked, with seriousness creeping into his tone, "Does he have Lance?"

"I don't know for sure, but I don't think so. Lance has a strong spirit."

Grant's shoulders relaxed.

"You and Sketch?" Brody asked.

"No," Sarah said, shaking her head.

The brothers looked at each other and shrugged. "Then who?" Grant asked.

"Afraid yet?" Sarah asked, staring into the flames as if searching for the answer. "Maybe you should be." She stood up and announced, "I have another spirit within me."

"Who? Our great-grandfather?" Brody asked and laughed. "Ew, that's disgusting."

"Max?" asked Grant uncomfortably.

Sarah paused. A hint of fear possessed her. The transfusion of Max's energy into her was a major detail she'd failed to mention to Grant. It was her secret—and her shame. The transfused venom of Max spoke to her—an ancient wisdom, a gravitational, earthly power—and fed her spirit.

"What is it?" Grant asked. She shrugged, tucked her worry aside, and managed a smile.

"I'm pregnant," she said and pointed to her belly.

Grant's mouth opened and closed like a goldfish's as his eyes blinked in awe. He placed his hand on her stomach and asked, "Are you sure?"

She nodded and smiled.

Brody said, "Sarah, we need to get you a dictionary, because that's not scary. That's awesome."

"*And* a little scary," she added.

The three hugged as the fire blazed. "I was wondering why you didn't want a beer," Brody said. "I thought you were turning into a lightweight in Lance's absence. I'll tell you what is scary, though—Grant has to tell Dad."

"I'll tell Mom first, and then she can tell him," said Grant. "Once Dad sees how happy she is, he won't be mad."

"Coward," Brody said with a laugh.

Sarah piled on. "Yeah, what's the deal? Too scared to tell him yourself?"

"It's not called fear; it's called tactics," Grant replied—to two people who knew the path of true bravery.

"If Lance were here, he'd say you were a coward too," said Brody.

"If Lance were here, I wouldn't have to tell Dad. Lance'd run into the house, wake everyone up, blurt it out, and then stand off to the side, laughing at the chaos he created."

They walked back to the house and stood outside.

"Everyone's asleep," said Grant, stating the obvious.

"Luckily for you," Brody replied. Just before opening the door, he turned to Sarah and said, "But when tomorrow comes, you're going to have to break the news—Grant may have stood up to Lance, but he's still a little boy when it comes to our father."

Brody entered the house. Grant hung back and squeezed Sarah's hand.

"How do you feel?" Grant asked her.

"Good," she said.

"Are you afraid?"

"A little," she admitted.

"Well, don't be—everyone is going to be so excited."

"Are you happy?" Sarah asked.

Granted hugged her in relief. "I'm more than happy. I'm traveling through space at light speed, witnessing everything beautiful all at once, and I can't understand why I haven't exploded into a million pieces yet. I had no idea I could feel this much happiness."

Their lips met, and Grant asked, "What's happening to me?"

"I think it's called love," she answered.

"I hope someday you'll marry me, because until you do, our lack of wedding rings will be the first and last topic of every conversation my family has."

"About that," she said, "I have a secret."

"What secret are you keeping from me—my beautiful, multi-dimension-traveling spirit-princess?"

"I've had a little fantasy about you for years."

"What kind of fantasy?"

"That you were my husband, and we had three—no four—kids playing in the yard."

"Really?" he asked.

"It's true," she said and smiled up at him.

"All this time you were playing hard to get."

She blushed. "But it was never going to happen without a very convincing apology. Consider that done. Apology accepted."

"Don't you think all that should be required is for a couple to decide to be married in order to be recognized as husband and wife?" he asked.

"Sounds good to me," she replied.

"Can I tell you something?" he asked, looking into his wife's eyes. She nodded. "You know that fantasy you had? I had the very same one." They kissed, long and deep.

Max stood in their shadow, hidden from the moon, witnessing their exchange. When they opened the door to go inside, Max said out loud, "Forgive my selfish interference in the orphan's journey—it is beyond my control. My lovely wild orchid—I saved her spirit, but now I cannot let her go."

Grant let the side door slam behind them and flipped on all the lights. In honor of his brave oldest brother and mentor, Grant called out at the top of his lungs for his parents to hear, "We're having a baby!"

Trucks and tractors pulled trailers and hauled yellow wheat under the bright Midwestern sun. The light breeze flipped the dog-eared pages of a book, *Nature's Secret Medicine*, held open by another book titled *Quantum Physics, Consciousness, and Multiple Universes*. A couple of empty glass jars in Sarah's collection tipped over in the wind and chimed as if calling souls to enlightenment. The many full bottles contained a multitude of botanical samples she had collected and studied for the last couple of years.

Sarah lifted the bottle labeled "Wild Mint—*Mentha Canadensis*" into the sun for a closer look. Amazing how the little flowering weed had spread all over the world, demanding to be noticed. Most people's reaction? Overlook it, trample upon its leaves, and douse it with weed killer. Luckily for humankind, this plant contained an unrepentant spirit disguised with an attractive purple flower and appealing scent.

The weed reminded her of another tenacious child of the land who was brave enough to continue to thrive—unwilling to retreat or be muted—in a world of distracted souls.

The medical community's entries on *Mentha canadensis* offered little more than a few superficial properties and undetermined findings—as if this plant could reveal its secrets by being isolated in a laboratory, dried, and stuck in a vacuum.

A tinted glass of diluted iced Indiana lemonade sat sweating on the table. She could not prove the mint was conclusively effective in neutralizing microbes in the Indiana well water. She had no idea whether the plant was effective as an antibiotic and did not know why it seemed to quench her thirst better than water itself. She supposed it was difficult to prove anything scientifically when there were so many combinations of chemicals in everything. But Sarah had come to know many things about the natural world that she could not prove. And she was working at preserving and documenting that knowledge.

They'd arrived together in Indiana two years after the plane crash, and Sarah had wasted no time in using the university's library after they registered for classes. Strange new wisdom spoke to her from within, and she was able to understand complex mathematical problems with a fraction of the effort she formerly had needed. She kept her new ability a secret. Her physical strength had more than doubled, too, but she also kept that a secret.

Sarah rubbed fresh wild mint leaves between her fingers and sprinkled the wet, oily grind over the lemon slice floating in the glass because she believed it would help her stay in harmony with the earth. When she stood, a gold-flecked, grayish-white owl tail feather—oiled, pressed, and covered in a thin transparent pouch—hung, protected, from her beaded belt.

She walked outside barefoot with her drink.

"Daddy!" the little boy shouted, pointing to an airplane flying overhead. Red highlights glistened in the boy's loose light-brown curls, and his eyes matched the blue of the sky. He ran to take off like a plane. Within a few steps, he fell and sprawled in the dirt. His hands searched for leverage to stand. Sarah saw his predicament and grabbed her tumbled boy by the belt loops of his denim jeans. She dusted the dirt from his elbows and lifted him off the ground. He extended his arms like wings and pedaled his feet as if he were on a Wright brothers' winged bicycle. Sarah swung him high into the air so he could feel what it was like to fly like his father. He reached for the sky as his mom spun him faster than a merry-go-round.

A crosswind picked up speed. In the distance, the first flash of lightning popped. Clouds and a dark sky were coming. A red, low-wing airplane launched upward at the end of the field and turned at 45 degrees until a 180-degree turn was completed. The plane descended flat above the knee-high plants, straight and level.

Sarah and her son stood hand in hand beside the house, watching. Sarah felt a wave of warm energy move up from the earth, through her bare feet and up to her waist. It encircled her there, electrifying the owl feather—changing its color to fluorescent white with glowing golden bands. The circulating energy flowed up and out along her arm and into the arm of the boy, whose face lit up with a knowing smile.

At that exact moment, Grant steered the plane to give his family a "wing wave," signaling to them it was the last field pass of the day—he was coming home. And Sarah knew, for the first time in her life, that she was not an orphan. She never had been.

EPILOGUE

THE TRANSIENT

A gangly man sprinted across the field into the dark woods, chased by a muscular hunter with long brown hair. The man cowered, hiding in the brush on the forest floor, and trembled. The unwelcome stranger's presence caused the beasts to growl and the earth to rumble. The canopy of the trees blocked the light, and animals scurried away, making their own escape from the wrath of the hunter.

A hatchet rose as the hunter with glowing amber skin bent under a low branch to track the intruder. A beg for mercy meant nothing to the hunter with the ax. The sharp flint blade swung in a mighty arc and descended. Breath stopped. Dim energy leaked from the man in the form of a heavy ground fog that was quickly soaked up by the forest floor. The shell of the man lingered only long enough for the wolves to argue over the scraps.

Max yelled into the forest for all to witness, "For the Orphan."

Max grinned, amused by an inner secret, and said, "She can't stay away forever."

ACKNOWLEDGMENTS

Thanks to everyone at Advantage and ForbesBooks. Where's my business book? Here it is. This book about how to achieve business success is disguised as a romance novel. Business is daunting, and *The Stealing* is gothic fiction. Business is the ultimate romantic journey, after all. Special thanks to Stephen Larkin for reviewing the draft manuscript and encouraging the completion of *The Stealing*. Thanks to the dedicated and professional management team: Kristin Goodale, publishing manager; Carson Kendrick, associate VP public relations; Nate Best, editorial manager; Carly Blake, creative director; David Taylor, creative manager; and Tracy Hill, print production coordinator.

Immeasurable gratitude to my editor, Andrew Wolfendon, for his keen attention to detail, patience, and vast experience. Thank you so much for the superb editing quality of my debut manuscript.

Thank you, Mitch Kolbe, for the most sublime, breathtaking cover illustration in the history of gothic romance novel covers. I'm awestruck and grateful for Mitch Kolbe's creative artistry. This cover is painted by a master fine artist, and the artwork is truly a precious gift.

Paulette Reddick Turner, a true leader, wrote the foreword. It is an honor. Paulette possesses the courage, strength, and faith to stand up to a fierce gale-force wind in America. "She faced the storm and refused to turn her head." Thank you for the encouragement and the inspiration—and for being a mentor and friend.

Thanks to the prerelease readers: Robyn R., Robert B., Camden L., Bianca G., Jerry K., Niti P., G. Kumpf, and Gary N. Special thanks to Debra Jordan for her expedited, detailed, and thoughtful analysis. Thanks to early reader H. Malik for offering so much enthusiasm for my writing style.

A special thanks to Helen Lewis, director of Literally Public Relations (literallypr.com), and the firm's expert team for significant early contributions in answering marketing, promotion, and public relations questions before the book was ready to promote. I appreciate your firm's quick, detailed handling and professional representation.

I'm grateful for the encouragement and support from extraordinary, successful entrepreneurial businesswomen Noemi Raines (consignmed.com), Alisa O'Banion (texasmicrofiber.com), Margaret Sevadjian (charlesalaninc.com), Christina Winters (cmwfinancial.com), Keri Smith (dotit.com), Ashley Altum (profitmatters.co), Robin Ford (showservicesllc.com), Christa Weatherby (dgqroofing.com), and Julie Gutic.

"I want to write a novel." Partners and immediate family members should fear the moment these frightening words are uttered by an aspiring author. I am thankful for my friends and family for illuminating so many cosmic causeways in the sky; my night is as bright as the day.

Thanks to Patricia Bryant for the encouragement to finish the book, lending an ear for hour upon hour, months on end, while I read recently drafted chapters. With that kind of enthusiasm and positive energy, the book was destined to be published. Thank you, Patricia, for being a wonderful, extraordinary friend.

The Stealing is dedicated to Loretta Adine Muntz, my first childhood friend, my lifelong friend, and my sister of the road. At five years old, we met at the kindergarten bus stop on Port Mahon Road. Our friendship taught me the beauty of the interconnected universe. It's inexplicable—to be certain of a beginning without an end. Without a doubt, we'll someday meet again at another bus stop, on another road, somewhere in the cosmos.

ABOUT THE AUTHOR

"Business is the ultimate romantic journey, after all."

As the founder and CEO of Cluso Investigation (cluso.com), Sharon Sutila is a licensed private investigator and expert in global identity deception.

Sutila successfully navigates the male-dominated industries of security and information technology. After receiving a bachelor's in engineering technology from the University of South Florida, she consulted for many years on the worldwide deployment of business process reengineering projects. Then, recognizing a need for reliable, quality-controlled background checks on global IT professionals, she built Cluso's proprietary hardware and software processing platform.

As with the main character of *The Stealing*, S.A. Sutila's journey began on a dead-end coastal road in Delaware.

S.A. Sutila is an entrepreneur, private pilot, conference speaker, and dedicated breaker of barriers for women.

Author website: SASutila.com
Book Website: TheStealing.com
Instagram: @SharonSutila
Tiktok: @SASutila
Twitter: @SSutila
Facebook: @SASutila
LinkedIn: SharonSutila

ABOUT PAULETTE REDDICK TURNER

Founder and President of Integrated Leadership Concepts, Inc.

Paulette Turner embodies her motto, "Standing Tall, Reaching Back," choosing to serve as a mentor and champion to benefit others. She earned a bachelor of arts degree in biology from Rockford College in Rockford, Illinois, and a master of business administration degree from Southern Methodist University in Dallas, Texas. She is a graduate of both Leadership Fort Worth and Leadership America.

Mrs. Turner is the founder and president of Integrated Leadership Concepts, Inc., which coaches and develops leaders to thrive in a changing world. An IBM Corporation retired executive, Paulette formerly led professional and leadership development for the IBM sales force across North America, Central America, and South America.

A facilitator of leadership change, Mrs. Turner designed, developed, and for seven years delivered PATHS *Forward*®, a leadership development program that prepares emerging leaders in the Fort Worth community in partnership with the Fort Worth Metropolitan Black Chamber of Commerce. She recently completed a six-year term as program director for Leadership Fort Worth. She is currently chapter chair for the Fort Worth Chapter of the Women Presidents' Organization. She uses proven professional and business development techniques to assist entrepreneurial women leading multimillion-dollar businesses in enhancing their personal effectiveness and achieving business growth.

In 2021 Paulette received the Trailblazer Award from the Greater Fort Worth Area Negro Business and Professional Women's Club and the Hometown Heroes Award from the Northeast Tarrant Chamber of Commerce. In recent years, she has also received the Dr. Marion J. Brooks Living Legends Award, the Girl Scouts of Texas Oklahoma Plains Discover Award, and the Fort Worth Business Press Mentor Award. The Paulette Reddick Turner Ambassador of Change Award, created in honor of her leadership, is awarded annually by her high school.

Paulette and her husband, Herb Turner, have one daughter and one grandson.

Email: pturner@ilc-inc.com
Website: ilc-inc.com
Twitter: @Turner_Paulette
LinkedIn: PauletteTurner

ABOUT MITCH KOLBE

Fine Artist

Mitchell Lee Kolbe hails from Charlotte, North Carolina. He has worked professionally as an artist since age fifteen. As a senior in high school, he was one of ten chosen nationally to receive the Art Merit Scholarship in 1973 to study at the prestigious Art Students League of New York City. After completing his studies at the league in 1976, he had his first one-man show in Charlotte, North Carolina. Work soon followed in the field of graphics, illustration, murals, sculpture, and fine art. By 1980, Mitchell was doing less commercial work and concentrating more on fine art and sculpture.

His works include paintings for the Florida State Governors Club, the Atlanta Cyclorama restoration work, all plant fabrication for Disney's EPCOT theme park, murals and sculpture at the Kennedy Space Center, murals for Universal Studios' Portofino Bay theme park, and sculptures for the 1996 Summer Olympic Games. In addition, Kolbe's work can be found in the collections of the Archbishop of Constantinople, the Bill and Melinda Gates Foundation, Antonio Banderas, and Richard Kessler, to name a few.

Purchase Kolbe's fine art easel paintings at the Kessler Grand Bohemian Art Galleries at Grand Bohemian Hotels in Asheville, North Carolina; Savannah, Georgia; Birmingham, Alabama; St. Augustine, Florida; and Charleston, South Carolina.

Poetry In Paint

Email : mitchkolbe@yahoo.com
Telephone: (727) 808-6869
Website: MitchKolbe.com
Facebook: @MitchKolbe
Twitter: @MitchKolbe

Q & A

Mitchell Lee Kolbe, Cover Illustrator

What style of painting do you prefer?
I love all styles of painting, but I guess I prefer the style of the late-nineteenth- and early-twentieth-century American, French, and Russian schools of painting, both in illustration, portraiture, and landscape painting.

What appealed to you to create the artwork for the *The Stealing*'s cover?
Both my morning and evening art teachers at the Art Students League were paper-back novel illustrators. So here it is forty-eight years later, and

this is my first gothic novel. The opportunity to paint one for the first time appealed to me.

What made this project a good fit for you?
I went to school for illustration and then moved to the fine art world; however, I always loved the old illustrators. This project was a nice departure from my usual landscape themes. Also, being able to paint a dark subject matter interested me.

What experience was most helpful in creating this painting?
Artists pour their life experiences into every painting they do. I pull whatever is necessary for that particular subject, at that specific time, dipping, as it were, into a collective pool of life lessons. Painting in Maine in inclement weather helped me a lot on this one.

Besides the book's story, does this artwork hint at something about you?
One of my all-time favorite artists growing up was Frank Frazetta. He was a master of dark subject matter, and I was probably conjuring Frank for this piece. There is a hidden, darker side we may mask from others. A painting like this can tap into dark dreams from long ago to capture the right feeling. The waves crashing against the rocks, for instance, were from a memory I had as a child of a painting my dad worked on—only mine was dark and forbidding, and his artwork was light and airy. Also, the swirling storm with the conjurer at the center is similar to a nightmare I had many years ago, appearing to foreshadow a real-life event.

After completion, stepping back now, what do you think about the painting?
Well, I rather like it. For my first gothic novel, I think it's pretty good. I like the lighting and drama and composition. It has a good design that draws you in and seems to flow. I am pleased with the mix of realism

and supernatural aspects of the piece and how it turned out. I believe I captured the dark gothic feel of The Stealing.

How do you interpret the meaning of this painting?
To me, the painting is a dream state. Sarah dreams or fantasizes about someone who can save her from herself and all the dangers, both internal and external. Her life is in turmoil. The painting captures the moment she may have found her "rock," but what she finds is either fleeting or not real.

What may be lost as book cover illustrations continue to abandon the more traditional approach and process to create *The Stealing*'s artwork?
CGI is great and getting better all the time. Where would cinema be without it? It's the way of the future; however, I believe there will never be a time quite like the golden age of illustration, with all the imagination and discipline that went into the art. Howard Pyle, N. C. Wyeth, J. C. Leyendecker, and Dean Cornwell, just to name a few. You can't touch those guys. But, on the other hand, I believe too much reliance on the computer can make one a little passive. The computer does all the work, and there seems to be a little less of the artist's input. If the computer artist learns the basics like those early illustrators did, I think it helps, but whatever approach is taken, the creative passion must surface or show itself in the art. In the end, an artistic soul is what I think may become lost over time.

How did you prepare before starting the painting?
For illustrations, when there is already a narrative, I first listen to the writer's ideas or read their book. From there, I next sit down with a newsprint pad and charcoal and hammer out some ideas for the picture. These are very small thumbnails and rough in the early stage, but they are often the heart and soul of the piece. This is where the initial thoughts and ideas are played out. From the roughs, I develop more refined sketches for the client's approval. Once the sketches are approved, I usually create a

little black-and-white or color sketch in oils to solidify my ideas. Sometimes I rely on my past artwork for ideas, and other times I research online.

What materials did you use?
The thumbnails were created on Canson newsprint paper, using different grades of vine charcoal. The finished sketches were applied on Canson tracing paper. The oil painting was done in oils on Strathmore plate illustration board with two coats of acrylic gesso. The coats of gesso were applied at ninety degrees to one another to replicate a fine linen surface.

Can you describe the techniques and process?
Once the client approved the sketches, I hired a young couple similar in age and description to the main characters in the story. Several photos were taken under different lighting situations and from different angles to capture my original thumbnails. Using both photos and drawings from my charcoal studies, I draw a more refined full-value pencil rendering three times larger than the book cover dimensions. Then, from this finished drawing, I traced a simple outline of the large shapes on tracing paper and transferred this "cartoon" to the finished board to paint on. To create the underpainting, I used a mixture of ultramarine blue and raw umber that approximates the look of warm charcoal.

When the underpainting dried, I painted over it with opaque grays and added black and white values. Once the black and white was complete and dry, I added an isolating coat of varnish. Then I painted the entire painting in oil colors, starting with my darkest darks and working to the lightest lights.

When the painting was completed and dry, I gave it one more final varnish and sent a photo for client approval. After final approval, the painting was sent to the photographers for a high-resolution image and format for printing.

CPSIA information can be obtained
at www.ICGtesting.com
Printed in the USA
JSHW020202160422
25004JS00006B/10

9 781642 252682